MW01600099

Canaaıan Historical Brides (Prince Edward Island) Book 11

Anita Davison and Victoria Chatham

Amazon Print 9781772998658

BWL Publishing Inc.

Books we love to write ...
Authors around the world.

http://bwlpublishing.ca

The Canadian Historical Brides Collection – Book List

Brides of Banff Spring – Book 1 Alberta
His Brother's Bride – Book 2 Ontario
Romancing the Klondike – Book 3 Yukon
Barkerville Beginnings – Book 4 British Columbia
Pillars of Avalon – Book 5 Newfoundland
Fields of Gold Beneath Prairie Skies – Book 6 Saskatchewan
Landmark Roses – Book 7 Manitoba
Fly Away Snow Goose – Book 8 Northwest Territories/Nunavut
On a Stormy Primeval Shore – Book 9 New Brunswick
The Left Behind Bride – Book 10 Nova Scotia
Envy the Wind – Book 11 Prince Edward Island
Where the River Narrows – Book 12 Quebec
Fly Away Snow Goose – Book 8 Northwest Territories/Nunavut
On a Stormy Primeval Shore – Book 9 New Brunswick
The Left Behind Bride – Book 10 Nova Scotia
Envy the Wind – Book 11 Prince Edward Island
Where the River Narrows – Book 12 Quebec

Dedication

BWL Publishing Inc. dedicates the Canadian Historical Brides collection to the immigrants, male and female, who left their homes and families, crossed oceans and endured unimaginable hardships in order to settle the Canadian wilderness and build new lives in a rough and untamed country.

Acknowledgement

BWL Publishing acknowledges the Government of Canada and the Canada Book Fund for its financial support in creating the Historical Brides of Canada collection.

"She had always envied the wind. So free. Blowing where it listed. Through the hills. Over the lakes. What a tang, what a zip it had! What a magic of adventure!"
From The Blue Castle by L M Montgomery

Chapter 1

Hampstead Village, North London, England March 1905

Grace sat bolt upright on the rigid chair set before an oak desk in the inner sanctum of Beech and Sons, Solicitors at Law. Her hands felt clammy so she removed her soft leather gloves and laid them in her lap, beneath her tapestry bag.

Rows of floor to ceiling bookshelves lined three walls, each one crammed to bursting with gold-tooled, leather bound volumes. Apart from the two chairs and a threadbare rug set before a black leaded grate, the room, although not sparse, was far from luxurious. A modest professional workspace that smelled of dust and stale tobacco smoke.

"Am I to understand you had no knowledge of your inheritance before yesterday, Mrs MacKinnon?" Mr Julius Beech the younger peering at her over his half-moon spectacles, occupied a chair opposite.

Grace guessed him to be in his late thirties, his appearance that of an amiable mole with his wide cheekbones, flat forehead and full lipped smile. His sombre black suit was broken by occasional glimpses of an embroidered yellow waistcoat beneath his coat.

"None at all, I'm afraid." Conscious that her maid guarded the front entrance, Grace darted a look at the wide window with a view of the High Street, pedestrians and traffic flowed past.

"I believe your parents were - ahem - tragically killed in a carriage accident in Oxford Street," he read from the papers spread on the desk in front of him. "Please accept my sympathy."

"That isn't necessary, sir. It was a long time ago." Grace shook her head, refusing to delve into a darkness avoided since childhood.

"I understand." He selected another document from the pile. "Forgive me if I repeat details with which you are already conversant, but your case is new to me." He cleared his throat, his round eyes dropping their gaze to the page. "After their - demise - you were made a ward of Angus MacKinnon, your father's business partner?" He formed the words as an enquiry.

Grace nodded. "I married his son when I was seventeen." She didn't know why she mentioned her age, possibly because she felt coerced into a situation she had been too immature to understand; and at the time, a refusal would not have been well received.

"Also, please accept my condolences on the recent loss of your husband.'

"Thank you." The stiff fabric of her black gown rustled, a reminder of what it represented. Widow's weeds: a symbol of her status in a society which abhorred women with no standing or power. Not that she had ever possessed any.

Mr Beech's sad smile sent a surge of guilt through her for having denied her husband the devotion he deserved. More like a brother than a husband, Frederick also suffered from his father's harsh, uncompromising rule. Although she would never admit it, Grace still felt angry with him at having escaped into death, leaving her behind to cope alone with his family.

"Well, Mrs MacKinnon." The solicitor leaned back in his chair, both hands crossed over his rounded midriff, increasing the impression of a mole. "By the terms of your father's will, it's clear you were granted control of your inheritance when you reached your majority. In fact, I'm at a loss to see why you have not been here to claim it before. You are, what age now?"

"Twenty-three." She inhaled a slow, deep breath and released the death grip on her tapestry bag. Almost twenty-four and yet still nervous as a child. "My father-in-law never discussed finances with me. Especially my own."

Angus MacKinnon always impressed upon her the expense of her upkeep was his personal burden. "That letter was amongst my late husband's belongings."

The thick bond envelope with the solicitor's seal had been attached to the underside of a drawer in Frederick's dressing room, along with a scrawled note addressed to her apologizing for his duplicity in keeping it from her. Unable to defy his father while he was alive, she liked to think Frederick's act of defiance as he lay dying had been done out of affection for her.

"I see," Mr Beech stroked his clean shaven chin. "And now you wish to take charge of your own affairs?"

"Would that I knew what those affairs were." She eased forward on her chair, lowering her voice. "Mr Beech, I don't mean to be disrespectful, but I have been here a full twenty minutes and you still haven't told me anything I don't already know."

"I apologize, my dear. I simply find the situation odd." The lawyer's chair creaked as he leaned forward, his plump hands folded over the pile of documents on the desk. "Mr MacKinnon received regular funds from the trust over the years, as well as financing your education at the

North London Collegiate School in Camden. Your attendance there was a condition of your father's will."

Grace smiled as one question at least was answered. Angus MacKinnon hated that school and regarded her expensive education an unnecessary indulgence. He called Miss Sophie Bryant, the headmistress, a radical, unnatural old biddy who made young women unfit for lives as wives and mothers. Whenever Grace asked why he sent her there, his answers were always vague and dismissive.

"Mrs MacKinnon?"

The sound of Mr Beech's voice brought her back to the present. "I'm so sorry, but would you mind repeating that?"

"With pleasure." His smile showed he was not in the least offended, or was she paying for his time by the minute? "I expect I was reading too fast."

"I leave to my only daughter, Grace Elizabeth Mary Aitken, the total of my investments in…." his voice droned on, flowing over her like sweet music as his words offered possibilities she never imagined would be hers. When he reached the end, he looked up at her with a benign smile.

"I regret what remains of the capital won't buy you a mansion in Kensington, but would certainly run to a pleasant villa in a quiet suburban neighborhood, somewhere like Chiswick, or Maida Vale perhaps. The remainder, if invested wisely, would provide you with a reasonable income. You would be entirely independent if that is what you wish." He folded the paper and returned it to the brown folder on his desk. "Now, what do you want me to do with your inheritance?"

"Do with it?" Grace stared at him. She had money. Not a fortune, but enough to live on without anyone's approval or permission. She blinked away sudden angry tears, her throat burning at the deception of her being forever dependent upon the MacKinnons.

"Oh, my dear, tears?" The solicitor looked stricken. He tugged out a drawer with a scrape of wood and withdrew a perfectly laundered and folded handkerchief that he thrust towards her. "It must be the grief, I expect. After all, your husband did not leave us very long ago. Two months is nothing at all."

"On the contrary, Mr Beech." Recovering herself quickly she summoned a weak smile. "These tears are entirely for myself." She dabbed at her cheeks with the handkerchief which smelled of old leather and laundry starch.

The night following Frederick's funeral returned with startling clarity. Summoned into her father-in-law's study, Angus MacKinnon's clipped voice cut into her from behind a desk every bit as vast as this one, though he had not invited her to sit.

"As my son's widow, and a childless one at that, you have limited status in my house. Therefore, I expect you to earn your place by taking charge of the housekeeping. At least your expensive education will be put to some use."

He neither sought her opinion, nor had she dared give it to a man who had never been challenged in either his business or his home.

She murmured something non-committal and retreated to the room she once shared with Frederick. One which, with its nine-foot high ceilings and a double height bay window became a vast, empty expanse she could not begin to fill. Her future stretched before her, days during which she would have to guard every word so as not to waken the self-righteous tyrant that dwelled in her father-in-law. The hours that stood between her and the next chilly dawn seemed never-ending, while rebellion curled in her belly like a malignant serpent. How could she endure such a future when she had no real past?

"Even so," Mr Beech's voice held sympathy. "You must miss him?"

"My husband?" She nodded. She did. "As a friend. A companion. A conspirator." Grace frowned, aware her selfish misery obliterated her feelings for Frederick, her only ally in that cold, forbidding house.

"Characteristics of any successful marriage I would say."

"I-I suppose so."

Now a single letter and the words of this kind but unprepossessing man of law changed everything. A raft of possibilities opened up in the space of a morning and she had no notion of what to do next. Or maybe she did.

Grace recalled dark winter evenings in front of the fire in their bedroom where they dreamed of going to Canada. Frederick longed to visit the great lakes, see snow as high as houses in a country that was new, exciting and as far away from Hampstead as either of them could imagine. When pneumonia took hold and he was barely conscious, let alone capable of speech, she sat on the floor beside the chaise longue where he lay propped up on pillows and wrapped in blankets, making up stories of what they would do when they got to Halifax.

"Mr Beech," Grace began carefully, "is my business with you completely confidential?"

"I beg your pardon, my dear?" He raised both hands from the desk in a gesture of surrender. "Why would it not be? We are quite alone."

"I didn't mean that. What I need to know is, if anyone asked you what we discussed this afternoon, would you be obliged to disclose it?"

"Certainly not." He relaxed back in his chair, removed his glasses and regarded her levelly, his forehead puckered in bemusement. "I'm only required to do so should you happen to be the subject of a police investigation. And even then, a court order would be required. I sincerely doubt that would be the case. Does that answer your question?"

"It does, thank you. Also, is there any way my father-in-law can override my father's will?

I mean, the part about the capital coming to me on my majority?"

"Indeed, he has no such powers. The money is yours to do with as you wish." He polished the lenses of his spectacles with a soft cloth he drew from a pocket. "The Married Women's Property Act has been in force for over twenty years and ensures that."

"I have another question." Growing excitement made her light-headed. "Do you happen to know how one would go about travelling to Canada?"

"Emigrating do you mean? In order to live there permanently?"

Grace nodded.

"I see." He stroked his chin thoughtfully. "I must say, my dear, I wasn't expecting that. Might I ask why you would contemplate such a course of action?"

"Are you acquainted with my father-in-law, Mr Beech?" She peered up at him through her lashes, adopting what she hoped was a look which required no explanation.

"Only by reputation, which I must say is considerable." His still youthful face flushed slightly. "My father handled his business affairs, and those of your family until his death last year. I believe Mr MacKinnon has always been a man of strong opinions and unbending resolve."

'A charitable description of him.' She offered a weak smile, but did not venture the adjectives that sprang to mind.

The lawyer appeared to come to a momentous decision, pushed a pile of files to one side and leaned both forearms on the desk, his shoulders hunched forward. "The Salvation Army arranges assisted passage for those with little means to begin new lives in places like Australia, Canada and so on." She went to interrupt him, at which he held up a hand to silence her. "I mention them simply as a means of obtaining information. However, I'm aware your position is entirely different. As an Englishwoman with your own funds, you have all you need to travel there. If that is what you desire."

Her desire? Could it really be that simple?

"It is, sir." As if he needed further explanation, she added, "My husband always wanted us to go to Canada." Her throat burned as she recalled Frederick's eyes when he spoke of their plans, only to cloud again at the realisation it would remain a dream, ending with a sigh and the words, "but Father would never let us go."

Even as a woman alone, there must be something she could do in a new and exciting country; it's most attractive quality being it did not hold Angus MacKinnon.

"I see." Mr Beech blinked several times, then coughed into a fist. "I assume you don't intend taking this amount of money to Canada on your person? That would be most unwise."

"Well no, of course not, but-" Grace hesitated. "What do you suggest?"

"That I furnish you with a letter of authority which you present to the bank of your choice on arrival. They will telegraph me to transfer the capital across as per the instructions you give them. Would that be agreeable?"

"It would indeed, Mr Beech." Excitement bunched beneath her ribs. She watched as he drew towards him from a tray on his desk a page of creamy bond paper. It bore the name of the firm in embossed gold. He dipped a pen into an inkpot and scrawled a few lines in bold script.

"Won't I need some cash in order to make travel arrangements?" Grace asked as Mr Beech signed the page with a flourish and dabbed the wet ink with a sheet of blotting paper.

"Indeed, I can provide you with an adequate amount right now." He withdrew a sturdy looking cash box from another drawer and proceeded to unlock it. Grace watched his fingers flicking through a satisfying pile of banknotes. He placed them, along with the folded letter of authority, into a thick brown envelope which he sealed with a damp sponge set in a small pot at his elbow.

Grace imagined her father-in-law's reaction when he realized her money was no longer available to him. The thought gave her a good deal of pleasure and, in some ways, she regretted she would not be there to see it.

"I assume you have weighed the possible consequences of this action?"

"Not really. It's all happened too fast for second thoughts or regrets." Grace took the parcel he held out. 'Although I'm certain I won't regret my decision."

He regarded her steadily for a moment, his round eyes above the half-moon spectacles unblinking. "I see." He tore a small square piece of paper from a pad on his desk and wrote something on it before handing it to her.

"This is the address of the Salvation Army office in Liverpool, together with the name of their chief Emigration Officer. They can help you put together the required documentation."

"That's most helpful, sir." She added the note to her bag and tugged on her now creased and damp gloves. "I feel quite equipped now to tackle whatever the world has to offer me."

"I have to admire your determination, my dear." He strode to the door and held it open for her. "However, I would warn you to be on your guard. A young woman of your obvious attractions and money is bound to be a target in a comparatively primitive environment."

Primitive? From what she and Frederick read about Nova Scotia, Halifax was a thriving city with beautiful architecture and a forward thinking society.

A clerk in the outer office scrambled to his feet as she appeared, his skinny limbs encased in skin-tight black reminding her of a spider.

Grace paused in the doorframe and turned back, lowering her voice. "By the way, Mr Beech. Why Liverpool?"

"It's the main port from where the immigrant steamships cross the North Atlantic."

He spoke softly, as if aware of her need for caution. "I have no idea when the next sailing is scheduled. However, something tells me that it would be wiser for you to wait there, than remain here with the threat of discovery." His brown eyes softened with sympathy.

He was right. If she was determined to leave, she must go as soon as possible.

"Thank you, sir. I'm inclined to take your advice." Her gaze flicked to the clerk and then back at the lawyer.

"Ah!" he held a finger to his lips. "Don't worry about my staff carrying tittle-tattle. My clerk is indentured, and therefore bound by the same rules of confidentiality which restrict me."

"That's reassuring." She inclined her head. "I'm most appreciative of both your assistance and your discretion, Mr Beech."

"My pleasure, Mrs MacKinnon. I was only a clerk myself when James Aitken was a client of my father's. I remember him very well. I'm gratified to see his daughter has a similar independent spirit."

Buoyed by his unexpected kindness, as well as the details of her changed circumstances, Grace descended the short flight of steps into Hampstead High Street.

"You was gone ever so long, Miss Grace." A lanky girl dressed entirely in shades of taupe and dun brown sidled up to her. "I was sure someone from the house would drive past and see me."

"My apologies, Annie." Grace strode along the High Street, her steps lighter and more confident than when she arrived, forcing the maid into a run to keep up with her.

"You look a lot happier than when you went in. It was good news then?"

"The very best. Now." She halted abruptly, causing Annie to collide with her. "I'm taking a trip, and I'll need your help."

"A trip, Miss Grace?" Annie's eyes widened. "Does the master know?"

"Not yet, but he will." Grace looked both ways as they reached the corner of Holly Hill, at the top of which the MacKinnon gothic mansion crouched. She surveyed the distant outline and shivered, which had little to do with the chill March wind that creeping inside her coat collar and biting her nose and cheeks.

"Where are ye going, Miss?" Annie's bonnet strings had loosened, sending her hat bouncing on her shoulders as she ran along beside her.

"Canada."

"But that's the other side of the world!"

"Not quite." Just then it felt like the perfect distance. "Annie," she lowered her voice, though the road was deserted. "I want you to hide a bag for me." She wouldn't be able to sneak a full size trunk out of the house without it being remarked upon. "Maybe two bags. I'll see what I can manage."

"What about your lovely gowns, Miss Grace? All your fine books and your mother's jewelry?"

"I'm not going to forgo this chance for a few dresses. I'll take my mother's jewelry as it can be sold if necessary, and a few of my favorite books. My everyday clothes and linens will occupy most of the space so there will be no room for ball gowns." Grace made a sharp turn into the lane that served as a shortcut back to the house.

"'Tis a dreadful shame, Miss." Annie sulked as she trudged along beside her. "You has so many lovely things."

"That's all they are. Things. Now, I rely on you to keep my secret, Annie. The best time for me to go would be this Sunday when everyone is at church."

"But you'll be missed. The master insists everyone attends service."

"I've thought of that. When everyone is about to leave, you'll go down and say I have women's problems. No one will question that. Nor will they want to be late, thus it's unlikely I'll be cross questioned."

"I could ask Jeb to help." Annie skipped ahead and pushed open the wrought iron gate that gave a small, protesting squeak. "He's sweet on me and will do anything I ask. He could borrow his father's gig. No one will miss it for an hour or so, what with everyone at church."

21

"Oh, would you, Annie? That would be a great help." Grace climbed the rear steps into the hall. "I'll give him five shillings for his trouble." And his silence. "I don't suppose you would come with me?" She felt compelled to ask, but instinct told her Annie would refuse. A widowed mother and younger siblings needed her wages.

Annie's face blanched, but before she could respond, Grace pressed her forearm. 'Don't worry, Annie. I know it's not possible."

"I'm sorry, Miss. Going to Canada sounds real exciting and I would, if it weren't for Ma and the girls."

"You don't need to apologize, I quite understand." Disappointment filled her, but not enough to spoil the anticipation of what she was about to do. There was no time to engage another willing maid she could trust with her secret, so Grace would have to face her future entirely alone.

Doubt pulled at her lower belly. What was she thinking? She had always lived in London. How could she contemplate travelling thousands of miles to a strange country where she knew no one? But then, she knew few people here apart from the MacKinnons, and she was running away from them.

"I will be all right." She pulled back her shoulders. "Hundreds of emigrants leave these shores every day for new lives. Why shouldn't I do the same? And you'll keep your promise not to tell anyone where I've been today, won't you, Annie?"

"I always keep my promises, Miss." Annie nodded gravely. "But what are you going to tell the master if he finds out you weren't at the church hall helping with the bazaar this afternoon?"

"Nothing." Grace lifted her chin, the brown envelope a satisfactory bulge in her bag bolstering her courage. "From today, what I do is entirely my own business."

Chapter 2

SS Parisian, Halifax Harbour, Nova Scotia

Grace braced a hand on the ship's rail, her other clamped onto her hat as a swell tilted the deck. Land was a blurred purple line beneath an overcast sky where seagulls wheeled overhead. White flashes on grey, they soared on currents of air on a single wing beat, then dropped like stones until they caught another current, climbing upwards again, their mocking cries triumphant, sharp and sad.

Spring had not yet arrived in the North Atlantic, and an icy north wind chased the blood from her fingers and stung her cheeks. After a week at sea, she fretted to be on dry land again. The steady thrum of the engines floors below kept her awake on her first night but now vibrated through her feet in a familiar, almost comforting, way.

Travellers strolled the boards of the upper deck; businessmen with their wives, nannies and their charges and elegant dowagers, their hats as wide as their shoulders. A tapestry of crimson red, turquoise and sapphire blue, primrose

24

yellows and sage greens, in fur-lined cloaks and overcoats against the chill, the day bright and almost windless.

Passengers from steerage sat in groups, sprawled on winches and packing cases scattered about the deck. Women in headscarves and men in long black coats, all eager for their first view of Nova Scotia. Couples strolled arm-in-arm with little space to move, many wrapped against the cold in the shipping company's grey blankets. Solitary young men in thick woollen sweaters leaned against the winch lines smoking homemade cigarettes and staring broodily out over the ocean, while children issued high-pitched shrieks as they ran between them.

Like sparrows and blackbirds, they flowed around the lower deck in contrast to the peacocks and birds of paradise on the upper levels.

Grace leaned on the railing, her gaze on the deck below and wondered again about those people, few of whom shared a common language, but whose ambitions for a better future than the life they left behind matched her own.

"Not long now and we'll be in Halifax." Priscilla, her stateroom mate, a diminutive blonde with a tendency to plumpness sidled up to her at the rail, a question in her vivid blue eyes. "Did the steward come and collect our luggage?"

Grace nodded, trying not to flinch at the heavy floral perfume the girl favored. Priscilla had left half her belongings strewn about the stateroom. Grace packed them for her before the steward arrived, but there would be little point mentioning it when she'd not get any thanks.

"Excellent. I knew I could rely on you." Priscilla waved a vague hand at the tween deck below them. "They're just like animals, aren't they? All huddled together like that."

"That's quite harsh, Priscilla." Grace rolled her shoulders, shrugging off Priscilla's remark. The girl's mean nature still surprised her.

"And must they make that infernal racket?" Priscilla's nose wrinkled in disgust at the jaunty notes of an accordion that struck up from somewhere.

"I quite like it." Grace smiled as a young man dragged a girl into a circle to dance; maybe in a last chance to establish a connection before they left the ship to go their separate ways in a strange country. "They might be poor, but they share the same hopes for a new life we do."

Priscilla was not listening, her attention having shifted to a group of affluent young men in blazers standing farther along the rail, their voices raised in the braying tone of the young and entitled.

A youth with fair hair that falling over his forehead tossed a handful of coins over the rail into the crowd below. A violent scramble ensued to retrieve them. A small, ragged boy was knocked to the ground by a larger, stronger youth, who took off with his prize, the brief scuffle eliciting loud claps and yells of encouragement from their audience.

"How cruel," Grace murmured under her breath.

"It's only a bit of fun," Priscilla tutted, one hand propped on a hip to give her audience a view of her voluptuous curves. "You're such an enigma, Grace." She issued a light, hollow laugh. "You speak and dress like a duchess but say the strangest things."

The young man who threw the coins caught Priscilla's eye, grinned and nudged the one next to him. The first one whispered something and in seconds, the others joined him.

Their open appraisal sent angry heat flooding Grace's cheeks and she turned away, but could still hear their lewd comments made in too loud whispers.

A crewman strolled past and requested the raucous group move aside. Grace harboured a vague hope he might reprimand them for their behavior. Instead, he passed them and halted in front of her. Priscilla's eyes lit with admiration, for the young man was tall and imposing in his immaculate uniform, with a neatly trimmed beard that appeared to be standard for the higher crew.

"Miss McKinnon?" He pinned her with an enquiring.

"It's Mrs MacKinnon." Grace's mouth went suddenly dry. What had she done to attract the attention of the crew?

"Telegram for you, ma'am." He thrust a small brown envelope toward her.

She eyed the envelope but made no move to take it. "There must be some mistake."

"No mistake, ma'am. You're the only McKinnon on board." He shoved it into her free hand, snapped a brief salute and strode off along the deck.

Her heart fluttering like a panicked bird, she slid a thumbnail beneath the seal. Her hand shook so badly, she could hardly unfold the slip of opaque paper inside, its corners curling inwards in the wind. She smoothed it out and read what was written by a juvenile hand in stark black capitals.

YOUR REPREHENSIBLE BEHAVIOUR DISCOVERED STOP MY AGENT WILL MEET YOU AT PORT OF HALIFAX STOP YOU ARE TO ACCOMPANY HIM TO HALIBURTON HOTEL STOP PASSAGE SECURED ON SS KENSINGTON FOR RETURN TO ENGLAND IN FOUR DAYS STOP.
ANGUS MACKINNON.

Her stomach clenched. The deck seemed to tilt beneath her, though the sea was perfectly calm. She closed her eyes until the dizziness abated. Briefly, she wondered what the wireless operator must have thought as he transcribed the uncompromising message.

"What's that you have there, Grace?" Priscilla drifted back to her side and attempted to read over her shoulder.

"Nothing important." Grace crumpled the slip of thin paper and shoved it into her skirt pocket.

"If you say so." Priscilla's sceptical gaze slid to a spot over Grace's shoulder and she gave an exaggerated sigh. "Really, it's too bad. How does she do that?"

"Who does what?" Grace looked to where a slender girl with long, curly black hair mounted the outside companionway wearing a well-made but worn coat which was a few inches too short. The coat was fastened to the neck, most likely to hide the shabbiness of the dress beneath.

Reaching the top of the companionway, the girl tossed the end of her green woollen shawl over one shoulder and gave the deck a slow, sweeping look before catching Grace's eye.

"That Effie girl does realize this is the saloon deck?" Priscilla made no attempt to lower her voice as the girl strode confidently towards them. "Steerage passengers aren't allowed up here."

"It's Aoife, and hush, Priscilla, she'll hear you." Grace summoned a smile, admiring the fact nowhere appeared to be off limits to the Irish girl.

"I did hear yer." Aoife insinuated herself between the two women at the railing. "And yer don't fool me with your airs and graces, Miss Prissie."

"Well, really!" Priscilla's cheeks flooded an unbecoming red. She looked about to deliver a withering response, but instead, flung away from them and joined the group of young men whose raucous laughter drifted along the deck.

Aoife's most startling feature was a mane of black hair that fell in tangled waves down her back, though her light brown eyes were too small, her nose too long, and her lips a little too narrow to be striking. Grace knew that when angry, her features screwed up like a cross fairy, only to transform with delight at small kindnesses offered by strangers.

"You shouldn't goad her, Aoife," Grace whispered, "This might be our last day, but she could still make trouble for you."

"I'm not scared o' the likes of 'er. Schoolmistress, my arse." Aoife swiped a hand beneath her nose. "She's a brasser if ever I saw one."

Grace suppressed a shocked gasp, wondering if the word meant what she thought it did, but was reluctant to show her ignorance by asking.

On her first day on board, totally lost by the various decks and corridors and unfamiliar with shipboard manners, Grace had wandered onto the steerage deck. While the other passengers stared at her and edged away, Aoife approached her with a bright smile and a cheery greeting. She had explained how the steerage and second stateroom passengers occupied separate areas of the ship and never mixed.

Apologetic but intrigued, Grace discovered that like her, Aoife travelled alone and over the next few days, the pair formed an unlikely friendship. One night, to the plaintive tune of a lone violin, she and Aoife huddled on a hatch cover and shared the cake Grace snitched from the second-class tea.

As pink fingers of an Atlantic dusk crept across the sky, Aoife revealed how she had answered an advertisement in the Liverpool Post for 'Ladies inclined to matrimony.' And embarked on correspondence with a farmer who lived in Marysville, New Brunswick. With an assisted passage granted by the Salvation Army in order to join him, Aoife talked of living under clear skies and fresh air instead of the choking fumes of a Liverpool slum.

"Even so, you should be careful coming up here," Grace warned, scanning the area nearby for members of the crew who strode purposefully across decks and scaled companionways, busy with the imminent arrival of the ship.

"They'll no' bother with me, not today."

"I cannot believe we are finally here.' Grace leaned both forearms on the rail, the paper in her pocket crackling as she moved, bringing her thoughts back to her pressing problem.

"You look a bit peaky." Aoife peered into her face. "Did that nor-eastern keep you awake last night?"

"A little, but never mind me, I had a relatively comfortable bunk to sleep in. I heard the crew ordered the hatches battened down. It must have been frightening for you below decks"

"It weren't so bad." Aoife shrugged. "Mrs Murphy's nippers got pretty scared, so I brought the youngest into bed with me."

Lying rigid in her bunk as the ship pitched and rolled, Grace found the whole experience terrifying, her hands gripping the sides of her thin mattress. She could not imagine what it must be like to lie in a room below the waterline stacked in bunks on top of one another in the dark; listening to murmured prayers and snuffling sobs of the children as the floor dipped and heaved beneath them.

A loud ripple of high, girlish laughter jolted Grace from her thoughts.

"Knew I was right 'bout her." Aoife nodded to where Priscilla preened for the benefit of her male audience.

"Never mind her." Grace nodded to where more couples joined the dancing on the tween deck. Someone played a harmonica and both young and old stomped the boards to its high-pitched, frantic tune.

"I'm surprised you aren't down there," Grace said. "It's become quite a party."

"I've said me goodbyes." Aoife's expression grew wistful. "I wanted to see you 'afore we arrived, but you don't look very happy to be here. You've been talking 'bout

Halifax all week, but you've barely said one word."

"I'm sorry, I don't mean to be miserable. It's just-' Grace sighed, withdrew the telegram from her pocket and handed it to her.

"What's this?" Aoife frowned, turning the paper over in her hands. "Who'd be sending you a telegram? You said no one knew you were on board?"

"It's from my father-in-law. He insists I go back, but I refuse to be treated like an upper servant in his house. I want my own life." Grace hated the whine that entered her voice. Her guilt for Annie resurfaced, the poor girl had doubtless been dismissed for helping her escape. Not that she could do anything for her maid now, what with her own future placed in jeopardy.

"You ain't his servant, he cannot make you go back." Aoife's gaze swept Grace's expensive wool suit, the string of freshwater pearls at her throat and the diamond ring on her finger.

"There are different kinds of subservience." Grace interpreted her look. "What if he's painted me as some sort of incompetent, or worse a fugitive? The authorities might let this agent he mentioned take me away without an argument. I have no friends or connections to speak for me in Halifax. I'll have to go somewhere Angus MacKinnon won't find me.

"Why don't you come to New Brunswick with me? They must have places there where the gentry live."

"I'm not gentry any more, Aoife, if I ever was, but I'm sure you're right The Provinces are vast, so it's not likely we would be neighbors in any case." She returned the paper to her pocket.

"No, thass true." Aoife's eyes welled. "I didn't think of it like that."

"I'm sorry, that was a harsh thing to say. You know I didn't mean it." Having cultivated few connections in her life, their short, unlikely friendship meant a good deal to Grace. Saying goodbye to Aoife would be hard, and she had no idea how to express it.

"Course you didn't." Aoife nudged her, grinning. "What are ye going to do?"

Grace sighed. "I really don't know. Yet."

Chapter 3

Grace glanced along the deck and stiffened at the sight of a young officer strolling leisurely towards them, pausing to exchange greetings with an elderly couple before moving on.

"Get behind me, quickly." She nudged Aoife with an elbow.

"What?" Aoife followed her gaze. "Oh bother, where did he come from?"

The officer nodded to the couple then moved on, his hands clasped behind his back. His gaze settled on Grace, eyes widening in admiration.

"Good afternoon." His mouth quirked into a smile and he halted in front of them, an eyebrow lifted in enquiry. "Have you enjoyed the voyage, Miss?"

"Thank you, I have. It's been quite an adventure." Grace didn't correct his address and looked away, hoping he might lose interest and find someone else to talk to.

Where was Priscilla when she needed her?

"Ah, I recall my first Atlantic crossing. London to New York five years ago." He sighed, resting his forearms on the rail beside her, apparently in no hurry to move on.

That's all she needed, his life story. Behind her Aoife suppressed a cough.

"How long will it be before we dock?" Grace asked, raising her voice slightly.

"An hour or so, no more. We're about to come up to the pilot station near Chebucto Head. There, the engines will be shut down and we'll pick up a pilot boat to guide us for the last mile or so. I gather you've not been to Halifax before?"

"Er-no." Well, obviously. "I'm looking forward to finding out what it has to offer." Not that she had any intention of staying there now Angus MacKinnon knew where she was.

"I'm sure you'll love Halifax, there's so much to see. Are you visiting family or friends perhaps?"

"Not exactly." Grace's smile wavered as the officer's gaze slid to Aoife, who stood with her back to them.

"Miss?" He frowned, his gaze sweeping Aoife's shabby coat. "I don't believe I've ever seen you on this deck before. Which stateroom do you occupy?"

"She's my maid," Grace said before Aoife could answer. "I know she shouldn't be up here, but I thought it wouldn't do any harm. Not when we're so close to arriving." She summoned a flirtatious smile.

"Even so, madam, third class passengers shouldn't be-"

"Is that quite right?" Grace directed his attention to another ship approaching from the east. "That vessel appears to be moving quite fast. Is that normal inside the harbour?" Grace gestured Aoife away with a discreet backwards wave.

The officer's attention went straight to the water, eyes shielded with one hand against the glare.

"I agree, it is odd. She faced the other way a few moments ago. I expect, like us, she's heading for the pilot station."

Aoife ignored the chance to slip away, her attention, like several other passengers nearby turned to where the ship moved steadily in their direction.

"I expect he'll change course any moment." The officer said, for the benefit of the line of curious passengers who now studied the other ship. "Um- their captain probably mistook one of the buoys and took the wrong direction."

"It's coming quite fast, whereas we don't appear to be moving at all."

What began as a ploy to distract him turned into a real concern as the ship ploughed through the water towards them, its bow frothing the water into a sharp 'v'.

"Uh, that's right." The officer glanced up at the bridge, then back at the water, his jaw set. "We stopped the engines to take on the pilot boat."

A ripple of murmurs ran through the passengers crowding the rail. Even the boisterous young men fell silent.

"Whatever is the matter?" Priscilla demanded, apparently annoyed to no longer be the focus of the young men's attention. "What's everyone looking at?"

"That ship's coming too close." A man nearby pointed out what everyone else must have been thinking. "What the devil is that captain doing about it?" he demanded of the officer.

"I don't like it," the woman with the irate gentleman said. "It's going awfully fast."

"Why don't they turn?" a grey-haired man asked.

"As far as I can tell, sir," the young officer replied, "the pilot boat has positioned itself too far away. It will have to steer back to us. I'm sure we'll be on our way to the quay at any moment."

"I don't mean the pilot boat, man!" the same passenger said. "I'm talking about that steamer out there."

"Grace." Aoife grabbed her arm, her voice low, intense. "It's coming straight toward us."

"I know." Grace chewed her bottom lip, praying the ship would veer away any second. She stared up at the bridge, where scared faces appeared and fingers pointed.

"Hasn't our captain seen him?" A woman in a violet hat voiced Grace's own thoughts.

"I'm sure he has, madam," the officer reassured her.

Grace wasn't convinced, confirmed by the fact the officer had apparently forgotten about Aoife.

"We're not in any danger, are we?" Priscilla clung to the officer's arm and stared up at him as more murmurings circulated.

'The name on the bow says she's the Albano," a man close to Grace said. "That's a German vessel," he added, indignant.

Grace gripped the rail and took a deep breath, murmuring, 'What difference does the nationality of a thousand tons of metal bearing down on us make?'

'What did you say, Grace?" Aoife asked but Grace shook her head, her gaze still on the other ship.

"Please, calm yourselves." The officer's gaze moved from one questioner to the next. "The other captain is bound to alter his course directly." He attempted to disengage his arm from Priscilla's clutches, but she wasn't about to release her prize.

"I feel much safer with you here," she said feebly, fluttering her eyelashes.

Behind the officer's back, Grace rolled her eyes at Aoife, who sniggered.

"It's not turning away," Grace said as the black hull loomed closer."

"I'm not sure," the officer replied without looking at her. "The wind is light, there's no sea running and no perceptible tide. She cannot be in difficulty," he muttered, as if talking to himself.

The accordion music cut off with a cat-like wail on the tween deck below them. The dancers stopped and drifted to the rail. Women covered their faces with their hands, or grasped children to their skirts, while others waved angry arms at the ship as if to signal it away.

Grace jumped as three loud whistle blasts came from the other ship. She clasped one hand in the other to stop them shaking, her nerves shredded.

"There!" The officer exhaled in obvious relief. "The Albano has signalled she's going full speed astern." He eased his arm firmly from Priscilla's grip. "Their captain must have realized his mistake. Now he'll reverse engines and steer the ship away."

"I'm so glad you're here to reassure us." Priscilla remained attached to his side, her chin tilted as she smiled into his eyes.

An anticipatory hush settled over the deck, all eyes strained as they waited for the ship to change course.

"Are you sure?" Grace swallowed nervously, the bow growing larger with each second. "She's not slowing at all."

The officer's knuckles whitened on the rail. "She's not been put into reverse," adding in a whisper, "if she hits the engine room amidships, we'll go down for sure." He pushed away from the rail and ignoring the barrage of frantic questions aimed at him, ran to the companionway leading up to the bridge.

Panic spread as doors were thrown open along the deck from which several crewmen appeared, taking off at a run in all directions.

Grace's nerves tightened at the sight of their grim faces, her thoughts going to the fact everything she owned was contained in the two bags the steward had collected less than an hour before. Her letter for the bank manager, her mother's jewelry and every shred of clothing she possessed as well as the money to pay her board for the next month; she would lose it all if they sank.

She wasn't much of a swimmer and, in her heavy skirts, she would probably drown. An hysterical laugh bubbled into her throat, and she fought it down. "I read somewhere that water at sub-zero temperatures can stop your heart in seconds."

Beside her, Aoife twisted the end of her shawl in her fingers, her frown deepening.

Suddenly a rumbling came from below as the engines roared into pulsing life and the Parisian began to move.

"What's happening?" someone shouted.

"There's no cause for alarm." The officer reappeared, his voice raised above the cries of dismay erupting all around them. "Captain Johnson has ordered full speed ahead, probably to put some space between us and the Albano so it will pass right by us."

"Can he do that in time?" Grace asked. Aoife moved closer, clutching Grace's hand in a vice-like grip. "Why doesn't the other captain turn his ship away?" A man in a fur hat pulled down to his eyebrows above a pair of terrified eyes asked.

"Maybe his steering has gone?" the lady with him suggested.

The Parisian surged forward about two hundred feet in an attempt to move out of the Albano's way, but even Grace could see it wasn't far enough. The sea boiled at the waterline and white topped waves curled outwards as the massive steel bow cut through the water, growing closer and more terrifying with every second.

She bit her bottom lip. This could not be happening. No more than five minutes had passed since she used the approaching ship to distract the officer from Aoife.

The passengers crowded to the starboard side, staring with disbelief as the painted name Albano came almost close enough to touch. Crewmen raced for the bridge or hung over the rail, waving frantically at the crew who stood, white faced on the deck of the other ship.

"We won't get out of the way in time!" a woman screamed as the black bow ploughed straight for them.

"It's going to hit us!" Aoife shouted, flinging her arms round Grace.

* * *

Grace gripped the rail until her fingers cramped and squeezed her eyes shut at the moment of impact. She gasped as a deafening, hollow clang came as the deck lurched, tilted then hovered for a heart-stopping second before it slammed back onto the surface of the water. A rush of spray climbed the starboard rail and rained down on the observers. A drawn-out screech of metal on metal followed as the two ships locked together, the forward momentum of the Parisian carrying the Albano alongside it through the water.

Grace hurtled backwards into the man in the fur hat, Aoife ripped from her arms as they slid for a few feet before coming to a halt in a tangle of limbs. Passsengers lost their balance and stumbled into one another, some in danger of being trampled as they were thrown to their knees or into the rails, winches and davits that secured the lifeboats.

Grace staggered to her feet, more shaken than hurt. She helped up the man had cushioned her fall and once reassured he wasn't injured, she clambered over and around people to where Aoife lay.

"Are you hurt? Grace grasped her hand and dragged her to her feet.

"Nah." Aoife scrubbed a palm against her elbow. "Are we sinking?"

"I don't know." Grace wiped salt water from her face as she ran back to the rail, where passengers had gained their feet and crowded the rail to see the damage.

The Parisian dragged the Albano for a hundred feet before shrugging her off with a juddering creak and a groan of metal. A gap rapidly formed between the two hulls and the German steamer dropped back, veering away in a sea that roiled with white tipped waves.

"Is anyone injured?" A crewman helped up a man who careened over a winch, the question greeted by shaken heads and bewildered, stunned looks. A lifebelt came adrift from its hook and fallen onto one of the youths who taunted the steerage passengers earlier. Others clambered to their feet more slowly, calling out for friends, or to enquire if anyone needed help.

Mothers searched for children and men separated from their wives called their names. White faces with strained expressions stared around in disbelief, but apart from the shock of impact, no one appeared badly injured.

The Parisian had levelled out, the engines ratcheted up a notch, and plunged smoothly through the water straight for the quayside.

"What happened?" A woman's voice rose in hysteria from farther along the deck.

"What do you think happened?" Aoife snorted. "That German boat bashed into us."

"Then why are we still going so fast?" The man in the fur hat demanded. "Is the ship out of control?"

"That was quite some bang, but we appear to still be afloat." One of the youths said as he disentangled his feet from where they had become entwined in the bottom rail.

"Maybe not." Grace pointed to the deck below them, where the stern dipped slightly on the port side. "We're listing, so there must be some damage below the water line. I cannot see properly from up here."

An officer who stopped to enquire as to injuries among the passengers was joined by another, who whispered something to him. The first man nodded, at which his colleague saluted and left.

"What was that about?" Aoife asked. "Is there something they aren't telling us?

Grace shook her head to tell her she didn't know, but hoped it wasn't bad news.

"Clear the boats!" The command came loudly from the bridge, sending crewmen running to lifeboat stations where they hauled at the tarpaulins.

"Looks like the captain's taking notice at last," the fur hatted man grumbled, brushing down the sleeves of his overcoat with both hands.

"There aren't enough boats for all of us." Aoife whispered, clutching Grace's arm. "We'll drown."

"Now stop that." Grace gave Aoife a tiny shake. "No one is going to drown," she said with more confidence than she felt. There were over nine hundred people on board and less than a dozen lifeboats. Aoife was right, they wouldn't hold everyone.

"We must be sinking if they are lowering the lifeboats!" This call was taken up by several others and in seconds the crowd surged in that direction.

"Stand back!" The young officer returned from the bridge and planted himself in front of the closest lifeboat, feet splayed and arms raised to hold them off. "It's just a precaution, ladies and gentlemen. Stay where you are."

"Let us get aboard," a woman with a whimpering toddler pleaded. "We're wasting time."

"Can't you see the deck's listing?" A man forced himself to the front.

"Be quiet!" The officer waved off shouts and tugging hands. "The engines would have to be shut down to load the lifeboats. Once stationary, the hold would rapidly fill with water. We're still a mile or so from the harbour, so our best course is to make for the pier at full speed. Captain Johnston knows what he's doing."

"Rubbish, man," a voice called out from the back of the crowd. "Get those lifeboats launched!"

The crowd divided into those who agreed the ship must keep going and those who harassed the crew to release the boats.

Voices were being raised in panic, and Grace anticipated a fight. Frantic, she looked around for a way out of the press of people, but she and Aoife were hemmed in on three sides, their backs to the rail. She searched the faces for Priscilla but couldn't see her.

"Perhaps readying the lifeboats is only a precaution," Grace whispered to a wide-eyed Aoife. "That officer is right. If we maintain this speed we'll reach the quay in minutes. It's possible the damage isn't serious at all." She tried not to look back to where the deck had dipped lower on one side and several passengers near the stern clung grimly to the opposite rail to stop themselves from sliding across the deck.

"What the devil is happening?" A moustachioed man accosted another officer. "No one is telling us anything."

"If you'll all calm down, I'll tell you what I know."' The officer waved both hands in a signal for quiet. "It appears the hull has been breached at number four hold abaft." He waited for the ripple of dismayed shouts and an occasional gasp to subside. "Fortunately, Captain Johnston was able to pull us forward enough for the point of impact to occur behind the engines and not amidships. We're still afloat, as you can see. The captain has given orders for full speed ahead towards the quay."

"Can't they send boats out to fetch us off?" The man in the fur hat's fear had turned to belligerence. "The harbour is only about a mile away."

"It's no different to the lifeboats, sir. To transfer everyone aboard a small craft, we would have to stop the engines. Captain Johnston is very experienced, and he knows the harbour well. He wouldn't have made this decision if he didn't believe it was the best course." He backed away rapidly. "Now, I must join him. You'll all be kept informed."

"I'm not staying on board until the ship sinks!" A terror stricken young man started to climb the rail. "I'll swim to the pier if I have to."

"Don't be a fool!" A crewman threw himself on the man and dragged him back. "You'll freeze before you travel twenty yards. That water was solid ice a month ago."

"It looks as if we'll make it to the wharf before we go down," Grace pointed to where the row of wooden warehouses loomed closer. "Even if we go into the water there's a chance we'll be pulled out."

"But I can't swim," Aoife whimpered.

"And I don't want to. This is my best coat," said Priscilla who reappeared from somewhere. "No one will be forced to swim." Grace reassured them both, while images of the cold harbour water closing over them flashed into her head. The list of the deck worsened and there was still a wide expanse of water between them and the dock.

The sound of distressed weeping came from a woman several feet away, being comforted by two others.

"Poor Mrs Simmons. She must rue the day she boarded this ship," Priscilla said, though there was little sympathy in her tone.

"Who is she?" Grace tried not to stare at the obviously hysterical lady who refused to be consoled.

"Don't you pay attention to what anyone says?" Priscilla tutted.

"Gossip, you mean?" Grace arched an eyebrow. "Not as a rule, no."

Priscilla shrugged off the implied insult. "A day out of Liverpool, rough seas swamped the deck. Her husband hit his head on the rail or something. He was killed outright."

"There was a death on board?" Grace gasped. "I didn't hear anything about that."

"I did." Aoife retrieved her shawl from the deck and shook it out. "I woke up at about dawn the next morning when the engines stopped. A woman in the next bunk told me it was for the funeral. Poor bloke was buried at sea."

"I had no idea." Grace thought the openly distressed woman looked only a few years older than herself. One of her companions patted her hand while the other whispered endearments, but neither appeared to have any effect.

"The crew kept it quiet," Aoife whispered. "A death on board's bad for business. Sailors believe in omens like that."

"I'm sure it's nothing to do with omens." Grace shuddered. Strange things certainly did happen at sea. The telegram in her pocket proved that, just when she hoped to have escaped her father-in-law's clutches. "What will happen to her?"

Aoife shrugged. "She's got two nippers. With no man to provide for them, she'll have ter go back."

"The poor woman," Grace sighed. 'To have all her hopes dashed so cruelly. And now this.'

"Looks like we'll make it!" someone shouted, redirecting Grace's attention away from the crying lady.

The quay, on which men in overalls had lined up wielding grappling hooks and lifebelts, lay little more than fifty yards away. A cheer went up on both decks, women hugged their husbands and children as the engines ground into reverse and then slowed. The ship came alongside the pier where shoreline staff rushed to secure lines and bolted the barriers into place with a clank of metal.

"We're still taking on water." Aoife indicated the now badly listing deck where passengers were making a dash for the gangplanks. "We'd better move or we'll not get off in time."

"I can't see Priscilla." Grace stared around but the girl had gone again.

"Don't worry about her. Nay doubt she'll be one of the first off." Aoife pulled Grace towards the crush of passengers making for the nearest gangplank. "Come on, let's go."

Chapter 4

Halifax, Nova Scotia

Silent, white-faced passengers crowded the rails as the SS Parisian headed at full speed for the jetty. Crewmen ran back and forth in response to orders to unhook the barriers ready for the gangplanks to be slid into place. The engines roared into reverse and the ship eased into the quayside where ropes were thrown from the deck to waiting dockworkers who wound them around the stanchions on the quayside, securing the Parisian

Grace's relief to have reached the relative safety of the quay was short lived, as with so many people still on board and only two gangplanks, it occurred to her they might sink right there in the harbour.

The panic of the race to the quay left no time for her to formulate a plan once she left the ship, but with so many fretful passengers clamoring to disembark, she might be able to lose herself in the crowd.

"I shouldn't be here, Grace," Aoife said. "I need to go down below. What if they're checking names as we get off? I'll be in trouble."

"It's safer here." Grace tugged Aoife into the queue lined up at the end of the nearest gangplank. The deck listed badly on the starboard side, and although it had only been stationary a few minutes, already the waterline crept further up the stern deck.

"You might become trapped if the water on the lower deck gets higher." Guilt filled her that the Irish girl's safety wasn't the only reason she wanted her to stay. The agent wouldn't be looking for two girls travelling together. Aoife was right. Her predicament was not her problem.

"I'll fetch my bag, then I'll come find you in the Customs Hall." Aoife nodded to where the first of the passengers were making their way along the quay. "There'll be quite a crush in there with everyone trying to get through at once, so it will be a while before the officers examine everyone's papers."

"Which is probably where this agent will be looking for me. But you're right. You should go, Aoife." She broke off at the sound of shouting from below. "What's going on down there?"

Frightened faces pressed against the metal gate that separated steerage from the main deck which remained locked. A crowd of angry men pressed against it, voices raised, and hands reaching through the bars. A crewman stood guard on the other side, but he kept shaking his head and ordering the people to step back. "Why doesn't he open the gate?" Aoife asked, nodding to the crewman. "They are below the waterline down there. If the water starts rushing in they'll be trapped."

"I don't know. Let's go and see." Anything to delay coming face to face with an official who might be looking for her.

Grace eased her way back through the queue of passengers who streamed around them towards the gangplank. Dragging Aoife with her, she ignored the annoyed murmurings and critical looks as they descended the companionway to the lower deck.

"Let them through!" Aoife demanded of the stone-faced crewman at the gate who ignored her.

"You can't leave them there, the ship might sink!" Grace said.

"Can't help that, miss." The sailor shrugged. "I've been ordered to wait until the saloon and second passengers are off, then there's the cabin baggage to be cleared."

"You must open the gate!" Grace insisted. The noise level from below deck had grown louder and more frantic. "There are four hundred people down there. The women and children at the back are being crushed."

"Not worth my job, miss." He shrugged. "I'll open it when I get my orders."

The ship gave a sudden creak and the aft deck sank a few more feet. A rivulet of water crept along the edge of the boards towards the steerage deck like a fast-moving snake.

"Please," Grace pleaded. "We're taking on water. If the deck tilts any more, they could be in real danger."

"Open that gate!" A loud, commanding voice carried over the din from behind them. Grace swung around, her gaze travelling from a sapphire blue vest upwards into the face of one of the handsomest men she had ever seen. A smooth shaven chiselled chin below a straight nose and grey eyes fringed with thick black lashes regarded her steadily. Her gaze went to a rogue streak of white that ran from his left temple and blended into straight, raven black hair that disappeared beneath his hat.

"There's a hole in the side of number four hold large enough for a man to walk through." The stranger said, pointing the silver top of a black japan cane at the crewman. "Do you want to be held responsible for any casualties if this ship does go down?"

"Er, yessir." The crewman's belligerent expression dissolved. "I mean, no sir. I wouldn't want to be held responsible. But I haven't had orders to open the gate."

"Consider this an order. The situation is an emergency. Those people need to get off the ship - now."

The crewman swallowed, touched his cap and executed a small bow. He withdrew a key from a breast pocket, unlocked the sturdy padlock and swung the gate open. A loud cheer went up from the packed companionway, followed by the clamour of booted feet ringing on the metal steps as a wave of steerage passengers surged through and spilled onto the deck, shoving the sailor aside.

Relieved, Grace stood back as women, the elderly and small children were swept along or dragged behind them. Fear and panic turned instantly to excited enthusiasm in their eagerness to get onto dry land.

The crewman's eyes widened in alarm and he darted to the front of the crowd, his arms waving in a feeble attempt to make them walk no more than two abreast across the gangplank.

The crowd ignored him as they thundered to the quayside. A half dozen customs officers on the dock sprang forward with shouted orders to direct them into the various entrances of the customs shed.

"That was kind of you step in like that," Grace said to the stranger. "Those people were beginning to panic."

"My pleasure." He tipped his hat to each of them in turn. "I suggest you ladies leave immediately. I don't know how long this vessel will stay afloat. We're still taking on water, and as you can see, we're listing badly." He nodded at the pressing crowd. "The customs men appear to be having a difficult time controlling them. You wouldn't want to get lost in the chaos." He inclined his head, turned and strolled off towards the bow end.

"That's where he's wrong," Grace said as they joined the diminishing queue at the gangplank. "It's exactly what we want." She unwound Aoife's emerald green shawl from her shoulders and wrapped it around her own head. "I have to keep my head down so tell me when we reach customs."

"Good idea," Aoife said. "Keep close to me."

It wasn't much of a plan, but better than Grace had come up with thus far. She pulled the edges of the shawl together beneath her chin and with her arm tucked through Aoife's, crossed the gangplank, keeping close to a chattering family of eastern Europeans in front, and a Sicilian woman hurling what sounded like abuse to her hapless husband close behind.

"I can't see where I'm going," Grace whispered.

"Hush, we're nearly there."

Grace stepped onto the solid quayside where she swayed on the firm ground. Had she been able to, she might have broken into a run, but the press of people forced her to shuffle along among calls of, "Move along there," and "Don't block the path, keep moving."

The customs area was little more than a wooden shed resembling a livestock market, long and low with wooden barriers marking the routes the passengers from different areas of the ship were to follow. Uniformed officers hustled the steerage passengers into an untidy line four times the length of the passengers on the stateroom side.

A low roar of voiced echoed through the shed as seven hundred steerage passengers chattered in their own language to each other or aimed incomprehensible questions at harassed customs men who attempted to maintain order, assuring everyone they would be attended to.

"Here's where we part company, Aoife." Grace nodded to a sign over the desk where uniformed officers stood. "I have to go over there to show my papers."

"All right, but I'll hang around at the back until you're safely through. By the looks of this lot, I'll be here a long time as we all have to be examined by a doctor."

"A doctor? Whatever for?"

"They don't want anyone with a disease comin' into their country. Don't look at me like that, I don't like the idea much either." That Aoife omitted the fact the stateroom passengers were not required to suffer the same humiliation did not escape Grace.

"I see, and what happens if they find something?"

Aoife shrugged. "I suppose they'll send me back to Liverpool."

"I'll hope that doesn't happen. Besides, you look healthy enough to me." Grace lifted the edge of the shawl, prepared to hand it back when her gaze caught and snagged a man in a stovepipe hat at the far end of the shed in conversation with a customs man. At intervals he would scan the shed with a penetrating gaze, his neck stretched to peer into faces. Once he grasped the arm of a female passenger, said something to her then when she shook her head, gestured her brusquely away again.

"What's wrong?" Aoife whispered when Grace didn't move with the queue.

"I think that's him. MacKinnon's agent." She nodded to where he approached a young woman at the rear of the queue behind them. "What do I do?"

"Nothing you can do. Don't look at him."

Grace's throat dried, and she tugged the shawl closer round her face, praying he wouldn't see her. The line moved slowly but steadily towards the desk where an officer examined passports and papers until it was almost Grace's turn. Her nerves on edge, she was about to check if he had come any closer, when a voice demanded, "Your papers please, Miss."

"Yes, yes, of course." Grace released the shawl that dropped onto her shoulders as she fumbled in her bag. She removed the sheet of paper with its official seal obtained in London with the help of Mr Beech's helpful contact at the Salvation Army office. Never having had a passport before, it surprised her how important carrying it made her feel.

Her heart beat rapidly as his disinterested gaze lingered on the details before he applied a rubber stamp before handing it back with a smile. "Thank you, ma'am, and welcome to Canada."

"Er, thank you." She shoved the paper into her bag and left the desk, looked up and froze.

The agent bumped into an elderly woman. She scowled at him and tapped him hard with her umbrella. He nodded in apology then forged on, his path blocked by a couple accompanied by a lady's maid.

Aoife left her place in the queue and joined Grace.

"Not that way, Miss." A customs man leapt forward and barred the Irish girl's way. "Steerage passengers must remain on the other side of the barrier. Do you have your papers?"

"That I have!" Aoife's eye widened. "I came to say goodbye to my friend. I'll be doing nothing wrong, sir."

"I'm sure you're aware we had some trouble in the harbour." Grace approached them. "This young woman helped me."

"Aye, well." The officer lifted his cap with one hand and scratched the wavy brown hair beneath it. "As far as I know, everyone is off the Parisian and safe, but regulations are regulations. If your papers are in order, madam, you may leave," he addressed Grace. "But you-" He jabbed a finger in Aoife's direction. "Get back behind that barrier."

MacKinnon's agent had negotiated all obstacles and stood a few feet away, watching the exchange with more than mild interest.

Grace kept her head down, her mind racing. Once the customs man left, he was bound to question her. What should she do? Deny she was the person he was looking for? Make a run for it? Before she could make up her mind, a strangely familiar male voice said behind her, "There you are! I've been waiting over there for you to finish. Is everything in order?"

Grace turned around to where the handsome man who helped with the gate stood smiling at her.

"Um, I-"

"No problem here, sir." The custom's man stepped between Aoife and the newcomer as if shielding him from unpleasantness. "A slight misunderstanding about procedures with this passenger, sir." His face blazed a self-conscious red. "Everything is under control."

"Forgive me, but it doesn't appear so to me." The handsome man eased him back with a wave of his cane. "Since when do you refuse entry to British citizens travelling second class?"

He wasn't as young as she first imagined, evidenced by tiny lines beside his eyes and deeply tanned skin that told of a life spent outdoors. His lips twitched into a smile as he returned her astonished look, his pupils widening as they roved her face.

"The lady hasn't been refused, sir. Her passport is in order and has been stamped." The officer's flush deepened, and he kept dipping his shoulders. Grace almost expected him to curtsey. "The query is with this young woman." He nodded to Aoife. "She hasn't shown her papers yet and has no business on this side of the barrier, I was just-"

"I will vouch for her myself, my man. You don't have to concern yourself."

"But sir, all passengers must show their papers."

"Agreed, but can't you see this young woman is suffering a debilitating case of seasickness?" He leaned closer to Grace. "Are you still feeling ill, my dear? It's very stuffy in here, with all these people, I can hardly breathe myself."

"Oh, I- uh, yes." Grace's throat dried. "I do feel quite faint."

"Then what are you waiting for," the handsome man whispered beside her ear. "Do it."

She had barely dipped a few inches in a feigned collapse before her feet left the floor and she was swept into a pair of strong arms.

"I must get her into the fresh air." The man glanced back and called to Aoife. "Come, girl, your mistress needs your help."

Grace's heart thumped with thrilled relief as she was borne through the door to the street. She summoned a pitiful moan and let her head sink onto his shoulder that gave off a smell of expensive cologne. It was all she could do not to press her face into his neck and inhale deeply to appreciate it more.

She sneaked a quick look behind them, but the officer was otherwise occupied and the man in the stovepipe hat questioned another woman passenger.

"You can put me down now, sir," Grace said as they stepped into daylight. That she was in no hurry for him to do so came as a surprise, and he bore her weight with no apparent difficulty.

"Are you sure, they might still be watching?" His soft breath on her skin sent a strange shiver through her. He made no attempt to do as she asked.

Apart from Frederick, no one had ever her before but his attempt at the threshold of their room on their wedding night ended abruptly when his back cramped.

"Well they ain't," Aoife said from behind them. "So, you can take your 'ands off her now. Not that it weren't kind of you to help an' all that." She retrieved her shawl that had slipped around Grace's elbows and trailed to the ground, dusting it down with firm strokes.

"Pardon me." The man set Grace down. Their eyes locked, her face inches from his due to the fact he kept his other arm firmly round her waist. "I didn't mean to cause any offence."

"You did not, and I cannot thank you enough, sir." Grace stepped back, conscious of the heat rushing into her cheeks. "And you did not, I assure you."

"You're welcome, although I confess, I'm curious as to why you needed to avoid customs.

However," he nodded to Aoife. "Your companion will still need to get through immigration."

Grace slapped down her skirt and poked stray strands of hair back into place beneath her straw hat. "I hope you don't think-"

"I assure you I wasn't thinking anything. Not that's it's any of my concern one way or the other." He lifted his hat and turned to leave.

"But I need to explain. I wasn't trying to avoid customs. My papers are in order, it's just that-" She glanced to where MacKinnon's agent watched her from the door. "Could you take me wherever you are going?"

"Grace!" Aoife gasped. "What are you thinking?"

"Is there no one here to meet you?" he asked.

"I'm afraid not."

"I see. He lifted his cane from the ground slightly to indicate Aoife. "And what about you, young lady?"

Aoife's eyes flashed. "You don't have to worry 'bout me." She folded her arms and adopted her cross fairy face. "I've made me own arrangements."

"I beg your pardon." He sketched Aoife a polite, if theatrical bow. "I meant nothing by it."

"I did have a reservation booked," Grace said, again feeling the need to explain. "But-" She dared not go to the boarding house the shipping agent had recommended. It was probably the first place Angus MacKinnon's agent would look. "My plans have lately become flexible. "Do you live in Halifax, sir?"

"Grace!" Aoife gasped, but Grace nudged her into silence.

"I do not," he replied, his mouth twitched as he fought a smile. "I shall be here for tonight. I leave for Prince Edward Island tomorrow."

"This island. Is it far?"

"About two hundred miles. My home is in Charlottetown. Why do you ask?"

"I see." Grace frowned, thinking. Two hundred miles should be far enough away.

"While you make up your mind, might I offer my services? My carriage is waiting to take me to my hotel. It's the third from the front." He waved the silver topped cane at the road. "If you have no accommodations arranged, I would be happy to obtain a room for you there."

"I accept."

"Grace!" Aoife gasped again.

"Shall I summon a porter to fetch your trunk?" he asked.

"My bags will be on one of the trolleys somewhere." She looked around vaguely. "Ah, there it is. The portmanteau and brown leather valise on the top there."

"I'll get my coachman to retrieve them for you. Perhaps we ought to introduce ourselves?" He raised his hat. "Andrew Jardine, at your service."

"I'm Mrs MacKinnon. Grace. And this is Aoife Doyle."

Aoife nodded, regarding him through narrowed eyes.

"I'll leave you to say your goodbyes." He replaced the hat, giving it a final pat. "When you're ready, Mrs MacKinnon, I'll be waiting at my carriage."

Grace watched him stride away, his long overcoat swaying round his ankles. The driver climbed down onto the road at his approach and after a short whispered conversation, the coachman approached the porter, and between them, unloaded Grace's luggage.

"What can ye be thinking, Grace?" Aoife tugged her shawl around her shoulders. "Goin' off with a stranger."

"I have few options if I don't want to be taken back to England. And did you know your Dublin accent gets stronger when you're angry?"

"I'm from Waterford if you wants to know." Aoife lifted her chin but didn't look at all insulted. "Though I ain't been there since I was a nipper."

"I apologize, and I've heard Waterford is quite lovely."

"Not the part I was born in," Aoife mumbled. "You'll be all right won't you, Grace?"

"I doubt I'll be in any greater danger than you are. You've agreed to marry a man you haven't yet seen. Anyway, you heard him. He's leaving for this Charlottetown place tomorrow.

If he takes me with him, maybe I'll settle there instead?"

"I'm going to be wed, while you're goin' off to some hotel with a man you just met. There's rules about how ladies should behave. It's different for me."

"Different, how?"

"I dunno. It just is." Aoife shrugged. "You got to admit though, he's a foine looking fella."

"I didn't notice," Grace lied, sneaking a look at Mr Jardine, then back at Aoife. "I suppose it's goodbye then?" She pulled Aoife to one side to avoid the stream of passengers hauling bags, suitcases and trunks behind them on an exodus towards the line of carriages.

"I suppose so." Aoife sniffed. The man in the stovepipe hat had disappeared, though the Customs officer lounged against the doorframe, staring at them. "I'll be there in a minute." Aoife gestured he was to wait.

Grace laughed and threw her arms around her. "I've enjoyed our short time together. I wish you luck in New Brunswick." Her voice hitched as it occurred to her they would probably never see each other again.

"Now don't you be goin' all soft on me." Aoife pushed Grace firmly away and wiped a hand under her nose.

"You'll be foine if you keep your money close and don't let fella-me-lad over there take liberties." She cocked her chin at the carriage, where Mr Jardine's coachman was loading Grace's meagre luggage.

"As if I would, but that's good advice." She blinked away tears as she gave Aoife a final, fierce hug. "You should go and join the line, or you'll be here all night." Aoife hauled her bag into her arms and with a final, cheery wave, sauntered back towards the hall, her green shawl billowing like a sail behind her.

At the door to the customs hall, she delivered a slow wink to the officer and skipped past him into the hall.

He pushed away from the doorframe and shaking his head slowly, he ushered her back inside.

Chapter 5

The Waverley Inn, Halifax, Nova Scotia

"When I said my carriage, I meant a hired vehicle." He settled onto the seat opposite Grace, one leg crossed over the other and his cane propped against the door.

"There's no need to apologize, Mr Jardine." Grace adjusted her hat which had collided with the doorframe as she climbed in. "This hackney is no worse than any found in London." Why he cared what she thought of his conveyance escaped her.

"Not quite, but I wouldn't want you to think I owned this one." He raised a sardonic eyebrow at the shabby upholstery and cracked varnish on the window frames. "My father-in-law keeps a very fine carriage, or at least it was considered so some twenty years ago. It's quite shabby now and the ride is so uncomfortable, even his sister prefers to walk, and she's a lady who is a stranger to exercise." Her smile at the memory died as the cab lurched forward onto the road, aware she had no idea where he was taking her. "Is - um, is this hotel you mentioned far?"

"A few streets away, although if you prefer, I could take you wherever you planned to stay this evening?"

"Uh, no, I had nowhere specific in mind,' she lied. The hotel where she planned to stay was too close to the harbour and bound to be known to the agent. "You won't be staying long in Halifax, Mr Jardine?" She recalled something he said earlier about going home.

"Only for tonight, I hope to be on my way to Prince Edward Island tomorrow."

"I see." She nodded, stricken by the thought that in twelve hours she would be on her own again with Angus MacKinnon's agent on her trail.

The harbour with its rows of wharves and warehouses behind them, the hackney entered a tree-lined street wider than any Grace had ever seen in England. A majority of the houses had boarded facades as opposed to brick or stone, most with bay windows covered verandas and porches, all freshly painted in pastel colors, like a child's toy village just out of its box.

"You are being very kind to me, Mr Jardine, when you know nothing about me. Are you not curious? After all, I might be a dangerous criminal."

"And are you?" He raised his eyebrows slightly.

"No, of course not." She lifted her chin, affronted by the suggestion despite the fact she invited it. "I've never done anything remotely illegal in my life." Reckless, maybe, even mischievous, but not criminal.

"Then I'm sufficiently confident I've not offered hospitality to an undesirable." He turned towards the window and lowered his voice. "In fact, you are exceedingly desirable."

"I beg your pardon?" Grace asked, feigning ignorance, although she heard him quite well.

"It's of no importance. Ah, here we are." Almost before the carriage came to a complete stop he leapt out onto the street, a hand extended to help her down where they waited in companionable silence for the coachman to unload their luggage.

The Waverley Inn boasted two square bay windows on either side of a short flight of steps up to a canopied front door with bevelled stained-glass panels. Pale painted clapboard clad the building and, from the lower ground floor up, a red tiled roof covered all three stories.

"It's charming." Grace's gaze took in the neat dimity curtains at the windows and the picket fence that bordered the front and sides.

"I always stay at The Waverley. It's a favorite of mine when I come to Halifax and not the sort of establishment a customs officer would frequent." He stood aside for the driver who unloaded their luggage and began transferring it through a side door.

"I wasn't evading cust-" she began, her voice trailing away as he had already crossed to the pile of luggage the driver placed on the road.

"You don't have a trunk? Just these two bags?" Mr Jardine nudged the scuffed leather bag gently with a toe of his shiny black shoe.

"Er-I plan to send for the rest of my things later," she repeated the excuse she used when Priscilla asked the same question.

"I see." He raised a sceptical eyebrow, then held open the door for her to pass ahead of him into a lobby that smelled of cinnamon and beeswax overlaid by the smell of something savoury from a kitchen in the rear.

A young man behind the front desk, greeted Mr Jardine like an old friend, then summoned a porter to take them upstairs.

"Your room is on the floor above mine," Jardine cocked an eyebrow, "in case you were worried."

She assured him she had not been, though the fact he mentioned it came as a relief. Pleading fatigue, she requested a light supper served in her room, to which he acquiesced without a word.

The heavy oak furniture and dark floral wallpaper were reminders of the English style. The high canopied bed with its thick mattress looked vastly more comfortable than her narrow lower bunk on board ship. At night her head had been regularly in danger of colliding with the communal vanity sink on the wall.

Once the door closed behind the maid who brought her supper of soup and sandwiches, Grace relaxed for the first time since she spotted the Albano's bow speed towards them. "She ate her meal and unpacked, arranging her silver vanity set on the bureau. It was one of her most treasured possessions as it had once belonged to her great-great grandmother.

From the comfort of the vast bed, she tore Angus MacKinnon's telegram into tiny pieces and tossed them in the direction of the wastepaper basket.

After such an eventful day, sleep came easily, only to be interrupted by a dream

Aoife emitted silent screams for help but remained unreachable as the water dragged Grace down. The ship's horn wailed in its final death throes and daylight faded into a diminishing beam above her.

At the point where blackness engulfed her, Grace cried out and bolted upright, the covers clutched beneath her chin. Panicked, she lit a candle with shaking hands to banish the shadows, repeating over and over that it was only a dream. She lay staring at the ceiling until her thoughts calmed and the candle guttered out.

She woke for the second time to the sound of brass rings being rattled over the curtain pole by a maid, flooding the room with wintery light.

'Good morning to you, ma'am." The girl set a pitcher from which a spiral of steam arose on the dresser.

"And to you." Grace propped herself onto one elbow, blinking against the sudden assault on her eyes. She slid from beneath the coverlet, pulled on her dressing gown, grabbed a few coins discarded on her nightstand and thrust them at the maid. The girl's start of surprise and deep curtsey told Grace she had been overly generous.

She had obtained the coins from the purser's office on the Parisian with only a vague idea of what they were worth. She would have to put that right if she was going to keep a close eye on her finances.

Once the maid left, Grace spotted a note had been slid under her door. The first fluttering of fear as she opened it was quickly dispelled when she saw it was from Mr Jardine. He informed her in a bold sloping script that he would meet her for breakfast in the dining room. She exhaled in relief, reminding herself that Angus MacKinnon was not all powerful. Neither he nor his agent could have tracked her down in so short a time. Even so, the sooner she left Halifax the better.

She dressed quickly, repacked her things and went down to the lobby where she asked the eager young man at the desk the location of the dining room.

"Please prepare my bill for me."

"No need for that, ma'am. Mr Jardine has taken care of it."

"I see." Frowning, she returned her purse to her bag and went to join him in the half-full dining room.

Andrew Jardine, reading a newspaper, occupied a table for two in the bay window. He looked up as she approached, refolded the newspaper and placed it on a nearby chair "Did you sleep well?" He rose and waited for her to take the chair opposite before sitting again.

"I did indeed, thank you." She cleared her throat and before she lost her nerve, said, "I appreciate your assistance with my - predicament, sir, but I'm not penniless."

"I did not assume you were." His brow furrowed. "Have I done something wrong?"

"Unwise perhaps. You paid my bill."

"Ah!" He adjusted his napkin on his lap. "I meant no insult, Mrs MacKinnon. The manager added your accommodation to my account for expedience." He lifted a silver pot in enquiry. "Coffee? And I've ordered for you. I hope you don't mind?"

"Thank you." She waited as he poured a dark stream of steaming coffee into her cup. "And I don't mind at all, but I wish you to know, I fully intend to pay my own way. In every respect."

"I apologize for the misunderstanding. In which case I hope you won't take offence when I say I have presumed again and taken a precaution on your behalf."

She took a sip from her cup; the brew was hot, rich and very welcome. "If you have a chaperone tucked away somewhere, I-'

"Nothing like that," he interrupted. "The manager has agreed to be discreet regarding your presence here."

"I appreciate your thoughtfulness." She replaced her cup in its saucer, both relieved yet embarrassed. It made sense the agent wouldn't give up looking for her when her name was on the passenger list, but the thought of how the manager must now regard her made her shudder. Hardly an auspicious start to her new life.

"It will take that customs chap some time to work his way through every hotel and boarding house in town and by then we shall be gone."

"As I explained yesterday, it wasn't a customs man I was-" she broke off as the waiter appeared and slid a plate in front of her which contained sausages, bacon, eggs and what looked like a beef steak. The server placed a slightly larger meal in front of her companion before he bowed and withdrew.

"This looks wonderful." She inhaled the heavy, meaty smell of sausages and bacon. "I ought to say that I couldn't possibly eat all this, but I rather think I can." She could hardly wait for the server to leave before she took a warm, floury roll from the basket in the center of the table and picked up her cutlery. "The ship was still sinking when we left the harbour. Do you know what happened to her?"

"I do. Fortunately the nine hundred passengers and crew disembarked safely. As a disaster at sea it doesn't register very highly. Not that the owners would agree. The damage was not quite as serious as it might have been. Pumps were set to reduce the leakage from the compartment and kept running all night. However, in the early hours of this morning the aft compartment bulkhead gave way and the two forward compartments were flooded. The stern deck was submerged, and water flowed into the engine room. I only hope they get it under control before it reaches the cylinders."

"You appear to know a good deal about it. Are you acquainted with the owners then?"

"Actually, I'm one of them."

Grace blinked, unsure how to respond. His clothes and demeanour certainly bore out the impression of wealth, but one could often be deceived by appearances. Perhaps it was a very small share. "But you said you were leaving today. Won't you be required to stay in Halifax to supervise?" her last small hope she was not to be abandoned disappeared with the shake of his head.

"Not necessary. There isn't much I can do. The company representative will take care of salvage operations."

"I hope you don't lose your ship - the part that belongs to you at least." Grace forked scrambled eggs into her mouth, delighting in their creamy taste. "Why did the Albano collide with us? It was as if their captain didn't know we were there."

"I've no idea. It will take a public enquiry to discern that." He cut into a thick slab of bacon as large as his hand.

They ate in comfortable silence, exchanging an occasional smile or a request to pass the salt amongst the low murmur of voices from other residents and the click of cutlery.

"Mrs Mackinnon?" His softened tone brought her gaze to his face. "I admit to a degree of curiosity. If the man on the quay wasn't a customs officer, why were you so determined for him not see you?" At her start of alarm, he added, "Not that it concerns me either way, but a spicy story might lighten my day no end."

She hesitated, knowing the question was bound to arise at some time. To leave him wondering seemed unfair, but how would he react to the truth? Would he agree with her father-in-law and march her to the nearest authority? Or sympathize and assist her to escape? A half-truth would be unlikely to satisfy him and perhaps she did owe him honesty.

"My guardian made plans for my future to which I objected. So I left. It's as simple as that." She stirred milk into her second cup of coffee. "That man you saw at the harbour was his agent, sent to escort me back to England."

"Does your guardian regard you as a bad influence? Because I have to say I find that hard to believe."

"Oh, I'm quite beyond help, Mr Jardine." She smothered a hysterical laugh. "I've scandalized that poor man on so many occasions, I really don't know how he put up with me for so long."

"Now I know you're teasing. Was he too harsh a disciplinarian?"

"Positively medieval." Not only with her either. As a boy, Frederick had been beaten for minor faults, a cruelty she had been spared.

"Then I'm glad to have rescued you from his clutches. Though I can still not imagine you being wicked."

"Talking of wicked." She pointed her knife at the quarter inch thick pancake on the side of her plate. "Pancakes for breakfast?"

He chuckled. "We Canadians have a liking for sweets in our harsh winters. Have you tried the maple syrup?" He pushed a small white jug closer to her plate. "I advise you not to skimp."

"You eat this with bacon?"

"Of course. Incidentally, aren't you too advanced in age to have a guardian?"

"He's no longer my guardian." She reached for the jug. "I'm simply accustomed to referring to him that way. He's also my father-in-law."

"Ah, the plot thickens. And is there a rejected husband in the background?"

"No. No husband." Grace concentrated on pouring a thick stream of amber syrup onto the pancake, taking care none ventured anywhere near the slice of bacon. "He died a few months ago."

"I'm sorry. Please accept my condolences." Sympathy darkened his eyes but was gone again in an instant. "You were about to tell me something you did which could be considered as reprehensible."

"Was I?" She paused to take a bite of pancake, and almost groaned at the soft texture combined with the sweetness of the syrup on her tongue. "Once, I brought a Women's Suffrage Movement pamphlet into the house which found its way onto the hall table."

"Found?" His eyes sparkled.

"All right. I put it there. I intended to deny all knowledge of the thing, but when a maid was singled out as the perpetrator, I owned up to save the poor girl's position."

"Is that all?" He cut a piece of bacon.

Grace shot him a look, unsure what to think of this man who seemed incapable of shock.

"I suspect you're deciding whether or not you can trust me." He peered into her coffee cup and seeing it empty, held up the pot again.

"Something like that." She held out her cup, regretting the fact everything which crossed her mind always showed instantly on her face.

"Are you still afraid of being discovered?"

"Er no, I don't think so, but I cannot stay here. Nor can I return to England." She nodded to her plate. "This pancake is truly delicious. It could become a habit." Though combining syrup and bacon still felt a step too far.

"Even if this agent does find you, is it a problem? Your father-in-law is thousands of miles away, he cannot compel you to return."

"That's what Aoife said, but MacKinnon doesn't like to be thwarted. He might accuse me of some crime, or say I was mentally unstable and had escaped an asylum. Anything to get his way."

"Goodness. Then we must make sure he doesn't find you, which will be easier than you imagine in a vast place like Canada."

"What about this island where you live?" Warmth crept up her spine at his use of the word. "Are there opportunities for widows with some resources there?" Grace mopped up the last drop of syrup with the remaining pancake and popped it into her mouth. Had she really eaten the entire thing including the bacon and sausages?

"Considerable ones I should think. Does Prince Edward Island interest you?"

"It does have a certain attraction, although I know nothing about it."

Grace wished she had spent more time studying her atlas. "I don't suppose we can we get there today?"

"Canada is not England. Distances between civilization here are greater and harder to traverse." He considered for a moment. "However, I feel Charlottetown is as good as anywhere to begin a new life. It has everything. Climate, beautiful countryside, a largely Celtic people."

"I'm English."

"Although your name is Scottish. In common with at least a quarter of the Island's population."

"My maiden name was Aitken, which is also Scottish. My parents died when I was young, and I know little about my real family."

"Then you cannot be sure none of them came here sometime in the past."

"I admit, the thought never occurred to me." The notion she might find a distant relative seemed remote. "Tell me more about the Island?"

"Let me see," he stared off for a moment. "We have one city, Charlottetown and one large town, Summerside, with smaller villages like Tignish, Montague and Souris, none of which hold more than a thousand people. Mostly the island is rural, with no part of it more than ten miles from the sea. Our seasons are not as extreme as on the mainland, although we have just come through one of the worst winters for years. The quality of the light is like nowhere else on earth, which as a traveller I can attest to. In fact, if you would allow me to escort you there, you could decide for yourself."

"You make it sound perfect." The main attraction being Angus MacKinnon wouldn't think of looking for her there. "I accept your invitation, Mr Jardine, provided you'll allow me to pay for my own ticket."

"Agreed. However, you won't need one."

"You said yesterday it was two hundred miles away?"

"It is, and as a rule I would take a train north to Pictou, then a ferry across the Strait of Northumberland to Charlottetown."

"But not today?"

He shook his head. "I have a friend who has been in Halifax for the last week or so on business. His steamboat is scheduled to leave from the harbour later this morning. He and his wife have invited me to join them on the last leg of their journey home. It will take us a little over a day to reach Charlottetown."

"But your friends haven't invited me, so perhaps I should take the train and the ferry instead?"

"Indeed, you could," he drew out the words slowly as if they gave his pause for thought. "Although I can promise you a far more entertaining trip. You'll also get to meet one of Charlottetown's most prominent and amiable citizens."

"In that case, how could I refuse?"

"I hoped you would say that."

Chapter 6

Halifax Harbour, Nova Scotia - SS Elizabeth

Chattering pedestrians and gigs loaded with people, all of whom appeared to be on their way to the quay, filled the road around them and, some ten minutes after the cab halted, Grace continued to peer through its window.

On the opposite seat, Jardine sat upright, one ankle crossed over the other, passing the time by reading a newspaper. He apparently felt no compunction to fill the silence with meaningless chatter, but from time to time he looked up from his newspaper and smiled as if acknowledging her presence. "I apologize for the delay, but according to a porter at the hotel, the morbid and the curious have been gathering here since daybreak. Somehow a rumour started that the SS Parisian sank with all lives."

"It's not your fault. Does the ferry to Charlottetown go from here?" she asked, suddenly nervous about her unexplained appearance on his friend's boat. "I'm quite happy to travel on public transport."

"Are you nervous, Mrs MacKinnon? Because the SS Elizabeth is a most seaworthy vessel and more than large enough to accommodate another passenger."

"Not nervous exactly, though I fear I shall be an imposition on your friend."

"I assure you he would be distraught if he discovered I did not invite you aboard and sent you off on a ferry. Ah, here we are at last."

As he handed her down from the hackney, two squabbling youths dashed past them, almost colliding with Grace. At the last second, Jardine pulled her to one side as the boys ran on, their voices raised in excitement in a bid to get a view of the half-submerged ship.

"Are you all right?" His eyes filled with concern as he steadied her, his arm closing around her waist.

"Yes, thank you." She pulled reluctantly away from his hold, righting herself. While she waited for him to instruct their driver as to disposition of their luggage, she strolled to where the stern of the Parisian sat lower in the water than the previous day, her hull and masts tilted towards the pier.

"She looks quite sad keeled over like that," Grace observed when he joined her.

"I don't like to see her like this either." He frowned and shook his head sadly.

"When I first boarded at Liverpool, I was so excited. I had never been on a steamship before. I remember thinking how noble she looked. Magnificent almost."

84

"And she will again." He turned away as if unable to look anymore and gestured to where a steamboat with a double smokestack nestled against the jetty; a gleaming red funnel and cream painted lifeboat attached to the upper deck.

"The SS Elizabeth." He nodded towards the boat. "Built in England by Earles Shipyard in Hull. One-hundred-and-sixty-five feet long with a twenty-one foot beam. Isn't she splendid?"

"She certainly is, yes." Bemused by the fact he imagined such details would mean something to her, Grace smiled. "And your friend owns her, you say?"

A wide promenade deck formed an enclosed passenger shelter forwards with a row of close set rectangular windows. What looked like a saloon was located forwards giving a panoramic view from a wide, curved window.

"He does." Jardine glanced past her as a steward halted a few feet away. "Good morning Mr Soames, is Mr Cahill on board yet?"

"His carriage has just pulled onto the harbour, Mr Jardine." He touched his peaked cap. "He'll be here directly, sir."

"Good timing then. Would you arrange for an extra cabin to be prepared for Mrs Mackinnon, who will be joining us for the trip?"

Grace licked her lips, half expecting a stern look and a refusal, but the steward simply smiled. "Of course, sir. Welcome aboard madam."

"Uh, thank you." She released a relieved breath.

A member of the crew approached them from behind a heavily loaded trolley that contained several expensive looking trunks, one of which she recognized as Mr Jardine's. Strapped to the top were her two bags, looking decidedly battered and forlorn.

Grace swallowed, as a rush of panic flooded through her at the sight of her worldly goods being trundled down the sloping gangplank onto the deck of the SS Elizabeth. "Is something wrong?" Jardine had stepped onto the gangplank but turned back and returned to her side, his eyes softening with concern. "I admit, it's still unnerving going on board another boat after yesterday, but it isn't that. The truth is, I don't know your friends, Mr Jardine. More to the point they don't know me." The prospect of climbing aboard another boat filled her with inexplicable dread. And with a man she had known less than a day.

"I'm sorry, I should have considered that it must have been a frightening experience for you."

"Wasn't it for you? Or have you almost been shipwrecked before?"

"No, but I do have more experience of being at sea." His rich, attractive laugh made her insides tighten.

"Why did you help me yesterday, Mr Jardine?" Grace planted her feet firmly, resisting the pull of his arm. "It's been worrying me all night. Gentlemen don't jump in and rescue young women from situations they know nothing about. And please don't say you needed something to brighten your dreary day."

"I disagree. Gentlemen do exactly that. Your compassion for the steerage passengers yesterday touched me. You disregarded your own need to get off a sinking ship and went to their aid."

"That was more Aoife than me. She had friends in steerage."

"But you did not. What struck me the most, was the terror on your face when you encountered that man sent by your father-in-law. I regarded it as a gentleman's duty to offer my protection. If I misunderstood, I apologize, but your relief at the time appeared quite genuine."

"It was. I-" Mortified by her own rudeness, tears pricked the back of Grace's throat. "You must think I'm stupid and flighty to have run away from home and travelled thousands of miles to a strange country?"

"Why on earth would I think that? I admire your sense of adventure. You may also be surprised to find Canada is not quite as strange as you imagined."

"I anticipated that. Which is why I read a lot of history books in my father-in-law's library about Canada."

"Though not my Island?"

"No, not that. I was surprised to find so many familiar names here, Halifax for one of course. Then there is Richmond, Truro, Dorchester, Yarmouth and even Liverpool."

"Also Bedford, Weymouth, Windsor, Dartford and Berwick. The Island was originally called Isle Saint Jean, but it was changed to honor Queen Victoria's father, Prince Edward, who was then commanding British troops in Halifax." His mouth twitched in response to her surprised stare. "You aren't the only one who likes to read history."

"Apparently not." Grace smiled into his eyes, surprised at how comfortable she felt in his company, as if she had known him for years.

"The islanders are friendly," he went on, "maybe too friendly perhaps, as everyone knows your business, but it's comforting that you are never truly alone."

"You obviously love it there."

"I do. It's my home and I cannot imagine living anywhere else."

"I-I apologize for being rude before. It was unworthy of me." Heat flooded her cheeks, making her feel silly for her sudden bout of panic. "Everything is all quite new to me, I don't know how to behave."

"A case of last minute nerves, I suspect." His voice softened, his smile sympathetic not mocking. "I understand if you wish to change your mind, but then what would you do? If your father-in-law is as determined as you say, his agent will keep looking for you. Evading him in an unfamiliar town won't be easy. However, if that's what you prefer, I'm quite-"

"No! That isn't what I want." Fresh horror rose at the idea of his leaving her. "And I'm sure your friend is everything you said. Please accept my apology and if your offer is still open, I would be delighted to meet him."

To return to Hampstead under a cloud would be tortuous, but her actions would be put down to her weak character and life would continue as before. The alternative was to step into the unknown, a prospect which terrified her in its enormity, and yet was exhilarating.

"You'll find John Cahill both charming and generous." Taking her hand in his, he slid it beneath his arm. "Association with him could only be beneficial. He's very influential in Charlottetown."

He nodded to where a hatless man strolled casually along the deck toward them.. He looked to be in his mid-fifties, possessed of the sort of manly good looks which only improve with time. Of a similar height to Jardine, his neatly trimmed moustache and beard was the same color as his full head of silver hair he wore brushed straight back to the base of his collar. His ankle length fur coat with wide lapels flapped open, against his broad chest. His leisurely stride and the jaunty swing of his cane declared him a man content with his world. He reminded her so much of an amiable bear, her fingers itched to stroke the white tipped pelt of his coat as he paused beside them.

"Good morning, John. Have you had a good trip?" Jardine asked as the pair shook hands with the vigour of long-term friends.

The newcomer raised his cane in salute. "I don't regard the semi-annual assault on my bank account as good, Jardine," he replied in a laughter tinged baritone voice that matched his bear-like appearance. "However, it had a number of agreeable moments." His gaze switched to Grace with a look of expectant enquiry. Jardine took his cue. "John Cahill, I would like you to meet Grace MacKinnon."

"It's a pleasure to meet you, my dear." Cahill shifted his cane to his other hand and grasped hers firmly, regarding her with bright blue, all knowing eyes that held her in a steady stare.

"I'm very pleased to meet you too, Mr Cahill." She imagined his moustache would have felt soft and pleasant on her skin, and experienced mild disappointment because she wore gloves.

"Mrs MacKinnon is lately from London and intends to settle in Canada, John," Jardine said. "I invited her to see Charlottetown, however I'm having trouble convincing her you would be happy for her to accompany us."

"I would be delighted. You hail from London, Ontario?"

"No, sir." Grace grinned up at him, all her former apprehension dissolving beneath his welcome smile. "The other one."

"Ah, what brings you all the way across the Atlantic to our beautiful island, my dear?"

"I suppose you could say, life, sir." She tried not to stare but his bright blue eyes and flirtatious smile held her entranced. 'Mine specifically. I find myself in need of a new direction."

"I do like a woman with secrets, and I'll wager you have an interesting story to tell. Perhaps we'll have an opportunity to get better acquainted during the trip?"

Grace hesitated, unsure how to react, but before she could summon a response, a high, female voice called from farther along the deck.

"Really John, can't you even wait for me to get out of the carriage?" A woman in a floor length silver fox fur coat sashayed along the deck towards them, several hatboxes bouncing on strings from her hands. She looked to be at least ten years Cahill's junior with small features, a pert straight nose above rosebud lips, her brows and lashes the color of dark honey.

"You might have helped me with my parcels, John. I shall be furious if anything is damaged." A fur hat that exactly matched her coat was pulled low on her blonde curls. Behind her trotted a plump, unsmiling woman, a bulky vanity case held in both hands.

Jardine inhaled a sharp breath, followed by a low disappointed groan. "Mrs Cahill," he said in response to Grace's enquiring look.

"She insisted on accompanying me on this trip," Cahill said, interpreting Jardine's look

91

before turning a lazy expression on the owner of the voice. 'Emily, come and meet Mrs McKinnon, who is joining us for the crossing."

"How do you do?" Her shrewd brown eyes swept across Grace from head to toe before shifting to Jardine where her bored expression disappeared, and her eyes sparkled with child-like delight. "Andrew!" She dropped the boxes on the deck and threw herself into his arms. "How lovely to see you. I had no. idea you would be joining us."

"Emily." Jardine's voice tightened as he disentangled himself from her embrace as if handling a wet dog.

"This trip is going to be so much more thrilling with you here," Emily gushed. Her attention went briefly back to Grace. "You must excuse me, Mrs - Um. I need to get settled in our suite. I expect we'll meet in the lounge for coffee presently." She gave Grace a taut smile, then turned to her maid, pointed wordlessly at the hat boxes before sweeping back along the deck.

The maid gathered the parcels from the boards, adding them to the vanity case, and with her burden awkwardly balanced, took short, rapid steps to catch up with her mistress.

"That's another thing I like in a woman." Cahill gave a low, throaty chuckle at his wife's stiff, retreating back. "A healthy dose of jealousy."

* * *

"Don't let Emily bother you." Jardine rested his forearms on the rail and stared out at the sea. "She dislikes anyone who deflects attention from herself."

His tone suggested he had no time for Emily Cahill, yet Grace had seen that manner before in men rejected by a woman they admired or had lost to another, more handsome or richer man.

She had not made up her mind which applied in this case when the crewman clicked the barrier into place. With a grumble and whir, the engines roared into life and the steamboat eased away from the jetty. As their speed increased, her stomach clenched as images of the previous day returned.

"Is that a castle over there?" she asked in an effort to distract herself, nodding to an outcrop of land nestling in the sea with a line of grey stones running around the perimeter. "I didn't know Canada had castles."

"It's a fort. Fort Charlotte, named for King George III's queen. It was built during Father Le Loutre's War to defend the strait."

"I kept up with you until the last part. Which war was that?"

"I shall have to educate you on our legendary heroes." He sliced a sideways smile at her. "It's required for anyone wishing to live on the Island. You have to name them all."

"Really?" Her breath hitched and he laughed.

"I'm teasing. But here's your first history lesson. In the mid seventeen-hundreds, Charles Lawrence and John Gorham, clashed with Louis Le Loutre who led the Mi'kmaq tribe and the Acadia militia against the British."

"Tribe?" She swung to face him. "There are Indians on Prince Edward Island?"

"Yes, there are. But they only raid the town once every few months." She glanced up at him and gasped, to which he gave a low chuckle. "I'm joking. There have been Mi'kmaqs in the west of the island for thousands of years. Long before the European settlers came. They're law abiding Catholics for the most part, a gentle, interesting people who contribute a good deal to our society."

"I didn't mean to imply otherwise," she replied, bridling slightly at the thought he was mocking her. "I was just - surprised."

"You're so easy to tease, Mrs MacKinnon. Were you aware your eyes change color when you are distressed or happy?" His sideways smile had a twist to it which sent a glow through her so intense, she looked away.

"Um – so I've been told. I would like to discover more about them. I-uh meant the Indians." Her nerves quietened as the deck settled into a familiar, solid vibration beneath her feet.

"It's a ferry ride from Charlottetown to the Mi'kmaq encampment on Rocky Point which is an excellent area for a picnic on a sunny day. For a real flavor of their culture you must be sure to attend the St Anne's Day celebrations which they host on the reservation at Lennox Island each July with a feast, singing, music and dancing."

"I shall have to remember that. It sounds fascinating." She chose her words, careful to avoid accepting his invitation when none was offered. "Incidentally, who won this war you mentioned?"

"The British, of course." He turned from his contemplation of the deep aquamarine sea with white topped waves. "You're looking distracted. Are you having second thoughts?"

"Er no - not really. I'm excited about going there, but-" At his wry look, added, 'I suddenly feel a long way from home."

"Isn't that what you wanted?" He twisted towards her, concern darkening his eyes.

"It is." She must stop thinking about England as her home. Especially when she was always little more than a guest in the MacKinnon's house.

"You look cold." He pushed away from the rail, an arm extended in invitation. "Shall we go inside?"

"Good idea." She hoped her nose hadn't turned an unbecoming red, a hazard with skin as pale as hers.

"Spring comes later to the Maritimes than Europe, and as I mentioned before, this winter was particularly hard. Snow towered over some rooftops and three weeks ago, the Northumberland Strait was frozen over. We were completely cut off from the mainland so the ice boats were employed to run between the capes."

"Ice boats?" Grace frowned uncomprehending.

"Rowing boats are dragged over the ice to deliver the mail in the winter. Even now we might have to take the odd detour to avoid a few ice floes off the coast, though hopefully none big enough to cause any trouble." He looked about to offer her his arm, but at the last second clasped his hands behind his back.

"There will be a spring then?" Grace hunched her shoulders against the sharp cold that cut through her coat. How bad did the winters become here?

"Indeed, there will be a spring, followed by a glorious summer." He guided her into a lounge that took up a third of the stern end of the deck; a window ran all the way around giving a panoramic view of the coastline from one side, and the open sea on the other.

A steward arrived with a tray loaded with a silver coffee pot and a platter of pastries. He placed the tray on a low table surrounded by plush red sofas, bowed and withdrew.

Jardine gestured to one of the sofas. When she was seated, he took a tub chair. "These look good, don't they?" He pointed to a plate that held a variety of Danish pastries, the swirls of icing and sugar gleaming in the light.

"Shouldn't we wait for the Cahills to join us?"

"Unnecessary." He held the plate higher "Besides, Emily will declare she's starving, then select the smallest one, but eat none of it." He gave a shudder. "I find it infuriating."

"What a waste." Grace helped herself to an almond cream pastry, taking a bite of the creamy delicacy. "Mealtimes were the one thing the MacKinnons didn't skimp on."

"How long will it take?" He poured coffee into two cups.

"How long will what take?" Grace removed a stray flake of pastry from the corner of her mouth and frowned.

"Before you stop talking about the man you came all this way to get away from?"

"I-I didn't realize I was doing it." Preoccupied, she did not notice the Cahills join them until they took their seats. They had removed their fur coats, the clothes beneath them no less impressive. Cahill wore charcoal grey with a mustard waistcoat sporting a thick gold watch chain. Emily wore a russet gown which complemented her golden curls.

"Oooh, lovely! Croissants, my favorite," Emily exclaimed. "I'm positively starving!" She selected the smallest pastry on the platter and dropped it onto her plate.

Jardine's mouth twitched and Grace almost choked on her first mouthful of coffee.

"Are you settled into your cabin, Mrs MacKinnon?" Cahill eased into the sofa opposite, his knees spread across the entire seat.

"I haven't seen it yet, but I'm sure it will be lovely."

"If there's anything you need, just ring the bell." He slid two pastries onto his plate, demolishing the first in one bite. "Has Jardine explained our route?"

"A little. I assume we'll follow the coastline east and then go north." His admiring look made her feel her time poring over the atlas wasn't wasted.

"Quite right. There are many islands in this part of the world so once we pass Canso on the tip of the coastline, we run north between Durrells and Janvrin Islands before calling in at Port Hawkesbury to refuel early this evening. We'll enter the Northumberland Strait by morning which will bring us into Charlottetown around early afternoon tomorrow."

"John, really," Emily pinched a small flake of pastry with her thumb and forefinger. "I'm sure Mrs MacKinnon doesn't want a geography lesson."

"But I do," Grace said. "I'm fascinated, and looking forward to learning all about the province. Thank you again for allowing me to join you."

"You intrigue me, Mrs MacKinnon." Emily dropped the piece of pastry onto her plate. "You're evidently of good family, I can always tell. But why are you travelling alone without even a maid or a male relative?"

"Emily!" Her husband muttered in warning, his coffee cup frozen in mid-air.

"It was a straightforward question." Emily's cornflower blue eyes widened in mock innocence "I only asked, because you don't look like a Sifton immigrant."

"I'm sorry?" Grace frowned and tore her gaze from the pile of crumbs accumulating on Emily's plate.

"Clifford Sifton," Cahill said. "He's our venerated Minister of the Interior. He has laid out a strict policy as to the type of immigrants he feels should be allowed into the country."

"He thinks they should all be white farmers wearing sheepskin coats," Jardine leaned forward to stir milk into his coffee. "Accompanied by several sturdy children capable of hard labor."

"Oh dear, does that make me ineligible?" Grace split a mischievous look between them. "I've never owned a sheepskin coat." This remark was greeted with a bark of uninhibited laughter from Cahill, a less exuberant one from Jardine and a sulky pout from Emily. Thanks to Mr Beech's advice, Grace had checked the immigration rules at the Salvation Army Office in Liverpool carefully before boarding the ship.

"In your case there's no question as you're British born." Cahill directed a withering look at his wife.

"Perhaps you're acquainted with the Highfield MacKinnons?" Emily asked. "Or perhaps you're related to the Lieutenant Governor, Donald MacKinnon?"

"Neither, I'm afraid," Grace said, instantly regretting her tone of apology. "The name is purely coincidence."

"Pity." Emily sniffed. "I might have been able to introduce you to my friends."

"Perhaps you'd consider obliging anyway, Emily?" Jardine avoided her eye, crossed one leg over the other and flicked a speck of dust from his trousers.

"It's not as simple as that." Emily gave a hollow laugh. "One must be careful to whom one exposes one's closest acquaintances."

The pair exchanged a long look which held something Grace couldn't define. "It wouldn't hurt to allow the misconception to spread," Cahill said. "There are plenty of MacKinnons on the Island." He addressed Grace. "It might even open some doors for you, my dear."

Grace smiled, but doubted she possessed the confidence to pull off such a deception.

"You didn't answer my original question, Mrs MacKinnon." Emily dissected a second pastry, having barely touched the first. "Why did you come to Canada? You aren't a runaway, are you?"

Jardine inhaled slowly and Cahill muttered his wife's name with a resigned shake of his head.

"I suppose I am in a way," Grace said, refusing to be cowed.

"There, you see, John." Emily flashed her husband a triumphant look. "You must tell me everything, Grace. I may call you Grace?"

"My story isn't very exciting, I'm afraid," Grace replied, aware she didn't offer the same intimacy. "After my husband died, I wanted to get away from old memories, although I have yet to make up my mind what to do here. I imagined I might open some sort of business."

"Not a hat shop I trust." Emily discarded the rest of her pastry onto her plate. "Sifton's not keen on shopkeepers."

"Emily is teasing, aren't you?" Jardine glared at Emily.

"Of course I am, Andrew, dear." Her tone was conciliatory but her eyes sharpened. "I'm merely curious as to how Grace intends to earn a living.' She brought her cup to her mouth and fluttered her eyelashes over the rim. "I assume she will need to?"

"I will indeed. But why does your governor despise shopkeepers?" Grace asked, aware she was being patronized, but her lack of knowledge rendered her ill-equipped to fight back.

"Sifton imagines that to make the Island a haven for foreign shopkeepers would signal the community's inevitable demise," Cahill supplied with a broad, cynical smile. "Not that Emily agrees. She likes nothing better than to shop. Don't you my dear?" He leaned across the space between them and delivered a friendly if heavy handed slap to his wife's knee,

Emily inhaled slowly, while Jardine held a ghost of a smile on his lips.

Grace looked away, self-conscious. She was unable to judge if his contemplation was critical, admiring or indifferent. The man confused her.

Turning back to her host, she found he too stared at her expectantly. "I beg your pardon. What was that you said?"

"I asked where you intended to reside in Charlottetown?" Cahill poured milk into his second cup of coffee. "I can recommend The Victoria Hotel."

"I'm sure I'll find something suitable." Grace buried her nose in her cup, aware the town's best hotels would be beyond her means.

"I admire your independence, my dear." He withdrew a calling card from an inside pocket and held it out. "It doesn't hurt to have connections, and if I can be of assistance, use this. Even if it's only to get the best prices at the mercantile."

Grace accepted the rectangle of pasteboard edged with gold from his square, blunt fingers, an exchange closely followed by Emily's narrowed gaze and tight jaw. She groaned inwardly. As twenty-four hours in the woman's company loomed ahead of her, she reminded herself to ask Jardine what a mercantile was.

Chapter 7

The rest of that afternoon passed amiably with a walk on deck, a game of cards and tea, followed by a rest in their respective suites before dressing for dinner. The cream and white bedroom assigned to Grace was larger than her accommodation on the Parisian, with ornate gilt mirrors and light fittings that exuded an air of opulence and style. The tang of beeswax polish, new paint and linseed oil told her the suite had been decorated recently, and all the surfaces vigorously cleaned.

An adjoining bathroom decorated in pink and cream with a marble basin set below a gilt bevelled mirror was equally luxurious. She lingered for a while, taking advantage of the pots of cosmetics laid out among perfumed soaps and fluffy white towels. These made up for the fact that she had left her bag in the lounge.

On her way back along the internal corridor she halted outside the dining room at the sound of her name and peered around the jamb to where the Cahills stood close together.

"It's not as if she's connected to any MacKinnon who matters, John," Emily said.

"People will think I'm trying to impose a fake on them. They would never forgive me."

"What nonsense!" John laughed. "Mrs McKinnon is a well-bred young woman who would benefit from an introduction. She has both the manners and the breeding not to embarrass you. I thought you would welcome the notion of making her your protégée." He ran a finger down her cheek. "Please. As a favor to me."

"It would have to be the right occasion." Emily pouted.

"Good girl." He turned the stroke from a sensual gesture into a patronizing one. "I knew you wouldn't let me down."

Grace clenched her jaw and darted behind the bulkhead. As if she needed a fatuous, cotton-wool brain like Emily Cahill to smooth her way. Giving them a few seconds to move away, she straightened her shoulders, took a deep breath and entered the room, almost colliding with Emily, who had not moved.

"Ah, Grace, there you are. I hope you'll call on me when you are settled in Charlottetown. The ladies of the Women's Christian Temperance gather at my house regularly. You must let me introduce you to them."

"It's kind of you to offer, Mrs Cahill," Grace replied carefully. "However, I shall be too occupied during my first weeks to attend 'at homes'."

Emily wrinkled her pert nose. "But what of your future, Grace? You're evidently well-educated, so perhaps you could be a schoolteacher? We have some excellent schools in Charlottetown for the worker's children. I'm sure John would vouch for your suitability."

"I don't think so, Mrs Cahill." Grace started to leave before she said something she regretted, but Emily matched her step for step.

"A governess then?" Her eyes lit up as if she had come up with the perfect solution. "English governesses are much sought after in the better homes." She brought a finger to her pursed lips. "Although you might find a certain reluctance in the mamas to their having a pretty woman in the house." She rested a hand on Grace's forearm. "A husband is what you need, my dear."

"That's the last thing I want at the moment," Grace said. "I'm still mourning the loss of my first one."

"You are? My condolences." Emily's voice held no sympathy as she gave Grace's sky blue jacket and skirt a pointed look. "Perhaps when your - um mourning - is over, perhaps you might reconsider my suggestion about being a governess."

"In which case, I could have found a position and a husband nearer to home." The effort of maintaining her smile made Grace's jaw ache.

"Ah, well, I'm sure you know your own mind, but I think you'll discover things here aren't quite the same as in London."

"You know London then, Mrs Cahill?" Grace levelled an innocent look on her, confident Emily had never left the Maritimes.

"Actually, no. I've never had occasion to visit Europe. Not yet anyway." Her gaze slid to where John stood, his back to the window as he perused a document that had been waiting for him when the boat docked at Port Hawkesbury. "It's your decision, of course. We'll talk later, I'm sure." With a vague wave in Grace's direction, she strolled towards her husband, possibly to inform him she had complied with his request, at least partly.

"You must learn not to do that," Jardine said from behind her.

Grace jumped and swung around to find him grinning at her.

"I didn't see you there." Grace's cheeks warmed, partly because she had been caught but also because his gaze bored into hers. "Were you eavesdropping, by any chance?"

"Shamelessly." He delivered a slow wink that sent her blood racing. "As were you in the hallway just now."

"And what is it I must learn not to do, Mr Jardine?"

"While you were talking to Emily, your jaw was clenched all the time she was talking. Then when she walked away, you shuddered."

"I did? Oh dear, that's not very nice is it?"

"I doubt she noticed, but someone more discerning and less in love with themselves might."

"And I thought you were one of her admirers." She slanted a coy look up at him, surprised at her capacity to flirt.

"No, you did not." He raised a sardonic eyebrow. "She's vain, and manipulative. Unfortunately, the one person who could have benefited from my counsel chose to ignore me." He nodded to where Cahill had finished reading and was pouring drinks for himself and Emily.

"He doesn't strike me as the sort of man gullible enough to be fooled by a pretty face."

"That's true. John is more than aware of the kind of deal he has struck with Emily. He has no illusions about her."

"You make it sound like a business arrangement rather than a marriage."

"Did you think it was anything else?" His mouth twitched at the corner into a cynical smile. "And if you did, you're too polite to say so." His eyes softened again. "But I'm being unsociable. You've not got a drink. Allow me to fetch you an aperitif?"

"Um, yes thank you. A sherry would be lovely." Did he approve of the nature of the Cahill's marriage, or despise it?

In his absence, she went to the chair she had previously occupied in search of her bag, but it was no longer there.

"Have you lost something?" Jardine asked on his return, two glasses in hand, one of which he handed to her.

"Um-yes, I'm sure I left my bag here, and now I-"

"Is this it?" He swept the navy-blue velvet pouch from the corner of a sofa behind her.

"Ah yes, thank you." Frowning, she took it from him certain that was not where she left it.

* * *

Grace woke next morning to a calm blue sea beneath a crisp clear sky. "Ah, Mrs MacKinnon." John Cahill gestured her to join him. "Come and have your first sight of Prince Edward Island." He nodded to where a purplish hump formed on the horizon. "That's East Point, from which we follow the coastline to Souris and then on to Georgetown. I'll point out the more interesting landmarks as we pass. Now, what would you like to eat?" He rubbed his hands together and approached a row of bain marie's on a side table.

"I think I'd prefer something light. Your hospitality is wonderful, but I've eaten far too much in the last twenty-four hours.

Their mutual laughter trailed off as the contrived cough from the doorway announced Emily's arrival. "What is it you two have found so amusing?" She flounced to the table and plumped down in her chair, barely acknowledging Grace's, "Good morning."

"Nothing important." Cahill winked at Grace, then glanced up again as Jardine appeared. "Ah there you are. Did you sleep late?"

"I did not." Jardine frowned, but good-humouredly. "I woke early, so I took a walk on deck." He greeted Grace and Emily in turn before he joined Cahill at the buffet where he loaded his plate. "Are we making good time?"

"Pretty good." Cahill helped himself to toast. "We were late getting into Port Hawkesbury due to a few stray ice floes near Isle Madam, but we are averaging eighteen knots, so should reach Charlottetown by late afternoon."

"You call it an Island, Grace began, "but how large is it? I mean, we regard the British Isles as one but it's over eight hundred miles long by over four hundred wide. The Isle of Wight, on the other hand is only twenty five by thirteen, but they are both called islands.

"Good point." Cahill held a finger aloft. "Prince Edward Island is one hundred and forty miles long and forty wide, which might give you an idea."

"Are the roads good?"

"Good is a subjective description," Jardine said. "The soil is mainly red clay, so when wet it turns to clinging mud and freezes in winter. If you plan to travel anywhere, make sure it's in spring and summer."

"We do have a railroad," Cahill interjected. "It cuts straight through the middle like a metal spine from east to west, but doesn't reach the more remote places. For those, you'll need a horse and cart. But forgive me." He touched her shoulder lightly. "This is all new to you and you'll likely not remember any of it."

"Not at all, I'm taking it all in and it's fascinating. I'll also be sure to add a horse and buggy to my list of essential requirements." Grace laughed. "What about motor cars, do you have many of those?"

"Not yet, I'm pleased to say," Cahill said. "Our roads are not suitable and the few we do have tend to frighten the horses. They are not very popular."

"I would love one," Emily piped up. "We saw lots in Montreal and everyone stands to stare when they pass by. Someone told me they can go as fast as thirty miles an hour."

"Which is precisely why I'm not paying seven hundred and fifty dollars for one, Emily. How would my horses feel if I bought an automobile? They would never forgive me."

"Oh, you and your precious horses." Emily huffed. "I'm sure you love them more than you do me."

* * *

The day passed very much as the previous one, with coffee in the lounge followed by luncheon which included an interesting byplay between Jardine and Emily which John Cahill ignored and watched by turns with a wry smile.

"Where are we now?" Grace asked as they adjourned to the lounge for coffee, arranging themselves on the sofas in front of the windows.

"That white clapboard building on the promontory, the one with the red roof, is the Wood Islands Lighthouse," Cahill said. "Then we turn north-west past Belle River onto Point Prim, past Governor's Island and then Charlottetown."

For the next hour, the SS Elizabeth glided through the strait along a shore of rose and golden sand that sparkled in the sunshine. Coves and small bays wound in and out, beyond which lay a patchwork of lush rolling fields, tidy gabled farmhouses and seaside villages scattered along the shoreline. The occupants of a small rowboat being pulled onto the beach halted to wave at the ferry, greeted by the captain with a cheerful whistle. A driver of a horse and cart raised his hat as he urged the horse into a trot along the coast road, while a group of boys in a field jumped up and down, arms waving frantically.

"Are all the inhabitants so cheerful and friendly?" Grace asked.

"I would say so, yes." Cahill leaned a hip against the edge of the sofa where she sat, his arms folded. "Most of them recognize the boat, but people on shore always wave to sailboats and the ferries. We're an island nation and the sea is in our blood."

"Those cliffs over there look red from here," Grace said. "But I expect it's a trick of the light."

"Actually, they are," Jardine said. "The sandstone has a high iron concentration which oxidises on exposure to the air and turns them into that warm russet color."

"That's not a very romantic explanation, Andrew." Cahill laughed.

"Perhaps not, but accurate."

"I've never seen anything like that before," Grace said. "It's beautiful."

"The cliffs are an excellent place for a picnic," Cahill said. "But make sure you have a blanket with you or the rust will stain your clothes."

"I'll try to remember that." Grace stored the snippet away for future reference.

"There's beauty everywhere you look, in the countryside, coves and small harbours all around the coast." Cahill sighed with pleasure. "There's a beach on the far eastern tip called Basin Head where the sand is fine and almost white. Some refer to it as the 'singing sands' as it squeaks when walked on."

"How fascinating. I must travel around the Island when I am settled here."

"That spring I promised you will begin in earnest in late April," Jardine addressed Grace, possibly to dispel the hard looks the Cahills gave each other. "Our climate is more moderate than in some provinces, due to the warm waters of the St Lawrence river, although you'll find it very changeable."

"You forget, I'm from England, where it's possible to experience all four seasons in one day."

He chuckled. "Then maybe Island life won't be so different."

"Charlottetown is around that point just up ahead," Cahill announced with boyish excitement. "You must come out on deck, Mrs MacKinnon, it's the only way to fully appreciate your first view of the town. You too, Jardine, Emily."

Jardine nodded, but Emily pulled a face. "Not me, it's far too cold out there." She gave an exaggerated shiver. "I have some packing to do. I'll see you all when we reach the harbour."

"I'll get my coat," Grace said. "And my hat, scarf and my warmest gloves. Oh, and a muff if I can find one."

Jardine's slow, rolling laugh followed her along the corridor back to her cabin.

Muffled up against the crisp, icy wind, Grace stood at the rail beside Jardine on one side of her and Cahill wrapped in his bear-coat the other. Her heart thumped with child-like excitement and her eyes strained to get her first glimpse of her new home. She could feel her muscles relax and her breathing slow as she took in the simple beauty of the vista ahead of her. It looked almost unreal, with unbroken coastlines and rolling green hills stretching away into the distance beyond the deep aquamarine water. A gentle, if sharp wind tugged at her hat and she couldn't keep the smile from her face.

"That expanse of green dead ahead is Victoria Park, but we'll veer off to starboard before that to make the harbour." Cahill kept up his enthusiastic commentary as the steamboat manoeuvred between two promontories into a natural harbour.

Beyond the wharfs and wooden sheds that made up the dockside buildings, the town's wide streets stretched into the distance. They comprised a jumble of wooden buildings painted in different colors, with odd brick-built structures and several church spires in between.

"The colors and the light are enchanting," Grace commented as the steamer glided towards the harbour where fishing boats and yachts scattered like toys as they passed. "It has a feeling of home, and yet I've never lived by the sea."

"I knew you would love it." Cahill's voice softened. "I always look forward to this view when I come home. I could not imagine living anywhere else."

"You're such a sentimentalist, John." Emily appeared at the door, her fur coat buttoned to the neck and a hat pulled down to her eyebrows. "My John has started a yacht club, you know. We already have a boating club, but this will be much more exclusive."

"Early stages, my dear," Cahill muttered. "Early stages. We had our first race last year, but I've yet to find a suitable location for a clubhouse. I'm hoping to organize it at Lords Wharf near where I berth the SS Elizabeth, but it's slow going."

"Would you ask a crewman to help Hilda with my luggage, John?" Emily asked, evidently bored with the conversation. She nodded to where her maid stood guard over a selection of bags, boxes and a steamer trunk, her arms encumbered with colorful packages. She huddled against the awning out of the wind, eyes narrowed as she hung grimly onto her burden.

Grace withdrew a handkerchief from her bag, using it to wipe away a spray of salt water that had caught her in the face, then frowned. All her familiar possessions were still there, but John Cahill's card which she had placed in an inside pocket was missing.

A thought struck her, and she glanced at Emily, who turned away quickly, heightened color on her cheekbones.

"Is something wrong?" Jardine asked. "Because it's time to disembark."

"Ah, no. Nothing." Grace allowed him to guide her off the boat and onto the wooden jetty where John Cahill waited to take his farewell. "I hope we meet again soon, Mrs MacKinnon." He held her hand in both of his own. "I meant it when I said you must call on me anytime."

"Thank you, Mr Cahill, and perhaps I shall." She withdrew her hand, meeting Emily's gaze for a long second. "It was so nice to meet you. I appreciate your kindness and hospitality."

"Not at all. I hope you enjoy your new life on the Island." Dismissing her, Emily raised her chin, turned and sashayed to their waiting carriage.

Bemused, Grace watched her. Emily must have removed the card when she was in her cabin. A childish trick, and a useless one as Grace had memorised their address and even the telephone number. Besides, John Cahill was obviously a leading character in Charlottetown so why would Emily think she could not find him should she wish to?

Unwilling to make an enemy of Mrs Cahill, Grace vowed not to ask for his help if she could avoid it.

"Are you sure I cannot escort you to a hotel?" Mr Jardine asked appearing at her side.

"I'm sure. I intend to start my new life as I wish to go on. Independent and relying on my own initiative."

"I hope that won't prevent us renewing our acquaintance? How will I be able to find you?"

"Perhaps I shall find you, Mr Jardine. Thank you again for all your help."

"Andrew!" Emily's shrill cry came from the open door of the cumbersome carriage. "We're about to leave."

"Stop fussing, Emily, we've hardly got far to go." Her husband said from the depths of the carriage.

Jardine smiled and Grace bit her lip. "Do you live far from here?" Grace asked him.

"No, not far. On the west side of town." He signalled to Emily that he would be there directly but showed no eagerness to leave. "I fear Emily has had her delicate nose put out of joint."

"How so?" Grace knew the answer but took a perverse pleasure in keeping Emily waiting.

"By your lovely self, of course. As you well know. I'm sure you've noticed how she hates to share male attention."

"The poor dear. That must keep her in a constant state of unease." She smiled in response to his uninhibited laugh. "Thank you again for all your assistance, Mr Jardine." She hefted both bags by their straps and started to walk away. "I hope we shall have occasion to meet again." Preferably when she had more to show for herself than a portmanteau, a reticule and an old scuffed leather bag.

"Mrs MacKinnon," Jardine called her back. "Might I suggest Mrs Mahoney's boarding house? It's a comfortable establishment, and the proprietor is, how shall I say, a gentlewoman?"

"Mahoney, you say?" She considered for a moment. "Is it far?"

He shook his head. "Follow this pier along Pownall street, past Water street then turn right at the next corner which is King street. About twenty yards down, you'll see a pale blue clapboard house that sits on its own plot on your left hand side. I've heard the accommodation is

117

modest, but the house is clean, and the food is good."

"Thank you, I shall try it." Grace set off along the wide street, calling back over her shoulder. "And now you will know where to find me!"

"Andrew." Emily called. "We really must go. The horses are getting restless."

Grace steeled herself not to look back, aware he was staring after her.

Chapter 8

Charlottetown, Prince Edward Island

Grace located the boarding house in a wide, tree-lined street of similar clapboard houses with flat roofs. The facade looked recently painted, with white shutters at the three symmetrical windows on each of the three storeys. The front door, with a fanlight above it sporting a design of a sailing boat, was in a covered porch at the side of the house.

Her bags had grown heavier during the short walk from the harbour, the handles scoring ridges into her fingers, so with some relief, she dropped them onto the bare boards, sending a flurry of dust into the air.

A tall, thin woman opened the door a few inches and peered through the gap. Her light blue eyes slid from Grace's hat down to her buttoned boots, then back up again to her face without so much as a flicker of welcome.

"Are you, Mrs Mahoney?" Grace heaved her portmanteau under her left arm and extended her right to shake the woman's hand.

"No, I ain't." She stared down at her hand but made no move to take it. "But this is her place. She'll be back later. Do you want a room?"

"Please, if you have one available." The woman eyed her brazenly a moment longer, then seemed to make up her mind and yanked the door wider. "She charges seventy cents a night, four dollars for the week."

"A week would be fine to begin with, if that's agreeable?"

She looked past Grace's shoulder. "On your own, are you?"

"Um-yes, I've just arrived on the Island. This afternoon in fact." A detail which plainly failed to impress the woman.

"I'm Marge. I cook and clean for her." She jerked her narrow chin, an invitation for Grace to enter an unexpectedly homely square hall decorated with a tiny flowered print wallpaper. An elongated version of the sailboat covered the boarded floor in bright jewel colors. A dog-leg staircase wound its way to the floor above, lit by oil lamps placed on various surfaces and small tables.

"In advance." Marge thrust her open palm out.

"Oh, I see. I don't have any local currency, but I do have English banknotes." Grace opened her bag to show the wad of notes Mr Beech had given her. "Please inform Mrs Mahoney that I'll visit the bank first thing in the morning and change them."

Marge narrowed her eyes. "All right then. But tomorrow morning, mind."

"Of course. You have my word."

"Your word don't mean nothing to me. I don't know you from Eve.' Her apathetic expression implied she had seen everything and expected the worst of everyone. A cotton print dress with mutton leg sleeves in hues of dark green and brown hung loosely on her angular body, a shapeless bun of frizzy russet hair streaked with white sat on top of her head.

Marge pointed a finger up the staircase on her left. "Room 6. First floor at the back. Supper's at seven in the back parlour. Latecomers go without," she recited like a mantra as she carried on along the lower hall to the rear.

"I'll take my luggage up myself then, shall I?" Grace called after her.

"Aye, because it won't get there by itself." Marge replied over her shoulder. 'And don't you be banging it about when you get up there neither. My man's sleeping. He's on the boats tonight."

Grace hefted the portmanteau in both hands and hauled it sideways up the staircase to the floor above, Marge's instruction almost impossible to obey as small tables bearing oil lamps and tiny vases of flowers proliferated wherever she moved along the upper corridor.

The door to Room 6 opened at a touch, which made Grace hope Mrs Mahoney would arrive with a key at some point, though the lack of a lock told her this was unlikely. The bolt on the inside made her feel slightly more secure.

The room was surprisingly spacious. A tall, thin window overlooked the rear garden comprised of a handkerchief of lawn surrounded by paving. There didn't appear to be any flower beds or statuary anywhere, only pots and urns in various shapes and sizes set on the stones.

A double brass bedstead dominated the room, two small tables arranged on either side with oil lamps on them, and a three drawer dresser and mirror to one side of the bed..

Grace couldn't resist running a finger over the polished wood surfaces, which came away clean, a faint fragrance of beeswax polish on her skin.

She heaved both of her bags onto the bed, delighted to find it neither creaked nor sank in the middle. She tested the mattress with a bounce, and then another, harder one, noting the sheets and coverlet were spotless and smelled faintly of lavender.

She must remember to thank Mr Jardine when she saw him next, and remembered with a jolt they had made no firm arrangement.

Mildly disappointed but refusing to allow the oversight to spoil her first day, Grace unpacked. With her modest collection of skirts, dresses and blouses stowed in a recessed cupboard, she arranged her beloved vanity set on the dresser. A third door which she assumed was another cupboard, on closer inspection led into a neat lobby with two more doors. One was locked when she tried it, but the other opened into a bathroom with a deep porcelain tub, and a hot water geyser attached to the wall above it. A washbasin and water closet with a chain pull completed the facilities. Not a private bathroom, but if she was lucky, she would only have to share with the boarder who occupied the room behind the locked door.

* * *

Grace emerged from her room at a little before seven, according to the grandmother clock at the end of the hallway. She crept downstairs and along to the rear of the house. Following the savoury smells of roasted meat and fresh bread, she entered what she assumed must be the parlour. The room was empty when she arrived, but the clash of pans and dishes accompanied by chattering voices indicated the kitchen next door.

A pine Welsh dresser ran the entire length of the room, the upper shelves containing plates, cups, saucers and serving dishes in a soft Provençale blue glaze with a single white flower sprig decoration while the lower ones held stoneware in a uniform shade of grey-blue. A scrubbed table set with eight plain chairs arranged in front of a small fireplace, a window on the opposite wall gave a view to the yard.

A slightly plump woman with fair hair halted in the kitchen doorway, a large tureen balanced in both hands. "Good evening m'dear. You must be my new guest?" Her rounded vowels and sweet expression endeared her to Grace immediately.

"I'm Grace McKinnon. Pleased to meet you."

"What a lovely thing you are, dear." She stared at the tureen in apparent confusion, then tutted and set it on a cork mat on the table top, rubbed both hands down her apron and thrust out her hand. "Pleased to meet you."

"She says she'll pay you tomorra'," Marge said at Mrs M's shoulder, a pile of earthenware soup plates balanced in the crook of her arm.

The dresser was crammed with the same crockery, plates, cups, saucers and serving dishes, each one in soft Provençale blue glaze with a single white flower sprig decoration.

"I don't have any Canadian dollars, I'm afraid," Grace explained. "You have my word I shall visit the bank tomorrow and pay you for the week."

"She tol' me that too," Marge said on her way to the table where she plonked the plates, rattling them ominously against the tureen. She raked Grace with a suspicious glance before marching out again.

"Oh, don't you go fretting about that, m'dear. You look like a nice young thing." She sent a swift look in the direction of the kitchen. "Marge can be a bit sharp, but she doesn't mean it. I'm Mrs Maureen Mahoney, but everyone calls me Mrs M. Now, if you take a seat over there at the end so we can all see you."

"All?" Slightly unnerved, Grace lowered herself into a wheel backed chair.

"I've two other boarders this week. Misses Ada and Ivy Dobson on their twice yearly visit from New York. They're regulars of mine, but I warn you they tend to complain a lot."

Grace stared around from the dresser with its neat rows of earthenware to the cosy fire that crackled in the hearth. "From what I've seen your house is extremely comfortable, what can they have to complain of?"

"Well bless your heart, but it's not my accommodation which bothers them. They find Charlottetown too provincial for their taste and not like they're used to."

"If they don't like the town, then why do they come?"

"They has to." Marge skirted the table, slamming cutlery onto its wooden surface in front of each chair as she went. "What with that brother of theirs holding the purse strings."

"Aloysius Dobson," Mrs M said in explanation. "He inherited all their father's money and came to the Island ten years ago. The sisters refused to leave the family home in Manhattan, so if they don't make the mandatory duty visits, Aloysius will cut off their allowance."

"Why don't they stay at his home?" Grace chose not to comment on the mean spiritedness of male relatives, a subject familiar to her.

"He's a resident at The Victoria Hotel and they refuse to pay their prices," Mrs M said.

"They charge more-n ten dollars a week to stay there," Marge said, obviously impressed. She dumped a basket of roughly torn bread in the center of the table.

"Yes, thank you, Marge," Mrs M said, a warning in her voice.

"I see." Grace glanced at the small wooden clock on the mantelpiece, noting it was already ten past seven. What happened to Marge's pronouncement that 'latecomers went without'?

"Suppers' a bit late," Mrs M said, following her gaze. "I'm not too strict where the sisters are concerned. They've never been good timekeepers."

As if on cue, the door opened again, and two middle-aged ladies bustled into the room.

Both well-endowed, they were far from fat, but looked nothing alike. One had brown hair and a dark complexion, wide spaced eyes the color of milk chocolate, a long thin nose and a high forehead. The other was ash blonde and fair skinned, her eyes set close together beneath a beetling brow and a snub nose. Their clothes were equally diverse, with the darker one in shades of purple and black while the fairer of the two favored a pale shade of pink with numerous flounces on the skirt and sleeves.

"Mrs M, we've had the most horrible day," the first lady said.

"We couldn't find any decent hats in the town," her companion added. "It's too bad, but we'll have to wait until we go home to find what we need."

"Ada would spend all her money on hats if she could, the fussier the better," the darker sister said.

"I like hats, Ivy." Ada waggled shoulders, fluttering the pink flounces on her blouse. Her eyes focussed on Grace. "Oh, and who have we here?" She tugged out the chair at right angles to Grace and perched on the edge, her chin jutted close to hers. "What's your name, dear?"

"You didn't mention you had a new guest, Mrs M," Ivy said with a slight sneer. "I thought we were your only boarders this week?"

"This is Mrs MacKinnon." The landlady busied herself arranging napkins and soup bowls, her refusal to look Ivy in the eye implied she did not feel obliged to explain. "She'll be with us for the week."

Grace was about to suggest this was yet to be decided, but left that discussion for another time.

"Where are you from?" Ivy demanded.

"Now, Ivy. You shouldn't question the young woman." Ada leaned closer. "Where are you from, dear?"

"England," Grace answered, "I arrived this afternoon."

Mrs M removed the lid of the tureen, releasing a cloud of steam that smelled of potatoes and herbs, filled a bowl with a ladle and passed it to Grace.

"I didn't know any steamboats arrived from Europe today." Ivy dragged out a chair on the other side of the table and sat down. "Which one were you on?"

"The Parisian," Grace said. "She arrived in Halifax yesterday."

"Not that ship that collided with another boat in Halifax harbour?" Mrs M dropped the ladle into the tureen with a splash. "I read about it in this morning's paper."

"It wasn't as dramatic as it sounds," Grace said. "The captain made a dash for the quay and everyone got off safely."

"I'm glad to hear it." Ivy slurped from her spoon.

"But all the same, it must have been terribly frightening." Ada's gleeful expression invited more details.

"Leave the girl alone, Ada. You can see she's safe and uninjured." Ivy rolled her eyes. "My sister has a yen for the dramatic. The Herald said the ship was still afloat and no one was hurt. Fuss over nothing if you ask me."

"Nobody did ask you, Ivy," Ada said.

"This is delicious soup, Mrs M," Grace ventured as the two sisters glared at each other across the table, savouring the delicate taste of leek and herbs with just the right amount of pepper.

"Thank you, dear. It's one of my Irish grandmother's recipes."

"We don't normally eat such simple fare," Ivy said. "We're from New York, you know. The cuisine there is far superior."

"I'm looking forward to exploring the town tomorrow," Grace said, embarrassed for Mrs M, who took this oblique insult in her stride.

"Provincial little place with not much to recommend it." Ivy sniffed.

"I come from a village north of London, so it might suit me perfectly," Grace said.

"That's not quite accurate, Ivy," Ada contradicted her just as Mrs M looked about to interrupt. "The architecture of the public buildings in Charlottetown is quite remarkable."

"You mean they used bricks instead of wood?" Ivy sniffed again. "Hardly impressive. It's too quiet here for my liking and the men seem to think more of their horses than they do their wives."

"Horses are valuable," Marge muttered as she set a platter of sliced roast pork on the table so hard a bowl of apple sauce toppled over, saved from spilling by Mrs M. "Wives ain't."

Grace bit her lip to prevent a laugh. What was meant to be a quiet supper began to resemble a theatre performance, with Ivy's scathing remarks diluted ineffectually by Ada while Marge threw the odd barb into the mix, the whole refereed by Mrs M.

By the time Grace finished her pork and roast potatoes, she was thoroughly enjoying herself. Mealtimes at the MacKinnon mansion were almost silent affairs which began with a prayer and ended with a lecture when Angus MacKinnon felt inclined to remind her or Frederick of their transgressions - again.

Thoughts of her husband made her wistful, followed by a stab of guilt that she hadn't thought of him at all lately. Not since Andrew Jardine had swept her into his arms in the customs shed at Halifax.

"Are you all right, dear?" Mrs M handed Grace a portion of peach cobbler. "You're looking a bit peaky. I expect you're tired. It's a long journey from Halifax."

"I'm fine, just reminiscing. This is a lovely meal. These peaches are delicious."

"Preserved, but quite tasty if I do say so myself." Mrs M beamed. "We do well for fruit here in the summer. I always buy a lot of everything as I do like to put aside my preserves."

"I shall have to pay attention, Mrs M. You could teach me a lot when I get settled."

"You intend to live here?" Ivy's spoon hit her plate as if this notion was unbelievable. "On the Island?"

"We thought you were a visitor. Like us." Ada included Ivy in her description.

"I do, and no, I'm not a visitor," Grace replied, mildly irritated by their continued disparagement of a place that was not only beautiful, but clean and well ordered. "I was told this is an excellent place to begin my new life."

"Really?" Ivy peered down her nose at her. "What was wrong with your old one?"

Grace made her voice hitch slightly. "My husband died." Past experience taught her death tinged with emotion was invariably a conversation stopper.

"How awful for you, and you so young." Ada's eyes welled with tears. She dragged a handkerchief from inside her sleeve and applied it to her eyes.

"Stop blubbering, Ada, you didn't even know her husband," Ivy snapped.

"What's that got to do with it?" Ada rubbed her nose hard with the scrap of lace. "One can still sympathize with another's loss."

"I agree, Miss Dobson," Mrs M interjected, scowling at the stone-faced Ivy.

"I suppose you are young to be widowed." Ada sighed. "It must have been devastating if you felt you had to come all this way to forget." She blew her nose nosily.

"With few friends and no family, there was nothing to keep me in England." None who cared for her anyway. "Prince Edward Island seemed a good place for a new start." Nor did she wish to forget Frederick, only to be able to think about him without a mixture of regret and guilt. She wanted to preserve the few happy memories of their years together.

"Then may I welcome you to our own little paradise, my dear. Life can be good here for those willing to work." Mrs M pushed both palms against the table and levered herself to her feet. "Marge don't stand there gawping at Mrs MacKinnon. Go and make the coffee."

Marge pushed away from where she slumped against the doorframe and returned to the kitchen.

Grace finished her last spoonful of the peach cobbler, replete and feeling quite at home in the cosy parlour with people who seemed genuinely interested in her.

After hot, rich coffee served with tiny almond biscuits, the Dobson sisters retired to their room a little after nine o'clock, still squabbling about trivialities as they retreated along the hallway.

Repeating her promise to visit the bank the following day, Grace wished Mrs M and Marge a goodnight and went to her room where she changed into her nightgown.

With her hair combed out over her shoulders, she stood at the window and looked out across the darkening rooftops to the black strip of ocean in the distance.

This was her home now, the place where she would perform her rituals of work, friends, disappointments and achievements. The red earth was very different, but the soft green hills she saw from the steamboat were reminiscent of where she was born. She sat unmoving as golden evening light faded to fingers of purple and pink that darkened to navy beyond the horizon, waiting for homesickness and regret to overwhelm her new surroundings. They did not come.

Chapter 9

The Dobson sisters did not make an appearance at breakfast the next morning. Relieved of their bickering, Grace enjoyed her porridge, tea and toast in relative quiet. While Marge laid the fire in the black leaded grate, Mrs M bustled back and forth from the kitchen offering advice on the prettiest route through town for Grace's intended walk, together with the location of the nearest bank.

"Not that I'm angling for payment, Grace, my dear. It's a pleasure to have you here."

"I like to settle my obligations, Mrs M. You have a business to run after all." She nodded to where Marge had finished setting the fire and now clattered pots enthusiastically in the scullery. "Marge sounds a little cross this morning."

"That's because her man, Rab was out until the early hours again. His first week off the night boats and he spends it drinking cold tea with his mates in some cellar. She's a bit peeved with him, though I wish she wouldn't take it out on my crockery."

A penchant for cold tea didn't sound much of a reason to be angry, Grace mused. Perhaps this Rab possessed other unpleasant characteristics?

Dressed in her thickest petticoats and best coat, Grace set off at a little after ten o'clock in search of the Merchants Bank, which turned out to be a short walk from the boarding house. An Italianate style three storey building of deep red brick with arched windows beneath a low hipped roof sat at the corner of Great George and King Streets. A thin, boyish clerk wearing too short trousers that flapped around his ankles greeted her with an oblique look when she asked to see the manager. At discovering she did not have an appointment, he appeared reluctant to oblige, until Grace informed him she wished to open an account.

In contrast, the manager, Mr Hill, received her cordially and having presented Mr Beech's letter of introduction, the atmosphere of the entire interview changed to pure business and ingratiating respect.

"Might I ask what your plans are for here in Charlottetown, Mrs MacKinnon?" Mr Hill asked once he had instructed the same clerk to make the appropriate arrangements to have Grace's funds wired from London.

"I haven't made any firm ones as yet, but I have a mind to buy a property." The idea only just occurred to her but spoken aloud sounded like a sensible use of her money. "I've only seen a small part of the town, but the houses are quite beautiful." The more she talked, the more appealing the notion became. If she could afford a villa in Chiswick, surely her money would buy her one of the pretty cottages in Charlottetown? Perhaps a pastel painted one with a veranda and bay windows?

"An excellent suggestion. Have you seen anything you like?"

"I only arrived yesterday, Mr Hill. I shall have to take a look at the market and become more familiar with the town."

"A wise decision." He studied her papers over his half-moon spectacles for a moment. "I see you reside at Mrs Mahoney's."

"For the time being, yes."

"An excellent establishment. And if you decide to invest funds to provide an income, I would be happy to offer some advice."

"That's very kind. I'll give it some thought." With confirmation of her first ever bank account tucked safely inside her bag, Grace strode back onto the street with a new spring in her step. The rest of the day was a blank page, so with no particular direction in mind, she wandered the wide, shaded streets, looked into shop windows and admired the numerous churches that proliferated on every other street.

She returned to Great George Street and walked north to the Market Hall, a square, two storey brick building that stretched over half a block. Its Gothic style sported a high-pitched roof with sandstone dressed gables. Curiosity drew her inside to where the ground floor was arranged as an indoor market, the stalls aligned in sections according to their type.

Cuts of meat were laid out on thick wooden tables, while whole carcases hung from hooks on racks attached to the wall behind them, the coppery tang in the air declaring the section to be the butchery. A layer of sawdust on the floor muffled footsteps and absorbed blood spillages. The fish section exuded the tang of salt, another designated for fruit and flowers in a fragrant array of color, among them garden smells of bay, thyme and earthy potatoes. Buyers crowded the aisles to browse and haggle for goods with the stallholders who called out entreaties to passers-by to purchase their foodstuffs. Set beneath the enclosed roof, the constant noise bore down on her until almost giddy, she stepped outside again and took a deep lungful of salt laden air.

At a bakeshop in the flour and meal section, she bought a hot pasty for her lunch, taking it into Queens Square next door to the market, where she occupied one of the long benches below a hexagonal bandstand, empty now, but which promised lively entertainment on summer days.

The pathways were flanked with neat, symmetrical flower beds she imagined would be filled with color when the warmer weather arrived. When she bit into the still warm pasty she realized how hungry she was. She ate slowly, savouring the layers of buttery pastry that enclosed tender slices of meat and a rich sauce, watching horse drawn carts, buggies and private carriages hurrying by, giving an almost pastoral feel to the town. The lack of motor cars seemed odd until she remembered what John Cahill said about them upsetting the horses. Lone gentlemen, couples and ladies in small groups strolled the square and adjoining streets, some of whom nodded a good day to her as they passed.

Grace smiled, at peace with her surroundings, made more intense by the fact Angus MacKinnon would never find her there. She liked to think that she had made friends, or at least acquaintances in Andrew Jardine and the Cahill's. Emily notwithstanding. She couldn't quite forget the removal of the business card, certain it was her doing.

As the afternoon progressed, the wind picked up and abandoning her perch, she wandered back along Queen Street towards the dark line of ocean in the distance and down to the jetties that reached like long arms into the Northumberland Strait.

The wind was stronger without the shelter of the buildings and with one hand clamped on her hat, she surveyed the harbour with its variety of fishing smacks, private yachts and ferries. When one left the quay, its horn sounding, an incoming vessel jostled for position against the wharf and disgorged a stream of eager passengers.

Seagulls screamed and whirled overhead, diving for scraps thrown from the boats unloading their haul of fish. Like Grace, ladies clamped their hats to their heads and ducked to avoid the swooping birds or harried their children towards the station to catch a train to far flung towns Grace didn't know the names of. Idly she wondered if the SS Elizabeth was still tied up at Lords Wharf and considered going to look for the boat, but to see it lying locked up and empty might tarnish her memories of the previous day, so instead, she set off back to Mrs Mahoney's.

It was mid-afternoon before she stepped through the front door, its stained- glass sailboat spread on the boards of the hallway in a rainbow of light. She hung up her coat and went in search of Mrs M, whom she found in the kitchen. Beneath the sharp eye of Marge, Grace counted out her payment for a week's board in Canadian dollars onto the table.

"I appreciate your promptness, m'dear, but I knew you were good for it." Mrs M scooped up the notes and tucked them into her pocket, giving Marge a clear I-told-you-so look which made Grace smile.

"You found your way about all right then did you, dear," Mrs M asked brightly.

"I did. It was remarkably easy with all the streets set out in a grid pattern, although the wind tends to funnel down them and cuts through your clothes."

"You wait until the summer comes, my love. You'll be glad of a breeze or two then. Not that it gets as hot as it does on the mainland. Did you buy some postcards to send home to England? I'm, sure your friends and family would like to hear you've arrived safely."

"Might I trouble you for some more towels, Mrs M?" Grace avoided the woman's eye. "I would like to bathe and wash my hair and my towel is probably still damp from this morning."

"Of course, dear. I suggest you do so before five o'clock, which is when the Dobsons will be back. They tend to monopolise the bathroom on your floor before supper."

"I'll do that," her question as to whom she shared the bathroom now answered. "And thank you for the bottle of lemon oil in my room. That was very thoughtful. I'll use some in my bathwater."

"That's not for bathing, sweetheart, that's for the bugs."

"Bugs?"

"Midges. You won't see 'em, but you'll feel 'em bite right enough.' Marge stretched on tip-toes to replace a pile of plates on the dresser.

"Invisible bugs?" Grace asked, mildly alarmed.

"Not quite but they're tiny." Mrs M laughed. "It's a bit early for them, but April is just around the corner and it don't hurt to be ready. I like to leave a bottle of lemon oil in each of the rooms for my guests. The critters come out at sundown and again around dawn, so on warm nights keep your legs covered. My lady boarders tend to suffer the most. Could be because we smell better than the men?"

"Is the oil to repel the bugs or soothe the bites?" Grace asked. "Both dear. Vinegar works just as well, but I doubt you'll want to smell like a pickle." Mrs M covered her mouth with a hand and giggled behind it. "Now as for those towels, I'll bring some up to your room presently."

"Thank you, but really, there's no need. I'm quite happy to come and fetch them. If you would just show me where they are."

"Um- all right then, dear. If you insist."

The woman's obvious reluctance puzzled Grace as she followed her along the hall and down four steps to a half-basement, at the end of which was a deep linen cupboard lined with tightly packed shelves of pristine white sheets, pillowcases and towels. A door opposite stood open to reveal a room with chairs laid out around the walls, strategically placed oil lamps on small tables set at intervals.

On a sideboard at the far end obviously full green bottles, their contents a mystery, stood behind a neat row of china teacups in various flowered patterns. Grace could see nothing which would explain Mrs M's sudden change of mood.

"There you are, dear." Mrs M selected a pile of fluffy white towels and handed them to her. "Should keep you going for a while."

"Are you having a party this evening, Mrs Mahoney?" Grace nodded to the open door.

"Oh, um, sort of." Mrs M's cheeks reddened and flustered, she pulled the door closed and stood in front of it. "Some friends of mine are due over for a light social. Church business you understand."

"How nice. I hope you have a lovely evening. Oh, and thank you for these." Grace hugged the towels to her middle and climbed the stairs to her room, bemused. Perhaps her landlady thought she was angling for an invitation to her soiree?

Chapter 10

At the beginning of Grace's second week in Charlottetown, she went down to breakfast to find the parlour empty, despite the fresh toast and pancakes laid out on the table along with a pot of hot tea. She was half-way through her second slice of toast, when the back door banged shut and Mrs M's voice drifted through from the kitchen.

"You'd best clear up the lower room before the guests come down, Marge, I need those bottles taken out before anyone sees them." She halted in the doorway, her eyes widening and almost dropped the milk jug she held. "Grace, dear. Is it that time already?"

"Good morning, Mrs M." Grace glanced at the clock, but she was no earlier than usual. "That's the third church social this week. The Parish Council certainly keeps you busy."

"That's right, dear." Mrs M retreated into the kitchen, reappearing a moment later. "There are always so many things to discuss."

Grace poured herself a second cup of tea, then held up the empty milk jug. "May I have some more?"

"Oh, what am I thinking?" Mrs M's cheeks flushed an unbecoming red. "I had the jug in my hand but took it right back out again. Silly me." She disappeared again, returning with the jug which she placed at Grace's elbow. "Did you say you planned to visit Victoria Park today, dear?"

"You might recall I went there yesterday. You were right, it's a beautiful spot with so many peaceful places with lovely views of the coastline among the trees, I could have stayed all afternoon."

"When I was a child, my Pa used to take us to the Battery every Sunday to listen to the military bands. I don't have the time for such things much these days." Mrs M wiped her hands on her apron and took a chair at the far end of the table. "Have you made any plans for the future yet, dear? Not that I want you to leave, but it's not right for a lady like you to be living in a boarding house. I imagine you're accustomed to a better sort of life." She eyed Grace's cameo and pearl brooch pinned to her hand-embroidered silk blouse.

Silently, Grace agreed. Mrs Mahoney's might be safe and comfortable but did not form part of any long-term plan.

"I have an idea, Mrs M, but it's not much of one at this stage." A sudden thought occurred to her and she glanced up in alarm. "You don't need my room, do you?"

"No, no dear, don't you fret on that." She splayed her work-worn hands in surrender. "I'm

143

not expecting any new boarders until Easter, and what with the Dobson's going home next week, I'm glad to have you." She twisted around in her chair. "Marge, fetch that package for Grace would you?"

"Yes, Mrs M." Marge entered carrying an oilskin wrapped package fastened with a length of string which she handed to Grace.

"I thought you might like a few sandwiches for your lunch." Mrs M beamed at her.

"That's very kind," Grace said. "The pasties from the market hall baking stall were very good, but I was becoming bored with eating the same thing every day." She held up the package. "These will make a nice change."

The sounds of mild squabbling from the hallway heralded the arrival of the Dobson's, prompting Grace to drain her teacup and scrape back her chair. "I'll see you later, Mrs M. Thank you for these." She swept up the wrapped parcel and made a rapid exit.

After another tour of the shops, churches and garden squares Charlottetown offered, Grace returned to Queens Square and sat on her favorite bench by the bandstand.

The elderly gentleman she saw every day waved his walking cane at her in greeting as he passed. Grace smiled and waved back, dismayed at the fact everyone appeared to have somewhere to go, whereas she had wasted another morning in aimless wandering and still not reached a firm decision.

She unwrapped Mrs M's parcel of sandwiches and picked one out, peering at the layer of mysterious brown paste between two layers of bread. She gave it a tentative sniff, then poked it suspiciously with a finger. It didn't smell fishy, in fact it didn't smell at all. She sighed, wishing she had bought a pasty after all.

Tearing off a piece, she threw it to a brace of beady-eyed seagulls that pecked at the grass nearby. The birds squabbled over their prize, the morsel consumed in seconds.

She tossed a second piece onto the grass, where two more gulls joined the first, creating an explosive ruckus as they fought for possession. The brown goo stuck to her fingers, and she absently licked them, surprised at the slightly rough texture on her tongue which tasted sweet, rich and nutty.

Curiosity drove her to take a bite of the second sandwich, then another. She chewed slowly, the flavor becoming more palatable as she ate. As she popped the last piece into her mouth, the seagulls squawked in protest and flew off.

"Sorry birds," she whispered. Refolding the oiled wrapping, she returned it to her bag. Traces of the paste lingered in her mouth and between her teeth, the flavor unusual, and strange but also satisfying. She must ask Mrs M what it was when she returned to the boarding house.

Leaving the square, she strolled up Prince street, admiring the pastel painted clap board houses with their picket fences and neat gardens, her thoughts troubled. Perhaps Emily Cahill was right, and she might have to make do with being a country schoolmarm after all. The prospect dismayed her, but if she didn't think of something quickly, she was in danger of drifting, precisely what she had run away from England to avoid.

She noticed a 'For Sale' sign on a post outside a three-storey house on the corner of Prince and Sidney streets with white painted clapboard and wood architraves on deeply pitched gables. Quite different from houses styles she was used to in England, but it reminded her of fairy tale houses in story books she read as a child, with its covered verandas and tiny balcony. A covered porch on one side led to a covered veranda across the front elevation, behind which were three square bay windows. A small balcony on the upper floor was supported by two columns, balusters and a gabled roof. The house looked hunched between its more affluent neighbors so as not to draw attention to itself. Much like herself in some ways. She tried to imagine what difference a few pots of colorful flowers arranged on the porch would make, and maybe a trailing vine or two hung from the eaves.

"Can I help you, madam?" a voice said from behind her.

Grace jumped and swung around to where a dapper-looking young man regarded her curiously from a few feet away. He wore a grey suit with a fine red stripe and a deep green tie, a brown fedora perched at an angle on his fair hair.

"Not really. The house caught my eye, so I stopped to admire it."

"This is indeed a fine property." He slapped a hand on the fence rail which wobbled beneath his touch and scanned the street quickly, frowning. "I was expecting a couple called Miller to see the house. Are you-?"

"No, I'm afraid not."

"Then I'm sorry to bother you, ma'am." His gaze slid past her to the street.

"Does it occur to you I might be interested?" Her hackles rose at his casual dismissal, although it was unlikely the house was within her budget.

"You?" His mouth twisted. "I doubt that, ma'am. But should the property be of interest, perhaps you might refer your husband to me? I'm always open to new clients." He flicked back one side of his open overcoat and delved into an inside pocket. "I have a card here somewhere." He frowned, slapped several other pockets, though no card appeared. "I must have left them in another coat."

"I don't see these clients of yours." Grace gave the street a swift look in both directions, doubting both his claims. What genuine broker left his business cards behind?

"They'll be along in a while, I expect. Fine properties like this don't come along often." He tucked his thumbs into the pockets of his waistcoat, his chin raised to survey the street.

"Not that fine. Unless of course you plan on fixing those shingles."

"Shingles?" He glanced up at the house, confused.

"The ones below the little balcony have rotted." She pointed to the upper story. "Most probably caused by the holes in the guttering. The whole building would also benefit from some new paint." Though the roof had no tell-tale dips which revealed damaged purlins, nor did the tiles have any patches of moss.

"Minor details, ma'am. None of which are serious defects in an otherwise sound property."

Grace smiled, confident in her own assessment.

One of Angus MacKinnon's passions in life, apart from the church, was buying up houses. He owned entire streets in Hampstead and Belsize Park which he rented out at punishing rates and one thing she learned from him was to always buy the worst house in the best street.

"The garden needs clearing out too. Is that an old sink over there?" She nodded to where an overgrown patch of weeds half concealed a corner of thick white porcelain.

"Er- It might be. This is a solid house, and I happen to know a gentleman brought up a family of nine here."

"Then it's a pity he didn't maintain it properly." His presumption made her disinclined to be polite towards him. "But I'm sure you're right, and I hope it sells soon. Good day to you."

"Now, there's no need to be hasty." He stepped in front of her as she went to move past him. "You strike me as a lady of discernment, Miss-?"

"It's Mrs. Mrs MacKinnon."

His eyes widened. "Of the Highfield MacKinnon's?"

Grace returned his steady stare, but stayed silent, following John Cahill's advice to let people assume a connection to one of the Island's leading families.

"Perhaps we could begin again." He lifted his fedora briefly before replacing it. "Charles Keogh, at your service. I would be happy to show you around the house. "

"I'm-I'm not sure" Instantly she regretted having goaded him when a refusal would make her look stupid. It couldn't do any harm to look, and it was a lovely house, although larger than she would need. "All right. But only until your clients arrive."

"Excellent." He pushed on the gate, which stuck so he applied some force to open it. He gave it a final shove, which produced an ear-splitting shriek as it scraped across the stone path. He unlocked a solid front door flanked with stained glass panels in an intricate floral design which threw long rectangles of color onto the tiled floor of an enclosed lobby.

She hesitated, her triumph at having bested him instantly replaced by apprehension. What was she thinking to agree to enter an empty house with a strange man? Her experience with Mr Jardine had turned out well, but that had been more sheer luck than judgment. She ought to take more care, but her desire to see the house overruled her good sense.

"Is there something wrong?" He frowned as he started to close the door behind her.

"Um-no, not at all. However, would you mind leaving the door open?"

"For the Millers of course. I should have thought of that. Then they'll see it is ready to inspect when they arrive." He strode into the hall, his hands splayed. "As you can see, this is an unusually grand entrance, not evident by the first sight of the house." The wide hallway with its arched cornices and a slate tiled floor was indeed an impressive entry. "The main rooms are over here. Follow me."

The rooms were large, square and featured cornice and crown moulding, parquet floors and Adam style fireplaces in both wood and marble. A solid oak staircase curved to the upper floors. A layer of dust on every surface and a few telltale cobwebs in corners proved the property had not been lived in for a while. An overall mustiness lingered although there were no signs of damp. All trace of personal items had been removed, but the heavier pieces of furniture were still in place; most with ornamental carvings and dovetail joints indicating time and expertise, expended in their making.

Her unease dissolved replaced by a sense of calm as she trailed through the rooms, each of which were flooded with light from full height windows, while Mr Keogh pointed out specific features in every room. During a stilted explanation of the function of the water closets, she bit her bottom lip to avoid laughing aloud at his flushed face. His stammered explanation put her more in mind of a nervous schoolboy than the arrogant man of business he attempted to convey.

"How many bedrooms did you say?" Grace mounted the second staircase to the upper floor ahead of him, partly to disguise her amusement as he tried to replace a doorknob that came off in his hand.

"Seven on two floors, plus an attic floor." He bounded up the steps behind her, almost tripping on the last one. "There are servants' quarters at the rear of the ground floor." He glared at the offending step for a second, recovering himself self-consciously.

"Seven," Grace mused, her mind working rapidly. Some of the bedrooms were very large and could easily be divided, while what he referred to as the servants' quarters were small, but could be combined to form an apartment. Removing a glove, she ran a finger across a mantelpiece. The cream marble shot through with streaks of chocolate was cool but smooth and soapy against her skin with no cracks or blemishes.

They returned to the ground floor for a second look of the main rooms, all of which contained wide, square bay windows. Two rooms of equal size were at the front, while a third ran along the back of the house overlooking a neglected garden, where overgrown shrubs and waist high grass blurred any impression of size.

With less dominant furniture, a row of French doors to replace the single half glazed one with cracked panes, and wall lights that washed pale painted walls with soft golden light, it would make a perfect dining area.

With her head full of ideas, Grace left her companion to follow and wandered back into the main hall, the open front door visible through the lobby which threw rectangles of jewel colored light onto the tiled floors. Grace exhaled blissfully. It was perfect.

"Er-Mrs MacKinnon." Keogh cleared his throat noisily. "What do you think?"

"There are some good features. A few bad ones of course." She surpressed her growing excitement beneath feigned banality. Never show you want something was a mantra her father-in-law drummed into her through the years.

Mr Keogh's face showed disappointment as he approached the open front door. "I expect the Millers will arrive presently, so if you have-"

"What does the owner want for it?"

"I beg your pardon?" He halted, staring back at her over his shoulder.

"I'm interested in buying it." A flicker of unease crossed his features and Grace sighed. "Why should that surprise you? Because I'm a woman?"

"You're serious?" He straightened, his gaze roving her face.

She shrugged. "Why wouldn't I be?"

"Well, um, in that case-" He quoted an amount, which, even after her rapid calculation into English currency, made her heart sink.

She stood in the porch and tugged on her gloves. No matter how much she loved the house, she could never pay that much. "I'll have to think about it. Did you find that card, Mr Keogh, so I might contact you when I have considered the matter further?" She doubted she would do any such thing but it struck her as the most business like thing to do.

"Ah yes, of course." Keogh patted his pockets again, just as a horse and buggy pulled up beside the front fence.

A bull of a man in a baggy brown suit with unruly ginger hair, climbed down onto the road and tied the reins to the 'For Sale' sign. His head down, he barrelled down the path and onto the porch as if the route was a familiar one He only looked up for a second so barely avoided colliding Grace. Swerving to one side, his stocky frame bounced off the doorframe and stumbled, his sour expression dragging down a set of heavy jowls.

"Mr Daly!" Mr Keogh bounced on his toes in front of the newcomer "I wasn't expecting you today."

"Have you sold the place yet, Keogh? You've had long enough," he snapped, giving Grace a stern up and down look before dismissing her. "I told you last week if I didn't have an offer by today I would look elsewhere for a broker." He was a man evidently uncomfortable indoors, as he carried the smell of fresh air and the stable about him.

"I know what you said, sir, but as you see, I've been showing this lady round this afternoon. She's most interested in the property." Belatedly, he performed a swift introduction, his eyes pleading with Grace to go along with him.

"Well?" Mr Daly glared at her, apparently a man with no time for niceties. "Do you want the place or not?"

"Actually, I do." Grace looked from Keogh's intense expression to Mr Daly's sceptical one. "Though the asking price is somewhat ambitious." She had no idea if this was true or not, but it was worth a try to see what he would say.

Mr Keogh inhaled sharply and was about to speak, but Mr Daly interrupted him, his bottom lip lightly held between a thumb and forefinger. "How much are you prepared to offer?"

Grace hesitated. Did she dare? But then what did she have to lose? He could only refuse her. She suggested a sum thirty percent less than the figure Keogh quoted.

"I must protest, Mr Daly," Keogh blustered. "I'm sure I could do better if you give me a little more time."

"You've had your chance, Keogh." Mr Daly silenced him again with a look. "Something tells me you've been charging too high a price to inflate your commission. You haven't had a bite in months. If the lady wants it, and has the money, she can have it."

"Thank you, Mr Daly." Grace's voice remained calm, but she had to resist the urge to throw her arms around the gruff owner. "If you would apply to Mr Hill at the Merchants Bank, he will confirm my financial situation and begin the paperwork." She had no real idea of what was required to buy a house but was confident that Mr Hill would oblige with all the relevant details. "Do you have any objection to a swift conclusion of the sale?"

"None at all." Mr Daly sniffed. "I inherited the place and it's nothing but trouble. I live in Tignish, and what with having to pay taxes and such, I need to get rid of it so I can concentrate on running my farm." He turned to leave, calling back over his shoulder, "I'll get the place cleared as soon as I can arrange it."

"Actually." Grace halted him mid-step. "I would be happy to take the heavier furniture off your hands. I'll give you more than you'd have to pay to get it removed." The beds, wardrobes and a handsome full-sized dresser that took up an entire wall in the rear reception room, were in excellent condition and would save her finding alternatives.

"Er-Mr Daly," Keogh bounced in front of the owner. "I have an associate who would sell the furniture for you."

Mr Daly ignored him, his grey eyes crinkled at the corners, his mouth lifted in a parody of a smile. He nodded. "I like you, missy. You're smart. And you have a deal." He jammed his crumpled hat back onto his head and stuck out a gnarled hand.

Grace accepted his brief, brisk shake before her hand was abruptly released. His hat lifted in salute, he turned and loped along the path back to the buggy.

Once the vehicle was out of sight, Keogh's ingratiating smile faded to an angry glare.

"You've just cost me a considerable portion of my commission, Mrs MacKinnon. That isn't a nice thing to do to a legitimate businessman."

"What are you complaining about, Mr Keogh?" Grace peered up at him, too delighted with her new acquisition to care. "You've sold the property, haven't you? Surely a lesser fee is better than none?"

"I suppose so," he conceded grudgingly. "But have I?" His eyes darkened. "What's your husband going to say when you tell him you've bought a house? Will he allow the sale to go through, or shall I find myself accused of unreasonable coercion?" The way the words tripped off his tongue made her think he had used them before.

"You don't need to worry. I'm a widow. And before you ask, I do have sufficient money."

"A widow, eh?" He stroked his clean-shaven chin thoughtfully. "In which case would you care to celebrate your new purchase? With a fine dinner perhaps at Queen Hotel?" At her sudden start, he added, "To discuss our new business arrangement, of course." He withdrew a key and locked the door behind them.

"What about the Millers, Mr Keogh?" she reminded him. "The couple you were waiting for when I arrived?"

"I'll catch up with them later." He gave a dismissive wave. "If not dinner, then how about tea? The Victoria is only a short walk from here."

Aware he referred to the large hotel in Great George street, she hesitated, suddenly nervous. She wasn't sure why, but something about this man put her on her guard. Mr Keogh was handsome, even charming in a self-satisfied way. Perhaps it was his eyes, which could change from limpid appeal to hard speculation in an instant.

His ingratiating smile made her suddenly feel foolish at having overreacted. After all, it was just tea, which would also give her an opportunity to see inside one of the town's best hotels. Something she could hardly do alone.

"All right. That would be nice, thank you."

Chapter 11

The Victoria Hotel straddled the corner of Great George and Water streets, built like many of the buildings in the town, with a clapboard façade with an open timber veranda running around the three sides that formed the triangular front. The corner section resembled a turret, with a second, smaller veranda two storeys higher, all beneath a pitched red tiled roof.

"What do you think of Charlottetown's finest hotel?" Mr Keogh directed Grace to an ox-blood leather wing-back chair at the far end of the hotel lounge. A dark panelled room of polished wood, leather and a combined smell of beeswax polish and old cigar smoke that reminded her of a library. When he removed his hat as they sat down, she noticed his wheat-colored hair gleamed with a liberal layer of pomade.

With an impatient click of his fingers, Mr Keogh summoned a server from whom he ordered tea for them both in a sharp, hectoring tone.

The waiter's eyes narrowed slightly, boring into Mr Keogh's neck before he ducked his head and left.

"So tell me." Keogh unfastened the last button of his jacket and eased back in his seat, his feet crossed at the ankles. "What does an attractive young widow want with a seven-bedroomed house in Prince Street? Or do you have a brood of children to accommodate?"

"No children," Grace replied. "I have an idea for a business venture, however I need to formulate a more structured plan before I feel comfortable enough to discuss it."

"Cautious, eh? I like that in a woman." Was it her imagination, or did his nonchalant grin mock her?

Her initial enthusiasm abated, leaving behind a mild panic. She had just committed more than half her capital to a building which needed further investment. She would have to plan the next step carefully.

"My plans are by no means definite, Mr Keogh. There is a lot to consider."

The waiter returned with a tray on which sat a china teapot, milk jug, sugar basin and two cups and saucers. He smiled warmly at Grace as he pushed the steaming cup toward her, but when he turned to her companion there came a tell-tale thinning of his lips before he bowed and withdrew.

"Do you know that waiter?" Grace asked once he was out of earshot.

"He's of no importance." Keogh took a small silver flask from an inside pocket, unscrewed the lid and tipped a measure into his tea. In response to her start of surprise, he added, "Purely medicinal. I have a certificate."

Grace shook her head, the certificate remark incomprehensible. "I was surprised because it's not yet four thirty." She removed her gloves and laid them on top of her bag in her lap.

"Never too early for a spot of rum." He held the flask towards her. "Would you care for some?"

Grace shook her head. In England, no one so much as opened a decanter until after six of an evening.

Keogh returned the flask to his pocket, plucked three lumps of sugar from the bowl and dropped them into his cup. "Perhaps you could convert the house into a school? Teachers for the offspring of the local gentry are always in demand." He flicked the bowl in her direction with a thumb and forefinger, so it rattled on the polished surface.

"It's certainly a consideration." Grace stirred milk into her tea, an eyebrow raised at the wobbling sugar bowl. "From what I have seen of Charlottetown it doesn't strike me as such."

"Then here's to your new venture, whatever that is." He raised his cup in salute, set it down again and rubbed his hands together.

"Now, let's get down to business. You'll be needing a sponsor, Mrs MacKinnon."

"I beg your pardon?" Grace stared at him over the rim of her cup.

"A sponsor," he repeated with a shrug, as if she might have misheard him. "A financial advisor. An agent to act for you in matters of business."

"I didn't know I needed one."

"Being new to the Province, you won't be familiar with how things are done here on the Island. As a woman alone you'll find it difficult to operate a business without any references to obtain credit. You'll need help with the legal requirements and tax obligations of a property owner. I could sort all that out for you." His brow cleared and he wagged a finger at her. "Ah, now I've got it. I knew there was something."

"I beg your pardon?" Grace's cup halted in mid-air.

"You're English aren't you?" He nodded, congratulating himself.

She sighed, replacing her cup in the saucer. "I am, yes."

"How long have you been in Charlottetown?"

"Not very long." She felt he deflected her to avoid her question. "You were explaining the functions of a sponsor to me, Mr Keogh."

"A simple arrangement." He shrugged. "You engage me to manage your affairs. I act

161

for you, negotiating major purchases, pay your bills and so on. For a fee, of course."

"Of course." Grace pretended to give the idea some thought, but she would never again allow a man to control her life. "I'll have to think about it. Perhaps when I've decided the manner of the business I wish to run, I'll let you know."

"That's your prerogative, naturally. But I ought to point out I do have other clients who occupy my time. If you leave it too long, I might not be able to accommodate you." He drained his cup, and pushed himself to his feet, indicating the meeting was at an end.

"How might I contact you?" Grace gathered her things and rose. "You did not give me your card."

"Oh, just ask for me here by name at the desk." He escorted her to the door at a much faster pace than when they arrived. "The porter will take a message and pass it on."

"You live at the hotel?" Perhaps he possessed better means than she thought?

"I negotiated a favorable rate." His slow wink conveyed something, but she wasn't sure what.

She had little time to speculate. Through the glazed lobby doors, she spotted a tall man on the street outside and immediately recognized the streak of white in his full head of otherwise black hair. Her breath caught in her throat as Andrew Jardine entered the lobby in the company of another man, the pair engaged in an intense discussion. As he came level, he, glanced sideways as if aware of being watched. He halted and did a swift double take, his eyes lightening. Her heart lifted as he looked about to speak, but then his gaze slid abruptly to Mr Keogh and he bit back whatever he intended to say.

His eyes darkened with what? Confusion? Anger? She couldn't tell. Only that what he saw displeased him.

His companion said something to him and Jardine nodded, then carried on past her into the lounge.

Grace stared after him, bewildered. "Is something wrong, Mrs MacKinnon?" Keogh asked.

Grace blinked, collecting herself, though her feet felt glued to the floor. "N-no, nothing. I thought I might have left my gloves behind."

"Are they not the items in question?" He pointed to her left hand where the gloves were squashed together in a shapeless lump."

"Oh, yes, of course," she murmured, her head down as she busied herself putting them on.

Without waiting for Keogh, Grace pushed through the door into the street, her throat tight.

"Now, dear lady, might I hail a hansom for you?" Keogh followed her out, evidently eager to get away.

"There's no need. I don't have far to go. I'll be in touch, Mr Keogh. "Thank you for the tea."

Without waiting for his response, she turned on her heel, her bag swinging on her wrist as she strode along the street, her steps quickening with each yard she put between herself and the hotel.

Why did Jardine pretend not to know her? He had been so kind all the way from Halifax, even attentive. She didn't imagine his interest then, or did she? Just now he looked genuinely pleased to see her, but then - nothing. Was his action to avoid having to introduce her to the man with him? She barely noticed where she walked, and when she next looked up, she found herself outside Mrs Mahoney's door.

She stepped into the hall, where the sight of the yellow sailboat spread out on the floorboards reminded her that she had bought a house today. A house she would transform into one of the best - no, the best small hotel in Charlottetown. And she would do it without Mr Charles Keogh, or, more importantly, Andrew Jardine. She could cut people too, and she would do exactly that the next time she saw him.

* * *

"There was a telephone call for you this afternoon, Grace dear," Mrs Mahoney said as she bustled through from the kitchen.

Grace's heart jumped the same way it had when that crewman handed her the telegram on the ship. Her mouth dried as she waited.

"From Mr Hill at the bank." Mrs M folded her arms beneath her bosom.

"Ah, I see. What did he say?" Grace removed her coat, giving her heart time to settle into a more comfortable rhythm.

"He wants you to call in to sign some documents. Something to do with your new account and funds being wired from London" She tilted her head like an eager bird. "You've decided to stay and set up home here then?"

"Did you think I wasn't going to?" Grace draped her coat over her arm and eased towards the stairs.

"You've been a bit confused since you arrived. But it seems you're sorting out your affairs. I was thinking, dear."

"Thinking what, Mrs M?" Grace halted on the second step and turned back.

"The Dobson sisters are going back to New York tomorrow, so I wondered if you would like their room? It's bigger than yours, and the furniture is newer. I could let you have it for another dollar a week. I know how fond you are of your daily baths, too, so I could let you have extra towels and linens for another fifty cents a week."

"That's kind of you to offer, but I'm more than happy in my room." Grace didn't know how long the renovations to the Prince Street house would take, so extra expenses were something she would rather not incur. "I wouldn't mind the linens, if that's still possible."

It was worth fifty cents for the luxury of not having to collect towels every day.

"Right you are, then. I'll send some up with Marge each morning."

Grace watched her over the bannister rail as she returned to the kitchen. Would Mrs M be as amenable when she found out Grace was opening a hotel?

Over a supper of roast chicken and spring vegetables, Ivy and Amy entertained her with stories of their parsimonious brother, whom they had not managed to persuade to increase their allowance.

"It's not as if he keeps them short," Mrs M said as the door closed on the pair, who retired early to pack for their departure in the morning. "They've bought two new dresses each since they've been here and goodness knows how many gifts and souvenirs to take home. It's always the same with them, money burns right through their pockets."

"You know what their problem is?" Marge said as she carried the used crockery through to the kitchen. "Those two are afraid Aloysius will propose to Martha Cooley, her who runs the library. I've seen them walking out together to church. Then they'll likely lose the inheritance they've been counting on."

"You'll miss them when they've gone, Marge." Mrs M wagged her finger at her. "You always do. Now, Grace dear, what are your plans for the morning? Off out again are you?"

Grace thought for a moment, wondering how much she should reveal. After her talk with the dubious Mr Keogh she debated whether to call on someone she could trust for business advice. Mr Jardine was the most obvious choice but she was reluctant to give him the impression she was chasing him. It made more sense to approach John Cahill, and the more she thought about it, the more it appealed. And if she was lucky, perhaps Emily wouldn't be at home.

"I'm going to visit a friend and his wife who live in West street. Is it far from here? I haven't decided whether to take a hansom or walk." She added, the 'wife' part to avoid any speculation on Mrs M's part. She wasn't a gossip, but she did have a keen interest in everyone's business.

"Friends in West street, eh?" Mrs M said, obviously impressed. "It's up to you, dear. You could walk it in twenty minutes, or take a hansom if it's raining. If you can find one this side of Queen square that is."

"It's not always been nice by the Government Pond," Marge said appearing abruptly from the kitchen. "Most people call it The Bog as it was on a swamp."

"I do wish you wouldn't sneak around like that." Mrs M jumped and glared at her. "Gives me palpitations, it does." She clapped a hand against her upper chest in emphasis.

"Don't pay any mind to her." Mrs M dismissed Marge with a wave. "It's where all the old shacks used to be. The Loyalists who settled here after the Revolutionary War brought their African slaves with them. When their descendants were freed, that's where they lived, though most have moved on now and the land around the pond itself is being tidied up. They've built some lovely houses there now."

"I was just saying, Mrs M," Marge said, defensive. "Grace told me she's interested in the Island history and I thought she'd like to know."

"Yes, all right, Marge, that'll do. Go and refill the coffee pot, would you, I'm that thirsty tonight." She waited until Marge had gone and lowered her voice. "Marge's grandma was from a Bog family. Not that you'd know with her freckles."

"No, you wouldn't." Marge's ancestry suddenly became more exotic than Grace had imagined. But I am interested, Mrs M. And there's no reason not to be proud of your heritage, Marge," Grace addressed a smiling Marge who had returned with the refilled coffee pot. "I don't know much about mine and would like to know where my descendants originated from." Apart from her Scottish name, Grace didn't even know if Scotland was where she came from. Angus MacKinnon always changed the subject when she asked.

"It's not only the Irish, Scots and English who made this place. There's the Africans, Lebanese, Turkish, and all sorts." Marge sniffed as she placed the coffee pot on the table. "There's plenty who call the Island home and The Bog is part of it."

"I would love to hear more about it sometime, Marge." Grace caught Mrs M's tightly clamped lips and decided to leave before an argument started. "Dinner was lovely, thank you." She scraped back her chair. "Oh, by the way, what was in those sandwiches you gave me this morning?"

"What was that, dear?" Mrs M frowned as she looked up from pouring her coffee.

"The-um brown concoction you gave me. I've never tasted anything like it before. It was quite - unusual."

"Oh, the peanut butter do you mean? It's made with steamed peanuts crushed and mixed with sugar."

"That's a strange name, when there's no butter in it?"

Mrs M shrugged. "Don't ask me why, dear. A Montreal man invented it, I'm told. An American salesman brought some from the World's Fair in St Louis last year and ever since, I've had some on order at the mercantile." She huffed a breath and patted Grace's hand. "Sorry, dear, it didn't occur to me you wouldn't have had it before. Perhaps I could make something else for you tomorrow?"

"Please don't worry. I admit it was a bit odd at first, but it was very tasty." And the seagulls loved it.

Chapter 12

Grace recalled the Cahill house was located on West street, but without the missing business card she had no idea how to get there or which house to look for. That early in the morning there were few people on the streets other than tradesman's carts, and the first one she asked spoke in such a thick Scots brogue she could hardly understand him.

Thanking him politely she backed away, then she spotted a postman on his rounds. No more than a youth, he was more than eager to share his knowledge of the town and gave her a detailed route to follow.

"The Cahill residence is fourth on the right as you enter the street. A double bay house with a covered porch and blue roof, Miss."

Thanking him, she repeated his directions in her head, walking north along Pownal and left at Rochford Square to an area of grassland with pathways beneath mature trees, but with none of the aesthetic features Queen square offered. Following the signs for Victoria Park, she found the street not far from the Governor's house, a small lake visible at the end of the road.

The unimpressive name had not prepared her for the half dozen or so mansions spread out along the wide tree-lined road which sheltered the roadways between larger than average plots with gardens, groves and hedges.

The Cahill residence was as the postman had described it; an impressive colonial style building with arched windows and a deep blue mansard roof, which gave it the look of a French chateau.

Her knock on the front door, set beneath an iron canopy between iconic columns, had not yet been answered when John Cahill strode around the side of the house, a soft felt hat askew on his flowing silver hair, a pair of secateurs in one hand.

He halted a few feet away, his eyes alight with recognition,

"Mrs MacKinnon!" His handsome face split into a wide smile. "How delightful to see you." He tossed the shears casually onto the porch and grasped her hand in both of his. "I was only saying to Emily last evening that we hadn't seen anything of that charming Mrs MacKinnon. Where have you been hiding, my dear?"

Grace could only imagine how Emily must have reacted to such a question.

"I'm also pleased to see you, Mr Cahill." Her voice caught in her throat, touched by his genuine welcome. "Did I interrupt your gardening?"

"Not at all. I was just idling away the morning with a spot of pruning. Making room

171

for the roses to bloom. What brings you to my humble home?"

Grace almost laughed. "I was hoping to ask your advice. And you did say that if there was anything-"

"Of course, of course. I'd be happy to help, in any way I can." He threw an arm lightly around her shoulder. "Hilda, you aren't needed," he addressed the maid who answered the front door. "Mrs MacKinnon is a friend. Bring us some coffee would you, we'll be in the study."

"Yes, sir." The maid bobbed a quick curtsey and scurried back into the house.

He led her into a double height entrance hall, in the center of which a wide staircase split at the top onto a gallery that ran around the entire upper storey.

"You have a beautiful home."

Her steps slowed as she stared at the Wedgewood blue walls and the ornamental white columns with scrolled corbels flanking each doorway. A sparkling multi-tiered crystal chandelier hung from the ceiling, each facet reflecting the light.

"Thank you, my dear. My father built it some fifty years ago. I always thought it was a little too grand for the descendants of immigrant Scots farmers, but Emily likes it."

"How could she not." Grace looked down at her shoes which sank to the uppers in the thick patterned blue and gold carpet.

The study reminded her of the reading room at the British Library, but prettier. A leather topped desk sat inside a full height curved window, the walls around the room filled with floor to ceiling shelves crammed with books. In contrast to most home libraries she had seen, the volumes were of uniform size and color with the appearance of never having been opened, let alone read. The phrase style over substance sprang to mind.

"What can I help you with, Mrs MacKinnon?" Avoiding the two chairs set on either side of the desk, he gestured her into a wing back chair beside an empty fireplace and sat on the one opposite.

"In the first instance, I've bought a house."

"Well, that's certainly an impressive beginning to your new life." His bemused smile emphasised the tiny lines beside his eyes.

"Not for me to live in. I mean, I do intend to live there, but only in part of it. I'm going to open a hotel."

"A hotel? My goodness, you are an ambitious young woman." The leather chair creaked as he eased further into it and crossed his ankles. "And you've only been here a few days. I'd be interested to see what you achieve in a year."

"It might sound as if I have come to you with a fait accompli, but I saw the house purely by accident. I had to act immediately, or I risked it being bought by someone else." Why was she justifying herself? She bit down on her bottom lip.

"I've made some of my best business decisions on impulse, Mrs MacKinnon."

"Please, call me Grace. And I'm so glad you said so because I knew the second I saw the property it would be perfect. I was able to obtain it at a lower price too."

"Well done, and where exactly is this house may I ask?"

"Prince street. On the corner of Sidney street opposite the Methodist Church. At least I think it's Methodist."

"Close enough to town to be convenient and yet far enough away from the commercial area with all the noise and activity." He nodded approvingly. "Sounds like an extremely good choice, Mrs - I mean, Grace. How can I be of help?"

"I need a sponsor. Someone to act for me in financial matters."

"Do you have the funds to secure this house?"

"Oh yes. I haven't come to ask you for money."

"What about a contingency for the renovation, running costs, staff and so on until you are established?"

"Yes, to all of those. I can afford to stay at Mrs Mahoney's until the work is done, providing it doesn't take too long. I'll miss the Easter trade, but if I work steadily, I can open in time for the summer visitors."

"Hmmm." He shook back his leonine mane of hair. "You'll certainly have to be organized with builders and so on. However, I'm not sure about this sponsor idea."

She frowned. "Why?"

"Quite simply, because you're British born, Grace, and soon to be a property owner which will give you automatic voting rights in municipal elections. You'll be a respected member of the community. I don't see why you feel you need anyone to sponsor you."

She brought a clenched fist down on her knee, her suspicions confirmed. She would have some harsh words to say to Mr Keogh if she ever saw him again.

"You appear to have the financial aspect adequately covered," he went on. "But I would suggest you engage a lawyer and a reputable accountant. I could arrange introductions for you if you wish? I know a few people who would give you a good, and more importantly, honest service."

"I thought you said I didn't need a sponsor."

"You don't, but women in business are considered less creditworthy than men. A mistake, as some of the best tacticians I know are women. Your suppliers are unlikely to extend you credit until you have shown the ability to pay your bills for a few months. They'll insist upon a cash only arrangement to start with."

"Isn't that how I keep a close eye on my budget? If I don't have it, I cannot spend it."

"A wise philosophy, my dear. But you're going to need accounts with your suppliers or you'll find your cash flow compromised."

"I would appreciate your recommendations as to people I could trust."

"Ah, here's our coffee." He rose and met the maid at the door where he relieved her of the tray. "Now we have the hard part out of the way, why don't we sit and chat over a hot cup of Columbian and you can tell me all about your new venture. Firstly, how do you like it here in Charlottetown?"

"It's beautiful, Mr Cahill. I-"

"Ah, no." He held up a finger of one hand and passed her a full cup of rich, aromatic coffee with the other. "If I'm to call you Grace, it's only fair you call me John."

"John, then." She tried out the word on her tongue, surprised at how natural it felt. "I'm staying at a very comfortable boarding house and have spent the days since I arrived exploring. Everything you said about the town is true and so different from where I come from. I love the wide streets and the gentle way of life here. It feels like being in a large village where people remember you after two or three meetings. Although I get the impression nothing you do stays private for long."

"You'll get used to that, though it's not malicious. We look out for one another." He paused with the pot over a cup and briefly raised one cynical eyebrow. "Well, most of us do." He resumed his seat and crossed one leg over the other. "And this hotel you wish to open, what sort of place would it be? Similar to the boarding house where you're staying?"

"No, I have something more stylish in mind. A small version of a London hotel with proper maid service and a reception desk where guests are greeted, and their needs are taken care of." She placed her half full cup on the table at her elbow and eased closer as she got into her stride.

"On the voyage over on the Parisian, there were several American ladies with one thing in common. They were subjected to stares and whispers at the hotels where they stayed, some were even refused service or shunted into a back room out of sight. Why should we continue to tolerate that behavior simply because we're women?"

"I can see you're quite passionate on the subject, and I admit I haven't given it much thought." He stirred cream into his cup with a tiny silver spoon that made his fingers look huge. "I was raised to believe ladies preferred to be sheltered from the coarser habits of the male population."

"We probably do, in some circumstances, but not when it makes us into virtual prisoners."

"Social change, if that's your aim, happens slowly. You cannot radically alter people's perspective with one hotel."

"I'm not a rebel, Mr Ca-John. I simply want to offer first class accommodation to ladies of means who wish to travel either alone or with a friend. My husband's aunt always had a fear of hotels as she never knew when she might run into some strange man coming out of the bathroom. For this very reason, all my rooms will have private bathrooms and a ladies' lounge where they can relax without attracting unwelcome male attention."

"You're making me think you don't like men, Grace." His explosive chuckle shot biscuit crumbs into his moustache. He brushed them away, only to re-position them on his waistcoat.

"Not at all. I have no intention of banning men. Married couples, for instance or a lady with her adult son would never be turned away. But primarily I want to attract ladies."

"I don't think you ought to put that particular requirement in the brochure."

"Brochure?"

"Advertising, the key to letting the world know you exist. I would recommend the newspapers in New York, Boston, Toronto and Montreal which will give you the best exposure."

"I'll remember that." Advertising. She hadn't thought of more than putting a card in the newly established tourist office in town.

"Do you anticipate making an adequate living from renting rooms to a few genteel lady guests? What you describe sounds as if you'll have heavy overheads. How many rooms are you thinking of?"

"I was thinking six double rooms, with possibly two singles if I plan the layout properly. I also envisage a dining room serving continental cuisine open to the public for extra income. The house has a large garden where guests can sit in private and enjoy the summer weather." She took a deep breath. "What do you think?"

He stroked a thumb and forefinger repeatedly down his moustache. "Have you taken into account that there are at least fifty small hotels and boarding houses in Charlottetown at the moment?"

"I have. More importantly, my daily walks have taken me to the harbour on most days. Even this early in the season the ferries are always full of visitors. I assume that number increases a good deal in the summer?"

"It does." He nodded, smiling. "The Island has been a tourist destination for many years."

"What I'm offering will fit in between a boarding house and one of the larger hotels. I hope to offer a novel alternative."

"I doubt there's a similar establishment anywhere on this island. I should be interested to see how you progress. I also know all the local suppliers, even own a couple. If you have any problems at all, just mention my name and refer them to me."

"I was hoping you could recommend a good builder. Someone who will do a first class job, within a reasonable time."

He leant across the space between them and patted her hand. "I know just the person. He's usually busy, as most good craftsmen are, but

I'm sure he'll be able to help you. I'll call him on your behalf."

"That would be wonderful, but I need to take ownership of the property first. I have yet to instruct my bank. I can hardly have walls knocked down until the legal side is completed."

"I agree, but it doesn't hurt to give prior warning." He held up the coffee pot. "Would you like some more coffee?" They spent the next hour discussing Mrs Mahoney, the eccentric Dobson sisters and Grace's daily request for more linens. "I'm sure she thinks I'm strange because I like to bathe every day. I'm determined to provide plenty of towels in my hotel rooms so guests won't have to ask for them."

"Don't forget to keep an eye on your laundry bills," he warned. "It's one of those expenses which can get out of hand if you aren't careful."

"I will. And thank you, you've given me confidence I'm doing the right thing."

When she took her leave, he escorted her onto the front step. "Feel free to call on me at any time. And even if you don't need me, do keep me up to date with your progress."

"I will, thank you." She hoped her association with John Cahill would also make her less vulnerable to the Charles Keoghs of this world.

"Only too glad to help. Ah, Emily." He turned as his wife drifted down the stairs towards them in a sage green gown, which flattered her peaches and cream complexion and enhanced her shiny honey colored hair, her steps slow and measured as if she entered a royal ball. "Grace came to call. Isn't it lovely to see her?"

"Isn't it?" Her smile did not reach her eyes which remained hard as flint as they tracked between Grace and her husband. "Had I known where she was staying I might have beaten her to it."

"Mr Jardine knew where I was," Grace said. "I'm sure he would have told you had you asked."

"I have something to attend to." John directed a discreet wink at Grace. "I'll leave you with Emily for now, but we must get together soon, Grace. Dinner perhaps?"

"I would be delighted."

"Well, well aren't you the veritable bloodhound?" Emily joined her on the front step, her attention on a carriage pulling up in front of a white house on the opposite side of the street.

"Not really, although I have a good memory." She caught a hardening of Emily's mouth at this oblique reference to the missing business card.

Smaller than the Cahill residence, the house had appealed to Grace when she arrived, possibly because it resembled a rectangular fantasy castle; a cream and white boarded façade with a turret at each corner. The entrance was reached via a wide covered veranda that ran between the two turrets. A row of round headed windows marched across the upper floor.

Grace followed Emily's gaze to where Andrew Jardine stepped from the carriage. He extended an arm back into the vehicle to help down a slender young woman in a forest green coat and matching hat. Behind her came a girl of about seven in a pink dress who reached up and gave Jardine a brief hug before taking the woman's hand. He placed a hand on the young woman's shoulder and all three of them walked the pathway towards the house.

"You seem surprised, Grace?" Emily's eyes widened in mock innocence. "Did Andrew not mention he and Mary were neighbors of ours?" She affected a gentle sigh. "Such nice people, the Jardines. And isn't Isla a beautiful child? She will be quite lovely when she grows up."

"I cannot tell from here, but I'm sure you're right."

It had not occurred to her that Jardine could be married or have children. He never hinted as much at The Waverly, or during their time on the SS Elizabeth, despite there being ample opportunity to do so. No wonder he snubbed her at the Victoria Hotel. He wouldn't want gossip circulating about his having a lady friend.

"I gather you haven't seen Andrew since your arrival on the Island?" Emily said, her intense gaze fixed on Grace's face.

"Not to speak to, no. But then I've been busy making plans and getting to know the town. I expect he's been occupied too." She tore her gaze away and concentrated on her gloves.

"He's been in Halifax most of this week. Something about a ship which nearly sank in the harbour." Emily gave a tiny gasp which was entirely unconvincing. "Wasn't that the same vessel you arrived on? He said that's where he found you."

"It's where we met, yes." Which explained why she hadn't seen him in town until yesterday.

"Andrew always says he meets some interesting scrapers on his Atlantic voyages."

"Scrapers? What are those?"

"Have you never heard the term? It's so amusing. It means those people you meet on board with whom you would never mix under normal circumstances." She wrapped a shiny blonde ringlet around a finger, a small smile playing on her lips. "They amuse you for a while, but once on land there's no inclination to see them again."

Grace descended the front step onto the path. "Do excuse me, I have business to attend to. Good afternoon, Mrs Cahill. It was so nice seeing you again."

* * *

Grace retraced her steps back the way she came in a daze, barely recognizing her surroundings, her chest so tight, she found it hard to breathe. Her feet pounded along the packed earth, vibrations jarring through her knees to the rhythm of her labored breaths. What a fool she was to think Jardine genuinely liked her. No wonder he revealed so little about himself. She was no more to him than an amusing creature whom he picked up on a whim to parade before his wealthy friends. Worse than her own hurt pride was the cruel triumph she saw in Emily's face.

Grace's fury grew as she relived the humiliation of Emily's scorn on the Elizabeth. All her superior smiles and the intimate asides directed at Andrew made sense now. But then, why encourage her to come to the Island, to the same town where he lived? She was bound to find out the truth; or was that all part of his plan? To keep her close, so at some stage he could make her his mistress? Or perhaps he had no plan and he simply didn't care she would occupy the same place as his family? Because she was nothing to him.

Her eyes welled, blurring her vision. She blinked hard to prevent real tears from forming.

In truth, she had made assumptions about Mr Jardine. He never said he wasn't married, nor had he expected anything of her. He owed her nothing, any more than she owed him.

Her steps slowed as her anger dissipated and she began to tire, surprised to find she had walked too far and was at Water Street. Realising her mistake, she halted, and released a frustrated sigh as she turned back to where King Street cut across the main thoroughfare, and almost collided with a man coming the other way. She glanced up, an apology on her lips which shrivelled beneath the arrogant stare of Mr Keogh.

"What a determined face, Mrs MacKinnon." He lifted his hat briefly, then replaced it. "How fortuitous to have encountered you here today."

"Good morning, Mr Keogh." Surely it was too much of a coincidence to see him again so soon? Had he been following her?

"I wondered if you had come to a decision about the house?" he asked.

"What sort of decision?" she snapped, unwilling to enter into that particular discussion. Not today.

"It occurred to me that having slept on it, the ramifications of running a business without a sponsor might have made you have second thoughts."

"For which I assume you would like to put forward a solution?" Irritation sharpened her voice. Were all men so oblique in their intentions towards women? Or did she attract the type somehow?

"I was about to suggest you sell the house on. I already have a prospect and could arrange the deal for you quite quickly."

"The Millers, by any chance?"

He shrugged, suddenly sheepish. "Mr Miller called to apologize for being delayed yesterday and is still keen to buy the house. I just thought-."

"That you would double your commission and inflate the price at the same time?" She was losing patience with him. Could she trust anyone?

"You do me a disservice, Mrs MacKinnon. I'm merely an honest businessman trying to make a living."

"I'm sure you are, a businessman, that is. And I appreciate the offer, but I intend to keep the house."

"I could still act as your agent. I know quite a few people in town and could get you some good prices on building materials, for example. You'll need paint, wood and supplies to renovate the building."

"I thought you said the house only had minor defects?"

He had the grace to blush. "Any property owner will tell you there is always something which requires work. I could also obtain furniture, linens, kitchen supplies. Anything you need, I can find for you. I have contacts in most businesses."

"I'm sure you do." A flutter of panic rose as the enormity of her task began to dawn on her. However, she would manage, somehow. She had no alternative. "And by the way, I discovered I'm not in need of a sponsor after all. I doubt our paths will cross again, so good day to you Mr Keogh." She made to brush past him but at the last second, he leapt into her path.

"There's no reason we shouldn't be friends, is there? Why don't you join me for dinner this

186

evening? I promise not to try and persuade you to sell the house."

His boyish grin tugged at something in her heart. Not in a romantic way, more in sympathy that she dashed his hopes of a lucrative deal and he was desperate to recoup his losses. Then an image of Andrew Jardine with his hand on a child's shoulder jumped into her head. "I don't think that would be wise, or necessary."

"Don't dismiss me so lightly, Mrs MacKinnon. I have a feeling our association isn't over yet." His grin faded as his eyes narrowed, rekindling all her former misgivings about him. Despite the warmth of the day, a shiver ran through her. Grace was about to ask what he meant, but he tipped his hat, turned and strode away, leaving her staring at his back.

Chapter 13

Putting thoughts of Andrew Jardine and Charles Keogh aside, Grace decided to forego her usual picnic lunch and went straight to the Merchants Bank where Mr Hill greeted her like an old friend and invited her into his office.

"Oddly enough, this morning I was visited by Mr Josiah Daly," he said once Grace informed him of her new purchase. "He's asked me to deal directly with his lawyer with regards to the paperwork. He also requested me to take charge of the keys to the property to avoid his having to come into town again. I'm to let him know when the formalities are completed."

"Would you be prepared to let me have the keys?" Grace asked. "I won't start the renovations until the property is legally mine, but it would be useful to have access."

He considered for a moment. "I cannot see any harm; after all you can hardly run off with a house." Chuckling at his own joke, he reached into a drawer and drew out a small bunch of keys tied together with a thin strip of leather. "The legalities shouldn't take more than a few days." He dropped the keys into her outstretched palm. "Have you had any further thoughts about investments, Mrs MacKinnon?"

"Not really, no. I've been preoccupied with my plans for this property." By the time her list of requirements for the hotel were fulfilled, Grace doubted there would be any funds left to invest.

"I've heard the silver fox industry is booming," Mr Hill winked at her. "The Island's pelts are in great demand, which means there's money to be made."

She considered profit from the slaughter of beautiful foxes distasteful, but politely promised to give his suggestion some thought. Tucking the keys into her bag, she gave the bulge they made a reassuring pat and thanked Mr Hill for his advice.

She walked north up Great George street to Queens square towards Wrights Furniture Company; an emporium she discovered on one of her earlier forays into town. Now with a reason to venture over the threshold, excitement pulsed through her as she pushed open the door.

Alerted by the jangle of the bell, a middle-aged gentleman in an ill-fitting suit strode forward to greet her, a speculative smile on his unremarkable features.

"May I assist you madam?"

"I hope so. I have acquired a property which needs to be furnished and you appear to have some interesting pieces." She stroked a side table polished to such a smooth gloss the wood felt waxy beneath her fingers. She looked around the vast room in which every inch of floor space was crammed with furnishings, from full-sized canopied beds down through chests of drawers, rugs and pot plant tables to chairs and antimacassars. The whole room smelled of linseed oil, beeswax and the added tang of vinegar.

"I'm confident we can be of assistance, madam. If we don't have everything you need here, we make items to order at our factory in King Square. Our motto is that we are always the best value in the city."

"That's most reassuring. Do you have any pattern books of fabrics and wallpapers?" Buying furniture would have to wait until she took possession of the house, but there was no reason she could not select colors and patterns for the rooms.

"Indeed yes, do come this way." He led her to a large table spread with piles of wallpaper samples, behind which stood shelves crammed with rolls of colorful fabric placed end on end.

"I'll leave you with these, madam," he said, then smilingly withdrew.

Left to herself, Grace browsed happily through the rich, colorful designs of William Morris and Arthur Sanderson which she remembered from home. From time to time, her attention was drawn to the delicate beauty of a woman a little older than herself in a plain navy-blue dress which skimmed her slender figure; a narrow sash belt encircled her impossibly tiny waist. Her perfect retroussé nose could have been drawn on by an artist, and her heavily lashed dark eyes, which frequently drew Grace's gaze, looked sad and inward looking, as if their owner was a spectator of her own life. Grace wondered if she too carried that same look.

Having chosen three Morris designs in various colors, Grace made a rough calculation of what she would need and placed an order with the salesman.

"Excellent choices, ma'am." He painstakingly transcribed the list into a vast order book. "Those particular designs will arrive in about a month. The fabrics will take a week or so longer."

"A month!" Grace gaped. "That long?"

"I could order them by express delivery for a small extra charge." His expression changed to pained regret. "But I doubt anything will be here inside three weeks."

"Oh, I see. I suppose that will have to do." Her exuberant mood dissipated. "Kindly let me know when they arrive. I'm staying at Mrs Mahoney's boarding house on King Street."

"Very good, Mrs MacKinnon." He saw her to the door. The woman Grace saw earlier was on the street, apparently studying the shop window next door.

Grace paused, deciding which way she would go, when the woman approached her. "I hope you don't mind," she said in a slightly breathless voice. "But I overheard you talking to the proprietor." She nodded to the shop Grace had just left. "Had you not spoken, I would have known by your dismay at being told the wallpaper would take a month to get here. You're from away aren't you?"

"I'm sorry?" Grace frowned. Away where?

"It's how an Islander regards someone not born here." Her smile banished the sadness in her eyes and she thrust out her hand. "I'm Maud Montgomery. Actually, it's Lucy, but that's my grandmother's name, which is far too frivolous for a serious writer. I much prefer Maud. Without an 'e'."

"I'm Grace MacKinnon." Charmed by Maud's friendliness, Grace returned the handshake with a broad smile. "That's Grace, with an 'e'."

"Oh, I Just knew I was going to like you." Maud hunched her shoulders in a girlish gesture which, strangely, sat well on her. "I love meeting new people, but I'm often too impatient to wait for a formal introduction. You don't mind, do you?"

"Of course not. I'm delighted to meet you, and as you have already surmised, I'm new to the Island and indeed I was a little disappointed about the wallpaper." Grace retrieved her hand. "It seemed such a long time to wait. Everything is readily available in London. Did you say you are a writer?" Grace asked, impressed.

"I like to think so. I've had some success with short stories, and I held a job as an editor once, although my real ambition is to write a novel. But enough about me." She gave an airy wave. "Do you really come from London?" At Grace's nod, she brought a delicate hand to her slender throat. "How wonderful. I've always dreamed of going there. Or anywhere in Europe to be honest. I've never been further than Nova Scotia, unless you count Saskatchewan, but I choose not to think about that." She shivered delicately, as if shrugging off bad memories. "But then I dream about so many things with little hope of achieving them all." Her eyes sparkled as she talked, her words tumbling over one another. "London must be especially fascinating with all that history and the ghosts of a thousand years behind it."

"I agree, there's nowhere like it," Grace said when Maud paused to take a breath. "Though where you live is no guarantee of happiness."

"You're a philosopher?" Maud's expressive eyes widened. "Then we are surely destined to be friends. My family have quite given up trying to understand me, not that they tried very hard, even when I was young." She sighed. "I'm sure I often confound my friends too."

"Do you live in Charlottetown?" Grace asked. Suddenly her day had taken a more interesting turn.

"Unfortunately, no. My home is a village in the north where I look after my widowed grandmother. In fact, some folks would say I'm 'from away' myself." Her musical laugh lit up her lovely face. "It's twenty-three miles but might as well be a thousand. I rarely get into town, so I try to make the most of it when I can.

I'm only here today to pick up some supplies for our family gathering on Easter Sunday. It's a tradition, which is nice, I suppose, but for me it tends to mean more work." The sadness returned to her expression, only to immediately lift again. "Anyway, what brings you to the Island? Your husband, I presume?"

"Er-no. I'm a widow." Miss Montgomery's beautiful eyes darkened, but Grace forestalled her. "Please, there's no need for condolences. Distance and circumstance have both played their part in changing my life completely. I look to the future now."

"Distance and circumstance," Maud mused, a finger held to her lips. "I would like to use that at some time." In response to Grace's bemused look she giggled. "Don't mind me. I collect phrases and store them away for future use." Her brow furrowed slightly. "I'm sure you have an intriguing story, Mrs MacKinnon, and I'm quite determined to root it out. Stories are my passion. May I call you Grace? Oh, please say I can, because I feel we shall be friends. And you must call me Maud."

"I should be delighted. Though I fear you are bound for disappointment. So far, my life has been less than fascinating."

"Nonsense, I'm sure I can find at least five interesting things to say about you."

"The only noteworthy thing I have done since arriving here is to buy a house. I'm not sure that constitutes a story. Not yet anyway."

"Well of course it does, I could write a thousand words about such an event. And maybe I will." Maud's wide smile revealed her even white teeth. "Tell me about it"

"It's here, in Charlottetown. I plan to turn it into a small hotel."

"A hotel? There you see, two fascinating things in two minutes. I would love to see this house. Where is it?"

"Not far, but it's quite neglected. Some of the woodwork needs replacing and the whole building could do with a coat of paint - or three. I'm afraid the garden is a mess too. In fact, when I think about it, the place is altogether unprepossessing."

"Oh, don't worry about that. I have a wonderful imagination. I have no idea when I can get into town again, so why don't we go there now?"

"Now? Are you sure?" Grace hesitated, though Maud's enthusiasm was catching. "I suppose we could. I have the keys. It's quite dusty, I wouldn't want your clothes to get dirty."

"If you're trying to discourage me, you've failed miserably." Maud tucked her arm through Grace's and surveyed the street. "Now, which way do we go?"

On their short walk to Prince street, Maud kept up a continual stream of questions, many of which she answered herself.

"As a widow, I assume you didn't come here with your parents? Or is it indiscreet of me to ask?"

"Not at all," Grace replied, admiring her directness. And no, they aren't with me. They were killed in a carriage accident when I was twelve."

"I knew it. We were meant to meet!" Maud halted and turned to face her. "When I woke up this morning, I knew something remarkable would happen today. But how tragic for you to have lost them so young. You'll think me quite awful, but you've given me a premise for another story right there. Were you brought up by some dreadful relative who didn't like children?"

"How did you guess? Only he's a guardian, and thankfully unrelated. He's also thousands of miles away, so I'm no longer accountable to him."

"Very wise and I so envy your independence. I've sought it myself in my lifetime, but somehow the Island always drew me back."

"I can see why. It's a beautiful place. But what about your family?" Grace asked, then regretted her question as a shadow crossed Maud's features, though it was gone in an instant.

"I never knew my mother. She died of consumption before I was two. My father went west. He remarried and produced a brood of children. I went to live with him in Prince

Albert in the North West Territories when I was younger, but I wasn't happy there. I did not fit in with his new family any more than I ever did here. I returned to my grandparents after a year. I missed the Island too much. I always do when I am away."

"Do you miss your father?" Although Grace didn't really know what it was like to miss anyone.

Maud shrugged. "It happened a long time ago. Anyway, he's dead now." Sudden wistfulness came over her though she didn't answer Grace's question. "I run the post office in Cavendish and look after my grandmother since my grandfather died. The advantage being that I can send my stories to magazines without anyone knowing. Nor do my payment cheques ever get lost." She laughed, a sound so infectious, Grace joined her, attracting curious glances from passers-by.

"Do you also believe destiny sent you to the furniture store this morning?" Maud asked. "I never go there, but for some inexplicable reason I decided to take a look around today."

"I'm afraid I don't believe in fate or destiny. I'm more inclined to think we choose our own path in life. The alternative doesn't bear thinking about."

"How free thinking of you. A young reverend of my acquaintance claims our whole lives are predestined. That we have no power of will to change anything. I must say I too find the concept disconcerting, but he's quite voluble on the subject. Is this it?" she asked when Grace brought her to a halt beside the sign which now bore a 'Sold' banner right across it.

"It will be when all the paperwork is complete." The facade looked shabbier in direct sunlight, but even the peeling paint and ragged garden couldn't spoil the thrill at the thought this belonged to her.

"Oh, it's beautiful." Maud clasped her hands beneath her pointed chin, her dark eyes shining. "You must be so excited."

"I am, if apprehensive too. I've never owned anything before and there is a lot of work to do." The gate gave with an ominous creak when Grace pushed on it but did not stick. "I did warn you about the garden, and don't look at that old sink in the corner. The entire house needs paint both inside and out, and some of the rooms need to be rearranged before I can open for guests."

"Mere details, Grace, all of which can be changed. It's so brave of you to embark on a business of your own when I am always being told as a woman, anything other than domesticity and good works is unseemly. I do try to conform, but sometimes I cannot help but have ambitions of my own. I even have to keep my journal secret."

"Your family disapprove of you keeping a diary?"

"It's a journal, only lonely people write diaries," she said, diluting the rebuke with a warm smile. "My late grandfather even disapproved of women being teachers. We had a few arguments about my taking a teaching diploma. As to my going to college, well the less said about that. When he was alive, I smuggled candles to my room, so I might continue writing into the night. It's difficult trying to please everyone when I have reached an age when I ought to please only myself."

"Everyone? Do you have a large family?" Grace experienced a deep sympathy for this young woman, whose only fault appeared to be a longing to simply be herself.

"Large, boisterous and enthusiastic. Aunts, uncles and cousins galore, but no one who is truly my own. I feel as if I have grown up watching a play in which I am a shadow moving in the background but never take the stage."

"I know exactly what you mean." Grace smiled in sympathy as she selected the largest key on the bunch given to her by Mr Hill and unlocked the front door.

Maud's vital and intelligent manner could not disguise the fact she was past the usual marriageable age for such an attractive young woman and yet she had not mentioned a husband or even a beau. Only a young reverend of her acquaintance. Grace wondered about that, but decided it was too early in their friendship to ask such a personal question.

"This is the first time I have shown anyone my new possession, so please be kind." She pushed open the door and ushered Maud inside.

"I'm always kind. But I warn you now, I won't flatter." Maud followed her into the hallway where all the doors stood open, the spring sunshine throwing rectangles of light across the floorboards.

"I hope to combine the five smaller rooms at the back into an apartment for myself," Grace said, leading the way. "It will be convenient for the kitchen, so I can keep an eye on my staff." At Maud's enquiring eyebrow, she added, "Oh, I shall certainly have staff. No hard labor for me. Someone I once knew always said you should work hard, but it is better to work smart. I shall be the ultimate hostess." Grace preceded her into the rear room that overlooked the garden. "This will make the main dining room. Over there, instead of a single door I would like three sets of French doors installed along the wall. In the summer they could be thrown open on warm days, giving the guests somewhere to sit outside."

"What a delightful room and how the light will flood in if you open it out!" Maud turned full circle in the center then ran to open the door to the garden. "The garden might be overgrown, but just think what you could do with it. You'll need screens to keep the insects out in the warm weather. The blackflies can be a nuisance in May, even in the town, I've heard."

"I'll remember that." Grace knew a little about mosquitoes and no-see-ums from Mrs M, but blackflies were an unknown entity.

"You've certainly worked it all out beautifully." Maud wandered to what looked like a chart cabinet, judging by its thin drawers. "Did you buy this monumental piece of furniture?" She began pulling out the shallow drawers which gave easily on smooth runners.

"No, it was one of the pieces which came with the house. I shall have to have it removed at some stage. It takes up too much space in here, and besides, it doesn't fit. Perhaps this room was used as an office at some stage?"

"These look interesting." Maud removed several large pages of thick cartridge paper from the third drawer down and laid them on top of the cabinet.

"What are they?" Grace picked up the first two in the pile. "They look like pictures of flowers."

"More than that. These are botanical watercolor drawings, perfect in every detail and labelled with the Latin name representing each plant. Aren't they beautiful? Look at these colors." Maud ran a finger over each one. "I recognize this pink flower, it's an orchid called lady's slipper."

"I know, we have those in England too, although I've not seen this one before."

"Wild lily of the valley." Maud nodded. "They are mostly found in the woodland areas. I don't know what the yellow one is, though I believe it's a type of wildflower. In fact, a few of these are wildflowers. That pale mauve one is a valerian." Maud held one of the drawings at arm's length, her head tilted. "These would look wonderful framed and hung on the walls in here. They could be your signature style and would make a welcome change from seascapes or views of the town squares."

"I'll have to buy a horticultural book and find out what they all are," Grace said. "But I agree they would make a lovely addition to the public rooms. They are lovely, and worth preserving. I wonder if Mr Daly even knows they're here?"

"I doubt they are worth anything, but as you bought the chest along with the house, they are yours now."

"I agree with your logic, but I feel I ought to at least ask Mr Daly if he wants them," Grace said. "I don't like to take possession of family heirlooms he thought had been lost."

"You are too good. In fact, you humble me because I should have thought of that. If Mr Daly doesn't want them, I suggest you take them to Haszard Moores photography shop and have them framed. It's the best place in town."

"I know you don't come into town often, but you know more than I do about suppliers. Where would I purchase fine wines in Charlottetown? I didn't see a wine merchant anywhere on my walks and I'm sure I have covered most streets."

"Ah. I'm afraid you have a conundrum there." Maud rolled the paintings carefully in a discarded sheet of brown paper, twisted the ends and set them to one side.

"What do you mean?" Grace sighed. "Don't tell me the best wines have to be shipped from Montreal? I suppose I could-" she broke off at the look of pained resignation on Maud's face. "Surely the local shopkeepers aren't averse to selling alcohol to women?"

"It's not so simple." Maud perched on a packing case in the center of the room, her elbow propped on a knee supporting her chin. "The Island is dry."

"I beg your pardon?"

"It means, you cannot purchase alcohol of any description."

"That's ridiculous." Grace slumped onto the packing case opposite. "You're teasing me, aren't you? You must be." Her chest constricted at the thought of her plans crumbling in front of her.

"I'm afraid not." Maud grimaced. "Families were being destroyed by men who spent all their wages on drink. The Scott Act made the Island dry twenty-five years ago but didn't include Charlottetown until five years later. The whole island is dry now and the provincial government employs inspectors who constantly check the law is being upheld."

"I cannot believe it!" Grace covered her face with her hands and stared at Maud through her fingers. "Why did I not know selling alcohol was illegal?"

"You can buy it from a druggist, but you'll need a medical certificate."

"Drink as a medicine?" Grace widened her eyes, although she recalled their doctor in Hampstead prescribed brandy as a restorative for her guardian's low blood pressure.

Maud shrugged. "Certain complaints are relieved with it, though I'm not sure what those are. Wine is allowed for communions, of course."

"I'll wager the church attendances are pretty regular," Grace muttered. In response to Maud's frown she shook her head. It also explained Mr Keogh's comment about possessing a certificate. "I don't understand. I was a guest on a private boat from Halifax where the stewards served us champagne and wine with meals." The men also drank brandy and whisky if she recalled.

"Strictly speaking you were still outside the Island, and being a private boat would make a difference, I imagine. Even a postmistress from Cavendish knows the lives of the wealthy are very different from those of everyone else. I imagine your host keeps a private supply, whereas the less affluent tend to rely on the services of bootleggers."

"Bootleggers?"

"Um." Maud lowered her voice though there was no one to overhear her. "Not everyone embraces abstinence. Their supplies come from unregulated sources."

"You mean smugglers?"

"Let me put it this way." Maud eased closer. "If you happen to be walking near a beach after sundown, you'll often see a line of lanterns bobbing in the fields close to one of the coastal farms. The rum runners bring the stuff ashore from small boats in kegs which are hidden in the grain stooks to be picked up later. Not that I know who they are, of course, I would never get involved in such activity but even I'm aware it goes on. The contents of the kegs are emptied into bottles and sold to people who gather in their backrooms to drink in private. My Uncle John calls them 'Blind Pigs'. If you ever hear someone order cold tea, that's what they arc asking for."

"Oh, good grief." That explained Mrs Mahoney's Church Socials, she was running a drinking den in the basement.

"Grace," Maude rested her crossed forearms on her knees and bent closer, her eyes bright. "Do tell me about this private boat you arrived on. I gather it didn't bring you all the way from England?"

"Er no. I came as far as Halifax on the SS Parisian."

"My goodness! That's the ship which was holed in the harbour by that German ship." At Grace's surprised look she added, "I devour all the newspapers when they come into the post office. I read all about it."

"I'll tell you the whole story one day. For now I have to work out what to do about this drink ban. I can't afford to become involved in anything illegal. What about my restaurant? No one is going to pay good rates for homemade lemonade. I was relying on wine and spirit sales to boost my income. What shall I do now?"

"It doesn't have to be a disaster." Maud switched seats and came to sit beside her, an arm around Grace's shoulders. "Why not use one of the smaller rooms at the front as a dining room exclusive for residents only. Then this room which leads to the garden could be an English tea room. If you open it to the public, you'll generate more income."

"A tea room?" Grace frowned. "Would the townsfolk patronise something like that?"

"I'm sure they would. The ladies especially. It would be somewhere for them to go after shopping expeditions, or to meet their friends."

"You know, I think you have something." Grace stared off through the window to the dilapidated terrace. "I could place some flower covered trellises set in alcoves beneath the trees for shade and privacy. Perhaps a Baroque style fountain would go beautifully in the center with the tables radiating from there. I could serve afternoon tea outside in summer and inside in winter."

"There, you see, Grace. You've taken my simple idea and injected it with inspiration." Maud squeezed Grace's shoulders. "It cannot fail, I'm sure."

"It mustn't. I've sunk most of what I have into this enterprise. And thank you, Maud. I'm not going to let some law devised by a group of pious women discourage me."

"I admire your spirit, Grace, but it wouldn't do to upset the WCTU. They're very influential. Who do you think campaigned to have the Scott Act passed in the first place? Their patronage will be useful out of season when the strait is frozen. Unless you intend going somewhere warm for the winters?"

"That's beyond my means at the moment, but it's definitely something to aspire to."

"Then don't slander the pious women." Maud pouted. "They could turn out to be your best customers."

"I hadn't thought of that."

Maud slid off the packing case and smoothed down her skirt. "Time is getting on and I must go. Uncle John will be waiting for me at the Market Hall."

"You will come back though, won't you?" The notion of her first real friend disappearing to the northern coast never to be seen again left her bereft. "You must return to see the hotel when it's finished."

"My time is pretty much taken up at the post office and with grandmother, so it's not easy for me to get away. You cannot work all the time, and perhaps you could visit me in Cavendish? The north coast is truly beautiful. The landscape there lifts one's spirits."

"You make it sound appealing."

"It is. We'll make a pact. In the heat of summer when you yearn for cool breezes and wide open spaces, you must come and stay with me. In the meantime, we'll write to one another.

I love writing letters almost as much as I do my stories."

"It will give me something to look forward to."

Grace locked the front door behind them, and with the roll of drawings tucked beneath her arm, they walked together as far as the next corner, where they parted company with affection and promises, as if they had known each other for years. She strode back to Mrs Mahoney's with a lighter heart at having made a new friend. With Maud's vision, her business venture was taking shape, prohibition notwithstanding.

Chapter 14

As a result of Mr Hill's diligent work, Grace became the legal owner of the Prince Street house within a week of her first seeing it. She occupied the following days with the practical aspects of converting it into the exclusive hotel she dreamed of. John Cahill's recommendations acted like magic on builders and tradesmen who produced, what up until that moment she had only seen inside her head, all delivered in good time and to exact specifications.

The wind from the sea lost its icy chill and the days grew warmer. The insects, midges or no-see-ums Grace was warned about came out in force in the month of May and the lemon oil came in useful to soothe the bites which appeared on her ankles and shins. She started wearing fine stockings at night which seemed to help as, once the first crop had gone, she wasn't bothered much after that. She heard somewhere they could not fly in breezes, so she kept the fan on in her room. She also learned not to walk too close to shrubs due to the fact they liked the moist under sides of leaves.

But the lemon oil Mrs M provided proved ineffective against the soreness of mosquito bites, so Grace reverted to white vinegar, which not only stung but smelled awful. Reluctantly, she avoided perfume during the warm, dry days, consigning her favorite lavender soap to a drawer. She was willing to try anything and made copious notes on various remedies in a leather bound journal bought for the occasion. There was so much to remember about life in this unfamiliar country.

"I keep those mossies down by pouring a few drops of cinnamon or lemon oil on the water butts and pond each summer," Mrs M told her. "Discourages them for a few summers, and the critters go elsewhere to breed. They can't breathe through the oil, you see. We haven't been bothered much these last few summers, but you can't avoid the odd one or two in the warmer evenings."

"It's much worse inland," Marge laughingly said when Grace complained of several bites on her shins that appeared like magic one morning.

When Grace felt almost comfortable dealing with the odd mosquito bite and learned not to panic at the sight of all flying things, the dreaded blackflies arrived. She had never experienced anything like them. Larger than an ordinary fly, she became convinced these fat, fast, noisy creatures possessed a malicious character with their sharp bites which turned sore, itchy and painful for days.

Grace's daily walk to supervise progress on the house grew more exciting. Windows, verandas and fences were replaced, plumbing renewed, and bathrooms constructed adjacent to every bedroom. A magnificent range installed in the kitchen. The overgrown garden was cleared, including the removal of the old porcelain sink. With the hard labor of four men working long hours a patio, brick pathways and a lawn emerged from the chaos.

She arrived one morning to find workmen with trickles of blood on their foreheads, arms and shoulders which they did not bother to wipe away. When she asked after them, they responded with blithe unconcern, and mild surprise.

"Pesky blackflies, but they'll be gone by June," she was told airily.

Her bank account dwindled in direct proportion to the number of tradesmen's carts arriving every day to disgorge furniture, crockery, linens, lighting and carpets, all forming untidy piles amongst builder's materials, tools and ladders.

In the lighter evenings, she replied to Maud's letters, the first of which arrived two days after their first meeting. Maud's neat script filled the pages with a description of her trip home to Cavendish on bumpy roads on a buggy with hard suspension and a squeaky wheel which drove her to distraction. Grace detected a note of dismay at the part which said she had taken up her duties as nurse and housekeeper to her grandmother, as well as postmistress, with only her role as church organist on Sundays to break the tedium.

"I think of our lovely day together often now all I have to brighten the hours is my daily stroll down 'Lover's Lane' towards Cavendish Road and across the fields to the sea. How I love this place, and how ungracious of me to complain when I have the good fortune to call this my home and now have you to write to, my dear Grace."

Grace sat over a blank page for a long time compiling a response to match Maud's eloquent prose, but all she was able to produce was a laundry list of tasks she had completed at the hotel and how much more there was yet to do.

Mrs M's enquiries as to what Grace did with her spare time became more difficult to answer. She had exhausted all the more interesting areas of Charlottetown and reverted to describing the churches and the market hall.

The questioning became less intrusive with the boarding house filled to capacity after Easter with what Mrs M referred to as her 'regulars'; the travelling salesmen who spent the spring and summer on the Island, arranging orders for old clients and establishing new ones.

Their constant demands created a buzz of activity which left Marge flustered and threatening to quit. The refrain, 'There's only one of me ya know,' echoed through the halls at all times of the day.

Grace shared the bathroom with a ferrety looking man called Timmins, who described himself as 'dealing in ladies' accoutrements'. He disguised his non-existent top lip with an outsized moustache that made Grace smile every time she saw him. Their contact was scant, apart from the time she mistakenly thought the bathroom was empty and came upon him bare-chested and in long johns. Fortunately, he had his back turned and she managed to close the door silently before he saw her.

"I hope it's still convenient to have me staying, Mrs M," Grace said after Marge revealed Grace's room was usually allocated to two guests due to the vast double bed it contained.

"That's quite all right dear, it's nice to have a lady to talk to apart from Marge. The men need more looking after than you do, what with all the mess they make of their rooms."

Maud's explanation of 'blind pigs' in basements provided Grace with a source of private amusement she chose not to share with her landlady.

"Another church social this evening, Mrs M?" Grace called over the bannister when she came upon her carrying a loaded tray down to the basement room.

"Only a small one this evening, dear." Mrs M flushed and hurried away, leaving Grace smiling at the way her untidy bun bobbed up and down on her head.

In response to a note delivered to the boarding house one morning, Grace set off for Wright's store. The wallpaper she ordered from Montreal had finally arrived and she wanted to inspect it before it was collected by the workmen and taken to the house. She set off under a warm spring sky free of clouds, dressed in a crisp white blouse and lilac walking skirt with a deep pleat at the back: a new straw boater trailed a matching mauve ribbon. A black belt encircled her waist which though small and fashionable, might never be as tiny as Maud's. She occasionally checked her reflection in shop windows, pleased with what she saw, her steps lightened by the warmer day with no need of her heavy wool coat.

Grace entered Haszard and Moore's, from whom she had ordered a book Maud recommended in her latest letter, described with an enthusiasm Grace now recognized.

"I have discovered a wonderful book which you must read. I know nothing of the author as it was published anonymously, but it has been hailed a success. You must read it, so we may talk about her anecdotal musings next time we meet. Elizabeth expresses her longing to be left alone by a judgemental society so eloquently and with humour. I understand her so well, and I am convinced you will too."

The young assistant spotted her when she entered the shop and raised his hand to catch her attention. "Ah, Mrs MacKinnon. That book you ordered came in yesterday." He disappeared briefly into a back room, returning with a slim volume bound in white cloth with the title in gold script which he handed her. "We've had a few requests for this one, though the author is something of an enigma."

"I'm looking forward to reading it." Grace tucked the book inside her bag, thanked him effusively and left the shop.

With her prize tucked into her bag, she called into Carter's Confectionery for a paper cone of humbugs. Unable to resist, she popped one into her mouth as she left the shop. The cloying sweetness reminded her of her childhood when she and Frederick would send a maid to fetch some from the tobacconists at the end of the road. Swearing the maid to secrecy, they would take them to a corner of the garden and share the sticky black and white confections.

Her smile deepened as she strode along, responding with polite greetings to those with an inclination to smile back, and some who were not.

Her steps slowed as an immaculate black carriage, drawn by two matched chestnuts with excellent conformation, pulled up beside her. Decals decorated the crimson trimmed door panels fitted with bevelled, slightly greenish glass windows. She paused to admire it but when the door swung open and Andrew Jardine stepped onto the road in front of her, her heart lurched. "Good morning, Mrs MacKinnon." He removed his hat and offered a polite bow.

She swallowed the remains of her humbug. The lump of candy stuck in her throat, making her cough to clear it before she made a complete fool of herself.

"Mr Jardine." She attributed the sudden leap of her heart to the unexpectedness of seeing him, bringing a hand to her neck to hide a blackfly bite she had discovered that morning.

How long had it been? Six weeks? And still she found difficulty breathing in his presence. It galled her to admit it, but she'd been unable to look at any man since without searching for that streak of white at the left temple and, when it was absent, a shaft of disappointment always ran through her. And now, without warning, there it was.

"I-uh see what you mean about hired hansoms not being your usual mode of transport." She nodded towards the carriage she vaguely recalled from her visit to the Cahill's.

"Ah yes. Quite." He followed her gaze briefly. "I hope you're well, and that life is proving interesting for you in Charlottetown?"

"How kind. But then you might have enquired before now, Mr Jardine. After all, you knew where I was staying."

"I didn't wish to intrude."

"I see." Intrude? A polite call on an acquaintance was hardly intruding.

"Actually, you don't." He twisted his hat in both hands. "I uh-" He broke off as a passer-by offered an aggrieved scowl at the open carriage door. Jardine held up a hand as a signal for her to wait, slammed the door shut and nodded to the coachman, with a brusque, "Meet me at Market Hall in an hour."

The driver saluted, flicked the reins and urged the horses to draw the carriage into light traffic.

"On the contrary, Mr Jardine, I do see," Grace said when the carriage disappeared along the quiet street. "We had a very pleasant trip together on the Elizabeth, but you have a life you had to go back to. Mr Cahill, however has been incredibly kind and has helped me a lot recently."

"So he has informed me. You have embarked on a new venture. A hotel no less?" Was that sarcasm or scepticism she heard in his voice? "But then I doubted you would settle for an easy life in a lowly position. Regardless of Emily's suggestions."

Ah yes, Emily. She wondered how long it would take him to mention her.

"Yes. It's kept me extremely busy these past weeks. I haven't opened yet, but hope to do so before very long."

"I should very much like to see it."

Grace wasn't sure what to say so she merely smiled, which seemed to disconcert him. He scanned the street before his gaze came back to her.

217

"Mrs MacKinnon, I hope you don't think I'm interfering, but I wanted to-" He paused and licked his bottom lip. "To advise you, that is, to be on your guard where Mr Charles Keogh is concerned."

"I beg your pardon?" Grace blinked, unable to reconcile the man's name on his lips.

"Only that I appreciate you are making friends in town," he rushed on, filling the sudden awkward silence. "I don't think he's the type of man with whom you should associate."

"I had no idea you were acquainted with the gentleman."

"I'm not. Well, not personally, although he does have a certain reputation I thought you should be aware of."

"Why is it of any concern to you with whom I associate?" Grace bridled at the cheek of the man. "In fact, I find it insulting you should even suggest someone to whom you have not been introduced does not meet your exacting standards." A torrent of rebuttal sat on her tongue, but she restrained for fear he would mistakenly think Charles Keogh meant something to her. Which might have suited her had she not already rejected him.

"I can see I've offended you, for which I apologize." His knuckles whitened on the rim of his hat. "I appreciate he's the type of man a lady might find charming, even attractive. His sort are always plausible, until we discover what their real aims are."

"His sort, Mr Jardine? Do you mean those who find making a living a more challenging task than you appear to, and therefore deserve your contempt?"

What was she saying? Keogh was quite clearly a man who couldn't be trusted, so why was she defending him?

"I simply urge you to be careful." In response to her incredulous 'tut' he added, "I only have your interests at heart."

"My interests? What an odd thing to say. I've been in Charlottetown for almost two months, and on the one occasion when our paths have crossed you had no time for me."

"Ah, yes that was unfortunate, and now I think about it, unforgiveable. But if you would let me explain, I-"

"I don't require your explanations, sir. Our association was pleasant, yet brief. And over. Now I must go. I am very busy. Good day."

"Mrs MacKinnon! Grace!" His insistent cry followed her along the road as she marched away.

She was almost a block away before she chastised herself for not asking after his wife, if only to see the look on his face.

* * *

Grace's hand shook as she let herself into the boarding house, closed the door behind her, and leaned against it; her eyes squeezed shut as she attempted to calm her rapid breathing.

219

She accepted that Andrew Jardine was out of her reach weeks before, so why did he have such an effect on her? The thrill of seeing him again combined with the resentment at his neglect confused her. As did his claim he only had her interests at heart.

"Grace!" Marge's voice broke into her jumbled thoughts and her eyes snapped open to where she beckoned from the rear hall. "Come here, quick!"

"What is it, Marge?" If she needed help setting up the cellar room she could think again. Grace had no intention of getting involved in anything illegal.

"I thought you'd never get back. Come with me, there's something you need to see." When Grace didn't move, she shuffled forward, grabbed Grace's arm and propelled her towards the kitchen. "See what?" Grace halted on the threshold. A figure sat at the kitchen table; a girl by the look of the mane of dark, tangled hair that obscured her face. Bits of grass sat among the thick tresses as well as something sticky Grace chose not to identify. She wore a shapeless cotton dress torn at one shoulder, sweat-stained and filthy; the skirt and hem ragged and ripped in places.

She sat with her head bent over a steaming mug held tightly between grime encrusted hands.

"She came to the back door," Marge said in a fierce whisper. "Mrs M is out but I couldn't leave her to wander the streets, so I brought her in.

"Which was very charitable of you." Grace couldn't imagine Mrs M objecting to a little Christian charity, not with all the church socials she ran. "Where did she come from?" Grace stared at the bedraggled figure with sympathy.

"How should I know?" Marge gave the back door a searching glance.

"Perhaps there's a mission in town we could take her to?" Grace whispered. "Or a church nearby which could offer her temporary shelter?"

"That's the thing," Marge said. "She mentioned your name."

"Me? But I don't-"

Grace looked past the grime and the tangled hair, and gasped. "Aoife?"

The dark head lifted slowly, and a pair of light brown eyes peered out of an extremely grubby face. "Hello, Grace."

Grace hunched down beside the chair. A hand reached for Aoife's forearm but drew back without making contact. "Oh, Aoife, look at you." She rose, scraped back a chair and sat on it, shuffling it closer, aware of an earthy, animal smell that emanated from her.

"No thanks. I already have." Aoife eased backward against the chair, released her death grip on the mug and held it towards Marge. "I don't suppose I could have some more of that tea?"

Her voice, complete with its familiar hint of mischief, brought a rush of emotion that made Grace's eyes well.

"Of course." Marge took the mug from her. "The missus won't notice. She's never grudge a body a cup of tea." She shuffled to the range and replaced the kettle on the hotplate.

"What are you doing here? How did you find me?" Grace asked Aoife. "I thought you were in New Brunswick?"

"The company wasn't what you'd call genteel." Aoife huffed a sarcastic breath. "So I left."

"In something of a hurry by the look of you. And where's your bag?" She scanned the floor but it was empty. Had she come all this way in only the clothes she stood up in?

"Give me a chance, Grace. I've only just got here and I'm that tired." Aoife took a careful sip from the mug Marge handed back to her.

Before Aoife gave an answer to Grace's question, the back door banged open hard enough to shake the frame and Mrs Mahoney strode into the kitchen in a whirlwind of indignation. She dumped her shopping bag on the floor which sent onions and potatoes rolling in all directions, her gaze going straight to Grace.

"Oh, you're here then?"

Grace rose and stepped in front of Aoife, shielding her. "Is something wrong, Mrs M?"

"I should think there is. What's this I've been hearing? Mr Hobbs at the mercantile tells me one of my boarders is opening a new establishment in Prince street." She propped both hands on her plump hips and glared at Grace. "He says you've had builders working on the place for weeks and been ordering all sorts of fancy wallpapers and light fittings. From Montreal, no less."

"Ah, did he?" Grace hesitated. "I was going to explain-"

"Explain what? That you're aiming to take all my boarders?"

Her eyes flicked past Grace and she pointed a shaking finger at Aoife. "And who's this might I ask?" Her eyes narrowed for a second while Grace hoped she wasn't about to order Aoife be ejected.

"Her name is Aoife," Grace explained, relieved when Mrs M circled Aoife's chair and tutted in sympathy. "I met her on the ship coming over. I've yet to discover how she got here and why, as I've only just walked in the door myself." Grace eased Aoife to her feet. "You can question me later, Mrs M. Right now, I need to take her upstairs and get her out of these filthy clothes. She'll need a bath too, so if I might have some towels? Lots of them."

"Then what are you going to do with her?" Mrs M demanded, though not unkindly. "There's no room for her here, and what about my boarders?"

"She can sleep in my room tonight. We'll work something out tomorrow; but don't worry, I'll pay you extra for the inconvenience."

223

"Huh! You'd have my whole linen supply if you had your way, Missy. But if you can vouch for the lass, and you're willing to pay, I suppose I could oblige." Her face softened with sympathy. "She's in a sorry state by the look of her. Get the towels, Marge, but not the best ones." Mrs M made shooing motions at Marge in the direction of the basement. "And while you're at it, take a bar of carbolic up with you. She'll need it."

Something awful must have happened to bring Aoife to her door in such a state. Grace wished Mrs M would stop talking so she could find out what it was.

"I didn't come here to make trouble," Aoife mumbled as Grace supported her along the hall.

"Don't worry. We'll sort everything out." Grace paused on the second step, addressing Marge over the handrail. "Is there a chance you could bring up some supper for us both later? It doesn't matter what it is. Even soup and bread would do."

"There's some leftover chicken stew in the pot," Marge said. "And I've got a bag of clothes I was collecting for the goodwill. I'll root through and see if I can find something to fit her." She continued talking as she descended the half-basement steps. "That dress she's wearing will have to be burned. Who knows what's crawling in it?"

Once they reached Grace's room, Aoife made no protest as Grace peeled the filthy dress from her shoulders, kicking it to one side as soon as it hit the floor. Her slip and undergarments were as dirty as the dress and, if possible, smelled worse. She had lost weight since Grace last saw her, with scrawny arms, and shoulder blades starkly visible through her skin.

"How did you get into this state, Aoife? Did you walk here from New Brunswick?" Grace tried not to stare at the bruises and welts on Aoife's shoulders and upper arms. Some had scabs and yellowing around the bruises, while others were more recent, sore and inflamed with streaks of dried blood.

"Pretty much." Aoife gazed round the small room with its cast iron roll-top bath and basin in the corner. "You've got your own bathroom?"

"Not quite, I share it with another boarder. It's a bit small, but it does what it's supposed to." She turned the knob on the hot water geyser that spluttered and coughed for a moment before a stream of steaming water flowed steadily into the tub.

"All I ever had was a tin tub in front of the kitchen fire," Aoife said. Grace stared at her and she laughed. "Don't get me wrong, I'm not complaining. I remember those Friday nights when I was a nipper as being cosy and full of laughter. But that woman was right, my dress is no good to anyone now. Not that I've got another one." She kept up a stream of trivial chatter, most likely to avoid talking about what happened to her since they both left the Parisian.

Grace eased off Aoife's scuffed boots, the soles worn to a wafer to reveal sore and grime encrusted feet, but did not press her. She would tell her when she was ready, and if she wasn't, perhaps it was her own business.

Aoife bent to remove her bloomers and Grace averted her eyes, though not fast enough to avoid seeing the raised welt across her narrow back as Aoife eased into the steaming water. The skin was broken in places and the marks looked inflamed, some caked with old blood.

"Ohh, that's lovely," Aoife released a deep sigh and smiled for the first time since arriving.

Grace wanted to ask if the hot water hurt her cuts, but didn't like to bring attention to them. "Shall I leave you to have your bath?"

"No, don't go. I'd rather not be on my own." Aoife lay passive, her bruised legs stretched out and her arms crossed over her chest, the slight swell of her breasts just visible above the waterline. She looked like a child with her head resting on a rolled-up hand towel.

"Of course, I'll stay." Grace retrieved a sponge from the sink and balanced on the edge of the tub.

"I have some violet soap which will make your hair smell lovely and won't dry it out." She gave the block of green carbolic a swift kick that sent it skidding behind the water cistern. "Put your hands over your eyes or it will sting." She worked up a lather and spread the suds into Aoife's tangled hair, trying not to grimace as the water turned dark brown around her waist with tiny bits floating in it.

She repeated it twice more, while Aoife endured being pulled this way and that, her eyes squeezed shut as the water streamed down her face.

"That's better," Grace said when the water ran clear. "Get out and rub it dry with a towel and I'll change the water."

"Again?" Aoife stared up at her, both hands braced on the side as she started to get out. "I've never in my life had two baths in a row."

"Why not? Just let me wash all this dirt away first." Grace plucked another of Mrs M's precious towels off the pile on the floor and applied it to the black ring round the bath.

"How did you manage to find me, Aoife?" she asked as they waited for the geyser to refill the bath with hot water for a second time. With her wide eyed, scrubbed pixie face and her hair hanging in black rat's tails over her shoulders, Aoife looked human again.

"I had nowhere else to go. I don't know anyone in Canada, apart from you. I remembered that Jardine fella mentioned he was going to Prince Edward Island so I assumed you would too. This was the fifteenth boarding house I tried." Aoife cocked her chin towards the door.

Grace listened without interrupting, finding it strange that their roles should be reversed and Marge be the compassionate one. She would think about that later. She turned off the geyser and helped Aoife climb into the fresh water, her wet hair wrapped tightly in a white towel on top of her head. Apart from a small cut across one eyebrow and a bruise beneath her chin, her face was clean and unmarked, if reddened by the sun and looking sore.

"I'm causing trouble for you, aren't I?" The sponge caught the edge of a cut which made Aoife stiffen and duck away. "Your landlady don't want me here. What if she throws you out? Then we'll both be on the street."

"Mrs M won't do that." Grace re-applied the sponge more gently. "She was angrier with me than she was with you, though it was for an entirely different reason."

"Why was she?"

"We'll discuss that later. Once you're clean and have had some of Mrs M's cooking, you'll feel much better."

Wrapped in more of Mrs M's towel supply, Grace sat Aoife on her bed and went in search of a nightgown she could lend her. The one she chose was too long and the straps kept slipping off her shoulders, but at least Aoife looked normal again.

Marge brought a tray of Mrs M's excellent leftover chicken stew, along with a pale blue dress with a yellow sash she found in the charity bag. "It's the nicest one I could find with no patches and look, it hasn't even been re-hemmed."

"You're very kind, Marge. Thank you."

Grace marvelled that her first impression of Marge as a surly, hard woman had undergone a complete reversal since then.

The two of them sat cross-legged on Grace's bed, the tray between them, eating bowls of hot stew.

"You can stay here with me for the time being," Grace tore a bread roll into pieces and dipped one into her stew. "It will give us time to plan what to do next." Her first instinct was to offer the girl a home, but Aoife was proud and her offer might backfire.

"I can't let you look after me, Grace. I need to work. Could I get a job round here? I was a good tweenie back in Liverpool. I was being trained as a lady's maid too. Not that I would go back there even if I could afford to."

"You were to be a farmer's wife, if I recall?" As Grace suspected, she would evidently take a little persuasion.

"Yes, well, that didn't work out so good, did it?" Aoife looked away, but her eyes darkened with sadness that reflected the pain beneath her skin.

"What about your husband?" Grace asked without thinking.

"He ain't my husband!" The spoon clattered back into the bowl, scattering brown drops onto the borrowed nightgown. "Oh, I'm sorry, Grace, I'll wash it for you, I promise." Her shoulders shook and a fat tear slid down one cheek into the remains of the stew.

Moving the tray to one side, Grace took Aoife into her arms, the girl's heart-wrenching sobs vibrating against Grace's chest.

"It's all right, Aoife," Grace crooned into her violet smelling hair. "You're safe now. No one will hurt you again."

Chapter 15

Grace was late down to breakfast the next morning, by which time the other boarders had already left for the day. Mrs M had thoughtfully set the parlour table for the two of them with her blue stoneware cups.

"How's that lame duckling who wandered in last night?" Mrs M closed a cupboard door and greeted Grace with a wry smile. "Got all her feathers clean and fluffed up have you?"

"Don't joke, Mrs M, she's had a very difficult time. The poor dear was exhausted, so I've left her sleeping. Would it be all right if I prepared her breakfast myself when she wakes up?"

"Marge will do that when she gets back from the Market Hall. She went to get some fish for tonight's supper, you miss out if you don't go early." She set a jug of milk and bowl of sugar onto the table. "What's this lass' story then?"

"I don't know yet. She didn't tell me much. She was supposed to have married a farmer in New Brunswick. They had been corresponding for months, but something happened which she won't talk about."

"One of those mail order brides, was she?" Mrs M slumped into the chair opposite, a steaming cup of tea in front of her as if prepared for a long chat. "Those farming types put advertisements in newspapers for wives to go and live in places no normal woman would want to be."

"The Salvation Army helped her with the passage but that's all I know." Grace ladled honey onto her oatmeal. "Would you mind if she stayed in my room for a few days? I'll pay you double."

"You could take Number 9. It's got two beds in there, but the bathroom is at the end of the hall. Mr Ross wouldn't mind going into your old room."

"That won't be necessary. I don't want to move, or disrupt Mr Ross. I think I was a comfort to Aoife last night. She is frightened of being alone." Whether that was because of her experiences in New Brunswick or an inborn aversion, Grace wasn't sure. "We'll be fine in Number 6. Look, Mrs M, I didn't mean to deceive you about the hotel. I was going to tell you, but I wanted to wait until I was sure it was real."

"And now it is?" Mrs M's homely face broke into a smile. "Don't fret, dear. I've had some time to think and maybe I overreacted yesterday. I doubt a lady like you would want to open a boarding house. Mr Hill's a man who doesn't fuss over anyone without money and what with all the calls he's made here lately, I assumed it was about more than a few dollars for your keep."

"There's nothing wrong with running a boarding house, Mrs M. You manage this one beautifully. I have no wish to compete with you. What I have in mind is a different sort of establishment."

"Different how?" Mrs M upended the stoneware teapot over an empty cup which she pushed towards Grace, then refilled her own.

"What I have in mind is a small, exclusive hotel aimed at lone lady travellers. Somewhere they won't be looked down on because they don't have a male escort or a maid."

"The Dobson sisters are single ladies who travel alone." Mrs M spooned sugar into her tea and stirred, the spoon clacking against the side of the stoneware mug. "No one looks down on them."

"I agree, and I don't mean to insult Ivy or Ada, but my establishment will be more - exclusive."

"Expensive you mean?" Mrs M raised one sceptical eyebrow.

"For ladies with means, shall I say, who like their privacy and want to spend a holiday in congenial surroundings?"

"Are you saying my house isn't congenial?" Her lips lifted on one side in a ghost of a smile.

"You know I don't. This house is lovely and welcoming. Like a home away from home."

"Ah, well, it's nice of you to say so, dear." Mrs M preened. "Though it sounds like a lot of trouble to me. Those ladies can be very demanding. The less they've got, the worse they are, if you see what I mean. Putting on all sorts of airs and graces. I'll stick with my travelling salesmen. A warm fire and two meals a day is all they need, and they're not under my feet all day neither. Oh, not that you are, dear, but you know what I mean." She held her cup in both hands. "I know plenty of places in town who charge more than me. They might have fancy things like chefs and chambermaids in uniforms, but they can't beat my dinners."

"Exactly, and it's those homely touches which make your establishment so attractive to your patrons. I promise, that if a travelling salesman in a bowler and suitcase turns up at my door, I'll send him to you."

"Bless your heart, Grace, and I hope you won't be a stranger when you leave."

The click of the door opening brought Grace's gaze to where Aoife hovered on the threshold. The dress Marge found for her was an excellent fit, if a little loose around the shoulders. With a few of Mrs M's meals inside her she would soon fill it out.

Aoife had plaited her wavy black hair and wound it into a knot on the back of her head. Apart from the boots she borrowed from Marge flapping round her ankles, she looked ready for church. Grace had thrown out the scraps of torn leather Aoife arrived in, so one of their tasks was to get her some new ones.

"And don't you look different, Missy?" Mrs M positively beamed. "I nearly didn't recognize you. Come and sit down, love, and have some breakfast."

"I see you found my hairpins," Grace said.

"Oh, I'm sorry if I-" Aoife's hand drifted to the back of her head.

"You're more than welcome." Grace waved a dismissive hand. "And your hair looks lovely."

Aoife took an empty chair at the table, but not before shooting Grace a wary glance.

"Mrs M says you are welcome to stay for a while, Aoife. As I explained, it was me she was angry with, not you. But we've sorted it all out."

"I had no idea you were a friend of Grace's, or I would never have been so harsh. But she did look like one of those Irish arabs we have round here sometimes."

Grace made no comment but assumed the term was uncomplimentary.

Mrs M poured her a mug of tea, the brew having stewed somewhat since Grace arrived. "Here you are, dear. Drink it while it's still hot."

"I didn't look much like anyone's friend yesterday, madam." Aoife accepted the tea with a smile. "You don't have to apologize."

"It's Mrs M, dear. And I'll let you into a little secret. Back in County Cork, oh, about a hundred years ago now, my best friend was called Aoife." Blinking rapidly, she patted Aoife's hand, scraped back her chair and rose unsteadily to her feet with a tiny grunt. "Ah well, I'd better get on. Can't sit here chatting all day."

"Was she crying?" Aoife asked after Mrs M disappeared into the kitchen.

"You know, I rather think she was."

* * *

Over the next few days, Aoife's cuts began to heal, her bruises faded, and her strength returned, as did her cheeky disposition and her inherent charm. She made herself useful by helping Marge change the beds and doing laundry, thus earning gratitude from both women. She also proved to be an accomplished cook. Grace frequently returned from her visits to Prince Street and found them laughing together over a batch of scones or fruit cake that Aoife produced for the guests' tea.

With her secret revealed, Grace no longer avoided the subject of where she was going each day. She even asked Mrs M's advice as to the best crockery for kitchen use and what design she should choose on the china for the tea room.

"I don't want it to be too delicate or fussy, but simple and essentially English to reflect the style. I'll take Aoife with me and see what I can find in town."

"I'll save you some time." Mrs M opened a cupboard in the dresser from which she withdrew a thick book she thumped onto the table, the cover bearing the words, Eaton's Fall and Spring Catalogue, in bold print. "Just about anything you want will be in there."

"What's this, Mrs M?" Grace leafed through the first few pages of pen and ink drawings of ladies in hats, blouses and walking skirts."

"A mail order catalogue. You'll find an Eaton's in most households." Mrs M resumed her seat. "Anything you cannot find in town will be in that there book. It's how we buy most things."

Grace continued to flick idly through the four hundred or so pages from embroidery supplies, furniture, baby carriages to clothes of all types for men, children and babies. "Goodness, this is quite a book. There are pocket watches, silverware, even engagement rings in here."

"It brings the best department store in Toronto to your fireside," Mrs M said with a knowing wink.

"Thank you, Mrs M. Eaton's should use that as an advertisement. May I borrow this?" Grace tapped the thick book with a fingernail.

"Of course, dear. Bring it back when you're finished with it."

"Why don't you come out with me for a walk, Aoife?" Grace asked later that morning. "Only a short one. The fresh air will do you good. You cannot stay inside all the time."

"I've been out in the yard hanging out the washing, haven't I?" Aoife said.

"That's not what I meant."

237

All Grace's ploys to tempt Aoife out of the boarding house since her arrival had failed. Aoife reminded Grace of a cat she once owned. The animal had been injured and abandoned, but even when restored to full health, he refused to venture beyond the garden. It was as if once outside, he was afraid he might not be allowed back in again.

She had not yet mentioned the existence of the hotel to Aoife, and asked both Mrs M and Marge not to talk about it either. When they asked why, she explained it would seem as if Grace was forcing her own good fortune under her friend's nose when she had little in the world to recommend her.

'Please, Aoife. There's something I want to show you."

"What sort of something?"

"You'll see when we get there. It's a surprise." Grace placed a straw boater on Aoife's head; another prize from the goodwill bag. The only thing missing was the shawl Aoife had always worn on SS Parisian. Grace always looked for that flash of emerald green as Aoife moved through the pressing crowd on the boat deck. She made a mental note to find one for her. Aoife wasn't Aoife without that shawl.

"All right, but I can't be gone long. Mrs M has promised to show me some of her Acadian recipes. Not that I know what an Acadian is."

"Someone once told me a little about them." Grace collected her hat from the row of hooks in the hall, recalling with a pang her conversations with Andrew Jardine on the subject. "They were the original French settlers who came to Nova Scotia in the sixteen-hundred's."

"They called their home Acadie, but when it was ceded to the British after the Treaty of Utrecht, the Acadians were systematically deported. Some Acadians came to live on the Island where they made their home." She pulled the front door closed behind them.

"Why were they deported? What did they do?" Aoife kept close to Grace's side as they walked along King Street, darting nervous glances around her.

"Now there's a question." Grace linked arms with her, and instantly Aoife seemed to settle. "They probably didn't do anything. But when countries fight over territory, it's never the people living there who benefit. Some Acadians came to Prince Edward Island to live, which was called Isle Saint-Jean in those days and still under French rule. From what Mrs M told me, it was a savage time, and many of the Acadians died on the voyage to France. No wonder they work so hard to keep the traditions and family names alive. Who wants history to forget you?"

"I had no idea it was so sad." Aoife watched her feet as she walked. "Mrs M said her husband's family had been here for two hundred years. Do you suppose they were among the original Frenchies?"

"It's possible. And it makes sense if she likes to make the traditional dishes."

"She wants to show me how to make chicken fricot for supper tomorrow. But I've no idea what it is. Apart from the chicken part."

"I remember she made it for the Dobson sisters one evening as a treat. It was a delicious chicken soup with dumplings."

They reached the corner of Prince and Richmond streets where Grace paused in front of the white painted house, bringing Aoife to a halt beside her. "What do you think?"

"Very nice. Much prettier than Mrs Mahoney's. You didn't say you were moving to another boarding house." Her eyes filled with fear as she glanced at Grace. "Or are you taking up a position?"

"Position? What sort of position?"

Aoife shrugged. "Like me, you ran away from home. So you'll need a position to support yourself. I cannot see you as a parlour maid or a skivvy, so it makes sense you would be a governess. Or is this a school and you're going to be a teacher?" Her eyes darkened with concern and Grace experienced instant regret at having kept her in suspense.

"No, Aoife, I'm not going to be either of those things. I've bought this house and intend to run it as a hotel." She nodded to where several workmen were visible through the windows, some perched on ladders or moving through the rooms. "Those men inside are renovating it for me."

"This is yours?" Aoife gaped at the newly painted facade. The formerly grimy upper

240

windows now gleamed in new, pristine frames. The rotted clapboards had been replaced and the roof scrubbed clean of all traces of moss. The front garden had been cleared and a new lawn laid. Raised flowerbeds built to hip level on either side of the path made a fragrant entry to a new front door with stained glass panels.

"You didn't tell me you were rich, Grace."

"I'm not, at least not now. This place was a bargain, but the renovations cost more than I thought. Though I believe it will be worth it."

"Can we go inside?" Aoife's mouth hung open again as her gaze swung from one side of the building, over the roof and to the other side.

"Of course. Why do you think I brought you here?" Her eyes watering instantly at the strong spirit smell that hit them like a wave, Grace led Aoife into a hall crowded with tools and pots of paint. Ladders were propped against walls, the rooms filled with laborers who carried tools and packing cases. As Grace and Aoife progressed through the house they were greeted by cheery voices and doffed caps.

"We'll start in the kitchen." Grace led the way through an inner hall to the east side of the house. "I'm rather proud of how this room has turned out. This will be the center of all my operations."

A wall between a small parlour and the original kitchen had been opened out to form a room sixteen feet square with the gleaming new cooking range complete with six hotplates and three ovens.

The dresser bought from Mr Daly had taken four men to dismantle and move into the kitchen. Sanded down and painted a matte bone white, it was a splendid piece of furniture which now occupied the opposite wall from floor to ceiling.

A solid pine table ran down the center of the room, its surface gleaming with recently applied wax.

"With all the cooking which will take place here, I expect that table to be as scarred and dented like Mrs M's within a few weeks," Grace said.

"It's a fine room." Aoife's voice was an awed whisper as she wandered to the black range and lifted pots arranged on the metal plates. "Who's going to do the cooking?"

"An interesting question." One which plagued her since she blithely told Mrs M that she would do the breakfasts herself because they were easy. Mrs M and Marge dissolved into almost hysterical laughter and after Grace's disastrous first efforts, she realized how wrong she was. Catering for the public would be no easy task.

"I'll need someone who knows what they are doing. I'll also need a good baker for the tea room too, although I could engage the services of local bakeries and buy cakes and pastries."

"Better to make them on the premises, Grace. Then they'll be unique to your place," Aoife said. "Why would anyone come to a tea room for a cake they can buy for a quarter of the price from a bakery?"

"That's a good point. I've put advertisements in the newspapers announcing the opening in June. Now all I have to do is wait for some firm bookings to come in. Perhaps I should advertise for a cook?"

"Pardon me for saying so, Grace. But you should have thought of that before now. Bookings and a fancy kitchen aren't much good if there's no one to make their dinner."

"Again, a good point," Grace conceded, flushing. Not for the first time did she wonder if she was competent enough to make the venture a success. "The walled yard is through that door on the left over there through which the deliveries will arrive via a rear lane. The cellar can be accessed through the kitchen and the yard so not everything has to come in through the kitchen."

"You've got it all worked out, haven't you?" Aoife sighed, her hands braced on the table as she stared around her. "It's a fine, grand house. I'm sure lots of people will want to stay here."

"I hope so. The garden furniture will arrive next week once the gazebos have been installed. The builder suggested I have a watertight shed built to put them all in for the winters, or they'll rot in all the snow they get here. More expense, but he convinced me. Did you know it snows here from November to April? I'll have to make sure we have plenty of boots and warm clothes."

"You could burn peat on the fires. Mrs M told me there are large peat bogs on the island but there's no coal. Strange that."

"I've had one of those heating boilers they make in America installed. It works by running hot water through pipes. It cost me a fair bit but worked out less disruptive than installing new fireplaces and chimneys to the rooms that don't have them. The Queen Hotel has a similar system, and I wasn't going to be outshone. My guests will have every luxury."

"Well, I never," Aoife said, impressed. "Though there's nothing like an open fire on a chilly day."

"I have those too in the lounge and dining room, more for atmosphere than heat. We'll be cozy here no matter what Canada's winters throw at us." Grace hoped she was right. The stories she'd heard about the Northumberland Strait freezing over each winter didn't bode well.

"I'll never forget the back kitchen in Falkener street on a January dawn." Aoife gave an exaggerated shiver. "My room was behind it and I could hardly feel my toes when I woke up of a winter morning." Aoife nodded to a door set in a deep alcove at the opposite side of the room. "Where does that door go?"

"My home," Grace said proudly.

"I thought this whole house was your home?"

"It is, sort of, although most of it will be open to paying guests. This," she strode to the door and flung it open, "is my private domain. I'm thinking of having a brass knocker on this door to deter unwanted callers."

Aoife followed her into a large sitting room where two sofas occupied the space on either side of a fireplace with a stone surround. A bay window, smaller than the ones in the main rooms, was still large enough for the circular table and straight-backed wooden chairs set in it. A roll of something which looked like a large rug was set to one side, and a bureau which still bore its delivery straps, ready to be placed wherever she directed.

"I love this teal and yellow wallpaper, Grace."

"Another of my favorite Morris designs. This one is called Pimpernel." Beyond the small lobby a bedroom the same size as the sitting room contained a vast canopied bed in pale wood which the salesman at Wright's told her was the finest ash wood.

"My own bathroom is through that door there, but it's the same as all the others in the house."

"It's all lovely and you deserve it after what you told me about that man MacKinnon."

"I still cannot believe it's all mine." Grace ushered her out of the room and closed the door. "Come upstairs, I have something else to show you."

"Do we have to climb all those stairs again?" Aoife asked. "We've already seen the bedrooms."

"A few stairs won't hurt you. Now, go on." Grace gave her a small push ahead of her.

Aoife tutted but obediently climbed past the two floors of guest bedrooms, then up to where the staircase narrowed to a hallway where the roofline sloped, requiring them to walk in single file.

Aoife passed through a door at the far end into a freshly painted, white attic room with a sloping roofline. "Well, what do you think?" Grace pirouetted in the center of the room which offered twelve feet by twelve feet of useable space between the eaves.

Aoife crept slowly forward. "It's an empty attic. What's it for?"

"Empty, yes. But it's been made watertight, plastered and painted. The workmen built in the cupboard at the end to follow the slope in the roof as no furniture would fit."

"As I said, what's it for?"

"I had intended this room for a live-in chambermaid. There's also a small bathroom and water closet next door to avoid them having to go downstairs. I rather thought it would be perfect for you."

"For me?" Aoife's eyes widened. "You want me to live with you here?"

"When it's finished, why not? This white paint is a little stark, but I have plenty of wallpaper. I ordered far more than I needed, but I was so keen to get started, I didn't think. You'll need a bed of course, a dresser, chair and a rug to soften these floorboards." Aoife had hardly said a word thus far, but her eyes sparkled from unshed tears. "I planned to move in at the end of next week. Why not come with me? If you want to, that is."

"Of course I want to." Two fat tears slid down Aoife's cheeks. "It's so kind of you, Grace."

"Good, because I thought for a moment you didn't like the idea."

"Don't be daft." Aoife's bottom lip quivered, and she swiped a hand beneath her nose. "I've been so scared, Grace. After leaving Marysville I burned every bridge I ever had and didn't dare think of what would happen to me when I walked all day and slept in hedgerows at night."

"No more hedgerows," Grace said softly.

"Why can't I stay here right now?" Aoife's wide brown eyes roved Grace's face. "I don't want you paying Mrs M for my keep longer than you have to. I'll be fine sleeping on the floor until the bed comes."

"But there are builder's materials all over the place, and there's the dust. It's not healthy. I intend to have the whole place cleaned before I move in."

"I've slept in worse. Leastways it's bright and warm here." Aoife wandered to the gable window. "I love that little turned around oval window."

"Elliptical." Grace smiled. The window had been one of the features that attracted her to the house. "I saw how nervous you were on your

247

way here after being inside so long. Are you sure you want to be on your own when the workmen leave for the day?"

"I don't mind being inside. The nights aren't too cold now and summer is on its way. I could also keep an eye on those laborers. Make sure they aren't slacking. I'll like it here, honestly. It will be the first place I've stayed in that's all my own."

"You've never had your own room before, Aoife?"

"Hah! I've never even had me own bed!"

"I'm afraid you don't have one - yet." Grace had to admit it might be useful having someone on the premises to keep an eye on things. "The construction work is done, it's mainly wallpaper to be hung and the painting completed. The gardening company started work today and the foreman will need instructions."

"Just tell me what you want, and I'll make sure they're not taking liberties."

"I'll make this room more homely for you, a curtain for that window might help."

"No, please leave it. I don't need the dark to go to sleep, and I like to wake up early and see the sun come up."

"All right. If that's what you want. We'll go shopping tomorrow. There are quite a few things you're going to need. More clothes for instance until the ones I sent for arrive."

Together they pored over Eaton's Catalogue for an hour that morning like excited children planning for Christmas. The cost of the final list horrified Aoife, but Grace insisted she needed to be appropriately dressed if she was going to deal with paying guests.

"I'll pay you back, Grace. Every cent. I promise," Aoife insisted.

"I know you will." Grace had been about to tell her it didn't matter, but Aoife's pride would never have allowed it.

They returned to the ground floor and wandered into the garden, where the trellis she ordered was being arranged by gardeners into intimate alcoves for tables and chairs beneath gazebos. The flowerbeds had been laid out but the plants had not yet arrived, so the garden was a patchwork of green and brown. "I wanted a fountain to go in the middle where the pathways meet, but I haven't found one I like."

"We'll have to take another look in that catalogue," Aoife said, her air of melancholy completely lifted. "There's everything else in those pages. Why not that?"

They sat side by side on an old wooden bench Grace planned to have removed, its layer of paint having faded and peeled a long time ago. Their companionable silence was broken only by birdsong, the occasional clop of hooves from the street and a muffled sound of banging from the house as the laborers continued their work.

"Aoife," Grace said finally. "You do understand, I'm not giving you the room so you'll work for me? You're my friend, not an employee."

"Why not?" Aoife sat with her arms wrapped around her drawn up knees. "Working as a chambermaid isn't much different to being a tweenie. And I was the best they ever had at Falkener street."

"I'm sure you were. But you didn't come to Canada to be a housemaid."

"I can't go back to Liverpool, even if I could scrape up the fare. I owe money to the Salvation Army for my passage over. I've no idea how I'm going to pay them back."

"You don't have to fret about that. We'll sort out what you owe. Although I'm not sure what sort of wage I can offer, not until I have some guests to stay."

"I'll work for bed and board. The house is looking grand, even if it isn't finished. Guests will be queuing outside when you open."

"I sincerely doubt that but having half the rooms filled would make a good beginning. And we'll be working together in the early days as I'll have to do a lot of the chores myself."

"It will be wonderful, I know it will. What are you going to call the place?"

"I've toyed with all the conventional names like, Belle Isle House, which is too ordinary and MacKinnon Towers, which is too pretentious, but nothing has really appealed so far."

"What about, 'Grace and Favor'?"

"Grace and Favor," Grace mused. "I like that, but I'm not sure it's appropriate. It means free, and I'm hoping to make a good living here."

"I doubt anyone who books in here will think it's free," Aoife scoffed. "Anyway, isn't 'grace' another word for kindness and 'favor' means 'service'?"

"How did you know that?"

Aoife shrugged. "I like to read. In my last place, the master let me borrow the odd book from his library on my day off."

"You are full of surprises, Aoife." That name might also become a talking point among the locals. "Grace and Favor it is. Now," she twisted on the seat to face Aoife. "Are you ready to tell me what happened in Marysville?"

Chapter 16

"It's all over and done with." Aoife ran a fingernail across a fold in her dress with fierce concentration. "Don't do no good to go over it."

"You had a good reason to run away. I saw the state you were in when you arrived. I've seen how you brood at times, so I thought it might help to talk about it."

"If I do, will you promise never to mention it again?" She raised her eyes. "Ever?"

"Of course I won't. Cross my heart." Grace made the sign with her hand and eased closer, lowering her voice. "It was really bad wasn't it? And don't pretend it wasn't I saw the bruises, remember."

"Humiliating more like." Aoife turned toward the window, where a shaft of morning sunlight highlighted the freckles across her nose. "The Salvation Army lady put me on a train to New Brunswick with a bunch of other girls going into the country. At Saint John station, this handsome man was waiting for me. He was really kind and so pleased to see me." Her voice hitched and she blinked away tears. "I thought of all those nights in the back scullery in Falkener street reading his letters. They made

252

me believe something good was going to happen."

"What changed?" Grace handed her a handkerchief.

"Nothing, not then." She dabbed at her face and sniffed. "He took me to a cart where this other man waited and put my bag in the back. I thought he must have been the driver as he didn't say a word. It wasn't until we were out on this country road when the younger one tells me his name is Seth."

"So who was the other man?"

"He was Cole."

"Oh dear, you must have been very disappointed?"

"It was a shock, mainly because Cole behaved as if I wasn't there. It didn't sit right what with all those letters he wrote me, but I thought maybe he was shy and didn't know what to say in front of Seth." She tugged the handkerchief between her fingers. "We left the town behind and were out in the country without a soul in sight, me squashed on the seat between them. I thanked Cole for all his letters, and that's when Seth explained to me that Cole couldn't read or write. Seth wrote every one of them. As a favor, he said."

"Oh dear. That wasn't a good sign."

"Looking back, I should have jumped off the cart and walked back to the station right then, but I thought, no, perhaps Cole won't be so bad once we get to know one another. I could even teach him to read if he me wanted to."

"You were prepared to stay?"

Aoife shrugged. "Why not? Close up he were all right. Older than I had imagined, maybe thirty-five."

"Positively ancient."

"I'm nineteen, so it is to me," Aoife bridled. "Anyway, he wasn't bad looking close up and he had all his own teeth."

Grace hid a smile behind her hand and waited for Aoife to continue.

"We drove for two days through some of the most beautiful countryside I've ever seen, camped at night under the cart and cooked bacon over a fire by the roadside in the evening. It was an adventure, of sorts. Cole hardly said a word, but Seth was chatty enough." She blew her nose noisily on the handkerchief. "We reached Marysville, which was when Seth told me I would be going the rest of the way with Cole. I tried to ask how far away that was, but he grabbed his bag off the back and walked off.

"We travelled for a whole day, with Cole not saying more'n three words to me. It was almost dark when we arrived. That's when I knew I'd made one helluva mistake. It were nothing but a one-room shack on an open prairie with a scullery tacked onto the side and a privy out back. Though they call them outhouses here."

"I know they do. What happened then?"

"I found out he had four boys."

"Four? Did he tell you he had children in the letters?"

Aoife shook her head. "They weren't children neither, but big strapping lads too, with no table manners. I've seen pigs eat neater from a trough than those boys." She wiped a hand beneath her nose. "They were quite nice to me, but their dad ruled them like a gang of skivvies. The youngest couldn't have been more than twelve. I felt sorry for them."

She swiped a hand beneath her nose.

"If they were big lads, Aoife it means Cole was probably more than thirty-five."

Aoife shrugged. "Probably. I didn't care by then. "

"You all slept in the same room?"

"There was a curtain down the middle, but you could have heard a mouse snore. The two youngest slept up in the loft but there was no wall, just an open platform."

"I gather Cole expected you to cook and clean for all of them?"

"Didn't take me five minutes to know that's why he wanted me there. I asked Cole when the wedding would be, and he said they do it different in New Brunswick. What with there being few churches and such. That all we had to do was swear an oath in front of his boys and some old bloke he called the reverend, but he didn't look like any minister I ever saw."

"That doesn't sound right. Did you believe him?"

"Did I hell, I refused, but that was when he took a belt to me."

This came as no surprise to Grace, having seen the damage on Aoife's back, but nevertheless, hearing her say it was a shock.

"What could I do?" Aoife shrugged. "I had no idea where I was or how to get to the nearest town. I held out for three days but finally gave in and swore his stupid oath. There was no register or nothing, and the reverend didn't wear a cassock either, just some old black suit. He smelled of whisky and kept slurring his words."

"That couldn't have been legal," Grace said.

"Which is what I said, but all I got for my trouble was a sore ear." She rubbed the side of her head in memory. "More of a cuff really, but it hurt a lot."

"A man should never hit his wife."

"It weren't him - it was the reverend who hit me. Cole just stood there."

"That's outrageous! And of course Cole was cruel. What do you call allowing this so-called minister to beat another man's wife? Not that I think you are his wife."

That she couldn't be legally tied to this man was the one redeeming feature of Aoife's experience.

"It weren't that bad. When my dad had six pints in him he had a stronger arm."

"Did you have to- I mean, did he-?"

"I know what you mean, and you're joking aren't you?" Aoife laughed. A harsh, scornful laugh filled with contempt. 'When he tried that, I taunted him. Told him I'd left better ones than that back in Liverpool when I was working the streets."

"You made him think you were a prostitute?" Grace gaped.

"Why not? Worked too as he shrivelled that quick, I-"

"I can work out the rest for myself, thank you." Grace grimaced.

"I learned from another maid at my last place that most men don't want to be compared between the sheets with another-"

"Aoife," Grace interrupted. "Enough. What did Cole do then?"

"Nothing. But he laid it on heavier with the belt after that. Maybe I should have been a bit nicer?"

"No, you should never give into that sort of abuse. You were brave to hold out. I don't know how you stood it."

"I didn't, I took off the first chance I got. Which wasn't easy."

"How did you get away?"

"I had a little money tucked away I didn't tell him about, but there were few chances to get any more. The tight-fisted git charged all his supplies to an account at what he called the mercantile."

"The general store," Grace supplied. "Many things have different names here."

"So I found out. He kept those boys of his poor, too, as they never had any money either; to stop them running away, I imagine. Cole kept chickens, so I sold a few eggs he didn't know

257

about to a neighbor. I did some of her laundry too and kept the money. I say neighbor, but it took me a half hour to walk to their farm. A nice woman who seemed to understand what I had got myself into. She said I was the third girl she'd seen there in the last year."

"The man was a monster," Grace muttered. "How did you manage to leave?"

"One morning, I waited until Cole and the boys went off to work in the lower meadow, packed me belongings and made my way to the nearest made-up road. Took me a day and a half to reach Marysville hitching rides in carts or walking. I got lost a couple of times. This country is so big, with miles and miles of open road between towns. I spent the night in a boarding house, but I knew my money wouldn't last long, so it was ditches and barns from then on. I kept heading east and one cart dropped me off at Moncton Station. I hid in a baggage car and got as far as Sackville before I was kicked off by a guard."

"You said you packed a bag, but you didn't have one with you yesterday."

"I fell asleep and some hobo stole it. Not that there was much in it. I found an old chap at the station who took pity on me. He said he was going as far as Port Elgin where I could get a ferry to the Island. I didn't tell him I had no money for the ferry, but I went with him."

"That was very dangerous," Grace said, but at Aoife's sideways glance, added, "I'm sorry, I understand you didn't have much choice."

258

"Exactly. I tried to sneak onto the boat, but they guard those things too well. Then I got talking to this lad on the pier; told him I'd been robbed, which was true. He said his dad had a fishing boat and he would take me to Prince Edward Island. He took me to a beach near a place called Victoria."

"How did you know you should come to Charlottetown? This isn't exactly the Isle of Wight. I think Victoria is over twenty miles from here."

"The fisherman said it was the largest town, so I hoped this was where you would be. I walked all day and started to make the rounds of the boarding houses asking after you. I almost gave up until Marge told me you were staying at Mrs M's."

"I'm so glad she did." Grace sighed. "My goodness, Aoife, what a time you've had of it."

"If I'd wanted to be a housekeeper and skivvy, I would have stayed in Liverpool. Working in a big house I got paid every quarter."

"What exactly did you think being a farmer's wife was all about?" Apart from the physical abuse, farming was never going to be easy.

"I dunno." Aoife shrugged. "I dreamed of a little wooden house with a veranda, painted light blue with a garden, lots of flowers and a duck pond. I imagined I would wave my husband off in the morning sunshine, throw grain for the chickens then tidy the house. Maybe kill a chicken for supper. I've done that before. But it wasn't anything like that."

"No, it wasn't. I'm glad you came to me." Grace wrapped an arm around Aoife's shoulders and smoothed her rough curls. "Cole isn't likely to come looking for you, is he?"

"I doubt it." Aoife snorted. "He's probably waiting at the station for the next train and another poor deluded soul."

"You weren't deluded, Aoife. None of this was your fault. You believed your decision to marry him was for the best."

"Didn't get me far did it?" Aoife pulled back her shoulders inside her loose fitting dress, Grace's handkerchief crumpled in one hand. "I'm not going to spend another moment fretting about it. I'm going to be a chambermaid in a beautiful new hotel, with a room of my own and everything."

"Yes, you are." Grace sighed. If only she could view life with such simplicity. Her own dreams had seemed straightforward, but behind the shopping and planning was a greater concern. What if she couldn't attract enough guests to her hotel to meet the running costs, let alone recoup her investment? Maybe no one would come? A shudder ran through her and she held Aoife tighter.

* * *

Grace and Aoife packed in readiness to move to Prince street, their combined belongings fitting easily into Grace's two bags. They brought them down into the hall where a tearful Mrs Mahoney waited.

"We'll only be a few streets away," Grace reminded her. "But we'll be sure to come back and visit often. You must come to the hotel to tea."

"I'll still miss the both of you." Mrs M snuffled into a handkerchief. "If there's anything you need, I'll be here. Oh, I almost forgot, I wanted you to have this." She stuffed the crumpled handkerchief in one pocket and delved into the other, from which she withdrew a small, cloth covered book and handed it to Aoife.

"What's this, Mrs M?" Aoife asked, flicking through the first few pages. "These are your recipes," she exclaimed, answering her own question.

"A few of my best Acadian ones too, including my mother's molasses cookie recipe. Use the best molasses you can afford but remember not to roll them out too thin or cook them too long to keep them soft."

"I'll remember, Mrs M. And thank you." Aoife slipped the book into Grace's bag before being subjected to another of the woman's fierce hugs.

Marge was nowhere to be seen when they left, although at the last moment Grace spotted her at an upper window from where she gave a small, sad wave. Grace gestured for her to come downstairs, but she shook her head, leaving them with no alternative but to blow farewell kisses from the street.

Grace always regarded Marge as the less sentimental of the pair, but over time, the two women's roles had been reversed, Aoife becoming a firm favorite with them both.

"Don't you find Marge a strange one?" Grace swung her portmanteau from one hand to the other and waved to Marge for the last time before she and Aoife turned the corner. "One moment she's snapping at you and the next she does something incredibly kind." She recalled the effort Marge went to in order to find a dress for Aoife the night she arrived. "I don't think I saw her husband more than three times while I was there. He was always coming in as I went out, so we hardly exchanged a word."

"Mrs M told me she and Rab don't talk much since their son died. When he's not out on the boats, he's in Mrs M's blind pig of a night." Aoife hefted Grace's other bag onto her hip. They had combined their belongings in order to transfer them to the hotel and could manage a bag each without too much difficulty.

"Church socials," Grace said, caught Aoife's oblique look and added, "Don't use that term or someone might hear and report her to the inspector."

"Church social then." Aoife shrugged. "Marge doesn't like it but there isn't much she can do."

"I didn't know they had a son."

"They don't. Not now. He drowned during the Galveston Hurricane five years ago when several boats were lost with all their crews."

"Oh, that's awful. And poor Marge. I had no idea." Her steps halted. "Galveston? That's in Texas. It must have been a bad storm to travel all that way." She would have to do some more reading about local history.

"Mrs M said Marge didn't want their boy to go out on the boats, but Rab said it was a family tradition and insisted. The lad was only fifteen."

"Is that why they don't get on? Because Marge blames him for his death?"

Aoife shrugged. "Must be."

"I wish I had known, not that I could have made any difference." She sifted through her memories in the hope she had not added to Marge's grief by an indiscreet remark.

"Oh, look, Grace," Aoife paused at the corner. "Doesn't the house look lovely with the picket fence painted white?"

"It does, but the front would look better with some color. This autumn, I'll plant some bulbs so we'll have a colorful display next spring."

"Fall, they call it fall here."

"Of course. I must remember." Laughing, she looked along the street to where Mr Charles Keogh strolled towards them. Her smile faded and a sinking feeling settled in her belly. "Oh no, not today," she murmured.

"Do you know that man, Grace?" Aoife eyed him with suspicion.

She didn't respond, but sensed her face warm as he halted in front of them.

"Good afternoon, Mrs MacKinnon." He removed his hat, and executed a mock bow, his feet planted apart. "You've made a very nice job of it." He inclined his head at the hotel, then gave the street a slow, sweeping glance. "Discreet, out of the way, and not too large so it is considered exclusive. A nice little business. I expect you'll do well." His gaze slid to Aoife with an expectant smile.

Grace handed Aoife her key. "Would you mind taking the bags inside? I'll be with you in a moment."

Aoife's eyes narrowed, and she stared at Keogh. She slipped the key into her pocket without looking at it; an enquiring eyebrow lifted at Grace.

"It's all right," Grace whispered. "I won't be long."

Aoife directed a final withering glare at Keogh, then grimacing at the combined weight of the bags, took short, labored steps up onto the porch.

"What can I do for you, Mr Keogh?" Grace asked once Aoife had disappeared inside the house.

"You didn't introduce me to the young lady." He waved a lazy hand behind him in a loose-limbed gesture, rocking slightly on his feet. "That wasn't very polite of you, Grace."

"That's right, I didn't." She flinched at his use of her given name.

"Best be on my way then. I only stopped by to wish you well."

"Now you have. Thank you. I must get on. There is still a lot to do." She stood her ground, waiting for him to walk on.

He didn't.

"Don't be so hasty, I deserve a fair hearing, don't I?" His upper lip curled, and he swayed closer, the unmistakeable smell of brandy on his breath.

"I have a proposition for you." He replaced his fedora low on his forehead, tipped his head back and peered at her down his nose.

"Mr Keogh," Grace summoned patience. "Our association is over. I appreciate your help in the past, but that is where it stays. "

"Oh, I wouldn't say that." He flicked a swift glance at the hotel again. "I take it your paying guests will include Americans?"

"I imagine some of them will be." Grace frowned. "Why do you ask?"

"Folks from away like to leave the sweltering cities behind and take advantage of our comfortable summers. They sail their yachts in our waters, stroll our beaches and enjoy the beauty of our countryside." His gaze returned to her face. "What they don't think much of, are our prohibition laws."

"Why is that a problem? They're on holiday - I mean vacation. Surely it's no hardship to do without alcohol for that time?" She knew she must sound naïve but refused to fall in with his line of thought.

"My dear Grace." His low, sarcastic laugh made her skin crawl. "You have to understand the nature of the affluent holidaymaker. What they don't like, is being told they can't have what is readily available at home." He ran a finger along her jaw, the movement so fast he gave her no time to avoid it. "If you want to make money, my dear, real money that is, you need to provide all the luxuries they desire. If not, they'll find an establishment that will."

"Thank you for the advice." Grace eased backwards out of his reach. "However, I intend to manage my guest's requirements and remain within the law."

"You ought to think about it, or you could find that fancy hotel of yours empty. And while you do, my invitation to dinner still stands. We could celebrate your new venture and discuss my proposition at the same time." He lifted his hat an inch and scratched his scalp beneath it. "When is this grand opening?"

"Quite soon, and it won't be grand. Even so, I shall be far too busy to go to dinner in the near future, Mr Keogh." She could barely refrain from a laugh but knew there was no point in antagonising a man who had been drinking. "But thank you for asking."

The expression in his eyes became ice cold, all traces of his false bonhomie gone. "Still aiming high, are you?"

"I beg your pardon?" Her mouth went suddenly dry.

"Don't play innocent with me, Grace. This town is not as large as you might think. People talk."

"Mr Keogh, I have no idea what you're talking about." She kept her voice light while eyeing the open door of the hotel, longing to leave but worried because he might follow her. How drunk was he?

"You arrived alone on the island, with no family or associates. No one knows who you are or where your money came from." He lowered his voice to a conspiratorial whisper. "I know about your cozy trip on the SS Elizabeth too, but sniffing round the Jardines and the Cahills will do you no good. They're Island born of families who've been here over a hundred years; almost aristocracy, or what passes for it in this province."

Grace inhaled sharply, a mixture of fury and disbelief robbing her of speech. How dare he? Several responses sprang to her lips, which she instantly suppressed. Any rebuttal would only amuse him, and probably fuel his malice.

"Good day, Mr Keogh. I doubt we'll cross paths again." Brushing past him, she stepped into the street, just as a horse-drawn cart rounded the corner and forced her to halt.

Her breaths came shallow and rapid as she silently pleaded with the cart to hurry. She had to get away from him. How could she have believed he was gauche but harmless? The man was evil.

The cart swept past her on a wave of animal sweat and manure, just as Keogh's voice whispered in her ear.

"Jardine's only interest in you, Grace, would be one thing and one thing only."

Freed at last, she walked rapidly across the street with his mocking laugh still in her ears.

Chapter 17

Aoife leaned against a doorframe, her arms folded and a sheaf of letters dangling from one hand. "Then who was he?"

"His name is Charles Keogh." Grace blinked at the wave of linseed oil, new paint and turpentine that greeted her. "He's no one of any concern. Are those letters for me?"

"Oh, yes, of course." Aoife held them out towards her. "I've put the bags in our rooms. Do you want me to unpack?"

"No, we'll do that later." She sifted through the sheaf of envelopes. It looked as if the advertisements she had put into the Halifax Chronicle, the New York Times and the Island magazine had produced results.

A blackfly zipped past her face causing her to jerk back her chin. "It might be an idea to open some of these windows to air the place, not forgetting the screens to prevent any more of those things coming inside."

She was unused to the hordes of flying creatures that inhabited this part of the world, sensitive to any nearby buzz or squeak.

Still distracted by an image of Keogh's leering face, Grace took the letters into the kitchen and spread them on the pine table.

"We'll never keep all these beggars out, no matter what we do." Aoife swatted at the persistent blackfly as she followed her in. "I'll swear these things like the smell of paint."

She pulled out a chair and sat, elbows on the table, her chin propped on them as she watched Grace slit the first envelope. "What have we got?"

"This is from a Mrs Cartwright from Connecticut who wants to bring her two daughters to stay in mid-June." Grace looked up from the page. "Do I put the daughters in one room and the mother in a second, or would they all wish to stay together?"

"Who knows? You'll have to prepare both and ask them when they get here. What else?"

"A Mr and Mrs Laskey from Saint John, want a room for four days next week." She handed it to Aoife who added it to the first one to form a pile. "A pamphlet from a milk delivery service. I'll keep that." She set it aside and opened another. "A Mrs Tenniel, who describes herself as a mature lady." Grace peered at the shakily written address at the top of the page. "She's from Boston and says she wants a short holiday after a bout of bronchitis."

"I hope she doesn't cough over the other guests and put them off." Aoife sniggered.

"She's quite recovered, or so she says, and hopes the sea air will restore her former good spirits. One thing this will teach me is the geography of North America. I'll have to buy an atlas and mark it to show where my guests come from. Here's an advertisement from a hansom cab company offering favorable rates to collect visitors from the harbour. That could be useful.

"Put it on the pile for safekeeping. The rest we can use for firelighters. Not a bad start, Aoife, three rooms booked, and we aren't open yet."

The letters in her hand, Grace headed toward the door to her private sitting room. "I'll unpack, then how about some supper?"

"First, I'll have to learn how to fire up that thing." Aoife indicated the shiny black iron stove that squatted on club feet at the far end of the room. "Where do I start?"

"The booklet that came with it is here somewhere." Grace rooted through a dresser drawer. "Ah, yes here it is."

"What's the round thing on the oven door?" Aoife left her chair and crouched in front of the stove.

"Um - says here it's a thermometer. There are also six removable cook lids and two back warming shelves as well as the ones on top. The firebox can take twenty inch logs."

Aoife straightened. "Wood and coal?"

"Don't scowl at me like that, Aoife, there's plenty of both in the yard. I'll help you bring some in. We'll fill up a couple of wicker baskets, so we don't have to keep going back and forth all day." She continued to read the booklet. "The foot rest is nickel plated. Not that we'll spend much time sitting in front of it with our feet up."

"Did you have to buy such a big stove?" Aoife swung open the door of the firebox and peered inside.

"Of course. When we are full, there'll be twelve people to feed, not counting us. Apart from preparing meals and baking, this monster heats enough water for bathing and will keep this entire ground floor warm in the winter."

"I'll see if I can get it going." Aoife took a white apron from a drawer and tied it over her dress.

"I wish you'd been here when the salesman called to install it." Grace set the booklet to one side. "He was such an enthusiastic chap and completely enamoured with his product. It was all I could do to dissuade him from cooking a meal for me to show me how efficient it was. He said that if I used the heaviest hammer I could find and managed to break the lid, he would not charge me for the stove."

"That's daft." Aoife scrunched up her pixie features. "What would you want with a broken stove?"

"Precisely. I suppose he was confident I wouldn't be able to do it." She slid a leaflet about painting fences to the back of the pile. "This one's from Maud, but it's got Mrs M's address on it."

"She must have told the postman we moved."

"I wish I could write so well," Grace scanned the page. "Listen to this."

You have restored my belief that kindred spirits are more numerous than I once believed. And what busy, productive women we are, Grace, you with your hotel and me with my novel. I am bereft at not being able to see the Grace and Favor on opening day, but Uncle John is too busy on the farm to mind Grandmother and I cannot leave her alone.

"My island home is a place of wonder and beauty which I miss dreadfully whenever I leave, and yet my lack of society also makes me a victim of creeping melancholy."

"What a shame. I was really looking forward to seeing her again. You'd think her uncle could accommodate her once in a while. Maud gets so little time away from the post office. She tries hard to hide it, but I'm sure she's lonely."

"Not that hard, she sounds right miserable to me." Sniffing, Aoife collected two plates from the dresser and laid them on the table.

'Don't you have a range to light?' Grace narrowed her eyes at Aoife, refolded Maud's letter and returned it to the envelope.

'Pardon me for the presumption, Miss Grace." Aoife bobbed a mock curtsey, a set of cutlery in each hand. "I'll remember I'm only the maid in future.'

'I'm sorry, I didn't mean that.' Grace bit down on her tongue until it hurt. 'You're much more to me than a maid. I'm disappointed Maud can't be here for the opening and nervous I've forgotten something vital. Perhaps having my own way all the time is making me selfish?"

"That's easily cured.' Aoife sniffed. 'Get yourself a cat. They'll always be ten times more selfish than you."

* * *

Grace unpacked her belongings in her room, which barely made an impression in the spacious wardrobe and dresser. Her encounter with Keogh repeated in her head. The way he brushed aside her attempts to discourage him with vague threats, though this time his meaning was clear. If she didn't sell alcohol to her guests, she wouldn't have any. Alcohol he was apparently eager to provide.

By the time she returned to the kitchen, it was filled with an aroma of melted butter and hot metal.

"Not a grand dinner, but it will do for tonight." Aoife stood stirring a pot of scrambled eggs on the hotplate. "Toast's a bit burned, but I'll soon get the hang of it." She slapped a plate of fluffy yellow eggs and still smoking charred bread in front of Grace.

"A bit?" Grace held up the offending item. "We don't have much time to learn. Our first guests arrive in a week. They cannot live on

274

toast and eggs." She dropped the toast back onto her plate.

"I'll get those new sheets unpacked and washed, Grace." Aoife forked scrambled eggs into her mouth. "They're all stiff and creased after being in the mail." She spread butter over the layer of black on her toast and took a bite. Grace opened her mouth to comment but changed her mind. "That will take you a while. I'd better give you a hand."

"I'll get them all done in no time with that new wringer you bought. Did you see the new china for the tea room had arrived?"

"I did, and I'm confident I made the right choice." The white china sprinkled lightly with tiny pink rosebuds was perfect. Delicate and yet robust enough to be in constant use. "I owe Mrs M a debt of gratitude for introducing me to Eaton's catalogue. I don't know where I would have got half the things we needed without it."

"Excuse moi," a voice said from the open door, followed by a tentative knock on the doorframe.

Grace swung round to where a young man in shirtsleeves rolled up to his elbows stood, a tweed jacket slung over one shoulder.

"There was no answer at the front door," he said shyly, performing a Gallic shrug. "It was open so I-er"

"-marched straight in without a by-your-leave." Aoife dropped her cutlery back onto her plate and stuck out her pointed chin.

"Can we help you?" Grace delivered a swift, but restrained kick to Aoife's shin while mouthing the word, "Guest?"

"I saw the sign outside saying the hotel is due to open in a few days." He swung the jacket onto his other shoulder and nodded toward the window.

"It is, but I'm afraid we aren't renting rooms until then." Grace stood. "Unless it's an advance booking you wanted?"

"Ah, I'm sorry but no. Actually, I wondered if you were hiring? My name is Leon Garnier." Apart from his name and opening words, he spoke in perfect, unaccented English.

"What do you do?" Grace inwardly cringed. She hated disappointing people, but his slender build and pale complexion indicated he spent most of his life indoors. She doubted he would be much good at heavy work. About the same height as her, he had sandy colored hair two shades from being carrot, and light brown eyes flecked with gold.

"I cook. Well, actually I'm a chef." He hesitated on the word, as if unsure of himself

"Might I ask how old you are?" Grace put him at about Aoife's age, thus his cheery, "Twenty-four, Miss," took her by surprise.

"I was born in Egmont Bay but I left when I was fifteen to train in Quebec City. I returned home a few weeks ago."

"Have you heard of the Chateau Frontenac?" He aimed a hard glare at Aoife.

"I have," Grace said, impressed. "A friend told me about it when I was on the ferry crossing. Built twelve years ago in the style of a French chateau on a hill."

"Fired you then did they?" Aoife's tone came out as sceptical, but Grace knew her well enough to recognize an underlying sympathy.

"Is that where you worked, Mr Grenier?" Grace asked, diluting his scowl at Aoife.

"Ah, no," he said, flushing. "At L'Hotel Artueil around the corner. A smaller establishment, but it has a very good reputation. My uncle died, so I came back to the island to care for my aunt because they brought me up."

"I'm sorry about your uncle, Mr Grenier, but after Quebec City, my hotel might be a little uninteresting for you." This time it was Aoife whose foot connected with Grace's ankle. She gritted her teeth and tried to ignore it.

"Not at all, Miss-?"

"Mrs MacKinnon."

"Mrs MacKinnon. This is just the sort of establishment I am looking for. You don't yet have a reputation so I can built one up based on quality from the beginning. How many guests do you accommodate at any one time?"

"When we open, we'll offer breakfast and dinner to a maximum of twelve residential guests and open a tea room. Would that be enough for someone accustomed to a French city hotel."

"I would say it was an advantage. I can work with less staff and more autonomy. Do you plan to take on other kitchen staff?"

"I hadn't thought about it." She groaned inwardly, aware it was one more thing she should have considered. "I suppose it depends on how busy we are." She gestured toward Aoife. "We'll both help in the kitchen to begin with, and I could serve at table"

"I could manage with one helper." He delivered a sly wink at Aoife. "I work fast, and you won't have to tell me anything twice."

"Well - um," Grace hesitated. "I have several prospective cooks, er-chefs to see over the next few days."

Aoife made a 'what-are-you-doing' face Grace pretended not to see. "Where may I contact you when I have made a decision?"

"At my aunt's. She lives near the station." He took a small black notebook from his pocket from which he tore off a pre-written sheet and handed it to her. "This is her address. I'm doing some casual work at the Railway Hotel, so if I'm not there she'll take a message."

"Thank you." Grace took the paper from him. "I'll definitely let you know."

"What do you cook, Mr Grenier?" Aoife demanded, mangling the pronunciation of his name.

"Um-all the classic French cuisine. The mother sauces, Béchamel, Velouté, Espagnole, Tomat and Hollandaise."

"Aoife, I don't think-" Grace began.

"Can you make chicken fricot?" Ignoring her, Aoife rose and closed the space between them.

"Of course." Leon's boyish face broke into a wide smile. "Also, Poutine, Rapure and meat pie."

"Even I can make meat pie," Aoife's upper lip curled.

"Ah." He held up a finger. "But do you put yeast in your pastry and let it rise before baking?" At Aoife's puzzled frown, he grinned. "I thought not. No, I make Tourtière. Acadian meat pie. You'll never taste better."

"You're hired." Aoife folded her arms and turned a triumphant smile on Grace.

"Aoife!"

"Grace!" Aoife mimicked her shocked tone. "The hotel opens in four days and we have guests arriving to stay soon after that. The only help you've taken on is that dumb girl, Tilly. I doubt she knows which way is up. You only took her on as a favor, what with her being Mrs M's granddaughter." She crooked a thumb at Leon. "If he doesn't do the cooking, who will?"

"I can find my way around any kitchen in a day." The young man took up Aoife's enthusiasm. "In three I can work miracles." He rubbed his hands together and advanced on the new stove. "Is this a Weir Glenwood?"

"It is, the latest model," Grace said proudly. "Do you know how to use it?"

"I can cook a gourmet meal on a wood fire on a prairie." He splayed his hands towards the

279

stove as if he was about to embrace the gleaming monster. "But this, this is a masterpiece."

Grace caught Aoife's wide-eyed, what-are-you-waiting-for stare.

"All right then. I'll give you a trial period. Then if we're both happy, we can discuss wages and hours."

"That's settled then." Aoife whipped his jacket from his shoulder. She draped it over a chair, then guided him firmly towards the door. "The storeroom is that way. Go and look around. If there's anything we've forgotten you may let us know. Your first job is to make breakfast for Miss Grace and myself tomorrow. My name is Aoife by the way, but you can call me Eva if it's easier."

"Thank you - Aoife." He pronounced her name the Irish way, saluted Grace then strode off in the direction of the storeroom.

"I'm not happy with what you just did," Grace said in a fierce whisper, reluctant to admit Leon Grenier appeared to be the solution to a situation plaguing her for days. "I'm the owner and I hire the staff. What do we know about him?"

"He lives with his aunt and works at the Railway Hotel. Both of which you can check," Aoife replied, unabashed. "If he messes up our breakfasts we'll know he was lying. Then we'll sack him."

"No, then I will sack him. He claims to have trained in Quebec and has a French name, but he doesn't speak with an accent."

"Not every Acadian does. Anyway, your 'a's and 'e's are different to most people's, but no one thinks you're not trustworthy."

"I suppose it's too late to find someone else. He'll have to do." Grace sighed. At the click of the latch on the storeroom door, added, "Hush now, he's coming back."

"I like your hotel very much, Miss Grace." Leon gave the room a slow appraising glance. "I could make some beautiful meals here."

"I'm glad to hear it." Grace accepted the compliment with a smile. "Can you bake by any chance? I was going to buy cakes and pastries from a bakery but my assistant," she cocked her head at Aoife, "thinks we should make them."

"And she's right." He bestowed an admiring smile on Aoife who accepted it with little reaction. "My ambition was always to be a pâtissier but the hotel I worked at didn't need one so they took me on as a sous chef. My gateaux are the lightest you will ever taste, and as for my pastries and desserts-" He extended his hands, palms upwards as if words were unnecessary

"You can certainly talk, Mr Grenier," Aoife interrupted, pronouncing it 'Groanier'. "But can you cook?"

He scooped his coat from the back of the chair and slung it over his shoulder.

"At seven thirty tomorrow morning I shall prepare my Eggs Benedict for you." He bowed to each of them in turn, dug his cap out of a pocket and jammed it onto his head. "Oh," he turned back at the door. "I'll need a fish kettle. Other than that, you appear to have everything I need."

"I'll see you out." Aoife followed him out, muttering. "And I'll lock the front door while I'm at it."

"What have I done?" Grace asked when Aoife returned. "Not that you gave me much choice."

"I'd say him turning up like that was a stroke of luck. Anyway, I like him. Although I've never heard of fish being cooked in a kettle. Won't the tea smell funny?"

Grace narrowed her eyes. Sometimes, she couldn't tell if Aoife was joking or not.

Aoife turned back at the door, her arms full of sheets. "What are Eggs Benedict?"

"I'm not sure. MacKinnon would never allow Cook to make it at home."

"Why ever not?"

"He said it was too papist for a Presbyterian household. Something about Catholics eating it during Lent. A pity, as I would have liked to be able to make an informed judgement of our Mr Grenier's attempt tomorrow."

Chapter 18

Grace braced both hands on the rail of the veranda and released a relieved breath as she surveyed the garden. Ropes of artificial flowers and ribbons wound around the uprights of white painted gazebos, their domed roofs and filigree balustrades resembling wedding cakes.

Her plan to use real blooms failed when they wilted too soon in the heat, resulting in a mad dash to fashion replacements out of white paper and wire.

Smiling, she admired the white wicker chairs in small groups around tables set with sparkling crystal, the edges of crisp white tablecloths lifting in the slight breeze.

Carts and carriages gathered in the street a full half hour before the tea room was scheduled to open, but instead of keeping them waiting, Grace gave instructions to open early.

At barely past two in the afternoon women in pastel colored dresses flowed through the main doors, their excited chatter mingling with the clink of cutlery against china, feathers and ribbons bobbing gently from their hats.

"I told you there was no need to fret," Aoife whispered at her shoulder.

"I know, but I had this awful dream last night that after all this work, no one would come," Grace said. "Have you noticed that although there are a few gentlemen here, most of our customers are women? There's a group of eight in the far corner who all arrived together."

"Isn't that what you anticipated?"

"It's what I hoped, but I didn't think it would be so obvious. It's an encouraging sign."

Behind them the main tea room was also full, the heat of the summer afternoon diluted with the help of electric ceilings fans. Grace had the foresight to add these at the last moment, as well as a pile of Chinese paper hand fans laid out for the use of the guests.

"How are the cakes and pastries going?" Grace asked.

"Can't bring them out fast enough. Leon's doing a grand job. He's had to make another three trays of madeleines and French fancies. I've made enough cucumber sandwiches to feed the whole town and Tilly's run off her feet."

"I'm glad that for now we don't have any residents to worry about. As a dress rehearsal this has stretched us to the limit. I might have to offer Tilly a permanent job." Grace nodded in the direction of a couple Tilly was serving with strawberry gateaux. "Not all of these people are genuine customers. Those two work at the Queen Hotel. I'll be willing to bet they were sent by management to snoop."

Grace turned at the sound of the shop doorbell, prepared to greet more customers, and froze.

Emily Cahill entered the main tea room, the full skirt of her pink chiffon dress billowing out from her waist, an oversized hat frothed with yellow chiffon sat on her blonde curls. She paused to survey the room before her gaze swung to the veranda where Grace stood, her stern expression softening into a smile.

"Grace, dear." Emily's loud greeting drew all eyes as she swept through the open French doors. "What a simply delightful place you have here. And a tea room, what an excellent idea." She waggled a white-gloved hand at the room behind her. "All this light wood furniture against the darker wallpaper is such a refreshing change from dun brown. How innovative of you." Despite her tone, Emily's narrowed nostrils indicated mild disappointment.

"Thank you, I took inspiration from your beautiful home," Grace lied.

"Really?" Emily's heavily carmined lips puckered slightly. "Perhaps it's time to call in the decorators," she muttered, taking in Grace's plain burgundy skirt and white, high necked blouse with a weak, dismissive smile.

Chosen to convey an air of professionalism, Grace had been pleased with the effect, but Emily's disdainful look made her feel underdressed.

"It was nice of you to come, Mrs Cahill." She returned her smile through gritted teeth.

"Oh, you must call me Emily. Surely, we know each other well enough? I brought Mary Jardine with me to show our support for your little venture." She searched the full room behind her in mild confusion, her eyes finally settling on a young woman who had stopped to speak to someone at one of the tables. "Mary do come and meet Grace."

Grace's breath caught in her throat as a young woman looked up at the sound of her name. She said something to a lady she was speaking to, then glided towards them, shepherding a child in front of her.

"We meet at last, Mrs MacKinnon." Mary Jardine's voice was low and sensual. "I've heard so much about you." Her luminous blue eyes settled on Grace without a hint of hostility, her cupid bow mouth and clear complexion free of the cosmetics Emily liberally employed. Her pale blue close-fitting jacket suit with wide lapels accentuated her slender frame, the high collar of the cream silk blouse beneath highlighting a slim, elegant neck. A pert hat, tilted jauntily to one side, sat on her swept up brown hair.

"I'm pleased to meet you too." Grace's mouth dried as she took her outstretched hand.

"And this is Isla." Emily rested a hand upon the shoulder of a child as pretty as her mother. Isla wore a white layered dress with a sapphire blue sash, a flat straw boater with a matching ribbon wound around the crown perched on chestnut hair that hung down her back.

The child curtseyed, then stared up at her with grey eyes so familiar, Grace suppressed a gasp.

"I-I'm so glad you could all come."

"We wouldn't have missed it." Emily smiled coyly from beneath the wide brim of her hat.

"Where would you like to sit?" Grace asked, recovering herself.

"Would you mind if we stayed out here on the veranda?" Mary asked. "The sun doesn't like me very much, but it would be nice for Isla to play in the garden."

"Aoife, would you find a table for these ladies?" A hard lump lodged in Grace's throat and stayed there. "Aoife will serve you. If you'll excuse me, I need to check on things in the kitchen." She fled through the main tea room into the kitchen, slammed the door shut behind her and leaned against it, a hand pressed to her bodice as she tried to calm her rapid breathing.

"Getting too much out there, is it, Grace?" Leon smiled in sympathy as he applied a piping nozzle to a row of cakes laid out on the table. He had dropped the 'Miss' from her name when Grace complained it made her sound like a matriarch.

It was bad enough when Tilly jumped to her feet each time she entered the room.

"I don't know why I didn't anticipate being so busy." Grace summoned a shaky smile. "Not that I'm complaining." The kitchen was hotter than outside, mainly due to the fired up stove from which an enticing hot sugar smell of baking emanated.

"I'll say not." He arranged half a dozen of the cakes onto a stand, then shouted, "Tilly!" in a sharp command that made Grace jump.

A slightly plump girl in a white pinafore and cap which only just contained her frizzy ginger hair darted forward.

"These are for table ten!" He swung the cake stand into her hand with such expertise, not one of them wobbled.

"Yes, Mr Leon." The girl bobbed a belated curtsey to Grace before backing through the door to the tea room.

"So that's her then?" Aoife said, making Grace jump for the second time in a minute.

She closed her eyes briefly. "I wish you wouldn't sneak up on me. I didn't hear you come in. Who are you talking about?"

"Like you don't know. Mrs Jardine and that blowsy woman who just arrived."

"I don't know why you sound so disgruntled. I told you Andr- Mr Jardine was married. It's not as if I had any expectations regarding him." She busied herself arranging the rest of the cakes on stands, refusing to look at Aoife.

"Course you didn't." Aoife rolled her eyes at Leon, who turned away to hide a knowing smile.

"Then you'll be going out there to talk to them?" Aoife asked. "Wouldn't be polite to ignore them, what with you coming over on the Cahill's boat."

"Naturally I shall. I was just taking a breather."

"Go on then. I've put them at table three on the veranda."

"I suppose I could spare her a few minutes." Grace hung around in the kitchen until Aoife's hard sideways looks drove her out into the tea room. She played for time by pausing to exchange small talk with a few patrons before she plucked up courage to venture onto the veranda.

Mary occupied a table beneath a flower covered archway, Isla sprawled on the grass at the bottom of the terrace steps, her arms wrapped around her drawn up knees. Emily was nowhere in sight.

"Did you enjoy your tea?" Grace asked, eyeing the single used cup on the table in front of her.

"Most refreshing, although there isn't much one can say about tea is there? Isla and I loved the madeleines. Didn't we, darling?"

Isla looked up from the grass and nodded, shielding her eyes with one hand.

"Is there anything else you need?"

"Some company would be nice." Mary tapped the arm of the peacock backed chair opposite. "Emily saw someone she's keen to impress and has deserted me temporarily. Not that I mind being alone, but if you are here, I shan't be approached by a committee member asking me to count bandages for the hospital."

"All right, just for a little while." Grace's nerves settled in the face of Mary's friendliness as she eased into the chair opposite. "I'm sure the kitchen can manage for a few minutes without me."

"This is such a beautiful setting and must be one of the prettiest gardens in Charlottetown."

"Thank you. I'm afraid all the flowers have been brought in, but hopefully I'll have grown some of my own by next year."

"John Cahill told us all about the work you have done, but it was hard to imagine. I'm so glad I came to see it for myself."

"You make it sound as if that was in doubt."

"It was Emily's idea. She insisted I accompany her, which came as a surprise as she usually ignores me." She laughed, a demure, gentle laugh which was barely louder than her speaking voice. "She never invites me to anything, even her 'at homes', probably because she finds me uninteresting. Not that I mind, those women aren't my sort. I'm a country girl at heart and I find them too superficial."

"You don't appear to have any trouble talking to me." Grace offered her one of Leon's light and spongy madeleines on the plate before them.

"That's because I feel I know you. Andrew has spoken of you often." She took the cake and bit into it, giving a tiny groan.

"He has?" Grace willed her to finish her mouthful of cake, eager to hear more.

"Oh yes. I heard all about how you pretended to faint, and he carried you off the ship to avoid that awful man your guardian sent to spirit you back to England. Such a romantic story."

"Not really." Grace felt herself flushing. "He could see how distressed I was and was merely being gentlemanly."

"That's Andrew all, over. The consummate gentleman."

Grace searched for sarcasm in her smile, but her expression was open and genuine.

"I suspected as much. He-uh seems the type."

"He is. Duty and responsibility are his watchwords." Mary sighed and stared off over the garden, treating Grace to a view of her delicate profile.

"You mentioned you were a country girl," Grace said, deflecting the conversation away from Andrew. She imagined hearing about him would fulfil a need but instead, his name on Mary's lips was almost painful.

"I was born and raised in Souris. That's on the eastern side of the island. It's pretty there and so quiet."

"You don't like Charlottetown?"

"I like the town well enough. The society, however, is not to my taste. I'm no good with these charity women with their never-ending committees and lobbying. I find them too - strident."

"I know exactly what you mean. I enjoy my work here at the hotel, but I savour my quiet times when I can arrange them."

"How nice to meet someone like me. I too prefer to stay at home with a book or piece of embroidery. Andrew loves Charlottetown. When he goes away on business he pines and wants to return. I doubt I'll ever prise him away. Then there's Isla's schooling. I wanted to hire a governess for her, but Andrew felt she would benefit from school. Andrew says a one-room country schoolhouse won't prepare her for the wider world."

"She's a lovely child." Grace looked to where Isla sat stringing daisies together from a tub of marguerites with fierce concentration.

"Like me she's quite shy but is blossoming slowly," Mary added. "To be honest, the only person's company she prefers to mine is Andrew's. He's wonderful with her."

"I'm sure he is." Grace suppressed a pang and looked away in time to see Emily mount their steps, a look of panic on her face on seeing them together.

"What have you two been talking about?" It was almost a demand as she split a speculative look between them.

"Mary was telling me about her home in Souris," Grace replied, defensive of Emily's unapologetic intrusion.

"That place?" Emily's upper lip curled in obvious contempt. "Mary, we ought to be going."

"Really?" Mary blinked, placed her plate on the table and rose. "What a shame. Just when I was enjoying myself too. And Emily, you haven't had any tea. You must try one of these excellent cakes."

"Is there something wrong, Emily?" Grace asked, taking in her quick, nervous movements and darting eyes.

"Er-no, but I've remembered something I need to do. I'll come for tea another time. Mrs Henderson is having her carriage brought round. She agreed to take us home since Andrew is using your vehicle this afternoon and John is away."

"We could take a hackney, which is how we got here," Mary persisted. "Mrs Henderson told me she planned to stay for the afternoon." She nodded to where a plump middle-aged lady appeared to be taking her farewells of a group of ladies gathered beneath one of the larger gazebos.

"She might have been then, but now she's happy to leave," Emily enunciated each word as if explaining to a child." Come along Isla," she called over the grass. "We're going now."

Isla clambered to her feet, a string of daisies trailing from one hand.

"Must we, Aunt Emily? I like it here." Her feet dragged on each step as she joined them,

"Yes we must, and don't call me aunt."

"Aren't you going to say goodbye to Miss Grace?" Isla asked, tugging at her arm as Grace accompanied them through the main tea room.

Why had Emily gone to all the trouble to bring Mary and Isla to the opening, only to drag them away at the first opportunity?

"What? Oh yes, of course." Emily halted and turned back briefly. "Good afternoon, Grace dear. Lovely place you have."

"Goodbye, Emily," Grace said. "And to you, Isla, I hope you'll come back and see me sometime."

"May I have some of that strawberry cake next time I come?" Isla stared up at Grace through eyes so like Andrew's she was momentarily speechless.

"I-I don't see why not. Let me know when to expect you and I'll ask my chef to make some for you."

"Thank you." Isla bobbed a charming, if wobbly curtsey before Emily ushered her into the street.

"I'm so pleased to have met you at last." Mary held back, a hand on Grace's arm. "Andrew was so right about you. I do hope we'll be friends."

"Thank you. I hope so too." A cold hand gripped Grace's heart and squeezed.

* * *

The rest of the afternoon passed quickly, with new visitors rapidly taking the place of departing ones. The tea room was a great success, with most attention on the garden, which was admired by everyone. Most patrons sought out Grace before they left to assure her they would come back often.

"It's so nice to have a place to bring one's friends," a matron expressed the sentiment Grace heard repeated all afternoon.

She escaped to the kitchen for a well-earned cup of tea and by the time she returned, there were only five or so tables occupied in both areas.

The tea room bell jangled, bringing a sigh from Aoife on her way past with a loaded tray. "I was hoping there wouldn't be any more customers."

"Don't worry, I'll see to them," Grace said. "Just make sure the urn has been replenished with hot water." She waved her away and turned to greet the new arrival only to come face to face with Andrew Jardine.

"Good afternoon." She swallowed, aware her breathing had quickened, but hoped he hadn't noticed. "Um-have you come to collect Mary and Isla? If so, I'm afraid they left a while ago."

He removed his hat, regarding her steadily. "Mary mentioned at breakfast she was to attend your opening, but I'm not here for them. I came to see you."

"Oh?"

"I felt our last meeting ended on a sour note. For a reason I cannot fathom, I appear to have intruded where I wasn't welcome."

"It's not important, really. I've forgotten all about it. There's no need to apologize." She held both hands up in surrender. "I would invite you to stay for some refreshment, but I'm horribly embarrassed to say the cake has all gone."

"Which is excellent news for your first day. I hoped to get here earlier but some business delayed me." He gave the room a slow appraising glance, then indicated the open doors onto the veranda. "May I?"

"Oh, of course." She stepped aside to allow him to walk through.

He strolled to the edge of the veranda from where he surveyed the garden. He rested one hand on the balustrade, the other he tucked into a pocket of his charcoal grey trousers, revealing a sapphire blue waistcoat the exact shade of the sash on Isla's dress.

Grace looked away quickly and swallowed.

"You have a good eye, Mrs MacKinnon." He turned his devastating smile on her, his eyes crinkling at the corners. "The way the hedges are placed to give privacy to the arrangements of tables and chairs is charming. Far enough away to discourage flying creatures but intimate enough for conversation. The gazebos are especially attractive. Allow me to congratulate you. I'm sure you are set for continued success."

"It's kind of you to say so." She kept her voice calm, but her heart felt as if it might leap out of her chest. "I could still offer you tea. If you have time."

"No, thank you. I need to get home, but I didn't want to let your first day go by without offering my good wishes."

"I appreciate that, thank you. Mary is a lovely woman," Grace blurted. "And what a delightful child Isla is."

"Thank you. I adore them both." He twisted his upper body towards her, his shoulder against a wooden upright. "Mary finds town too busy, but it's the best place for Isla. She's enrolled into Edgehill School for Girls in Windsor for when she's older."

"I assume that isn't the Windsor I'm familiar with?"

"Ah, no. It's in Nova Scotia." His spine-tingling laugh drifted out across the garden, knotting Grace's insides.

She wished he would leave and put a halt to the torture of his presence, but at the same time dreaded his going.

"Do I see a familiar face?" His gaze slid past her to where Aoife issued change to a departing customer. "Surely that's the young lady you sailed over with. The Irish girl with the quick tongue?"

Grace smiled. "Aoife Doyle, yes that's her. Things didn't quite work out for her in New Brunswick."

Aoife caught them looking at her and wandered over. "It's Mr Jardine isn't it?" she said with her usual unguarded friendliness. "Nice to see you again, sir."

"And you, Miss Doyle."

"Aww, no one calls me that. Aoife's what I answer to. I hope you'll be a regular here, sir. Miss Grace was saying the other day-"

"Aoife," Grace interrupted. "I think those people by the door wish to pay their bill." She gave her a discreet but firm shove.

"I'm going," Aoife muttered, both hands held palms outwards as she backed away.

"She hasn't changed." Jardine smiled at her retreating back. "If I recall, she travelled on an assisted passage. Would you let her know for me that if she has any unfinished business with the Salvation Army with regards to reimbursements, complaints for misrepresentation and so on, I would be happy to assist where I can?"

"That's very kind of you to offer. I'll pass that on." Grace searched for something interesting to say, but in truth she was quite happy to stand and look at him. "What happened to the SS Parisian? I know she didn't sink, but were you able to salvage her?"

"We did indeed. I've spent some time recently going back and forth to Halifax to deal

298

with the investigators. Unfortunately, the dispute will take at least a year to get settled."

"From where I stood on the deck it was obvious who was at fault. That German boat made no attempt to slow down and we were stationary."

"Where money is concerned, nothing is obvious." They fell into a companionable silence, both contemplating the garden, now almost cleared of patrons. Grace sneaked covert looks at his profile, unable to work out exactly why he had come.

"I hope you'll allow me to call again," he said finally. "Perhaps I'll come earlier next time when you have made more cake."

"Of course. After all it's a public tea room. I look forward to seeing Mary again too, she's such a sweet woman."

"I didn't mean - uh, never mind. I'll convey your sentiments to her when I get home." He bowed and replaced his hat. "If you find yourself in need of help, I hope you won't hesitate to call on myself or John Cahill."

"I've already asked Mr Cahill's advice." Grace frowned, sensing there was something he wished to say but couldn't bring himself to do so. "What sort of help do you feel I need?"

"Advice then. Remember we will always be here, and that you should not trust every offer you receive."

Grace was about to ask him what he meant, when he added, "It was nice seeing you again, Mrs MacKinnon, Grace." He nodded at Aoife who hovered at the far end of the veranda. "And you, Aoife."

"What was all that about?" Aoife drifted back to her side once he moved away.

"I've no idea." Grace watched Jardine as he made his way through the tea room and out to his waiting carriage.

"You could have been a bit nicer, Grace," Aoife said. "You hardly said a word to him."

"I don't think that's true." Though on reflection, she was probably brusque without meaning to. Perhaps he already regretted his visit?

Grace remained at the door, seeing out the last of the customers who issued thanks and congratulations. Grace locked the door behind the last of them, and turned the sign to read 'closed'. Through the glazed door she noticed a man on the corner who appeared to be studying the tea room. He wore a baggy brown suit, his face, apart from a heavy moustache, barely visible beneath a pulled down homburg hat.

She beckoned Aoife closer. "Do you see that man? Was he one of our customers?"

"I don't recognize him." Aoife studied the distant figure. "I think I remember him though, he was standing right there when I opened the tea room. He hasn't moved."

"Perhaps he's waiting for someone?"

Dismissing him, Grace pulled down the blind and followed Aoife into the kitchen where Leon and Tilly stood among piles of freshly washed crockery set out in neat piles ready to be put away.

"He's a fine-looking man, that Mr Jardine," Aoife said, heading for the china storeroom with a tray loaded with cups.

"Who's Mr Jardine?" Tilly asked, her face bright with expectation as she balanced several plates.

"No one," Grace snapped. "Tilly, be careful, that pile is too high, you'll drop them."

Chastened, Tilly reduced the pile and set off after Aoife.

"I still think you were a bit short with him," Aoife whispered, returning for another pile of crockery.

"I'm no marriage wrecker, Aoife," she whispered back.

"If you say so, though to my mind, if a man likes you as much as that, he deserves some encouragement."

"It cannot be, and that's an end to it." Grace straightened her shoulders and began sifting through a stack of receipts but didn't take in any of them.

Her memories of Andrew Jardine were bitter-sweet, what with Emily Cahill's obvious ploy to goad her by parading Mary and Isla in front of her. What made matters worse, Grace genuinely liked Mary. The last thing she would ever do was hurt her, or Isla. Then there was Keogh's remark that any interest Jardine showed in her would be of a particular kind; and it wasn't marriage.

She slapped the pile of receipts back in the cash box and slammed the lid, annoyed with herself.

It was her own fault she misunderstood Jardine's intentions, which were no more than those of a generous friend. A friendship she would be churlish to reject. If only she didn't like him so much, but how did one stop hankering over someone they could not have?

Chapter 19

"We might need more staff soon," Grace observed, running a finger down the ledger she studied at the kitchen table. "We've more bookings over the next few weeks, and we'll be full for all of July."

"We'll be pushed to deal with them as well as running the tea room," Aoife banged a wicker basket on the table, shunting the ledger several inches sideways. "How about a waitress or two?" She splayed her fingers inside a pair of gossamer fine white gloves, her head tilted to admire them; a gift from Grace to celebrate the opening of the tea room.

"Some extra help in the kitchens would be welcome," Leon said, appearing at the door of the storeroom, his jacket slung over an arm. "I wouldn't mind getting off on time on occasion."

"Noted, Leon and thank you for all your hard work." Grace pointedly shifted the ledger back to its original position.

"Good night then, Grace. See you tomorrow, Aoife." Leon touched his hat to both of them before he disappeared through the back door.

"One more waitress then, and a kitchen hand. I'm surprised you get on so well with Tilly," Grace said. "I would have expected you to be less tolerant of the way she flirts with Leon." Their cook had taken one of his rare evenings off, so Grace felt comfortable enough to mention his name. Usually when that happened, he would pop up from wherever he was hiding and catch her.

"And just about every other tradesman who walks through the kitchen door." Aoife sniffed. "Ach, she's such a mouse, and don't have the nose for a good spat. It's only worth doing if they fight back."

"Hush, Aoife, Leon might be out, but Tilly is upstairs. You know how sensitive she is to criticism. You look lovely by the way." Grace smiled as she took in Aoife's dress with its marigold colored skirt overlaid with primrose moiré silk that floated as she walked. "Are you off to this basket social with Jake?"

Aoife recently began attending the Catholic St Dunstan's in Great George street, less for its spiritual life, Grace suspected, and more because the Irish youth of the area congregated there for social occasions.

One evening she brought back to the hotel a young man whom she introduced to Grace in a way which revealed she longed for approval. She need not have worried as Grace took an instant liking to Jake Brennan, a stocky young man unable to sit still. He either jiggled his knee or drummed his fingernails on a table top. Keen

304

brown eyes shone in his cheerful, bronzed face shadowed by the peak of his ever-present cap.

He always leapt to his feet whenever Grace appeared and addressed her as ma'am, or Miss Grace, though she told him repeatedly that both made her feel old.

His father had worked on the fishing boats and was taken in the same hurricane which took Marge's son, making him the main provider for the family.

"I am, but don't you go reading anything into it," Aoife insisted. "Jake's a friend and he's going to stay that way."

"Marrying your friend is often the guarantee of a successful marriage."

"Mebbe, but it helps to have a man who's worth looking at too."

"I know what you mean." She nursed a secret smile as an image of Andrew Jardine jumped into her head.

"Is that another letter from Miss Montgomery?" Aoife indicated the corner of an envelope that peeked out from beneath the accounts book.

"It is. She's invited me to visit her in Cavendish. Maybe a day beside the sea would do me good."

"We are beside the sea; it's only a block that way." Aoife cocked her head towards the street.

"I meant long deserted beaches and wide open countryside."

"Then you should go, Grace. You're all work these days and don't have any fun. You wouldn't even come to hear the band play at the Queen square bandstand last night with Jake and me."

"I wasn't in the mood. Besides, I enjoy working here with all of you. The Grace and Favor is my life."

"Well it shouldn't be. It will do you good to take some time away. The only letters you get apart from supplier's bills are from Miss Maud."

'Who else would write to me? You know I have no family,' Grace replied, mildly irritated.

Aoife had a point. Were all her friends destined to be passing acquaintances like the Cahills, or people she employed? Aoife was young, so there was every chance she would seek another life before long. Perhaps with Jake Brennan. She was too much of a free spirit not to.

'You must have friends," Aoife persisted. "People you knew in London. Don't they want to know how you go on?'

"Possibly." Though at that moment Grace couldn't put a name to anyone she could regard as a real friend. "They have no idea where I am." Not that she dared write to anyone in case it alerted them to where she was. The shadow of Angus MacKinnon still hovered on some days.

She refolded Maud's letter and returned it to the envelope. She couldn't explain why, but lately she had begun to miss England. Not her father-in-law or his self-obsessed wife, or his fussy sisters, but the village where she spent most of her life. She even missed Frederick on occasion. The sound of his laugh, which had been all too infrequent, reminded her that one person cared about her. Once.

"Incidentally, what exactly is a basket social?" she asked, changing the subject.

"I didn't know either until Jake explained it," Aoife wandered to the mirror above the sink and pouted at her reflection. "All the girls take a basket full of their best home-cooked food which is auctioned off. Only the men don't know which basket belongs to which girl. Whoever bids the highest amount gets to eat the food with you."

"Suppose you don't care for the man who wins your basket?"

"Don't you worry, I shan't be leaving anything to chance. Jake will know which is mine."

"And if a person bids higher than Jake?"

"Huh, he won't let that happen. Not if he knows what's good for him." She hung the basket over her arm and headed for the back door. "I'll be back by ten so don't lock me out."

Grace took Maud's letter out again and re-read it, hearing her friend's voice inside her head, the only sound in the room the tick of the stove as it cooled.

Uncle Leander informed me that unlike most years, he won't be bringing his family to stay with Grandmother and me this summer. I tried to appear sad, when he told me, but he cannot imagine my relief. He has spared me having to cook, clean and tend to my boisterous cousins, not to mention aunts and uncles for days on end. My days shall be so pleasant and peaceful I feel quite amiable. It would be a perfect time for you to take advantage of my altered mood and come to stay.

Do tell me you will come, Grace. I should love it if we can spend some time together before winter closes in and I become isolated again. If this winter is anything like the last, I should surely expire. The snow was as high as the roof and the house gloomy as dusk all day. We didn't leave the fireside for weeks.

I am so glad to hear the hotel is doing well even if I cannot be there.

Your true friend in spirit.
Maud

Grace replaced the letter in the envelope and stowed it away safely in the box in her room where she kept all of Maud's correspondence. She returned to the kitchen and her invoices, receipts and lists of supplies, one eye on the bell board for any guests who might require a late night drink or more towels.

The desk in her sitting room had been arranged as a private place to work, but she preferred the kitchen with its atmosphere of activity and sociable chatter and enjoyed Aoife's cheerful banter with the guests, or her gentle teasing of the shy Tilly, while Leon entreated them to try another of his recipes.

The clock in the hall chimed ten. Grace closed the ledger with a thump, her arms stretched over her head, frowning at the fact Aoife was later than promised, which was unlike her. Grace put the kettle on the hob to boil water for tea, then took some old newspapers into the yard. She was about to come back inside when the sound of raised voices reached her.

She eased open the gate and peered round the jamb to where three people stood talking in the lane. The figure in a pale dress was recognizable as Aoife, the one beside her was undoubtedly Jake. They stood with another man Grace did not recognize. She couldn't make out their conversation, only the timbre of their words which was clearly confrontational. Had something happened at the church to upset them?

Aoife wagged a finger in front of the second man's face but was immediately pulled away by Jake.

The man turned and moved off down the lane, though he appeared to be in no hurry.

Aoife called after him. Her words sounded as if she was casting doubt on his parenthood before Jake grasped her by the shoulders and propelled her towards the gate.

Before they saw her, Grace darted back into the kitchen, just as the kettle boiled. She busied herself making tea when Aoife stormed into the room, scowling at Jake who followed her in.

"Did you have a nice time?" Grace asked, frowning as she watched Jake carefully lock the door.

"You didn't have to haul me away like that." Ignoring Grace's question, Aoife dumped the basket onto the table and turned furious eyes on Jake.

"You shouldn't have been quite so sharp with him," he replied. "Doesn't do to upset the likes of him."

"The likes of whom?" Grace asked, pouring hot water into a teapot.

Aoife shrugged. "No idea who he was. But he had a brass neck." She nodded at the basket. "How much do you suppose I got for it?"

"The basket?" Grace raised an eyebrow. "By the look on your face, I would say you did very well."

"That I did, I got Jake to bump up the price to four dollars." She hooked a thumb at the young man who hovered by the door. "Then I passed out some of Leon's leftover pastries to those who hadn't brought along any dessert. Told them where to get them, too."

"You'll have Leon selling them out of the back door at this rate." Grace smiled, wondering how she could ever manage without Aoife. "This man you were talking to. Was he the same one hanging around outside the tea room the other day?"

The man Grace spotted on opening day had come back several times since.

On one occasion Leon took off across the road to demand what he was doing, but he wasn't fast enough, and the fellow slipped away before he got there.

"No, it weren't him." Aoife shook her head. "This bloke was younger. He had the cheek of the devil too." She pronounced it 'divil'. "He wanted to come inside to talk business, or so he said. I told him to sling his hook."

"What did he want to discuss?" Grace asked, filling three cups with strong tea, mainly to stop her hand from shaking. She had a fair idea of what the man wanted to talk about but hoped she was wrong.

Aoife bit her bottom lip and Jake flushed and looked away.

"If it has anything to do with illicit liquor, you were right to send him away. I'm not interested," Grace said.

"Not his liquor, Miss Grace," Jake interjected. "He's a messenger working for someone else."

"Who?" Grace asked, the name on the tip of her tongue

"Does it matter? Whoever he is, it doesn't do to upset the likes of him," Jake warned.

"Most of my guests are ladies." Grace filled a jug with milk and set it on the table. "The few gentlemen who come here don't seem like hard drinkers. I doubt I'd be able to sell much even if I tried."

"Some places just sell it under the table and pay the fines," Aoife said. "It's worth the risk to some."

"Well, I don't intend joining them," Grace said. "I'm still an outsider here and don't wish to draw unwelcome attention to myself. They can keep their rum and sell it elsewhere. From what you say there are plenty of people willing to do so."

"There are, but you should still watch out," Jake said. "The rum runners might have accepted your refusal for now, but they're the types not to take no for an answer. When they can see a lucrative outlet, they are reluctant to give up and American money is a huge draw." Jake picked up two of the cups and handed one to Aoife.

"You seem to know something about it, Jake?" Grace said. "Are you trying to persuade me?"

"Not me, Miss Grace. I'm just warning you. He might not take kindly to a second refusal."

Grace gulped a mouthful of tea which burned the roof of her mouth. Jake's words sounded too much like Keogh's for her liking.

Was she being naive to think she could avoid the bootleggers forever?

Chapter 20

Grace made a concerted effort to banish Andrew Jardine from her mind by burying herself in work at the hotel. The rooms were continually full, so much so that Grace turned people away. Leon was busy all day producing cakes for the tea room and gourmet dinners for their discerning guests at night. Never much of a cook, Grace even learned how to make Mrs M's molasses cookies which proved very popular with the customers taking morning coffee.

She employed a new chambermaid who came in each morning to make up the bedrooms and a middle-aged woman to keep the kitchen and storeroom as clean and tidy as Leon demanded. Aoife had graduated to the front desk where, under Grace's tutelage, she greeted guests and kept the bookings in order.

The hot July days were exhausting and after a particularly busy morning, Grace handed over the afternoon customers to Aoife and went for a walk to clear her head.

"I'll be back before the dinner service," she called through the kitchen door as she left.

Avoiding the bustle of Queen square where families gathered to listen to the band on a summer day, she headed to the quieter, less aesthetic Rochford square with its open spaces and haphazard arrangement of trees. She chose a bench beneath a low hanging branch of an ancient oak where she settled down for a quiet read of her copy of Elizabeth and her German Garden, the book she had bought at Maud's urging. The smell of freshly cut grass and meadow flowers added to the atmosphere.

Before long she was immersed in a charming story of a woman's love for her garden to the exclusion of all other company apart from her children.

The author's frustration showed through when unwelcome callers unanimously viewed her as being a wife abandoned by her husband to rot in the country, too loyal to him to complain.

Grace giggled at the writer's rejection of her German gardener's insistence to plant flowers in straight rows, ignoring all her instructions for a wilder arrangement.

Leaving the square, she planned to collect a picture from the stationers on the way back to the hotel. Haszards had made a wonderful job of framing the botanical drawings she found in the house, which were now displayed proudly in the dining room. However, one of her first guests, the silent couple from New York, removed one from its hook for a closer look and dropped it, smashing the glass.

"I'll wager she threw it at him," Aoife said when she saw it; thus condemning their marriage to a swirling maelstrom of discontent. Grace reached the corner of Dorchester and Pownall streets when a shout alerted her to a commotion ahead. A small crowd gathered at the corner. With the intention of offering help if she could, she eased her way to the front, just as she heard a strangled voice call her name.

"Grace. Oh, Grace, thank goodness you're here." Mary Jardine crouched beside her daughter. "Please help. It's Isla."

Isla Jardine lay on the boardwalk, pale and semi-conscious but no injury as far as Grace could see. Her face was flushed, each breath accompanied by a strangled croaking noise.

"Poor little thing," said a matron who stopped to assist them. "I think she needs to be taken home, dear, and put to bed."

"What happened?" Grace bent beside Mary. "Is she hurt?"

Mary shook her head. "She had a sore throat this morning, that's all. I was taking her for ice cream to cheer her up, but she just collapsed onto the road."

Grace eased Isla into a sitting position, hoping it might make the child's breathing easier. "Isla, can you hear me?"

"I don't think she can!" Mary's bottom lip quivered. "She doesn't seem to know I'm here. I need to get her home and send for a doctor, but I can't see a cab anywhere." She gazed along the street filled with tradesman's carts and buggies, though no hansom or a hackney in sight. "There could be one in the next street, it's busier than here. Could you go and look for me, Grace?"

"Where's the nearest hospital?"

"What?" Mary's eyes widened. "Why, what's wrong with her?"

"There's a crackle in Isla's breathing. We need to get her medical attention." The words "before she stops altogether" Grace left unspoken.

Mary covered her face with her hands, not moving.

"The hospital, Mary, where is it?" Grace urged.

"There's the new one in Kensington Road." The helpful matron pointed to the road behind them.

Grace lifted the child into her arms. Isla lay limp, her head thrown back, and her arms flung out to her sides. For such a small figure she was heavier than Grace anticipated.

"No, the Catholic Hospital on Haviland street is closer." Mary gathered herself and clambered to her feet. "It's only a few minutes from here. We can walk there." She swept her bag and Isla's hat from the road where they had fallen. "We aren't Catholics, but I trust the Sisters of Charity. They looked after Andrew's mother during her last illness."

Though only a few minutes away, the frantic walk to the hospital felt like an age with Isla's limp form growing heavier with each step. Mary hurried alongside clutching the child's hand which made progress more hazardous, though to ask her to step away would only distress her more.

"Here it is." Mary pointed to a square white clapboarded building which looked more like two ordinary houses knocked together than a hospital.

Grace mounted the five shallow steps, turning sideways to push through the double doors into the entrance hall where, breathless, she halted.

"Could we have some help please?" she gasped to the grey-garbed nun seated behind a desk.

The nun did not hesitate, and gestured to another, younger nun who entered through a side hall, possibly in response to Grace's frantic plea.

"Sister Conceptua, find Dr Bateman and tell him to go to examining room four," the nun said, beckoning Grace along a short corridor and around a corner to a door on the right.

The room held a metal bed, a chair and a nightstand but nothing else apart from a window with a white blind half pulled down.

"Place her here." The nun drew back the cover on the bed. "Would you wait in the hall until the Doctor has examined her?"

"But I want to stay with her!" Mary pleaded.

"Let them do what they have to. We won't be far away." Grace wrapped an arm around her and guided her back into the hall just as a man in a white coat eased past them into the room. Without acknowledging them he walked straight to the bed.

"I'll come and take your details in a moment," the nun said, ushering them outside.

"What's wrong with her?" Mary sobbed onto Grace's shoulder as they returned to the main hallway where the desk stood. "How did she become so ill this fast?"

"I'm not sure, but she's where she needs to be. The doctor will look after her."

"I didn't know what to do." Mary slumped onto the bench. "One minute she was walking along beside me and the next-" She broke off to submit to another burst of distressed sobbing.

"You said she had a sore throat?" Grace eased down beside her.

"Not much of one. She was more lethargic than usual and complained of a headache. It didn't occur to me it could be anything this bad. Oh, Grace, what do you think is wrong?"

"I don't know," Grace lied. "We'll have to wait for the doctor." She had seen Isla's symptoms before but hoped she was wrong.

"Andrew!" Mary's eyes flew open and she grabbed Grace's arm, so tightly she winced. "I must tell him. He'll want to be here."

"Of course he will. Is he anywhere near a telephone do you know?"

Mary nodded. "He's at home. The nuns will know how to reach him."

Grace approached the desk, where a third nun now sat, this one in the pinafore and white half veil which denoted her as a novice. She gave Isla's name and Mary's, then requested the nun telephone Andrew Jardine and ask him to come to the hospital straight away.

As time passed, Mary grew more restless, no longer accepting Grace's assurances that the doctor knew what he was doing. She questioned every nun who walked by but received the same answer.

"The doctor will be with you when he has completed his examination."

Finally, a white-coated figure walked slowly towards them, his expression unreadable, giving no clue as to whether his conclusion was good or bad. "Mrs Jardine?" He looked from Grace to Mary and back again.

"I'm Mrs Jardine." Mary rose to her feet and hiccoughed, her face tear-streaked and puffy.

"I'm Dr Bateman. I've examined your daughter." He turned watery blue eyes on Grace in enquiry. "Might I ask who you are?"

"I'm a friend who happened to be there when Isla collapsed," Grace said.

"I would prefer to discuss this with members of the family only," the doctor said gravely.

"Never mind that," Mary snapped. "I want her here. What's wrong with my child?"

"Ah, I see." He cleared his throat before continuing. "The situation as it now stands, is that a false membrane composed of bacilli and dead cells has formed in the child's throat. Combined with the already swollen tissues underneath, her airway is becoming obstructed."

"What does that mean?" Mary turned anguished eyes on Grace. "What's he saying, Grace?"

"He means Isla has diphtheria, Mary." Grace tightened her hold on Mary's shoulders, the doctor's next words lost in Mary's wail of anguish.

"What are you going to do?" Grace asked him. The diagnosis came as no surprise. Isla's swollen neck and her rasping breaths were symptoms she had seen before.

"I need to intubate her."

"What? But that's a horrible procedure," Grace said. "Especially for a child."

A ten-year-old neighbor of the MacKinnons in Hampstead had been intubated in London Hospital. His father always maintained that the hard rubber tube inserted into the child's throat had caused his death.

"I'm aware of that. But if I don't, the child could suffocate."

"You can't let her die!" Mary cried. "You can't."

"Is there no other way?" Grace asked.

"There is one." Dr Bateman didn't sound confident. "An antitoxin is available with which we've had some success in the past, but it's far from proven."

"It's worth a try, isn't it?" Grace said. "Intubation is a temporary solution but isn't a cure. You simply put that tube into the throat and wait?"

"It's not quite as simple as that, but in effect-" He left the sentence hanging.

"What do you think, Mary?" Grace asked.

"I don't know what to do." Mary slumped back onto the bench where she rocked back and forward her clenched fists held to her mouth "Where's Andrew? I want to hear what he thinks."

Just then the main doors flew open with a bang and Andrew strode into the hall, his face a picture of angry concern. He halted beside the doctor, his gaze going from Mary to Grace.

"Grace? What are you doing here?" For a moment, Grace thought he was about to embrace her, but at the last second, he dropped his hands to his sides. "Did Mary call you?"

"No, I -" Grace began but Mary cut her off.

"Isla collapsed in the street and Grace helped me bring her here. She's been wonderful. I don't know what I would have done without her."

"What happened? Where's Isla?" he asked of the silent doctor.

"She's being well taken care of," Dr Bateman replied. "If I might talk to you privately, Mr Jardine." He drew Andrew to one side where the two men conducted an intense, low conversation.

"What are they saying?" Mary asked.

"I cannot hear them. Whatever it is, they don't think we deserve to be included in the discussion. Mary? Has Isla been at school this week?"

"No, as I said, she had a slight sore throat, so I kept her at home." Mary stared up at her from red rimmed eyes.

"For how long?"

"Two days maybe. Why?"

"Oh, nothing. I wondered how long she's been unwell." Grace knew the disease to be highly contagious and perhaps Isla's school friends were also at risk. The incubation period before symptoms showed was about four or five days. Hopefully she might no longer be infectious.

"What is this antitoxin the doctor mentioned?" Mary asked in a whisper.

"It's a medicine, but as far as I know it's quite new and has only been in use a few years."

"What kind of medicine?" Mary sat rigid, small lines of tension on her forehead.

"I read about it in a magazine on the ship coming over." The article had fascinated her at the time and she searched her memory for details. "As I understand it, diseases like diphtheria are being injected into horses. This stimulates an immune response in the white blood cells producing an antitoxin to fight the infection."

"They give diphtheria to horses?" Mary's eyes widened.

"Only in small enough doses so as not to harm them. They harvest the antitoxin that forms in their blood and inject it into people who have the disease. It helps the body fight the infection."

"I don't understand any of what you just said." Mary dragged a handkerchief from a pocket in her skirt and blew her nose noisily. "Will it make Isla better?"

"It might, if given in time and in the right dose."

"And if it doesn't?"

Grace sighed. "I'm sorry, Mary I don't know exactly how it works. I'm not a doctor." She looked up to see Andrew approach them, his face grim.

"What's happening, Andrew?" Mary pleaded.

"Bateman is going to consult with a colleague to obtain another opinion. I don't think he should intubate Isla unless it's absolutely necessary."

Grace released a relieved breath, but said nothing, aware she was hardly qualified to give any opinion. Whatever they chose as a treatment for Isla was entirely his and Mary's decision.

"What about this antitoxin Grace told me about?" Mary asked.

He shot a wary look at Grace. "That isn't an option. Four years ago, in St Louis, Missouri, ten out of eleven children died from contaminated diphtheria antitoxin."

"That was an isolated incident," Grace interjected, unable to help herself. "The article I read said the antitoxin was contaminated because the horse from which the toxin was derived had tetanus."

"What's to say there aren't other, similar incidences?" He pinched the bridge of his nose as if in thought. "No," he said after a few long seconds. "It's too experimental. I don't think we can take the risk."

"Mary? What do you say?" Grace asked.

"What if we make the wrong decision which harms her?" Mary shook her head hard, sending her hair into disarray. "No, I can't. Andrew must decide."

"If you do nothing, both of you will harm her," Grace whispered, reminding herself yet again that this wasn't her daughter. If she persuaded them against their instincts, Isla might still die and would either of them be able to forgive her?

While they were debating, Dr Bateman returned. "My colleague has no more experience of the antitoxin than I. Our opinions as to its effectiveness are in conflict. I'm afraid the decision is yours."

"Where would we get this antitoxin?" Andrew asked.

"We have some serum on hand in our pharmacy. I'm sure you are aware we have several cases of this disease every year. Children are especially susceptible."

"Andrew, what shall we do?" Mary asked. "Should we let them use it on Isla?"

His eyes reflected his worry, but Grace could see he had yet to make a decision.

"I would urge you to hurry, Mr Jardine," Dr Bateman said. "Whichever form it takes, Isla needs treatment."

"What do you think, Grace?" Andrew asked.

She met his steady gaze, her mouth working but no words came for a moment. "I-I can't decide for you. My only experience of this situation was one where intubation was traumatic for the patient and did not help at all. In fact, it made things worse. The antitoxin might not work, but it gives her a chance. I would think a chance, no matter how small, is worth taking." He was about to speak but she cut across him. "But she isn't my child. Don't take my word unless you are certain you are prepared to accept whatever the consequences are."

"I understand." Andrew eased onto the bench. "Mary?" he said, his voice soft. "Do you want them to give her the antitoxin?"

"I don't know what to do for the best." Mary's voice hitched. "All I want is for Isla to be home and healthy again."

Andrew sighed, his gaze lifting to the doctor's face. "Give her the antitoxin."

Dr Bateman nodded, and without a word hurried back down the hallway.

"Suppose she dies?" Mary expressed Grace's own thought.

"Then everyone concerned will have done all they could." Andrew's gaze met Grace's over Mary's bent head, in their blue depths a heartfelt plea mixed with hope and something else. Acceptance? Forgiveness? Whatever it was she couldn't look away while Mary sobbed quietly on Andrew's shoulder.

Chapter 21

His hands in his pockets, Andrew paced the floor, pausing occasionally to scuff at a loose tile with his shoe like an impatient schoolboy.

Mary huddled on the bench, her hand clasped firmly in Grace's, from which she appeared to take some comfort.

No one spoke, the tense silence broken only by the relentless tick of the clock on the wall. Grey garbed nuns glided through the hall at intervals, each one treated to an anticipatory glance, only for them to disappear again without a word.

Just when Grace felt they could not stand much more, the now familiar click of Dr Bateman's shoes on the tiled floor heralded his appearance long before he reached them.

Grace studied his approach, but his leisurely stride and bland expression betrayed nothing of what was going on in his head.

"We've given Isla the antitoxin," he said, halting in front Andrew. "Although the outcome is by no means certain, she's doesn't appear to be getting any worse."

"But will she recover?" Andrew asked.

"It's too soon to tell, I'm afraid. We shall have to wait and see."

A nun gently called the doctor's name. He raised his hands in a gesture of apology before hurrying back the way he came.

"How can he not tell?" Mary clenched her fists in her lap. "He's the doctor."

"Mary, you're exhausted." Andrew rubbed the back of her neck. "The carriage is still outside. Why don't you go home and get some sleep?"

"I want to be here for Isla, but I'm so tired."

"Perhaps there's somewhere here she could lie down for a while?" Grace suggested.

"I'll ask the staff." Andrew rose and approached the desk where he conducted a brief conversation with a gentle faced nun.

"Would you stay, Grace?" Mary pleaded. She looked to where Andrew approached them and lowered her voice adding, "Andrew doesn't handle this kind of thing very well. He hates to feel useless."

"Of course, I'll stay if that's what you want."

"Please, I would welcome it too," he added, joining them. "And Mary, the sister says there's a room down the hall you could use."

"That's kind of them." Mary dragged herself to her feet and smoothed down her crumpled dress. "If you hear anything, you must wake me."

"I promise." Andrew encircled her tenderly with his arm and escorted her along the corridor after the nun.

When he returned, he took a seat further along the bench, leaving the space where Mary sat to gape between them like a chasm.

Grace clasped her hands in her lap and sent wishes for Isla's recovery to whatever deity looked down sympathetically on sick children, while sneaking swift looks at Andrew. He sat with his eyes closed and his head tilted back against the wall. He'd loosened his collar, revealing an expanse of throat, his lips moving silently in either a prayer or a curse, she could not tell.

The silence expanded, making her feel they were in a church rather than a hospital, accentuated by the soft footfalls of the nuns in their grey habits and white wimples.

"I forgot to thank you for being so kind to Mary." Andrew broke the silence, his head turned away from her.

"I just happened to be there. I couldn't leave them."

"Even so." He pushed away from the wall and twisted to face her. "It's kind of you to keep vigil like this. You barely know Mary, or Isla."

"Who wouldn't feel compassion for a child in peril?" She glanced at the clock. "I should have been at the hotel ages ago." She twisted the straps of her bag in her fingers. "Do you suppose the nuns would let me telephone them to explain?"

"Of course. I'll arrange it." As if glad of something to do, he strode to the desk and made the request.

The nun called Sister Conceptua showed Grace to a wall mounted telephone, where after a wait for the exchange to put her through to the Grace and Favor, she explained to Aoife what had happened. 'You stay as long as you have to," Aoife's voice crackled down the line.

"Everything all right?" Andrew asked when she returned.

"Aoife is confident they can manage without me for a night, and she says everyone sends their best wishes to Isla."

"That's kind of them." He eased forward, his forearms resting on his splayed knees. "This is awkward, isn't it?" He skewed his gaze sideways at her.

"A little. Perhaps it might help to talk about something to distract us. It will help make the time go faster."

"You could be right." He pushed himself upright. "What do you suggest?"

"Why don't you tell me about yourself?" she said gently. "We discussed so many things on the SS Elizabeth, including my reasons for leaving London. But I know nothing about your life or family. What were your parents like?"

"My father had a tougher upbringing than I did. Days when there wasn't enough food or warmth, which meant he dragged himself up by his bootstraps. When he reached a level of society he felt was more acceptable than the one he came from, he married a woman who already belonged to it to secure his right to be there."

"You didn't get along with your father?"

"That obvious, eh?" he chuckled. "He was one of those men who thought a son should be strong, unsentimental and ruthless. Like him. He bred silver foxes when I was a boy which was a steady but not very lucrative business in those days. I used to play with the pups and it broke my heart when he killed them. I always felt when it came to the slaughter, he would always choose the one I liked the best."

"Didn't you like all the cubs?" Grace recalled trying to choose from a litter of kittens, unable to favor one over the others. Not that her sensibilities mattered, as McKinnon hated cats and had ordered them all destroyed.

"I suppose I did." He shrugged. "But at the time, I believed he did it on purpose. I couldn't bear to be around when it happened and would make sure I was as far away as possible. I would wander back at dusk and pretend the fox had simply run away so it wouldn't hurt as much."

"Did that help?" Grace's chest tightened with sympathy for the boy Andrew's pain.

"No." His slow smile appeared, turning her insides to water. "Then he would taunt me, say I was spineless and didn't understand the way of the world. That I should toughen up and be a man."

"Is the ability to kill beautiful animals without feeling anything the mark of a man?"

"In his mind, yes. I could never do it. Have you ever seen a silver fox?" He braced a hand on his thigh and turned towards her.

Grace shook her head.

"Beautiful creatures and if you gain their trust, they are almost tame. Almost but not quite. Some are completely black except for a splash of white on the tail, some are bluish-grey with coppery lights, their pelts are thick and unusually silky to the touch, bred to remove all traces of brown. They're a lot like dogs in some ways, in that they respond to affection and have unique characters. The vixens are good mothers and if they lose a cub will become distressed until they are reunited. My father disregards all that and sees them as a commodity. He thinks me weak to attribute them with feelings."

"Does he still feel that way now you are grown up?"

"He does, and is now justified as silver fox pelts are bringing in good money, more than he ever dreamed of."

"What about your mother? Does she feel the same way?"

"Mama was sentimental, like me, but she would never go against Father's wishes." Grace registered the past tense with a pang, but felt it inappropriate to offer condolences when she didn't know when it happened. "She didn't like to anger him and hid her own feelings. She died trying not to bother him and slipped away before he noticed."

"Is that why you chose shipping as a career instead of the family business?"

He nodded. "Ever since I was a boy I've always loved the sea and became fascinated with boats and ships of all kinds. I spent hours at the harbour watching them come in, using the money I earned from chores travelling back and forth on the ferry all day. The skippers knew me by name. When I left university in Halifax, I used an inheritance from my mother to buy a share in my first steamship. I'm now a partner in a few cargo vessels and I even own two leisure craft outright. It hasn't always been easy, especially when you take into account the Texas hurricane."

"I've come across two people since I arrived here, both of whom lost relatives in that storm."

"That doesn't surprise me." He nodded slowly. "One of my ferries was damaged beyond repair, which proved to me that nothing is certain in this life." He released a long sigh and massaged his forehead with one hand before glancing up at the clock. "Goodness it's two in the morning. I cannot believe we've been here so long."

Faint stubble had appeared on his chin since he first arrived, his usually immaculate hair in disarray from his hand repeatedly being pushed through it, the streak of silver loose and curled onto his forehead. His slightly dishevelled appearance stripped the years away, making him almost boyish, though she still didn't know his age. Mid to late thirties maybe? Older?

"What about you?" His smile was warm and intense. "I cannot see you being like my mother, suppressing your dreams and intelligence beneath a veil of meek domesticity."

"I did to some extent. It would have been harder still had I not been able to see through that veil to what beckoned me. It was what I held onto but made me more discontented as well. I've found it though, in the Grace and Favor."

"You had to come to the other side of the world to do it."

"I didn't have to. I chose to. That way I didn't have to keep looking over my shoulder. I only regret one thing."

"Which is?"

"That I will never see the look on Angus MacKinnon's face when he learned I was finally out of his reach."

He laughed, the joyful, uninhibited laugh which knotted her insides.

Grace stared at her lap, giving herself time to formulate her next words. 'Strangely, I don't mind talking about the MacKinnons with you. The only other person I feel so comfortable with is Aoife."

"You feel at ease with me?"

"I do, yes. Which surprises me. We don't know each other very well."

"Thank you, because you, Mrs McKinnon, make me as nervous as a sixteen-year-old."

"Why? I'm not as complicated as you imagine."

"You're still something of an enigma. Since our first meeting on the SS Parisian, you've occupied a good deal of my thoughts." He braced his shoulders against the wall and eased his neck, oblivious of the effect his words had on her.

She fidgeted in her seat, telling herself he couldn't have meant what he said in the same way she heard it. He was simply being kind. She had not seen him at all during the week's voyage from Liverpool. But then that wasn't surprising since he travelled in First Class and she spent most of her time with Aoife in steerage.

"So tell me what the story is with Emily," she began, mainly to hide the flush she could feel creeping up her neck. "Are you one of her former beau's?"

"Good God, no!" Jardine straightened, turning shocked eyes on her. "Whatever gave you that idea?"

She shrugged. "Women's instinct, perhaps?"

"Emily is an opportunist," he said. "Though I'm, reluctant to tell stories about a woman. It smacks of ungentlemanly behavior."

"I'll not tell a soul. Though I'm someone who likes to know her enemies. If you have any weapons in your arsenal, I might be able to use, I would appreciate it."

"You really are full of surprises aren't you, Grace?" He chuckled, his gaze roving her face. "All right, because she does seem unsettled by your very presence. Emily came to the Island on a vacation four years ago as a lady's companion to the middle-aged wife of a New York Banker."

"Really?" Grace's eyes widened. A Companion. No wonder Emily had wanted to reduce her to the status of a governess. "Do go on."

"On meeting John, she discovered how wealthy he was and when the couple returned to New York, she stayed behind. She gave John Cahill a sob story about being abandoned and having no money, but when I made enquiries, the banker informed me Emily left them without notice and the wife, whose health was delicate, was distraught at losing her. There were also a few personal items missing from the mistresses' luggage which Emily claimed to know nothing about."

"Did you tell John Cahill that, or did you allow him to be deceived into being her rescuer?"

"I wrestled with the dilemma for a while but decided to tell him. He wasn't at all shocked, nor even surprised. As I said before. He knows what he's got with Emily. A few weeks later, he married her."

"You disapprove?"

"Not exactly. He grimaced, as if the question was still under debate. "As long as John wasn't under any illusions, it's entirely his own business. My main problem is John is a dear and close friend, which means I'm often forced to spend time in Emily's company being fawned over. I hate it, but John treats it like entertainment. Mary avoids her at every opportunity too as the woman is so false." His laugh turned into a wide yawn and he eased his back against the seat. "I suppose they both made compromises, which if they make them happy, who am I to criticize?"

"You could say that's true of us all," Grace mused, recalling her own circumstances. "You look tired," she said, more relieved by what he had said about Emily than she should be.

"I am, but then so must you be? You're a working woman these days, not a lady of leisure."

"I'm all right." She belied this statement with a yawn. "I'm not even hungry, although I haven't eaten since luncheon. I'm too worried about Isla." The reason they were there came back to her with force. "They would come and tell us as soon as they know anything. Wouldn't they?"

"I do hope so, Grace." His hand slid across the bench where her hand lay. He laced his fingers with hers and gripped her hand.

Grace dared not look at him, hoping to prolong the moment. If she met his gaze now, he might realize what he was doing and

337

embarrassment would make him move away. At the same time her chest hurt with a truth she could not avoid. She loved this man, but he was lost to her. And worse, if Isla died, the pain would separate them forever.

The hours ticked by, during which the muscles in Grace's back cramped from sitting in the same position. Sister Conceptua brought them tea and toast at around six in the morning, which was received gratefully. The nun returned to collect their dirty plates just as a door at the far end of the hall opened and Dr Bateman emerged.

"Mr Jardine!" He strode briskly along the corridor towards them. His face grim.

"Oh no, please no," Grace muttered under her breath, both hands gripped on the edge of the wooden bench on either side of her knees, aware of a vast empty space beside her as Andrew left his seat.

She couldn't hear what they were saying, but the doctor's face was unreadable, his voice low and rapid. Andrew listened in silence, nodding now and then, his gaze on the floor.

With a final nod he gave the doctor's hand a firm shake. The doctor inclined his head, turned and strode away.

Andrew walked back slowly to where she sat - too slowly.

She squeezed her eyes shut, only aware that he bent over her when she felt his warm breath on her forehead.

Raising her head, she looked into his eyes, mere inches from hers.

"Her fever has broken, Grace," he whispered, his voice thick with emotion. "She's going to be all right."

She exhaled a held breath and slouched forward, the tension draining from her tight muscles as she let the tears come.

He lowered himself onto the bench, his arms closing around her shoulders and pulled her sideways into his embrace, his weight pressed against her side as she sobbed gently.

She covered her face with both hands and whispered through her fingers. "I look terrible when I cry."

"You could never look terrible. Distress makes you vulnerable, but so lovely."

She swallowed a sob as fat tears squeezed between her eyelids and onto her skirt, leaving dark droplets on the pale fabric. "I could have been wrong about the serum. Then you might have lost her."

"We can only be thankful for that and ignore the rest. There's nothing to be gained by 'what if's,' Grace. You were right, the serum was her only real chance; I see that now. Without it she would certainly have died. I would never have blamed you for the outcome."

She didn't quite believe him. In his place, would she have been quite so magnanimous if things had turned out differently? Would anyone?

"We must tell Mary." Embarrassed, Grace pushed him away and swiped tears from her cheeks. As if on cue, Mary appeared from around the corner at a run. She looked refreshed after her rest, but her hair was awry and her gown a mass of creases. Grace realized for the first time what a crumpled, messy figure she must look, having huddled on the bench all night.

"Have you heard anything? How is she?" Mary grasped Andrew's shoulders as he rose to greet her, staring into his eyes with such pleading, Grace had to look away while he explained.

"It's good news. The antitoxin seems to have reduced the swelling. Isla's throat is no longer so badly constricted."

"Then she'll be all right?" Mary asked, her eyes welling with tears.

"She has a way to go before they can call it a full recovery, but the doctor is pretty confident."

"Oh, thank the Lord." Mary buried her face in Andrew's shoulder, the lapels of his jacket gripped in her hands. "I've had the most terrible thoughts since last night. I was convinced we would lose her."

Andrew stroked her back, whispering in her ear words Grace couldn't make out, but could imagine. Mary straightened, visibly recovering herself. She released her death grip on Andrew's jacket and took a step back. "Can we see her?" Her voice was strong and in command again.

"Dr Bateman said it would be all right for a few minutes. Though she isn't awake."

"I don't care. I just want to see her."

Andrew slid his arm around Mary's waist and led her toward the door Dr Bateman had disappeared through.

Forgotten, Grace turned away and slipped quietly through the main doors into a street waking up to a summer morning.

A tang of salt filled the air and seagulls called from the harbour a block away, while smaller birds chirruped in the trees lining the street as she strode back to Prince Street. Her eyes blurred with her own tears which she blinked back, thrilled that Isla would be well again, though a deeper sadness broke through her smile as she walked, causing a tightness in her chest. By the time she reached the hotel, she had decided to take up Maud's invitation to visit her in Cavendish.

A change of scenery was exactly what she needed.

Chapter 22

The MacNeill Farmhouse, Cavendish Village, Queens County

The buggy Grace hired to take her the ten miles from the station at Hunter River to Cavendish Village swayed precariously with each bump, the wheels juddering over deep dips in the soft earth.

"This red clay is easy to cut roads in but tough to travel on, Miss," her driver declared cheerfully as the cart canted alarmingly to one side, sending clouds of red dust over her skirt from her knees down to her boots.

Despite the uncomfortable ride, the scenery was spectacular, with miles of verdant fields bordered by lush woods, the verges bursting with wildflowers while birds wheeled and dived overhead beneath a clear sky.

"The McNeill farmhouse, Miss." The driver nodded at a lone clapboard building behind a picket fence in an almost deserted road. A plain, utilitarian building which doubled as the Cavendish Post Office, it fitted with Maud's description of her stern grandparents, its stark rooflines softened by the summer foliage of the nearby trees.

After assisting her to the ground, the driver circled the cart and retrieved her bag from the flatbed, setting it down on the road before leaping back onto the seat. With a final backward wave, he turned the cart full circle in the road and headed back the way he came. Grace watched him disappear in a cloud of dust, hoping he would remember to return and take her back to the station on the following day.

She paused at the gate, both hands braced in the small of her back to ease her sore muscles just as the door of the house opened and Maud approached at a run.

"You're here at last!" She encircled Grace with both arms, threatening to throw her off balance. "I've been waiting all morning for you to arrive. Was it a truly horrible journey?"

"Not really," Grace lied, summoning a smile. "Only the last part, but more than worth it to see you." The prospect of enduring it all again tomorrow loomed but she pushed it away. "I was sure we would get lost as there were so few road signs, but the driver found his way by using schoolhouses as markers."

"That's because there are over four hundred of them so you are rarely far from one." Maud tucked one arm through hers, hefted Grace's bag into her other hand and led her through the main post office. The room held a desk on which a scale sat to weigh letters. Behind it hung a bank of wooden pigeonholes into which the mail was sorted. They were all empty now as the thoughts and news of the writers had been distributed to be pored over with their breakfast oats and tea.

"Come into the kitchen. It's cosy in there and we can sit and eat while we share our news. Not that I have much news."

"Is there anything I can do to help?" Grace asked, removing her hat, which Maud took from her and placed on a hook by the door.

"I wouldn't dream of it, you are my guest. Besides, it's all prepared." She flitted about the room as she talked, collecting cups and plates from the wooden dresser which she arranged on the neat table.

Maud had taken some trouble with luncheon; prettily dressed dishes of cold meats, sliced tomatoes, cheeses, and freshly baked bread had been put together with much thought and were perfect for such a hot day.

"I'll take a plate in to Grandmother when we've eaten," she said in response to Grace's question about the health of her maternal grandparent. "She finds this weather tiring. And to be honest, I've looked forward to your coming so much, I don't intend to share you."

Leaving her to it, Grace wandered to the writing table, the surface empty except for a pristine notebook and pencil.

Attached to the wall above the desk was a photograph of a girl, her soft features in profile, and a flower pinned above her ear. "Who is this?" Grace traced the girl's face with a finger. "Is she someone you know?"

"In a manner of speaking." Maud came to stand beside her, wiping her hands on a cloth. "She's an actress called Evelyn Nesbit. I cut that picture from an American magazine. I'm using her as my muse for Anne."

"Anne who?" Grace frowned, then memory returned, and she gasped. "Oh, Maud, you're writing your novel?"

"I am, and since the McNeill's and Campbell's have left me to my own devices this summer, I cannot tell you how glad I am to be set free to write, stroll to all my favorite places and dream. Anne has become quite the chatterbox. I can barely get all her thoughts down before they dance away again on the wind. On other days she's infuriatingly silent, then she will wake me in the middle of the night and I have to light a candle and scribble it all down on paper before it flies right out of my head."

"Tell me how you see her."

"She's an orphan, brought up in an orphanage in Newfoundland, or maybe New Brunswick, I haven't decided." Maud dragged out a chair and perched on the edge, the cloth draped across her lap "A child who is homely looking apart from the rich color of her hair, which is like fall leaves. Her head is full of contradictory and yet profound thoughts which will enchant or infuriate everyone around her. She has a unique ability to make people see everyday things differently, her unhappy past concealed beneath a veil of optimism."

"I would love to read it." At Maud's start, she added, "Not until you've finished it, naturally."

"That's the problem. I never quite know when it's truly finished."

"When you're a published author, I shall be the first to buy a copy and ask you to sign the flyleaf for me."

"You are more optimistic than I, Grace." Maud sighed. "Sometimes I feel Anne's story will never be shared with anyone."

"Have more faith in yourself. You've already achieved some success. This book might be the next step."

"I hope so." Maud discarded the cloth with a smile. "Even as a child I felt that no matter what my obstacles were, I had a capacity for success. As an orphan yourself, you must have felt the same on occasion, Grace?" She posed the question without false sympathy and a genuine interest in the answer.

"Sometimes. I had Frederick of course, but he was at school. There were the holidays to look forward to, but I was never allowed to invite school friends back to the house, so they drifted away."

"I had my cousins, which was nice, some of the time." Maud sighed. "But whenever a squabble broke out or something got broken, I was always to blame."

"Always?"

"It felt like that." She shrugged. "They tried to be kind, but I would see them shake their heads when they thought I wasn't looking. Not having a mother to defend me against spite or malice made me vulnerable. I went to work in Halifax for a year as an editor on a newspaper, but when I came home, Uncle John said I hadn't changed much in a manner which hinted he was disappointed because I had not."

"Why did you not stay there if you were working? Didn't you like it?"

"Oh no, I loved it. But Grandfather died so I had to come home and take care of Grandmother."

"Couldn't your Uncle John do that?"

"No. He had the farm to look after. There was only me."

"I think you made a great sacrifice, Maud. I hope they appreciated it."

Maud shrugged.

"I do sympathize. The MacKinnons decided I must be quite wicked; as if the carriage that killed my parents removed any good qualities I might have. I remember when I first went to live with them in Hampstead. I was twelve and it was deepest winter. I woke one morning to a blanket of snow carpeting the garden. I was so excited, I rushed downstairs and burst into the sitting room to tell them, only to find my guardian entertaining the vicar and his wife. They had arrived early to inform him of the death of an ancient aunt of his. Three sombre faces like walnuts turned toward me in absolute horror. MacKinnon was furious, the fact that I was in my nightgown was considered especially heinous. I was given ten bible verses a day to memorise for a whole week."

"Only ten?" Maud laughed. "You got off lightly."

"It didn't feel like it at the time."

"I think those who are loved by many people don't feel slights and insults the same way we do. Their words linger in our heads like fish hooks, always able to hurt."

"That's true," Grace gave this some thought. "I brood on the slightest rejection, even when it isn't cruelly meant." The hurt she felt when Andrew ignored her at the Queen Hotel returned with all the desolation she experienced then.

Maud sighed. "We appear to have begun a competition to see whose childhood was the most miserable. The worst of it is, we're enjoying it."

"Then we must vow to talk only of happy things from now on." Grace joined Maud's delightful laugh, relaxing properly for the first time since she left the hospital the day before.

"The moment I summon one happy thing, I shall do exactly that." Maud ushered her to the table and settled her in a chair. "Let's eat, and then afterwards, we'll take our walk."

* * *

The path through the dune wasn't wide enough for them to walk side by side, so Grace followed behind Maud. The grass on either side grew so high she had only to reach out her hand to run her fingers through it, the fronds soft against her skin.

"Did you know this lane was called a portage?" Maud turned her head to ask.

"I'm not familiar with the word." Grace waved a persistent bee away from her face.

"I was about to explain. When the Island belonged to the Mi'kmaqs they forged these walkways to carry their canoes from one body of water to another. Another one runs through the Haunted Wood. I could show it to you tomorrow. I find all the mysteries and magic here, with all its silvery sounds."

'Silvery sounds?" Grace's buttoned boots caught in a rabbit hole, forcing her to crouch down in the grass to wrench it free. "All I can hear are blackbirds and distant waves, which in their way are magic enough.' She examined the boot for scuffs but saw none.

"You have to use your soul to hear them." Maud paused a little way ahead, waiting for Grace to catch her up.

"My soul is too battered right now, my head being full of food orders, washing sheets and buying china to replace the ones Tilly has smashed." She hauled her feet up to the top of the dune where Maud stood, grinning at her.

"Why are you laughing, I - Oh!"

Spread below them was an expanse of pristine sand of an unusual pink color, beyond it the deep blue-green sea, the surface glittering with thousands of tiny points of light beneath a crisp azure sky. The wind flowed over her in a warm caress, rippled through the tussocks of grass that clung to the dune and puffed up the sand in between.

"Lovely, isn't it?" Maud sighed. "Sometimes I feel as if I am the only person in in the world when I am up here. At sunset, the cliffs turn a deep, glowing red. It's an almost spiritual place which makes me think God must have made it entirely for his own pleasure."

"Then it's a shame He spoiled it by putting mankind on it." Grace brushed sand from her skirt, smiling at Maud's shocked expression.

"I'm joking, take no notice of me, the journey here must have tired me more than I realized. And you're right, this must be one of the most beautiful places on earth.'

"You're a long way from home, Grace. I always get homesick when I'm away. Don't you?"

"Never." Grace shook her head, wrapped her skirt around her knees and sat on the sandy grass, her face lifted to the sun. "In England, I would have become a drudge without gratitude or thanks."

"Like me?" A shadow crossed Maud's delicate features as she joined her, her legs stretched out beneath her skirt.

"I didn't mean it like that." Grace's heart sank. "I'm sure your family love and appreciate you."

"They need me, which is a different thing entirely. How did you find the courage to escape, Grace?"

"Through an act of compassion. My husband, Frederick, hid a letter where only I would find it."

"A letter declaring his love?"

Grace snorted a laugh. "Our marriage wasn't that kind. No, it was addressed to me from a solicitor with details of my inheritance which my guardian kept from me."

"Why didn't he give it to you so both of you could have benefitted?"

"I'm not sure. Maybe because he was already ill. It doesn't matter now, but I shall be forever grateful to him."

"You're so fortunate, because without money, it's impossible for women to forge their own lives. Men, even impoverished ones, assume the right to tell us what to do. You were given the chance to carve your own path, Grace. That course isn't open to me."

"I had to be widowed first. And forgive me if I wish ill of your relatives, but your grandmother won't live forever."

"True. But can one ever forget the dark years? Don't they color everything you do?"

"I have to forget, in order to forgive, or the injustice will always have the power to hurt me."

"I so envy your ability to cast off the bad things. Did you ever lose faith that life would improve?"

351

"Many times. And don't envy me, Maud. You may as well envy the wind. It moves wherever it wills and will either carry you to adventure or leave you behind."

"Envy the wind," Maud whispered. "I could use that phrase. Do you mind?"

"Of course not." Grace smiled, she could almost see Maud turning the words over in her head. "Words don't belong to anyone."

"Have you managed to read Elizabeth and her German Garden?"

"I have, and now I know why you wanted me to read it. Because Elizabeth wants to be her own person, as we do."

Maud delved into her bag from which she withdrew the white cloth covered book identical to Grace's own copy, but hers was more dog-eared, with tiny slips of paper inserted into the pages at intervals. "I like the part where she refers to a woman's tongue as a deadly weapon, and the most difficult thing in the world to keep in order?"

"I can imagine her saying something outrageous to one of those callers she finds so unwelcome, then remembers it with embarrassment long after the guest has left."

"That has happened to me on occasion. I've had to learn not to say the first thing which comes into my head. Anne, however, suffers no such inhibition."

"Elizabeth also refers to her husband as 'The Man of Wrath'," Grace said. "Do you suppose that's the author's real husband or her imagined one?"

"Oh, her real one, most definitely. She's too strident on the subject to have conjured him in her imagination." Maud closed the book and placed it on the grass beside her. She folded her arms over her bent knees and fixed Grace with a penetrating stare. "I've waited all afternoon for you to tell me what is troubling you. Now I have no option but to ask you outright."

"What makes you think anything is wrong?" The breeze shook strands of hair from Grace's bun and swept them across her face. Impatient, she brushed them back.

"Because like me, you hide your misery beneath sarcasm and denials but it's clear something has made you unhappy."

"Talking about it will make it real, and I'm not ready to face the hopelessness of truth." Grace rested her cheek on her knees, her gaze following the gentle lapping of waves on the sand; not a soul in sight but the two of them.

Maud waited, her dark eyes soft with understanding. "It's a man isn't it?"

"Oh yes, it's a man." Grace sighed. "All right, I'll tell you. His name is Andrew Jardine."

As the setting sun turned the horizon to a blaze of orange, crimson and yellow, Grace talked about the first time she had seen Andrew Jardine on the SS Parisian. She went on to describe every moment she spent in his company up to and including the night at the hospital when they were unified in their fears for Isla.

"I've tried to stop thinking about him, but I know how useless it is. Yet, I also feel that should I give him the slightest encouragement, he would tell me he felt the same way. I see it in his eyes each time I look at him. Every touch of his hand, and the way he becomes awkward in my company."

"You don't think your own desires are exaggerating his reactions?"

"I've told myself the same thing, but there's something there, Maud, I know it. He fights it as hard as I do. But nothing can come of it. Of us. There's Mary and Isla which makes things so much worse as I like them both. Isla is the most delightful child and Mary a gentle, charming young woman with no pride or pretensions." Maud's raised eyebrow made Grace laugh. "I know. I have my own and maybe a few pretensions. But she's so lovely, Maud. What kind of woman would I be if I came between them?"

"A dreadful one, whom I couldn't possibly regard as my friend for another moment." Her expression belied her words. "Though I know you, Grace, you're fundamentally too good a person to act dishonorably."

"Is that what I am? Honorable? What a sombre word. But it's so tempting at times to forget everything else and be close to him." And it could be so easy. Too easy.

Maud rolled onto her back, a hand braced behind her neck. "On the whole, I've found men to be something of a disappointment. They're either too arrogant or childish, or so manly, that they appear cold. I was engaged once, to a clergyman."

"Really?" Grace propped herself up on one elbow. "Why have you not mentioned him before?"

"There was never an occasion to. His name was Edwin Simpson. I had such high hopes of him, but he did not stir my heart. Then I met Herman, who gave me an insight into what real love between a man and a woman could be. You could say he spoiled me for Edwin."

"You've not mentioned Herman to me either."

"Have I not? Ah well, he's dead now so it's not relevant."

"Oh, I'm so sorry. I had no idea."

"I met him during the year I taught school at Lower Bedeque. I boarded with the Leard family across the road from the school house. Being with him was a wonderful interlude, but we had little to sustain us for a lifetime. When we are young, we treat everything lightly, assuming better things await us farther on. Then nothing does come along, and the chance has already slipped away."

A comfortable silence stretched as each of them were occupied with their own thoughts, broken only by the gentle swish of waves on the sand. Grace's thoughts turned to Frederick, as

355

they often did these days. Would their marriage have grown? Or would their affection have withered to resentment and finally contempt as the years passed?

Maud rolled over onto her stomach and propped her chin in her hands. "Would you accompany me to Sunday service tomorrow, Grace? I want you to meet someone."

"Really? Who?"

"A young man who preaches at our church. I should like your opinion of him."

"If he's your friend, why would my opinion matter?"

"Perhaps it doesn't, but I would still like to show him off."

"I warn you that I, too, was raised Presbyterian. I find clerics sanctimonious and judgemental while claiming to preach forgiveness. They twist everyone's motives into a penchant for evil, then claim they are purely altruistic when the opposite is true."

"I'm sure you'll change your mind when you meet him. And your opinion means a lot to me."

"Then of course I shall. Is he the same reverend you told me about when we first met? The one who believes we are all destined before birth to be saved or lost, no matter what kind of lives we lead?" Grace didn't like to point out that she regarded this particular Calvinist doctrine represented the dark side of Presbyterianism.

"It is. He says to aim for perfection is to invite failure, because our lives are not truly our own."

"And what do you think?" Grace wasn't sure she would like this man but would reserve judgement for Maud's sake.

"That there is no Hell, Grace. At least not one that has not been invented by men's evil hearts."

"Perhaps you aren't the only one to think that? Have you voiced your belief to other members of the congregation?"

"Certainly not." Maud gaped at her, genuinely shocked. "Like most of what is in my head, this must be hidden from the good people of Cavendish. To criticize church doctrine is - unthinkable."

"You do make me laugh, Maud. But I relish the idea that our thoughts are so aligned. Are we doomed, do you think?"

"Only if you think men know everything. And I do not," Maud said.

"Even your young reverend?"

"I do believe you're trying to vex me, Grace." Maud lifted her chin, but only pretended to be affronted as her lips twitched.

"Is he handsome?" Grace asked, changing the subject.

"He is, yes, and yet I've found the more interesting men tend to possess homely looks. Isn't it a pity we can't have two husbands? One to look at and one to talk to."

"Husband?" Grace stared at her.

357

Maud flushed and looked away. "Oh dear. I wasn't supposed to reveal that, which proves one's dearest wishes always find a way to express themselves. Don't look at me like that, Grace. You must have had some idea."

"How could I? You've never mentioned a beau in your letters."

"Beau's aren't for old maids like me. Have you forgotten I'm thirty-one?"

"Hardly reason enough to pledge your life to a man. Are you in love with him?"

"I'm not sure what love is." Maud stared off towards the horizon, her brow furrowed beneath her hat. "With the beaus of my youth there was always something missing; either they kept their true hearts from me, or I from them. I admire Ewan. He's handsome and respectable."

"Is a country minister your last, best hope for marriage?" Grace found the very idea of the man depressing, but perhaps he had some redeeming qualities.

"Why not? My life hasn't turned out the way I hoped. If it weren't for my imagination it would be pure agony."

"Few people achieve the life they dream of, Maud, but agony?"

"Perhaps I exaggerate." She shrugged. "But then I often do. Like my Anne. I live inside my head most of the time. Don't look so worried for me." She nudged Grace playfully. "I'm not sad all the time." She smiled, but the truth lay in her eyes. "I have days of complete perfection when my writing goes well, or I sell one of my stories.

Anne is my other half; introspective but unfailingly optimistic. Life has given her so little, she believes things can only get better. She weaves scenarios around simple events with a happy ending for all. She can even see magic in tragedy."

"She sounds destined to be misunderstood and doomed to disappointment."

"Not at all. She simply sees the possibilities in every situation."

"As I said. Doomed to disappointment."

"I didn't take you for a pessimist, Grace."

"I prefer pragmatic." She recalled having said much the same thing to Mr Jardine and he had been equally sceptical. "That way, life doesn't hit me so hard and I can take pleasure from small things."

"I prefer Anne's philosophy, to see a thing of beauty in a wildflower, not a weed to be crushed underfoot."

"What about your young man?" Grace asked. "Is he a wildflower or a weed?"

"A little of both, I think." Maud plucked a blade of grass and inserted it between her teeth. "You're younger than I am, Grace. When you too are past thirty, you will realize compromises need to be made about everything."

"Marriage might not be what you imagine. Not all marriages are happy. Living contentedly within one is not always easy."

"If I try hard enough I can achieve whatever I want."

"That sounds like Anne talking, not you. And incidentally, what is this paragon's name?"

"He's the Reverend Ewan Macdonald."

Chapter 23

The church service with all its familiar hymns, prayers and responses was reminiscent of those Grace sat through in the past. The only difference were her surroundings; a wooden building with light flooding through the end window as opposed to the chill of a stone church. Alone in the front pew, she exchanged frequent conspiratorial looks with Maud who was seated at the church organ.

During an hour-long sermon which Angus MacKinnon would have approved of, Grace studied the Reverend Ewan Macdonald so closely, anyone watching her would have thought she was hanging on his every word. In truth, she was trying to fathom what it was about the man to whom Maud as willing to pledge the rest of her life.

He was handsome enough in an unremarkable way with wide cheekbones, a square jaw and what a writer might describe as long eyes. His upper lip was thinner than his lower one, the meaning of which Grace had read somewhere denoted a vitality for life; a quality she saw little of in the unsmiling cleric.

He spoke well, if in an overly theatrical manner to an audience, who without exception appeared entranced.

When the service ended, the congregation filed out of the little church into the sunshine where they stood around in groups. The matrons hung back to talk to the reverend while the younger women and girls stood a little way off, giggling amongst themselves while throwing him longing looks from beneath their hat brims.

"Well, Grace," Maud's voice made her jump. "What do you think of Ewan?"

"Goodness," she brought a hand to her throat. "I didn't see you there. I thought you were still inside the church."

"There you see," Maud laughed. "You were so busy staring at him you didn't notice me. You're enamoured of him already. Admit it." She looked up and gasped. "Oh, hush, Ewan is coming towards us."

He had broken away from his admiring crowd of matrons and glided towards them, an air of calm about him belied by a slight twitch at the corner of his mouth.

"Reverend Macdonald," Maud said, her voice slightly breathless. "I would like you to meet my very dear friend, Mrs MacKinnon."

"A pleasure, Mrs MacKinnon." He grasped the end of her fingers briefly in a firm, warm grip. "Have you enjoyed your short holiday in the country?"

"I have, thank you. Maud is a very entertaining companion. I see things differently when I'm with her."

"You do?" He frowned, his puzzled gaze sliding to Maud. "A unique point of view, certainly. I find Miss Montgomery possesses all the qualities of a dutiful, God-fearing young woman. She is to be admired for having devoted her youth to caring for her grandmother. She's also a pillar of the church, not to mention an exemplary organist."

"You flatter me, Reverend." Maud flushed, a delicate hand going to her throat.

"Is that all you see?" Grace said in an attempt to shake him out of his complacency. "There's a good deal more to her than that."

"Grace is being overly complimentary." Maud flushed, tucked her arm firmly through Grace's elbow and guided her away. "It's time we should be going. The buggy will be waiting at the farmhouse to take you back to Hunter River. You don't want to keep it waiting."

"Goodbye, Reverend," Grace called over her shoulder. "It was a pleasure to meet you."

"He sees me as a perfect example of womanhood," Maud whispered, although they were out of the reverend's hearing. "I don't wish to disillusion him, or he might change his mind."

"Disillusion him? About you?" Grace's steps matched Maud's, their skirts swishing as they walked along the lane, sending dandelion wings into the air. "Why, are you uncertain of his feelings?"

"I don't know. But there's no reason to plant doubt in his mind, is there?"

"If his heart is sincere, nothing I could say would alter it. I promise to mind my tongue from now on." She hugged Maud's arm into her side unwilling to cast a shadow onto a relationship that meant so much to her friend.

"You still haven't told me what you think of Ewan, Grace."

"I hardly exchanged five words with the man. But you were right, he is handsome, even if he is too serious."

"He's a minister, his life is taken up with grave matters."

"Surely even men of the church are allowed to laugh?" Grace said when they set off again. "There's no spark in him, and I'm afraid he might extinguish the one in you. Your writing needs to grow and flourish, not be subsumed by someone else's demands."

"I want to be free, which I can be as a married woman. Even at my age I'm still subject to the whims and will of others, particularly those of my male relatives. As Ewan's wife, I shall have a home of my own and if I wish to write, I shall, with no whispers and accusations of it being an unsuitable occupation. My husband will protect me from my critic's barbs."

"Either that or he'll have ones of his own to throw at you," Grace said. "What does Ewan feel about your novel?"

A starling burst from a grass verge in front of them, taking to the sky with a frantic flap of wings. Startled, Maud cried out, halting. "The subject hasn't come up," she said as they watched the bird wheel into the sky and disappear. "I shall tell him, of course. When I'm further along with the story. I'm sure he'll be supportive."

"I hope you're right." Grace conjured up Andrew Jardine's lightness of spirit and capacity for laughter, neither of which she saw in the Reverend Ewan Macdonald.

"Don't look so solemn, Grace." Maud laughed. "What other course is open to me? As you mentioned yourself, what happens when Grandmother is no longer with us? Uncle John cannot wait to take over the farmhouse, which is rightfully his according to the terms of my Grandfather's will."

Grace was horrified. "Your uncle would throw you out?"

"I doubt he would do that." The hesitation in her voice told Grace otherwise. "No doubt I shall be welcome to visit, but he wouldn't want me as a dependent."

"You could move to Charlottetown. Then you would have the freedom you crave."

"I might be able to earn a living with my writing, it's true. But I'm lonely, Grace. I want someone of my own to love."

"I sympathize." Grace hugged Maud's arm. "I love the hotel and I have Aoife, Leon and others around me. But when I retire to my room after a long day, there's no one with whom to watch the night sky through my bedroom window."

"You see. You do understand. Did you watch the night sky with your Frederick?"

"No." Grace wrinkled her nose. "He hated the stars, he said they made him feel insignificant and lost. I would watch them on my own while he snored."

"Oh, dear. That would have spoiled Ursa Minor for me forever."

"Exactly."

Later, when Maud waved her off outside the McNeill farmhouse, Grace couldn't shake away the conviction that Ewan Macdonald was too much like Angus MacKinnon to make any woman truly happy; especially a complicated, tortured soul like Maud.

* * *

That evening, Grace arrived back at the hotel, hot, tired, dirty and ready for a bath. She literally ran into Tilly in the hall, resulting in the girl's high-pitched, garbled apology that exacerbated Grace's mild headache.

"Don't worry, Tilly, it wasn't your fault. Where's Aoife?"

"Upstairs, Miss Grace, getting the new visitors settled. Shall I send her to you when she comes down?"

"No, it's all right. I'll talk to her later." Tilly rushed away, her nervousness making Grace briefly fear for the state of her crockery. She carried her bag through to the kitchen, waved to Leon who was busy preparing the evening meal and headed for her sitting room.

"Miss Grace," Leon called, his voice lacking his habitual goofy humour. "Might I have a word with you?" He wiped his hands on a towel and approached her, his brow furrowed in anxiety.

"Is something wrong, Leon?" She halted in the doorway and turned back.

"I'm afraid so, Grace. Mr Keogh called while you were away."

Grace groaned inwardly, summoning a smile. "Really? And what did the gentleman want?"

"He's no gentleman." At Grace's start he added, "Aoife told me to watch out for him, so I was prepared when he turned up."

"Quite." Relieved she did not have to uphold the facade, she nodded. "Thank you, Leon. I hope you showed him the door."

"I did, but he didn't take it well."

"What do you mean?" She removed her hat and dropped it on a chair, her stomach knotting. "I don't understand. What did he say?"

He sighed, snapped the cloth over one shoulder and braced one hand on the back of a chair. "Perhaps you should sit down."

"Leon, tell me!" Her nerves stretched to breaking point. How bad could it be?

"Jake came over early this morning to help stack the dry goods in the storeroom," Leon began. "We heard a noise out in the yard but as it was a Sunday, we weren't expecting any more deliveries. We went out to see what was going on and we found the lock on the outside cellar door broken."

"Is anything missing?" Grace asked, her pulse racing. They had never had any break-ins before. Was this the sort of thing she should expect? "Have you notified the police?"

"I thought it best not to. When we got outside, two fellows were unloading crates from a cart."

"What sort of crates?" Grace's pulse raced as a dreadful thought occurred to her.

"Twelve cases of rum."

"Didn't you try to stop them?" Grace demanded, both furious and frustrated.

"Jake did, and got a black eye for his trouble."

"Oh, no, poor Jake." She brought a hand to her mouth. "How did you know this is Keogh's doing?" Not that she doubted for a second it was anyone but him.

"Because about an hour after the cart left, he turned up. He asked if his product had arrived safely. He didn't wait for an answer, simply told me to tell you he would be back for his payment tomorrow at midnight."

"Midnight? That's a bit melodramatic. And how does he expect-?" She pushed a hand into her hair. "Have you been down into the cellar since he left?"

"I have, but you'd better take a look for yourself."

The cellar door swung silently inwards on oiled hinges as she pushed it open, her heart thumping. She clattered down the short flight of steps into a low-ceilinged room. The only light was from a window at head height which threw a rectangular shaft of evening light onto the concrete floor.

Stacked all along the back wall were twelve wooden crates, each filled with green bottles, their clumsily inserted corks leaning drunkenly askew.

"How dare he do this? Who does he think he is?" Grace cried, fighting tears. "Does Aoife know?"

"That you'd gone into bootlegging?" Aoife appeared beside Leon at the top of the steps, her arms folded across her chest. "Not until this lot arrived."

"This is no time for jokes, Aoife!" A sob rose in her throat as terror overcame her fatigue. She turned to mount the stairs, but her foot slipped on the edge of the second tread. She staggered forward, jarring her knee and collapsed onto the step, too dispirited to move.

"I cannot believe he expects me to sell this poison through the hotel."

"Might not be poison." Aoife clattered down the steps and slumped next to her. "My uncle made good pochine in a cave back 'o his house. The whole street used to come and-"

"Yes, all right! Well, it's not happening here. I'll hire a cart and have the whole lot shipped back to Keogh at the Queens Hotel. I'll dump it in the street if I have to."

"You can't do that." Leon stood above them, his hand on the rail. "You cannot afford to be caught anywhere near this, Grace."

"All right. Then I'll have every bottle taken out onto a beach somewhere and hurled into the Strait."

"Which won't work either." She sensed Aoife's firm shake of her head. "You'll still owe Keogh money, so you have little choice."

"What if I pay him for this load, but refuse to handle any more?" Grace looked from Leon's grim expression to Aoife's anguished one.

"Pay once and he'll have you," Leon said. "Then you'll never get out from under."

"Then I'll refuse to pay him at all."

"Grace," Aoife said on a sigh. "You're such an innocent. This ain't a parcel o' books delivered to the wrong house. It's serious business run by dangerous men. You renege on a debt and he'll send his thugs around. They'll get their money one way or another, either from you or the hotel."

"What shall I do, Aoife? I'm not going to allow that man to control me." Grace inhaled a shuddering breath as she fought for control, determined not to go to pieces in front of them.

"Tell Mr Jardine," Aoife whispered. "He'll know what to do."

"I can't. He already suspects I have some sort of connection with Mr Keogh, even though it's not true. He'll think I deserve all I get and walk away."

"Give the man some credit." Aoife wrapped an arm around Grace's slumped shoulders. "He ain't stupid. He must have a pretty good idea of what Keogh is. He thinks the world of you, Grace, I've seen it in his face. He'll help."

"No. I can't go running for help at the first sign of trouble." Especially not to Andrew Jardine

"Mr Cahill then? He's a man of the world. He'll sort out the likes of Keogh."

"I couldn't. He's been so good to me, I'd be too embarrassed to admit I had dealings with a man like Keogh." She buried her face in her hands. "What should I do?"

The sound of Tilly's voice from the kitchen was followed by Leon's, who moved from the door to intercept her. After a brief, muffled exchange the room fell silent again and Leon reappeared at the top of the steps.

"I sent her into the dining room, but I think she's suspicious. She won't tell the other staff though, she's a good girl."

371

"That's a small blessing anyway. I can do without everyone knowing." Grace took the handkerchief Aoife held out and blew her nose.

"Jake knows some 'o them rum runners," Aoife said. "What if he can get the stuff sold elsewhere so's it don't get tracked back to you?"

"That's no more legal than what Keogh is doing," Leon gave a derisive snort.

"What do you suggest?" Aoife scowled up at him.

"Don't snap at Leon, this isn't his fault." Grace rubbed Aoife's back gently, her stiff shoulders revealing her own worry despite her chirpy comments. "And Jake's been hurt already. I don't want anything worse to happen to him."

"What, that little shiner?" Aoife said. "That's nothing. Jake wouldn't run from a good scrap. Did Leon tell you he also broke one of the bloke's teeth?"

Leon raised a satirical eyebrow, and Grace couldn't help but laugh, which turned into a dismayed sob. "There must be a way out of this."

"There isn't." Aoife chewed her bottom lip. "Keogh will have a hold over you whatever you do."

Chapter 24

A firm knock at Grace's bedroom door pulled her from a restless sleep. "Who is it?" she groaned as the early morning sun prised her eyelids open.

"It's me," Aoife's face appeared round the door. "Are you up yet?"

"Does it look like it?" Grace yawned. "I had an awful night. What time is it?"

"Breakfast time. But don't worry, Tilly can handle the tables this morning." She directed a pointed look to where Grace's crumpled dress lay on the floor. The previous day's events had so exhausted her, she left it where it fell and crawled beneath the coverlet in her chemise and drawers. Sleep had lasted only a short time before she was wide awake again, terrifying images running through her head. "What is it, Aoife?" As if she did not have enough to think about today.

"There's someone here to see you."

"It's not Keogh is it?" Grace slid from beneath the covers, her heart thumping.

"No, thank goodness. It's that Mr John Cahill. He wants to talk to you."

"What, now?" What could make John make an impromptu call so early?

Aoife nodded. "He's waiting for you in the guest lounge."

"Would you ask him to give me a few minutes?" Leaving Aoife to make excuses on her behalf, she fled to her bathroom, her head full of questions.

Did John Cahill know about Keogh? Or worse, was he aware her cellar was full of illicit rum and had come to tell her he was about to report her to the authorities? Her fingers shook as she stripped off her underwear, leaving another trail of clothes across the floor and fled to her bathroom. Washing quickly, she dressed and brushed out her hair, securing it into a loose bun on the back of her head with a tortoiseshell comb.

She swept her discarded dress from the floor, inwardly cursing at the film of rust colored dust that clung tenaciously to the fabric and hoping it wouldn't stain.

Pausing outside the guest lounge door, she smoothed down her skirt and took several deep breaths before entering.

"John," she glided towards him, both hands extended in greeting. "How lovely to see you. And what a surprise."

"Good morning, Grace." He took her hands. "I'm sorry not to have called before, but I've been in Toronto on business for a few weeks."

"There's no need to apologize. I know what a busy man you are." She studied his face for any signs this visit was more than a social one but could detect nothing but friendliness.

He had paid a recent visit to a barber; his silver hair and beard were neatly trimmed and shorter than usual. His smile was still the same and made her feel he was genuinely pleased to see her.

"You've done a wonderful job here, Grace." He took in the room. "The place looks magnificent."

"Thank you. Have you eaten breakfast, or may I offer you some coffee?"

"I've eaten, thank you. Young Aoife has just told me you returned from a trip to the north of the Island a little while ago."

"Yes, I came back last night. I have a friend who lives there."

The door opened to admit an older lady dressed in maroon accompanied by a much younger one in eau-de-nil organza.

"Good morning, Mrs Lennox, Miss Lennox," Grace moved to one side of the door to allow them past.

"Hello, dear," the older one spotted Grace at the last moment. "We're a little early, I know, but we're quite famished. Aren't we Mathilda?" She addressed the younger one, whose features were almost identical. "We plan to take a trip to Victoria Park today to watch the military band. We so like outdoor music, don't we, Mathilda?"

"Yes, Mama," Mathilda confirmed in a bored, long suffering tone. "And it cannot be described as a trip. The park is on the other side of town."

"I'm sure you'll have a lovely day, Mrs Lennox." Grace interrupted the older lady's stammered protest. "Would you excuse us?" She lowered her voice to address John. "Shall we go onto the veranda? We'll have more privacy there."

"Good idea," he whispered back. "I hope you enjoy your day, ladies." John delivered a theatrical bow to both women, rewarded with their shy blushes.

A pre-dawn rainfall lingered on the gazebo roofs that glittered with droplets, the grass and trees looked clean and greener, the sun having dried the patio and pathways in the already warm morning air.

"I heard about your heroic efforts with Isla." He waited for Grace to take her seat before lowering himself into the peacock backed chair at the far end of the veranda. "Mary tells anyone willing to listen that you single-handedly saved her daughter's life. She cannot praise you highly enough."

"Hardly heroic. I happened to be there at the time and stayed to support them. How is Isla?"

"She's recovering nicely. They hope to bring her home in a week or so."

"I'm so glad. Diphtheria is such a dreadful illness."

"Andrew said you slipped away from the hospital the other morning without a word to anyone." His warm smile removed the sting from what might have been an accusation.

"I-I didn't want to intrude." She ran her fingernails along a fold in her skirt, her head down. Seeing him comfort Mary had grated at her heart.

"Did I misjudge the situation, Grace?" he asked gently.

"I'm not sure to which situation you refer." She brought her gaze back to his face, aware she blushed.

"I think you do. I detected a strong attraction between you and Andrew Jardine while we were on the SS Elizabeth. However, he says he has barely seen you since your arrival in Charlottetown. That on the few occasions when your paths have crossed, you appeared less than pleased to see him."

"There was a misunderstanding when I first arrived, but lately we've been quite cordial." Grace fidgeted. "I've also been busy with the hotel, and in any case, he's done nothing to seek me out. And indeed, why should he?"

"Andrew talks of you often. Was I wrong and in fact you have no affection for him?"

"What do you expect me to say? Surely you don't see me as a woman who would come between a man and his wife?"

"Wife?" John's eyes darkened with genuine confusion. "You must be mistaken, my dear. Andrew has never been married."

"I-I don't understand." Her pulse raced, her mind filling with questions. "Emily told me that-"

"Ah, Emily." He sighed and leaned back in the chair, crossing one leg over the other. "My wife is - mischievous. She likes to be the center of attention and regards Andrew as her personal acquisition. I should have seen this coming as she saw you as a rival from the beginning."

"But there's Mary. And Isla?" Grace tried to make sense of what she was hearing. "At the hospital Andrew was frantic. They both were."

"Of course they were. It's natural that he should be distraught about a niece he has raised like his own daughter."

Like his own daughter. All her fears of Keogh, rum and policemen flew from her mind as one thought dominated. Andrew isn't married.

"How could I have been so wrong?"

"If Emily had a hand in things, I doubt it was your fault." John gave a cynical laugh.

"To be fair to Emily," Grace began, "she didn't actually say Mary was his wife. I must have misunderstood."

"Hah! You have no reason to be fair to her, she's rarely fair to anyone else. No, my dear, you were manipulated. As I said, Andrew talks about you often. A fact which annoys my petulant little wife a good deal."

A couple of hotel guests passed by the veranda on a leisurely stroll around the garden. Glad of the distraction in which to marshal her thoughts, Grace inclined her head in acknowledgement. She waited until they moved on before speaking.

"Even if what you say is true," Grace said when they were alone again. "Andrew has never made any approach to me."

"Did it occur to you that he's a shy man where you're concerned? You give the impression of being an independent, strong-willed young woman. A challenge for any man."

Shy? Andrew? Was he talking about the same person who had literally swept her off her feet, on the quayside? The charming man who had been so animated at The Waverley and then again on the steamboat? The day outside Wright's Furniture store came back in full force and she cringed. "Oh dear. Come to think of it, I might have also been at fault."

"It appears that you have misunderstood each other. May I suggest you talk to him?"

"I'm not sure what I would say." Suddenly the door which had been closed to her opened up and she could see a very different path in front of her. "But if Mary is his sister-in-law, what happened to Andrew's brother?

"Ah, there's a story." He stared out over the garden for a moment. "Alasdair was the younger, indulged son who left school early; always looking for the pot of gold which didn't exist. He married his childhood sweetheart, Mary in '97 and they had Isla a year later. He bought a large house, filled it with expensive furniture, bought a fancy carriage, all with the inheritance his mother left him, and some which Mary came into from her grandfather."

"I presume they exhausted the inheritances?" Grace said.

"Yes, they did. It resulted in the house being sold to pay his debts. Jardine senior wasn't prepared to throw good money after bad, no matter how much he loved his son. Alasdair rejected his father's suggestion to join the family business. Instead, he decided to search for gold in the Klondike. Leaving Mary and Isla in his father's care, he went to Alaska. To everyone's surprise, including his own, I imagine, he struck gold. He returned months later with his pockets bursting, threw parties and played the part of the conquering hero."

"What happened?"

"He had to return to Alaska to organize the mining operations and booked passage on The Islander in August '01, intending to be away three months, but the ship hit an iceberg. Alasdair was one of the forty people who drowned."

"Oh, how awful!"

"Indeed. Mary was inconsolable, and Jardine senior became a broken man, shutting himself away on his silver fox farm. Andrew didn't like to see such daily misery, especially for a child, so he brought Mary and three-year-old Isla to live with him."

"Surely he doesn't blame himself for Alasdair's death?"

"In a way he does. He believes he should have supported his brother financially and not let him go off to die."

"Then Alasdair would have expected Andrew to support him forever."

"Probably, but Andrew's view is that his brother would still be alive. Isla would have a father and Mary a husband."

"What about Alasdair's gold claim? Or was that just a story?"

"Oh, it was real all right, but the seam ran out during the second year. Andrew invested the money for Mary, and for Isla when she's older."

"What a sad story. Somehow, I forgot other people don't have perfect lives any more than I do. Sadness makes people very insular. If I did speak to Andrew, what would I say to him? That I've been cold because I thought he was insincere?"

"Give him credit, Grace." His repetition of what Aoife had said gave her pause. "You'll know when you begin. Actually, that wasn't the only reason for my visit."

"Which is?"

"I believe you are acquainted with a man named Charles Keogh?"

Grace's heart did a painful leap. What did John know? "Distantly. He arranged the purchase of this house."

"Is that all? Have you had contact with him since then?" His eyes seemed to see right through her. Dare she tell him? Or was it a trap?

"I've had little to do with him. I don't trust the man."

"I'm pleased to hear you say that, my dear. If I were you, I would continue in that vein. The man has a certain reputation." She was about to reassure him, when he added, "I'm aware of nothing definite, I've never met him, but one hears things."

"Then why are you warning me against him?"

"Because Andrew asked me to."

"Oh!" Grace frowned.

"Now, I must go." He pushed himself to his feet. "I have a meeting to attend this morning. I'm glad we managed to get things sorted out."

Once Grace had waved off his carriage, she collected her hat and bag from her room.

"Where are you going?" Aoife waylaid her in the hall.

"I won't be long. I need to see someone. Can you and Tilly manage the breakfasts while I'm away?"

"I've already said we can. But what about-" She pointed a finger at the floor, whispering, "You know."

"I don't know, but I hope to have a better idea of what to do when I get back."

Grace strode along West street, where medium sized merchants and builders' homes made way for imposing residences with large covered porches, multiple turrets and front drives on expansive plots of the more affluent. Having identified the Jardine house, she

382

checked the street for curious bystanders, but the wide tree lined road looked empty. While waiting for a response to her knock at the vast black-painted front door, the memory of her previous visit made her glance across to the Cahill house opposite, just in time to see a figure step back quickly from an upper window.

Emily.

Suppressing an urge to wave, she turned back just as the door was opened by Andrew Jardine in dark trousers, waistcoat and rolled up shirtsleeves.

"Oh, I-." She swallowed the speech she had prepared for a reluctant butler. "I didn't expect-"

"To see me open my own front door?" He regarded her with mild surprise. "Today is my manservant's day off. Come into the library." He stepped aside to allow her entry into a light and elegant hall decorated in earth and cream tones. Less flamboyant than the Cahill's, the house gave the impression of comfort and warmth with a glass lantern in the ceiling of an upper floor that allowed light to flood the hall.

"I assume you've spoken to John?" He held open a door to the right which led into a book lined room. Smaller than the one in John Cahill's house, it was an entirely masculine domain, the same cream and buff shades with touches of burgundy, green and gold in fabrics and the rug on the polished wood floor.

"Yes, he called on me first thing this morning. He explained about Mary being-"

"My sister-in-law."

"Yes. Why didn't you tell me?"

"I had no idea you thought so until yesterday, when Emily let it slip to Mary at the hospital. Emily tried to pass it off as a joke, but she forgets, we know her very well. Mary told her exactly what she thought of her. You would have been proud of her."

"I treated you so coldly when you were so nice to me. What must you have thought?" It also explained Emily's panic when she saw her talking to Mary at the tea room.

"I was puzzled, but not vain enough to feel I had any rights over you. I was content to be your friend."

"Were you?" The way he looked at her said otherwise.

"Actually no. I don't know why I said that." His shoulders lifted in a wry shrug. "I called at the hotel on Saturday to see you, to ask you why you left the hospital without a word, but that girl with the red hair-"

"Tilly," Grace supplied.

"Is that her name? She told me you had gone to visit a friend."

"You came to the Grace and Favor to see me?" At his nod her shoulders slumped. "I had no idea. No one said anything." But there hadn't been much time, and everything had been frantic since she returned the night before. "Where is Mary this morning?"

"At the hospital, of course. She stays all day at Isla's bedside."

384

"John said Isla was recovering. I would love to go and see her."

"She's still very weak and uncomfortable but is improving daily. I'm sure Mary would welcome a visit. And of course, so would Isla. Now, please sit." He indicated two wing-back chairs on either side of the fireplace. "I'd like to explain a little about-."

"No, not yet if you don't mind." She stepped away from him to the window that looked onto a garden, larger than the one at the hotel, though less cultivated.

It was more like a park with a circular lawn surrounded by shrubs and trees. On the far side of the lawn, an irregular shaped pond with an arched bridge straddling its narrowest part, shimmered in the sunlight.

"I didn't come here to demand explanations. Well, I did, but there's something else." She turned to face him, her fingers gripped around her bag. "I need your help. But first, I want you to say you trust me."

"Of course I trust you. You can confide in me about anything, Grace." He remained standing beside the fireplace, his folded arms resting on the back of a wing chair. "If I didn't make that clear in the past, I do now."

"You'd better wait until you hear what it is first." She paused, licked her lips and inhaled a deep breath. "I have twelve cases of illegal rum in my cellar."

"Oh, good grief." He straightened, his arms falling to his sides. "I didn't expect that."

"I didn't have anything to do with it. I promise you. I-"

"I believe you. Really I do." He closed the space between them in two strides and grasped her upper arms, holding her away from him. "Is this the work of that man Keogh?"

She nodded, tempted to sway towards him and rest her head against his shoulder. Embarrassed, she pulled away, determined to tell him everything before she crumbled.

"These men turned up at the hotel with a cart and unloaded the cases into my cellar despite attempts from my staff to prevent them."

"If you recall, I tried to warn you against that Keogh chap, but you gave me the impression I was interfering."

"It wasn't your advice I was rejecting, but the manner in which you gave it. The first time I saw you after the SS Elizabeth, you pretended not to see me and the second, you practically ordered me to have nothing to do with him but didn't explain why." All the pent up frustration of the last weeks entered her voice.

"Ah, yes. I apologize for that. I didn't handle things as diplomatically as I might have."

"No, you didn't! Although it appears we've both caused each other unnecessary anguish." She repeated John's comment earlier. "Had I known I could count on you, I might have been less scared of Keogh." She gave an involuntary shudder as she recalled the way he taunted her.

"He frightened you?"

"It's not important. But what am I to do?"

"Had you previously made it clear to Keogh that you wanted nothing to do with his illicit liquor?"

"Of course I did!" She hesitated. "Well - I might not have actually said so. He implied I wouldn't have any business if I did not, but he wasn't very specific. It was all suggestion and vague threats."

"Which might make it more difficult to prove he's behind this when you have had previous dealings with him. It's your word against his."

"I'm not involved with him, no matter what you might think."

"I accept that, Grace, but I need to know the facts. Since I heard the name, I've asked questions about him. He can be charming and manipulative when he chooses but he's quite ruthless."

"You don't have to tell me! He was nice at first but changed when I made it clear I wasn't interested in him or his dubious business practices."

"You're angry?" His gaze roved her face and he smiled.

"Furious!" She gripped her bag tighter, dismayed when the stitching on the fringe gave. "I've had a very difficult night. My staff are all terrified and looking to me to sort out this problem. That man is coming back for his payment tonight and I have no idea what to do." She left out the midnight part, which seemed too comical to repeat. "There's something else. Both Aoife and I believe someone is watching the hotel. Aoife thought he was a policeman, but what if he's one of Keogh's men?"

"That's more likely, but whoever it is creates a problem which we have to take into consideration. How many people know about this cache of yours?"

"It's not mine!" She brought her chin up and glared at him. "There's Aoife and Jake, Leon, Tilly probably knows if her nervousness last night anything was to go by. Other than that, no one."

"Have you told John Cahill? He might be willing to help."

"I thought about it. But to be honest, I was ashamed to admit I had got myself into such a situation. What if he called the police?"

"John would never do that. He could be your ally if you let him."

"He's helped me in the past and I don't want to take advantage of his good nature." Besides, she did not want to generate more hostility from Emily.

"My first instinct was to hire a cart and have Jake take the lot to the harbour and throw it in the sea."

"Who is Jake?"

"Oh, sorry. He's a friend of Aoife's who is eager to help. I suspect he knows more about rum running than he admits to, but I don't want to involve him."

"I agree. Should Jake be stopped by a patrolman, or observed disposing of the bottles, it would seem he was trying to destroy the evidence of illegal rum running. Not only that, but you would still owe Keogh money - then you'll never be rid of him."

"Leon, that's my cook, and Aoife said the same thing. What do you suggest I do?"

"I don't know - yet. I have to think about it. In the meantime, don't do anything."

"Nothing at all?" Grace asked, disappointed.

"I'm sorry, I know this might seem inadequate, but you need to be patient. I've only just learned about this, I need to ensure Keogh is held responsible without ruining your reputation or your business."

"I realize this is a lot to ask, but I cannot stop thinking about all those bottles sitting there waiting to be discovered. I want them gone."

"Was Keogh present when the assignment arrived?"

"No, Leon said Keogh turned up after the rum was delivered."

"We need proof he's directly involved, and for that we must catch him in the act."

"We don't have much time. He'll be back for his money at midnight tonight."

"Midnight? Who does he think he is, Dick Turpin?"

Grace giggled. "I thought the same myself. But that's what he told Leon."

"You don't have the money? Because if not I could always help you?"

"Of course I do, but I refuse to hand a cent over to him."

"That's more like the Grace I know," he whispered, sliding an arm around her shoulder. "If we're going to stop him, you need to be patient. When Keogh returns, go along with him. What he wants now is your co-operation."

"Huh! From our past encounters, that isn't the impression he gave me."

"I see. Then do your best to keep the conversation on a professional level. Say you have reconsidered and need the extra income and will sell the rum through the hotel as he demands. Keep him sweet, Grace. Don't make him nervous."

"Don't make him nervous? What about me, I'm shaking. Look." She held her hand out to demonstrate.

"Shall I send for my carriage to take you home?" He grasped her hand in both his and pressed it against his chest.

"No. I don't want that man hanging about outside the hotel to see your carriage, especially as Mr Cahill's has been there already this morning. I'll walk back to the hotel."

"You appear more confident than when you arrived, Grace. Even though we don't yet have a firm plan."

"I know, but strangely I feel better. I needed someone on my side."

"Pity. I thought you were going to say you needed me?" He held her gaze steadily and did not release her hand.

"I do. That's why I'm here." Was his touch meant to be a comforting gesture or something more? She daren't ask, while wishing she could. "I won't let that awful man best me.."

"I rather like this forceful side of you. It's impressive."

"Did you expect me to collapse into your arms and weep?"

"I suppose I did, yes. I have to admit, I'm a little disappointed."

A bubble of laughter worked its way up into her throat as he rested his forehead against hers. She closed her eyes, breathing in the fresh linen smell of his shirt and the cologne he wore, the same one as he wore on the ship. His lips brushed lightly against hers as if testing her reaction. When she didn't move away, he increased the pressure and when she kissed him back, he wrapped his arms tightly around her. Finally, he pulled back a few inches.

"Thank you," he said, his voice a whisper against her mouth. "For trusting me enough to ask for my help."

"After John's visit, what else could I do?" She looked up into his face. "You do realize that was our first kiss?"

"Was it a disappointment?"

"Not at all, but I wasn't prepared for it. Would you mind repeating it?"

"With pleasure."

391

Chapter 25

After Grace left Andrew's house, she returned to the hotel through streets which looked brighter and more beautiful than they had on her way there. She could barely keep the smile from her face which attracted both odd and bemused looks from passers-by.

At the door of Grace and Favor, she called a bright good morning to a couple of departing guests, taking time to accept their compliments and thanks for a wonderful stay.

"Well, you look happier than you did this morning." Aoife looked up from where she sat at the kitchen table with Jake.

"That's because I have everything in hand." She pulled a chair out from the table and sat. "Good morning, Jake. How's your eye?" His cheek was puffy and purple up to his eyebrow, but the skin was not broken.

"Morning, Miss Grace." Jake looked suddenly wary. "I've had worse."

"In hand?" Aoife scoffed. "What does that mean?"

"I can't explain just yet," Grace replied as she helped herself to tea from the pot on the table. A pot which was always being refilled but it had become a habit she quite liked.

"Everything is going to be all right. You'll have to trust me."

"Whom do you trust?" Aoife dragged her chair closer to Grace. "The alcohol inspector could turn up any minute, not to mention the police."

"Aoife!" Grace warned, shooting a quick look at Tilly who was on her way past with an armful of clean linens. She shot each of them a frightened look before hurrying out.

"That won't happen. We'll carry on as usual and no one is to go into the cellar."

"I need some flour and raisins," Leon said from his position at the stove.

"With one exception then." Grace smiled at him.

"I could get rid of the rum for you," Jake volunteered.

"Thank you, Jake, but I've already been told trying to dispose of it could make matters worse. I'm going to do what I was told."

"Told by whom?" Aoife asked, apparently still suspicious.

"Never mind. If it works you'll see for yourselves. Everyone back to work. It's almost time to open the tea room."

They dispersed slowly, muttering to themselves, obviously not happy with Grace's half-hearted solution to a problem which affected them all. She couldn't blame them. Like her, they had expected a rescue party to come swooping in and solve the problem.

The day wore on with no message from Andrew or, thankfully, Mr Keogh. Grace dealt with tea room customers, residents and tradesmen with false smiles and quiet, if nervous attention.

"Why don't I stay here for the next couple of nights?" Leon suggested as he was about to leave after dinner. "Only until this business is sorted out. I could put up a truckle bed in the storeroom."

"Thank you for the offer, Leon. Jake has already suggested it," Grace replied. "I don't think either of you should be on the premises in case something goes wrong."

"Well, you know where to find me if you need me." Leon nodded his goodbye, shrugged into his jacket and left.

"Where did you go this morning?" Aoife set mugs of tea in front of them at the kitchen table after ushering Jake out amid protests and sent Tilly to her room to listen out for residents' bells calling for late night drinks.

"Mr Jardine's house." In response to the girl's suggestive look, she added. "I was wrong about him. He isn't married. Mary is his sister-in-law."

"Ain't that a turn up for the books?" Aoife put the mug down with a thump. "Of course. He could be a bootlegger himself, I'll bet he knows all the right people."

"Whatever makes you say that?

"Don't look so shocked. It might not be so bad to marry one of the more successful bootleggers on the Island. They do pretty well from what I've heard."

"It would be a bad idea!" Grace snapped, though deep down she knew she would take Andrew on any terms, no matter how flawed. "And what makes you think he'll ask me to marry him?" Her casual tone belied the wish inside her head. "Even if he does propose, and I'm not intimating for a second that he would. What if he wants a large family? I doubt I can give him that."

"How do you know?" Aoife looked up from her tea, her eyes round. "Have you ever tried?"

"Not tried exactly, but I was married to Frederick for five years and I didn't conceive once. My father-in-law always insisted it must have been my fault as no man in his family ever failed to breed."

"Your husband's health was delicate wasn't it? Did he have the mumps as a nipper?"

"Mumps? I don't-. Actually yes, he did, along with every other childhood illness. But he was hardly a child then, he was twenty-two."

"Uh-huh, and did his, you know," she made a vague wave at her nether regions. "Swell and get tender?"

"Really, Aoife, what a question." Grace's cheeks warmed, and she buried her nose in her tea.

"Well, did they?"

"What do you mean, they? Oh, I see. Yes, now you mention it. He was in considerable pain for a while."

"There you are then."

"What do you mean by that?"

"It were your fella that had the trouble, not you." In response to Grace's puzzled frown, Aoife sighed. "My second brother had the same thing. His face blew up like a frog and he was sore - down there - for days. The doctor told him he wouldn't be having any more bairns. Not that he cared as he and his slattern wife already had five."

Grace clamped her lips together to prevent a laugh, while her eyes pricked with unshed tears. Could it be possible she might one day be a mother after all? After Angus MacKinnon's censure, she had always assumed she was not destined for that role in life.

The clock on the mantel ticked away the minutes as they sat there, absorbed in their own thoughts.

"Stop kicking the chair, it's irritating," Grace snapped.

"I'm restless. Why did Mr Jardine tell you not to look in the cellar?"

"I don't know. Why do you ask?"

"Mr Keogh is coming back tonight. What's he going to do about that?"

"To be honest I don't know. All he said was he would sort things out. He didn't explain how."

"It's getting late, Grace. Maybe Jardine isn't coming at all?"

"Shh." Grace cocked her head, listening. "Did you hear something?" Was it a bump, or the gate to the yard opening? She couldn't tell. Whatever it was it set her nerves on edge.

"No. What did it sound like?"

"I'm not sure."

"Well I'm not just sitting here all night." Aoife rose and moved to the cellar door.

"No, Aoife, he said-" But Aoife had already gone.

Grace followed, gingerly descending the steps onto the concrete floor.

"Maybe this is why." Aoife nodded towards the back wall.

Grace hardly dared to look. When she did, her heart leapt into her throat. Apart from wicker baskets of root vegetables and sacks of dry goods stacked in one corner, the cellar was empty.

"Oh my God. It's gone." Grace clutched the rail. Did Jardine somehow get Keogh to take back the rum? Or was it stolen by another gang of bootleggers? Frantic, she grasped the wooden rail to stop herself keeling over.

"Suppose it was all a double bluff and Andrew is a bootlegger with his own operation and this was his chance to put Keogh out of business?" Aoife said.

"We have to think about this," Grace said, trying to be reasonable, though she was terrified. "Maybe Andrew threatened to expose Keogh and made him take the rum back?" She couldn't think the worst of Andrew. Not now. He wouldn't be that cruel.

"Or another gang of bootleggers found out and they took it."

"Did Jake tell anyone it was there?"

"He wouldn't do that. I know him." Aoife twisted her hands in front of her, wrestling with the idea. "Look, why don't I go and find Jake? He knows some bootleggers. Maybe he knows who took it."

"What for? It's not as if I would want it back." Grace snorted.

"If it was another gang, chances are they're more scared of Keogh than their own boss, so we might be able to get out of this. Turn the scum against each other and let them fight it out between them."

"That's one way to resolve the problem, I suppose. If I could be sure it would work, I might let you do it."

"We've still got time, it's only nine-thirty. Let me go and talk to Jake. I won't be long."

"Wait. Let me telephone Andrew first. He might be able to tell me what's going on."

"If he was going to, he would have done that already. Not just helped himself. No, Grace, if it was him he'll only give you some story. You're mazed enough about the man to believe everything he says. Let me see what I can find out from Jake first."

Indignation, doubt and confusion took turns to make her unable to decide what to do. By the time she did, Aoife had gone.

She returned to the kitchen and poured away her cold tea and occupied herself with washing up the cups.

Should she call Andrew anyway? If he did not answer, she would doubt him more. Aoife was wrong. Andrew couldn't be involved. Confusion muddled her thoughts. One moment she had a cellar full of rum she did not want, then it was gone as if she had dreamt it. She suspected everyone. A sudden thought occurred. She went to the front door, turned off the porch light and peered into the gathering gloom.

The man on the corner was no longer there. When had she last seen him? Earlier that day? Before? She couldn't remember.

Was he a policeman, or one of Keogh's men? If a policeman, were they on their way to arrest her?

She returned to the kitchen, her elbows propped on the table and her chin in her hands, her mind such a turmoil that a headache throbbed behind her eyes.

Dread churned her insides at the thought she might have ruined her future in this country and be sent back to England. There was nothing left for her there, and the Grace and Favor was her own achievement, one she couldn't bear to part with.

She loved the Island and all the people she had come to know here. Aoife, Mrs M, Leon, even Tilly. Then there was Andrew, whom she loved.

The clack of the door latch made her jump. She looked up, expecting to see Aoife but Charles Keogh stood with his back to the door.

"Hello Grace."

Chapter 26

Grace removed her elbows from the table and leaned back in her chair as the tension drained out of her, leaving her strangely calm.

"All alone, I see Grace. Or were you waiting for me?" He gave the immaculate kitchen a slow, almost possessive glance.

"You're early." She rose slowly from her chair while at least ten scathing insults ran through her head. None of them reached her lips.

"I couldn't wait." His shoulders lifted in a casual shrug. "Sorry about the unexpected visit, but I had to unload the stuff quickly and you had all that cellar space empty."

Not as empty as it is now.

"I would have thought you had no trouble finding willing distributors for your - product. Why me? Why my hotel? I couldn't sell that much liquor in a year."

"Ah, Gracie, so stubborn. So angry, when you could have made this all much easier." He moved closer, resting his hand on the table.

She winced at his abbreviation of her name and backed away, keeping the vast pine table between them. She silently pleaded for Aoife, who had only been gone a few moments, to return. Tilly was a heavy sleeper, but even if she weren't, she would be of little use to anyone in a situation like this.

Keogh crept closer, apparently in no hurry. "Had you accepted my offer in the first place, I wouldn't have had to resort to this sort of behavior. I'm not fond of strong arm tactics myself."

"A pity that you have used them now." She took another step, so the entire length of the table was between them.

"A means to an end, perhaps?"

"What end?" she asked automatically, aware he wanted much more than money.

"Oh, come on, Grace. You're not a child. I have a particular liking for widows. They know what to expect and you don't get all that shocked indignation when it comes right down to it."

"Trust me, Mr Keogh. We shan't be getting down to anything."

"Now that's not very cordial, is it? Considering what you owe me." He skirted the end of the table unhurriedly, apparently enjoying himself.

Grace matched his stride in the opposite direction. "Owe you?" She debated whether or not to mention the rum was no longer in the cellar. Or would that make things worse?

"I don't give my product away. And besides, the margins are good. You could make quite a bit from what I supplied. I'm not greedy, so seeing as it's your first consignment, I'll give you a better rate."

Grace swallowed. Andrew had had all day to arrange something, anything. Surely he hadn't planned to leave her alone with this man?

Where are you?

"Why do you keep looking at the door, Grace?" He eased closer with a smug smile. "There's no one there. I saw that Irish chit leave a little while ago and I know your staff don't live in. Oh, apart from that little red-haired lass. Not that she could do anything. How about you relax and spend some time with me? I'm in no hurry to collect."

Her skin crawled, her first instinct being to run from the room but she resisted. Andrew would be here. He must. She had to play for time and hope he was on his way.

"I don't think so, Mr Keogh. Just tell me how much I owe you and then go." She released an understated sigh and turned to leave, showing she wasn't afraid to turn her back on him. "Or you could simply take your rum and leave."

If you can find it.

It was a mistake. He let out a bellow of fury and circled the table in two strides. His fingers closed on her shoulder and he swung her around, tearing the sleeve of her blouse.

"No! I tell you when this meeting is over." A muscle twitched involuntarily at the corner of his right eye, his lips thinned to a grimace. "In fact, I think you should be a whole lot nicer to me. Who do you think you are anyway? You're nothing but Jardine's tart."

403

She gasped, a combination of pain and the shock of his grip on her flesh. Her stomach knotted as he hooked his hand at the back of her neck and pulled her close, his breath laden with spirits.

"Get away from me!" Terrified, and yet furious, she scored her fingernails across his face as hard as she could, tearing two in the process.

"Ach!" He flung his head away, releasing his hold on her. His hand went to his face where his cheek oozed blood from three long scratches.

For long seconds, he stared at the red stain on his hand in obvious disbelief. "Bitch!"

With a snarl, he slammed his balled fist into her cheekbone.

She saw the blow coming and tried to duck, but wasn't quick enough, releasing a sharp cry as her head jerked, the force of the blow sending her backward against the table. Pain radiated through her hip and she half turned, braced both hands on the top in an effort to remain standing.

"I'd better not have a scar." His voice was harsh as he brought an arm around her waist from behind and pulled her against him.

Grace struggled to free herself but he was too strong, his hip ground into her back making her want to retch. Frantic to break away, she flicked a foot up behind her, catching his knee cap.

He gave a furious yell but did not let go. He pushed his other hand into her hair, gripped it at the roots and twisted, pulling her head painfully backwards.

"Feisty one, aren't you?" he whispered, his breath warm on her neck. His fingers tightened in her hair, his feet spread to prevent her kicking out again. Her stomach cramped as he pressed her harder into the table, but she refused to cry out. His arm around her waist tightened, forcing a bone in her corset to dig into a rib. Through pain and anger she searched for a way to fight back but she couldn't move.

Her struggles were useless, her breathing grew rapid with terror and revulsion as his hand moved from her waist slowly upwards. She summoned all her strength and braced to throw her weight backwards, when without warning, he released her. His hand dropped from her midriff, his fingers slid from her hair and his weight no longer pressed against her.

Grace froze for a long, uncomprehending, second. She registered a dull thump and swung around.

Keogh lay on the floor. Aoife, her face screwed up into her cross pixie expression as she stood over him, held an iron skillet in both hands.

"You all right, Grace?" she said, her voice oddly calm as she glared at Keogh's immobile form, the skillet still held ready.

"I-I think so. I doubt you need to hit him again. He's out cold."

"Just makin' sure."

The sound of hoof beats sounded in the lane beyond the backyard, followed by voices shouting. In seconds, four uniformed men in peaked caps strode into the kitchen, followed by a white-faced Jake with an equally horrified Andrew Jardine.

"Blimey!" Jake stared at Keogh. "Aoife, I said you were to wait." He appealed to Grace, his hands held out to his sides. "When the police jigger and horse drew up, I told her to stay in the lane, but she ran past me."

"No time to explain," Aoife responded, stone faced. "I knew something was up."

"I'm very glad she did." Grace swayed on her feet as blood rushed to her head.

Andrew Jardine pushed roughly through the policemen and wrapped her in his arms. "Are you all right, Grace?" At her nod, he turned on the man in charge, evident by the stripes on the arm of his dark jacket. "I told you Keogh would probably come early. You should have listened to me!"

"We had our own enquiries to make first, Mr Jardine. Then we had to secure the consignment." He gave Grace a swift up and down glance. "The lady looks unharmed to me."

"That's all you know!" Grace stared back at him, a hand cupped to her face where Keogh hit her.

"No thanks to you." Andrew elbowed him away, a protective arm clamped around Grace.

"You're here, which is what counts. I think I'll fall into your arms now," Grace murmured as she half collapsed against him.

Did I hear right? The police took the rum?

"About time," Aoife muttered, her pixie face exhibiting a broad smile.

"I must admit I expected more than four policemen to come to my rescue." Grace said into his jacket that smelled of the outdoors.

"What do you mean?" Andrew drew in his chin, smiling down at her. "I brought half the Charlottetown Police force with me."

"Half? You only have a force of eight in this town?"

Andrew shrugged, and Grace rolled her eyes.

Keogh started to come to, moaning, a hand clamped to the back of his head. Two policemen hauled him roughly to his feet, holding his arms tightly behind him.

He glared at Grace, swaying a little between the officer's grip. "I want that Irish slut charged for assaulting me," he snarled. "What's it come to when a chap visits his lady friend and gets his head bashed in?" He laughed, a harsh, mirthless sound, adding. "What's the matter, Jardine? Don't like to share, eh?"

"You bast-" Andrew jabbed a clenched fist at Keogh's face so fast, no one saw it coming. Especially Keogh, whose head snapped back, and his eyes rolled upwards in their sockets. The two officers released him abruptly and for the second time in five minutes he had a close view of the kitchen floor tiles.

One of the policemen sighed, the other propped his hands on his hips and gave Andrew a 'did-you-have-to' look.

"What are you waiting for," their commanding officer shouted. "Get him out of here!"

"He might have a point," Grace said as Keogh was dragged from the room slung between the two policemen. "What are you arresting him for?"

"A little matter of a dozen cases of rum found in Mr Keogh's warehouse will do to begin with, Ma'am." The sergeant saluted Grace and Andrew, nodding in Aoife and Jake's direction before he re-entered the yard, the fourth policeman trailing behind.

"You can put that down now, Aoife," Andrew smiled, indicating the skillet in her hand.

"Oh, yes. Sorry." Sheepishly, she returned it to the stove.

* * *

While Aoife went to see if any of the guests had been disturbed by the commotion going on in the kitchen, Jake secured all the locks. Grace excused herself to her room where she changed her torn dress and did her best to repair the damage to her hair which had been tugged free from its pins.

"Tilly didn't even wake up," Aoife said, miffed. "And wait 'til I tell Leon about this. He'll be sorry he missed all the excitement."

With the premises secured, the four of them sat down at the kitchen table.

Despite repeated enquiries, Grace convinced them she was unhurt, although the tingling in her cheek told her she would have a bruise in the morning. She and Jake would make a fine pair.

"Did I hear that policeman say they found the rum in Keogh's warehouse?" Grace accepted a steaming mug of tea from Jake, whom Aoife had enlisted to help. "So he did take it back?"

"No. Actually I did," Andrew said. "I engaged some friends of mine to remove it earlier. For the plan to work, the rum had to be found somewhere registered as Keogh's property. I could hardly have it delivered to the hotel he uses as his address."

"Isn't that a little unethical?" Grace winced and eased her painful hip that was crushed against the back of the chair.

"Would you prefer the police to have found it here?" Andrew's lips twitched, and Grace looked away, knowing he was teasing her.

"How did you know he owned a warehouse?" Aoife tidied away the empty cups, replacing them with clean ones.

"Um-there's a man in a brown suit with a very sore head at the police station who told us. Eventually." Andrew said.

"So the man watching the hotel was Keogh's man?" Aoife nodded, as if answering an internal question.

"The same. As soon as we got it out of him, we transferred the cases from your cellar into Keogh's warehouse and then came here."

"How long can they keep Keogh in jail for owning some rum?" Grace asked.

"That's not the issue. He'll be out of commission for some time once those he employed make statements against him. And they will. He might even be drummed off the Island."

"I hope it will be that easy," Grace sighed. "I sense drinking is something most people don't regard as a crime." Mrs Mahoney was evidence of that.

"I'll wager there'll be plenty more like him waiting to take his place," Aoife said.

"Don't be cynical, Aoife," Grace frowned at her. "I should have avoided him from the start, but then if I had, I might not have this place."

"When you told Keogh about opening a hotel, my guess is, he saw you as a likely prospect, whether you agreed or not," Andrew said

"He's done this sort of thing before?" Grace asked, unsurprised.

"It appears so. He makes an unsolicited delivery, then pressurises the victim for payment. If they refuse, he threatens them with exposure. Most people are too scared of him and his thugs to go against him. The man is too clever and keeps just the right distance between himself and the people who work for him."

"I'm impressed by the police acting on your word and keeping me out of it."

"Maybe it has something to do with Marshall being my godfather."

"Who's Marshall?" Grace looked up from her tea. The hot brew was doing its job reviving her, although her cheek stung, and her scalp was sore from Keogh pulling her hair.

"Charles Cameron, the Police Chief, but everyone knows him as 'Marshall'"

"So there is such a thing as Prince Edward Island aristocracy?"

"Maybe." Andrew grasped her hand beneath the table and they exchanged an intimate smile.

Aoife scraped back her chair and gave an exaggerated yawn. "Time you went, Jake. It's late and I have to work in the morning."

When he didn't move, she punched him lightly on the arm. "What already?" He stared at her, indignant. "I haven't finished my tea."

"Stop mithering and sling your hook. I'm worn out by all the excitement." Aoife cocked her head to where Grace and Andrew sat before ushering him unceremoniously into the yard. She locked the door behind him and her gaze fixed straight ahead of her, retraced her steps back to the door to the hall, calling as she went, "Goodnight then. See you tomorrow, Grace." She paused on the point of pulling the door closed behind her and turned back. "Goodnight, Mr Jardine and thank you."

"You're very welcome, Aoife," Andrew inclined his head, smiling.

Aoife flushed shyly, delivered a wink at Grace and closed the door behind her.

"Are you sure you're all right?" Andrew cupped Grace's face with his free hand and ran his thumb gently beneath her eye. "This is going to look spectacular in the morning."

"The one you gave him will be equally as colorful, I expect." She removed his hand from her sore cheek and brought his fingertips to her lips. "I was more furious than scared. I've never wanted to hurt someone so badly, but I was powerless. I'm better now you're here."

"Do you plan on keeping the Grace and Favor open when we are married?" Andrew asked.

"What did you say?" Grace pulled her chin back, bringing his face into sharp focus.

"I think you heard me." He took her hand. "I'm not very good at this sort of thing."

"As a proposal, it's not a very good one."

"I knew I wouldn't do it right. I've been trying to work out a strategy for weeks but didn't know how to ask you."

"And that's what you came up with? A fait accompli?"

"Hmm, it does sound like one doesn't it? Perhaps it's because I'm not used to people saying no to me, so I assume they'll go along with my decisions."

"I didn't say I wouldn't go along with it, but I might need some time to mull it over?"

"What for? Everyone loves the idea. Mary and Isla are delighted."

"Are they? You've told them already?"

"I might have mentioned it. Once or twice." His gaze held momentary panic.

He was so obviously unsure of himself that she loved him all the more. Nor was she disappointed that he had not proposed properly. But then, Frederick hadn't either. Angus MacKinnon simply announced their betrothal at breakfast one morning having convinced Grace she owed him gratitude for his years of protection.

Perhaps this was the way her life was meant to be. Unconventional, impulsive, but still utterly romantic in its own way. It would be a story to tell their children one day. She couldn't wait to tell Maud.

"Why did you wait so long?" Grace asked. "I don't mean for me, but surely there are other young women in Charlottetown you could have chosen?"

"It's only recently I realized marriage and a family was something I wanted."

"How recently?" Her new confidence in his feelings made her want to flirt.

"Since the day I met you."

"And those feelings didn't change, even when I wasn't very nice to you?"

"Hmm, I did wonder at times if I was on the wrong track. But then Mary told me you were jealous of her and I was determined not to be put off. Thus I enlisted John Cahill to give you a little nudge in the right direction. Now, never mind all these diversions. You haven't answered my question."

"Yes," she whispered.

"Yes, you'll marry me?"

"Yes, I want to keep the Grace and Favor after we're married. Which means I do want to marry you. It occurs to me we might need it if you lose any more of your ships."

His burst of uninhibited laughter was interrupted by the kettle Aoife had refilled coming to the boil.

"Would you like more tea? I think there are some of Leon's pastries in the tin."

"Tea and pastries aren't much of a celebration. By rights we should toast each other with champagne." Andrew slid an arm around her waist and pulled her to him.

"I'm afraid it's all I have since someone stole my rum." Grace leaned closer and kissed him lightly on his lips.

"Are you sure?" he asked, his eyes sparkling with laughter. "Because I have some rather fine Dom Pérignon in my cellar."

"Andrew!"

The End

Bibliography

Acknowledgements and Sources

A Writing Life - A biography of Lucy Maud Montgomery by Mary Rubio and Elizabeth Waterston
If You're Stronghearted - Prince Edward Island in the 20th Century by G Edward Macdonald Associate Professor of History at PEI University.

This book provided me with some fascinating reading into a unique view of what life was like during the early 1900's on Prince Edward Island. His insight in the minds of the Islanders' personal pride in their history and way of life drew images for me which have made me long to visit a place I only know through books and the internet. Of the now extinct railway, he says:

'Special trains were put on to shuttle mourners from funerals to cemeteries; to carry hockey teams and their raucous supporters to critical matches; to take chattering excursionists, complete with brass bands, to any one of the Island's yearly crop of tea parties. School children were made to memorize the stations along their stretch of the line. Fares and timetables were part of the everyday lexicon. Housewives and field workers timed their day by the train whistle. More often than not, it was the train that freighted Islander's produce to market, and the train that carried their emigrant sons and daughters

away to distant places. The train stood for what had been on Prince Edward Island and what still might be. What matter if it ran a deficit?'

Elizabeth and Her German Garden by Elizabeth von Arnim.

This, her debut novel was published anonymously by Macmillan in 1898

Australian Marie Annette Beauchamp became Mary, the Gräfin von Arnim on her marriage to Graf Henning von Arnim-Schlagenthin, a member of the Prussian aristocracy.

Her future works were usually published with the phrase 'by the author of Elizabeth and her German Garden' as the only guide to their authorship.

She also wrote 'The Solitary Summer' [1899] 'The Benefactoress' [1901] 'The Caravaners' [1909] 'The Pastor's Wife [1914] 'Christine' [1917] 'Christopher and Columbus' [1919] 'In the Mountains' [1920] 'Vera [1922], 'The Enchanted April' (1922) and 'Mr Skeffington' [1940] as Elizabeth von Arnim's memoir, 'All the Dogs of My Life' [1936]

Books by Anita Davison

From BWL Publishing Inc.

The Woulfes of Loxsbeare
The Rebel's Daughter, Book 1
The Goldsmith's Wife, Book 2
Royalist Rebel - Published by Pen and Sword
Books
https://www.pen-and-sword.co.uk/
[under the name Anita Seymour]
The Flora Maguire Mystery Series Published by
Aria Fiction
https://ariafiction.com/
1 - Murder on the Minneapolis
2 - Murder at Cleeve Abbey
3 - A Knightsbridge Scandal
4 - Murder at St Philomena's
5 - Murder at Paddington - October 2018]
Published by MuseItUp Publishing
Trencarrow Secret
Culloden Spirit

As a Londoner constantly drawn back to the
city, Anita connected with its history at a young
age. When the rest of the school trip were busy
throwing the contents of their lunch boxes
across the school coach, Anita daydreamed

417

about men in high white wigs, long coats and petticoat breeches climbing into sedan chairs on the cobbles of Paternoster Row, where the sight of Christopher Wren being lowered down the outside of the half built St Pauls Cathedral in a basket was a daily occurrence.

BLOG: http://thedisorganisedauthor.blogspot.com
FACEBOOK:
http://www.facebook.com/anita.davison?
GOODREADS:
http://www.goodreads.com/AnitaDavison
TWITTER: @AnitaSDavison

Books by Victoria Chatham

His Dark Enchantress, Berkeley Square Book 1
His Ocean Vixen, Berkeley Square Book 2

Loving That Cowboy
Cold Gold
On Borrowed Time
Shell Shocked
The Buxton Chronicles Boxed Set

Manufactured by Amazon.ca
Bolton, ON